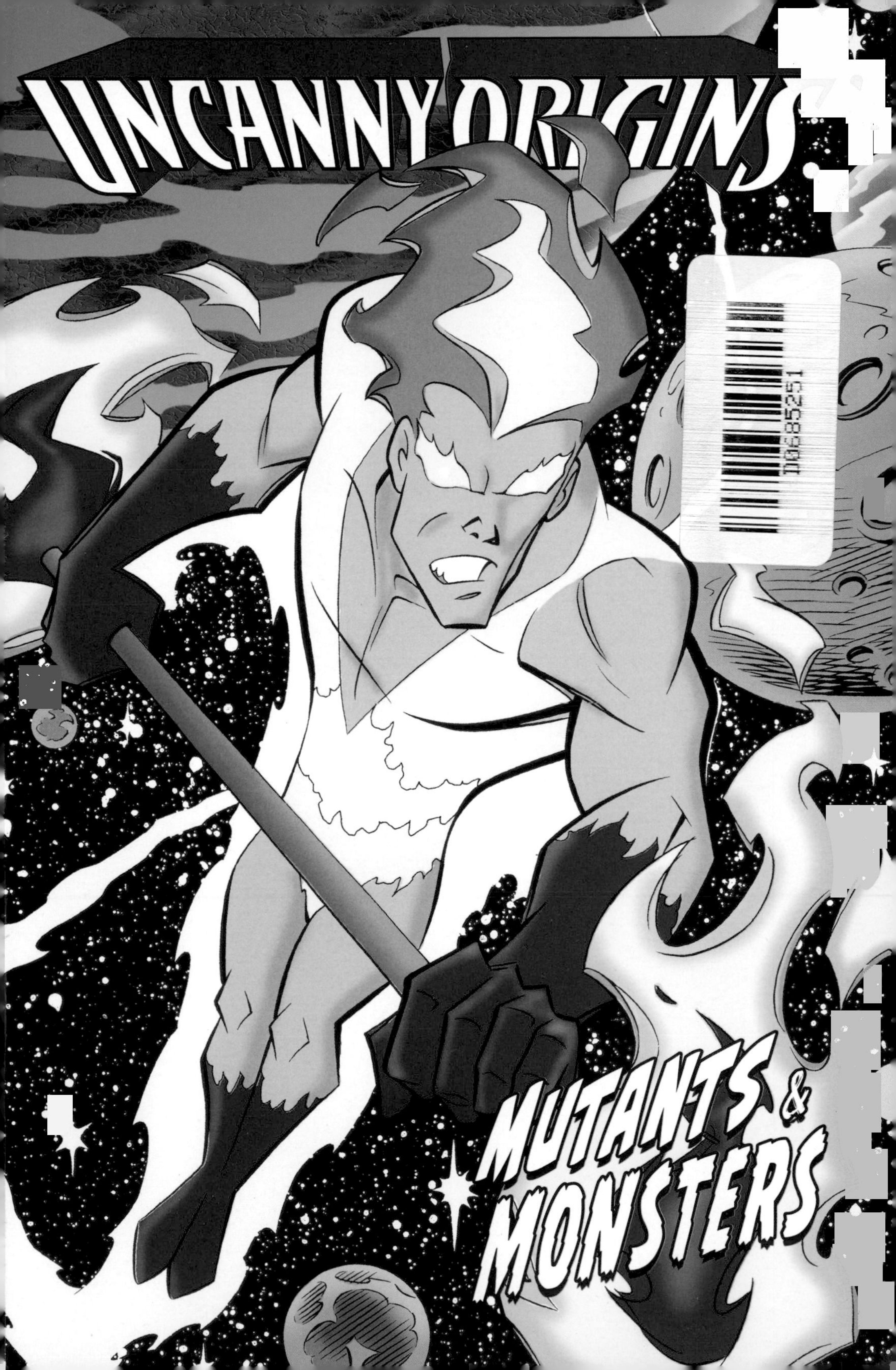
UNCANNY ORIGINS
MUTANTS & MONSTERS

UNCANNY ORIGINS
MUTANTS & MONSTERS

BEN RAAB, GLENN HERDLING, MATT IDELSON, JAMES FELDER,
GLENN GREENBERG, MICHAEL HIGGINS & BOB BUDIANSKY
WRITERS

DAVE HOOVER & PABLO RAIMONDI
PENCILERS

BILL ANDERSON & DON HUDSON
INKERS

BOB SHAREN & KGM GRAPHICS
COLORISTS

JACK MORELLI & JON BABCOCK
WITH JANICE CHIANG
LETTERERS

NANCY POLETTI & MATT HICKS
ASSISTANT EDITORS

MARK GRUENWALD & TERRY KAVANAGH
EDITORS

DAVE HOOVER & BILL ANDERSON
COVER ARTISTS

COLLECTION EDITOR MARK D. BEAZLEY
ASSISTANT EDITOR CAITLIN O'CONNELL
ASSOCIATE MANAGING EDITOR KATERI WOODY
ASSOCIATE MANAGER, DIGITAL ASSETS JOE HOCHSTEIN
SENIOR EDITOR, SPECIAL PROJECTS JENNIFER GRÜNWALD
VP PRODUCTION & SPECIAL PROJECTS JEFF YOUNGQUIST
RESEARCH & LAYOUT JEPH YORK
PRODUCTION JOE FRONTIRRE
BOOK DESIGNERS SALENA MAHINA WITH ADAM DEL RE

SVP PRINT, SALES & MARKETING DAVID GABRIEL
DIRECTOR, LICENSED PUBLISHING SVEN LARSEN
EDITOR IN CHIEF C.B. CEBULSKI
CHIEF CREATIVE OFFICER JOE QUESADA
PRESIDENT DAN BUCKLEY
EXECUTIVE PRODUCER ALAN FINE

SPECIAL THANKS TO DOUG SHARK OF MYCOMICSHOP.COM

UNCANNY ORIGINS: MUTANTS & MONSTERS. Contains material originally published in magazine form as UNCANNY ORIGINS #1-7. First printing 2019. ISBN 978-1-302-91983-2. Published by MARVEL WORLDWIDE, INC., a subsidiary of MARVEL ENTERTAINMENT, LLC. OFFICE OF PUBLICATION: 135 West 50th Street, New York, NY 10020. © 2019 MARVEL No similarity between any of the names, characters, persons, and/or institutions in this magazine with those of any living or dead person or institution is intended, and any such similarity which may exist is purely coincidental. Printed in Canada. DAN BUCKLEY, President, Marvel Entertainment; JOHN NEE, Publisher; JOE QUESADA, Chief Creative Officer; TOM BREVOORT, SVP of Publishing; DAVID BOGART, Associate Publisher & SVP of Talent Affairs; DAVID GABRIEL, SVP of Sales & Marketing, Publishing; JEFF YOUNGQUIST, VP of Production & Special Projects; DAN CARR, Executive Director of Publishing Technology; ALEX MORALES, Director of Publishing Operations; DAN EDINGTON, Managing Editor; SUSAN CRESPI, Production Manager; STAN LEE, Chairman Emeritus. For information regarding advertising in Marvel Comics or on Marvel.com, please contact Vit DeBellis, Custom Solutions & Integrated Advertising Manager, at vdebellis@marvel.com. For Marvel subscription inquiries, please call 888-511-5480. Manufactured between 7/26/2019 and 8/27/2019 by SOLISCO PRINTERS, SCOTT, QC, CANADA.

10 9 8 7 6 5 4 3 2 1

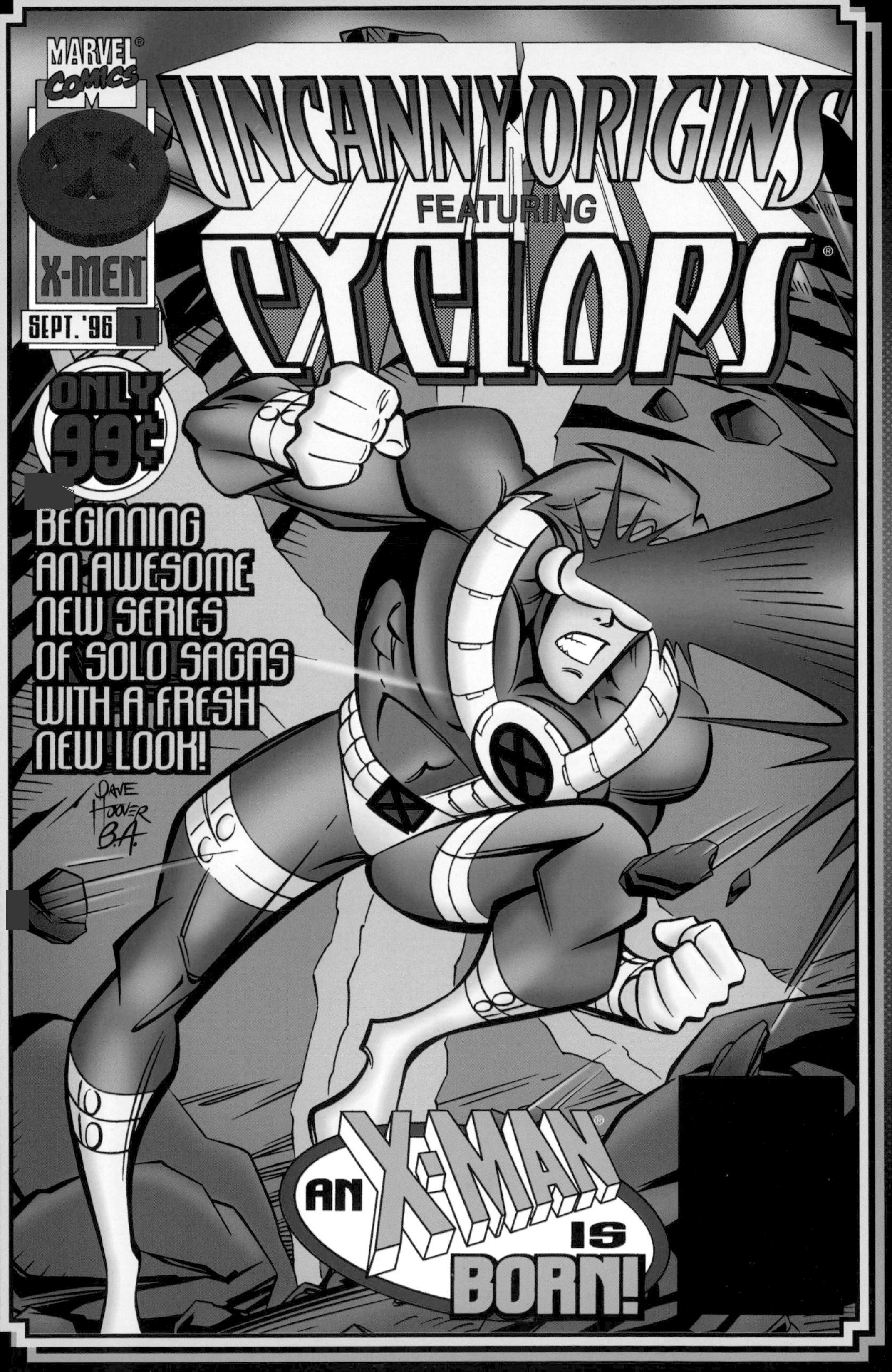
MARVEL®
COMICS
X-MEN
SEPT. '96
1
UNCANNY ORIGINS
FEATURING
CYCLOPS®
ONLY 99¢
[redacted]
BEGINNING AN AWESOME NEW SERIES OF SOLO SAGAS WITH A FRESH NEW LOOK!
DAVE HOOVER B.A.
[redacted]
AN X-MAN® IS BORN!
[redacted]

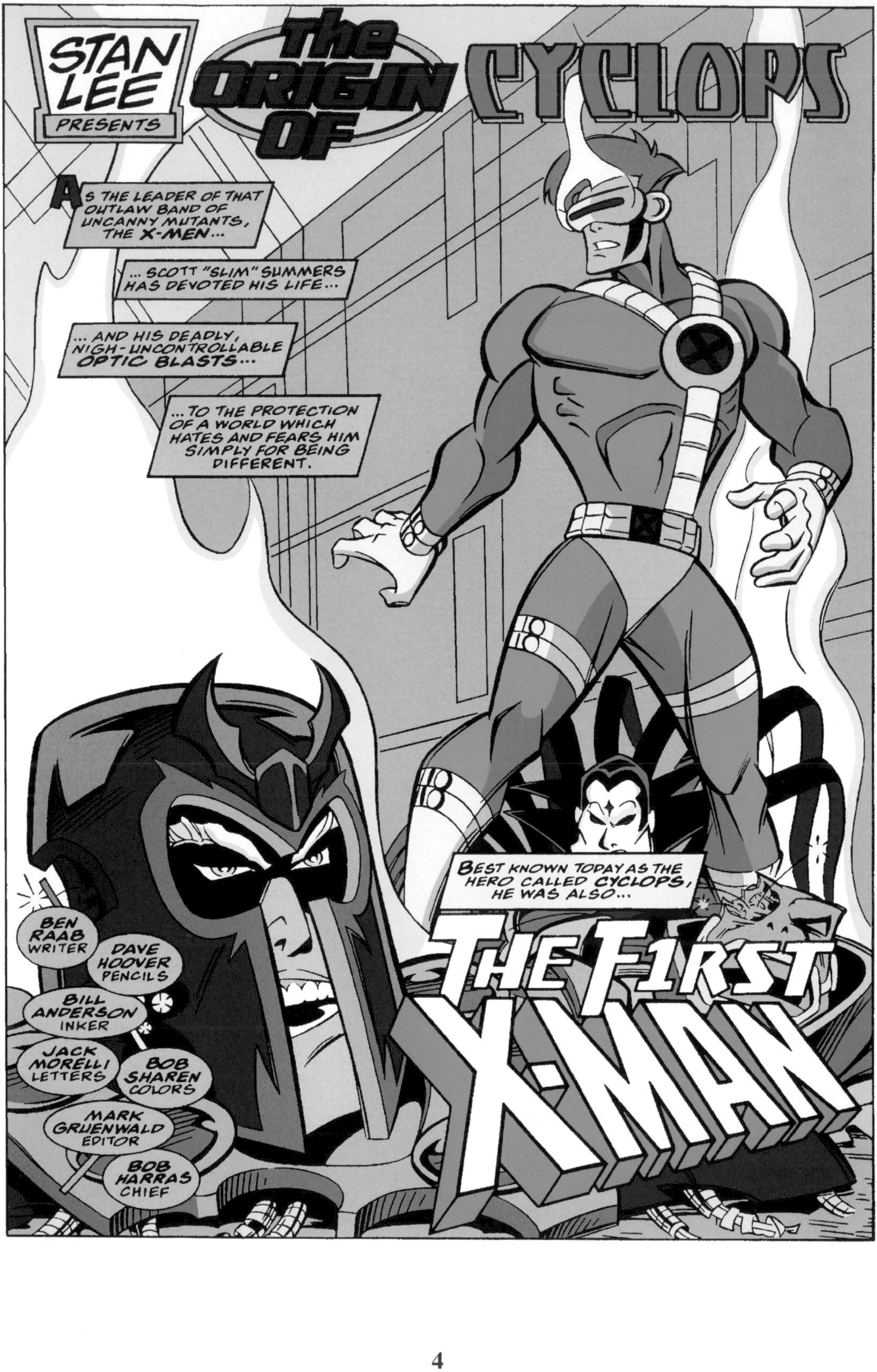

STAN LEE PRESENTS
THE ORIGIN OF CYCLOPS
AS THE LEADER OF THAT OUTLAW BAND OF UNCANNY MUTANTS, THE X-MEN...
... SCOTT "SLIM" SUMMERS HAS DEVOTED HIS LIFE...
... AND HIS DEADLY, NIGH-UNCONTROLLABLE OPTIC BLASTS...
...TO THE PROTECTION OF A WORLD WHICH HATES AND FEARS HIM SIMPLY FOR BEING DIFFERENT.
BEST KNOWN TODAY AS THE HERO CALLED CYCLOPS, HE WAS ALSO...
THE F1RST X-MAN
BEN RAAB WRITER
DAVE HOOVER PENCILS
BILL ANDERSON INKER
JACK MORELLI LETTERS
BOB SHAREN COLORS
MARK GRUENWALD EDITOR
BOB HARRAS CHIEF

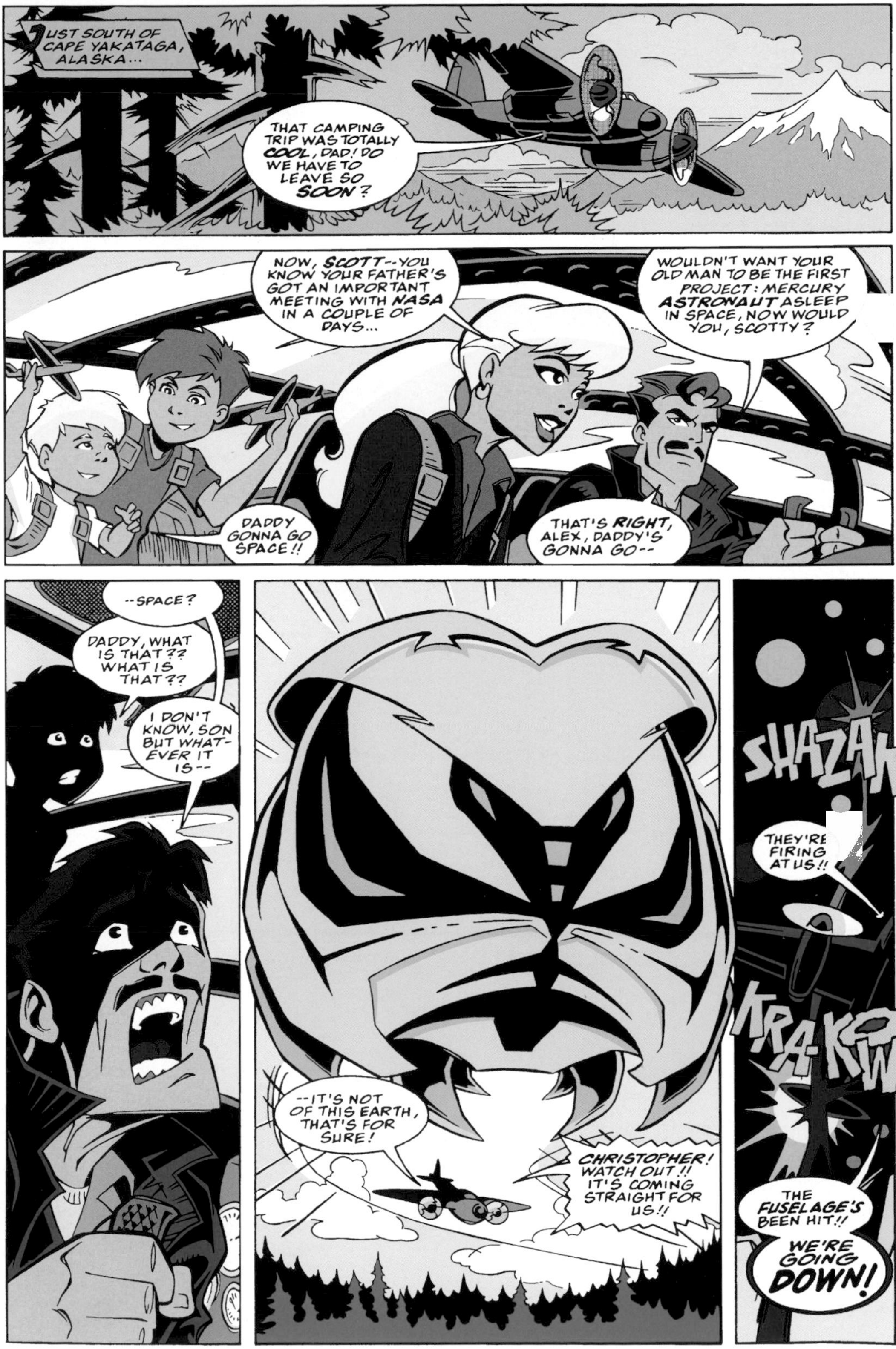
JUST SOUTH OF CAPE YAKATAGA, ALASKA...
THAT CAMPING TRIP WAS TOTALLY COOL, DAD! DO WE HAVE TO LEAVE SO SOON?
NOW, SCOTT--YOU KNOW YOUR FATHER'S GOT AN IMPORTANT MEETING WITH NASA IN A COUPLE OF DAYS...
WOULDN'T WANT YOUR OLD MAN TO BE THE FIRST PROJECT: MERCURY ASTRONAUT ASLEEP IN SPACE, NOW WOULD YOU, SCOTTY?
DADDY GONNA GO SPACE!!
THAT'S RIGHT, ALEX, DADDY'S GONNA GO--
--SPACE?
DADDY, WHAT IS THAT?? WHAT IS THAT??
I DON'T KNOW, SON BUT WHATEVER IT IS--
--IT'S NOT OF THIS EARTH, THAT'S FOR SURE!
CHRISTOPHER! WATCH OUT!! IT'S COMING STRAIGHT FOR US!!
SHAZAK
THEY'RE FIRING AT US!!
KRA-KOW
THE FUSELAGE'S BEEN HIT!! WE'RE GOING DOWN!

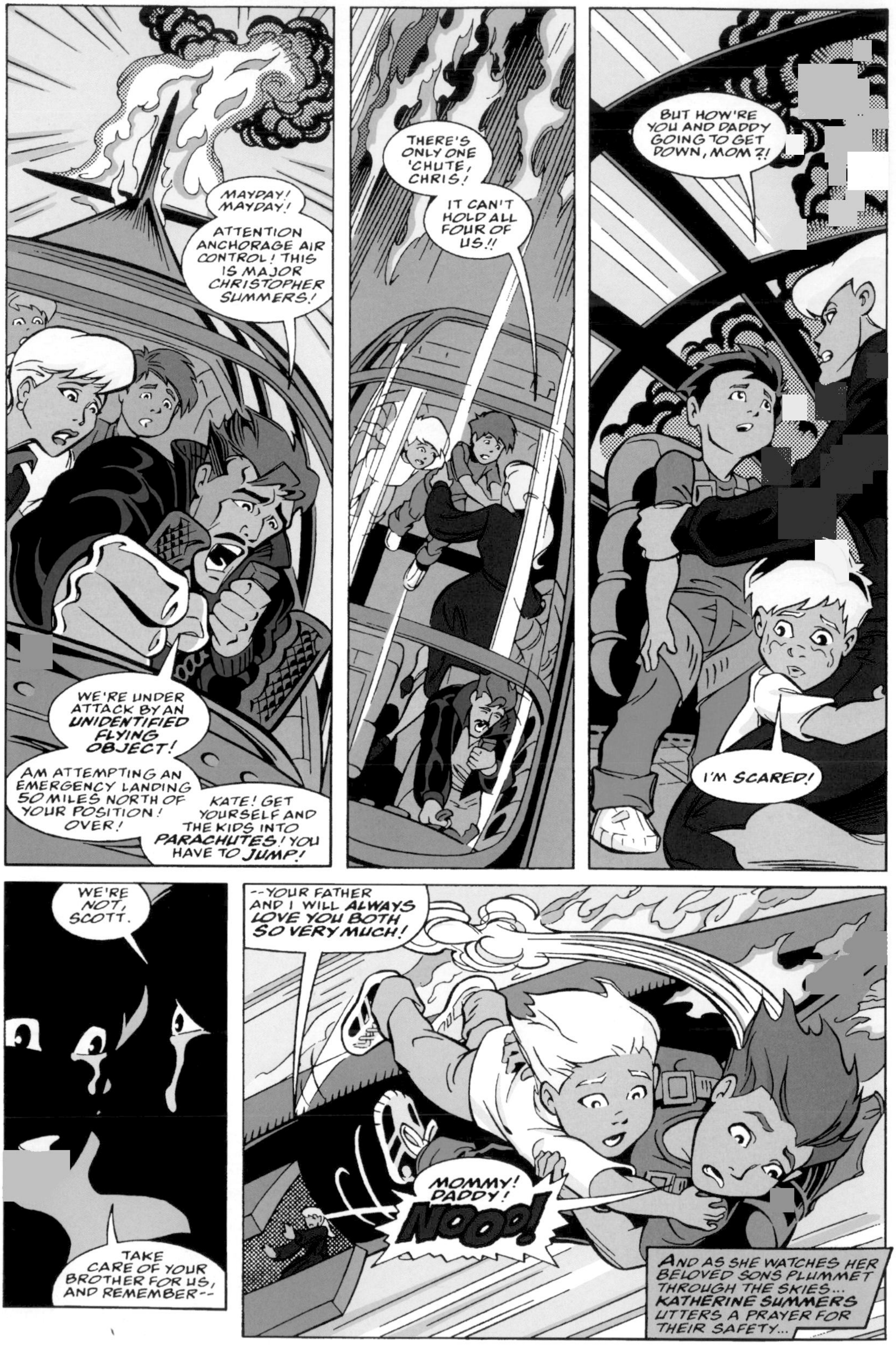
MAYDAY! MAYDAY!
ATTENTION ANCHORAGE AIR CONTROL! THIS IS MAJOR CHRISTOPHER SUMMERS!
WE'RE UNDER ATTACK BY AN UNIDENTIFIED FLYING OBJECT!
AM ATTEMPTING AN EMERGENCY LANDING 50 MILES NORTH OF YOUR POSITION! OVER!
KATE! GET YOURSELF AND THE KIDS INTO PARACHUTES! YOU HAVE TO JUMP!
THERE'S ONLY ONE 'CHUTE, CHRIS!
IT CAN'T HOLD ALL FOUR OF US!!
BUT HOW'RE YOU AND DADDY GOING TO GET DOWN, MOM?!
I'M SCARED!
WE'RE NOT, SCOTT.
TAKE CARE OF YOUR BROTHER FOR US, AND REMEMBER--
--YOUR FATHER AND I WILL ALWAYS LOVE YOU BOTH SO VERY MUCH!
MOMMY! DADDY!
NOOO!
AND AS SHE WATCHES HER BELOVED SONS PLUMMET THROUGH THE SKIES... KATHERINE SUMMERS UTTERS A PRAYER FOR THEIR SAFETY...

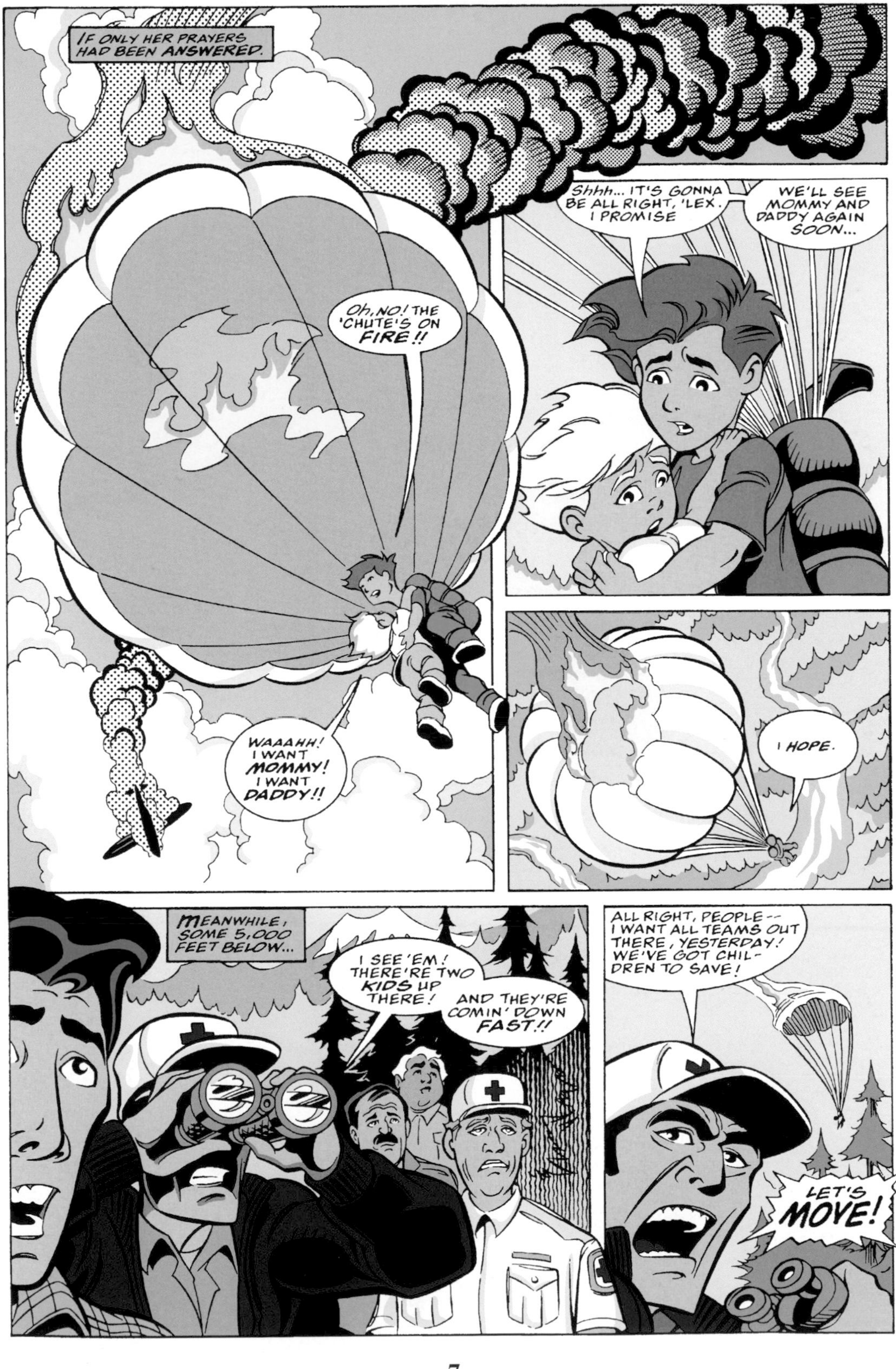
IF ONLY HER PRAYERS HAD BEEN ANSWERED.
Oh, NO! THE 'CHUTE'S ON FIRE!!
WAAAHH! I WANT MOMMY! I WANT DADDY!!
Shhh... IT'S GONNA BE ALL RIGHT, 'LEX. I PROMISE
WE'LL SEE MOMMY AND DADDY AGAIN SOON...
I HOPE.
MEANWHILE, SOME 5,000 FEET BELOW...
I SEE 'EM! THERE'RE TWO KIDS UP THERE!
AND THEY'RE COMIN' DOWN FAST!!
ALL RIGHT, PEOPLE-- I WANT ALL TEAMS OUT THERE, YESTERDAY! WE'VE GOT CHILDREN TO SAVE!
LET'S MOVE!

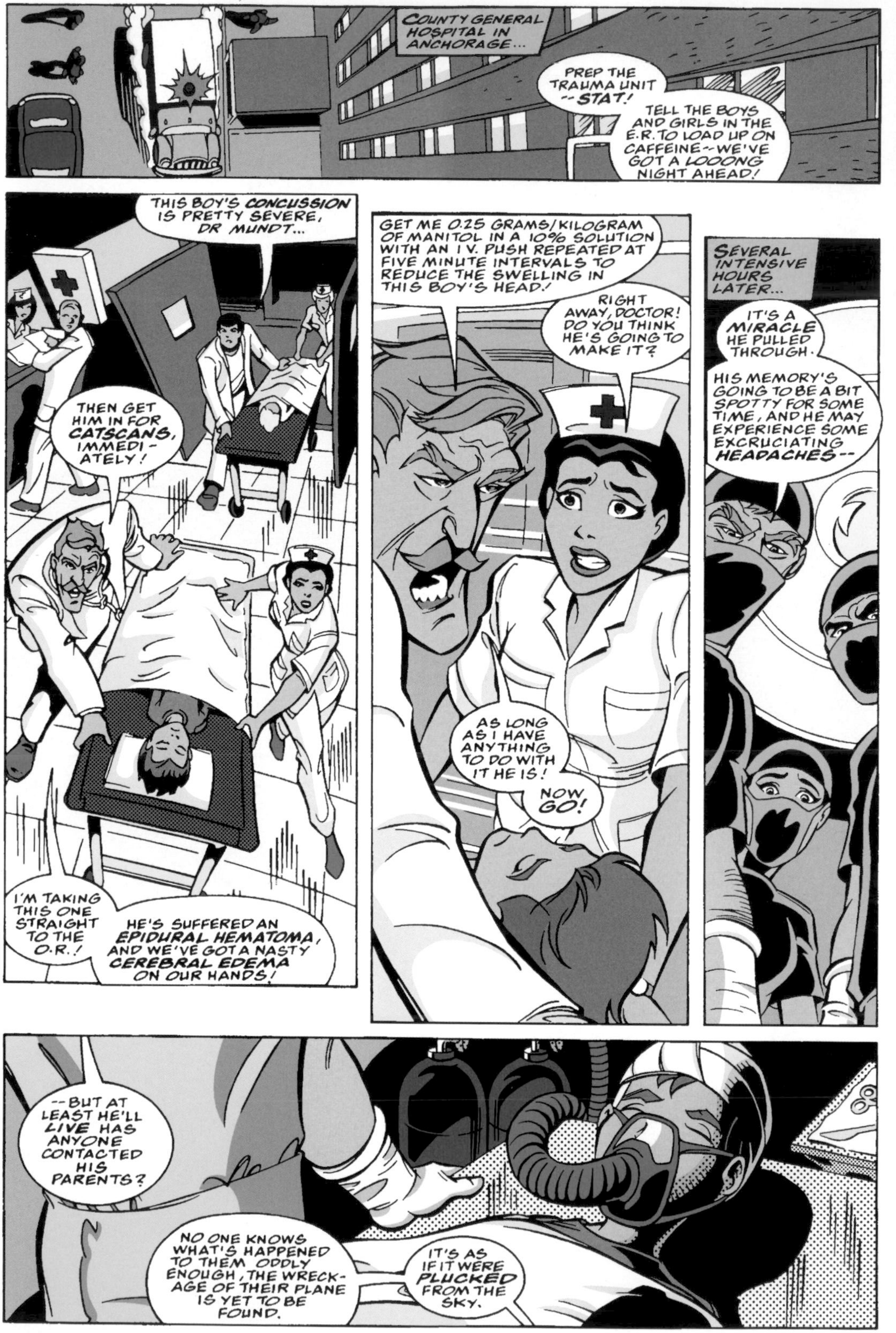

COUNTY GENERAL HOSPITAL IN ANCHORAGE...
PREP THE TRAUMA UNIT --STAT!
TELL THE BOYS AND GIRLS IN THE E.R. TO LOAD UP ON CAFFEINE--WE'VE GOT A LOOOONG NIGHT AHEAD!
THIS BOY'S CONCUSSION IS PRETTY SEVERE, DR MUNDT...
THEN GET HIM IN FOR CATSCANS, IMMEDI-ATELY!
I'M TAKING THIS ONE STRAIGHT TO THE O.R.!
HE'S SUFFERED AN EPIDURAL HEMATOMA, AND WE'VE GOT A NASTY CEREBRAL EDEMA ON OUR HANDS!
GET ME 0.25 GRAMS/KILOGRAM OF MANITOL IN A 10% SOLUTION WITH AN I.V. PUSH REPEATED AT FIVE MINUTE INTERVALS TO REDUCE THE SWELLING IN THIS BOY'S HEAD!
RIGHT AWAY, DOCTOR! DO YOU THINK HE'S GOING TO MAKE IT?
AS LONG AS I HAVE ANYTHING TO DO WITH IT HE IS!
NOW GO!
SEVERAL INTENSIVE HOURS LATER...
IT'S A MIRACLE HE PULLED THROUGH.
HIS MEMORY'S GOING TO BE A BIT SPOTTY FOR SOME TIME, AND HE MAY EXPERIENCE SOME EXCRUCIATING HEADACHES--
--BUT AT LEAST HE'LL LIVE HAS ANYONE CONTACTED HIS PARENTS?
NO ONE KNOWS WHAT'S HAPPENED TO THEM ODDLY ENOUGH, THE WRECK-AGE OF THEIR PLANE IS YET TO BE FOUND.
IT'S AS IF IT WERE PLUCKED FROM THE SKY.

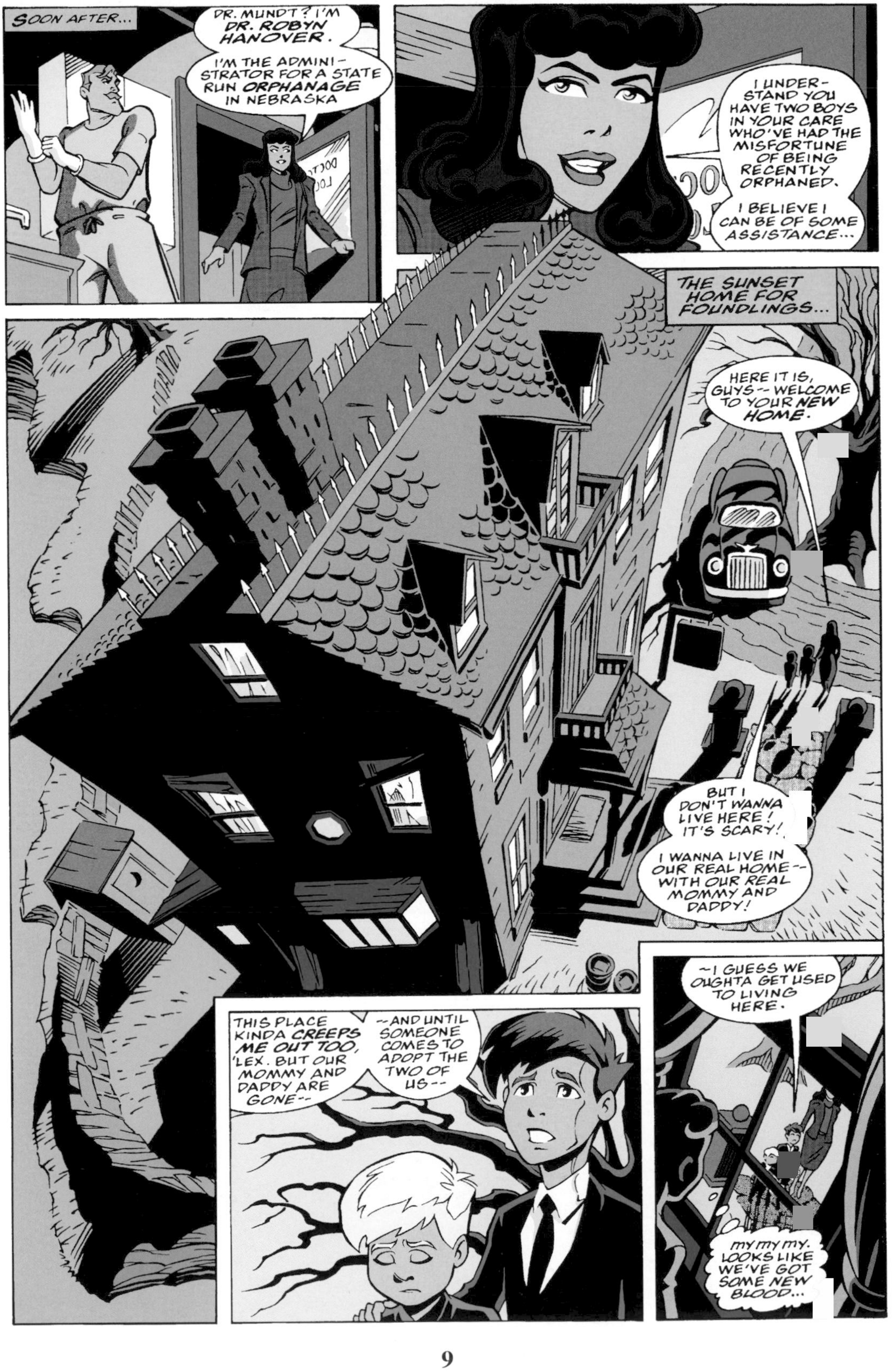
SOON AFTER...
DR. MUNDT? I'M DR. ROBYN HANOVER.
I'M THE ADMINISTRATOR FOR A STATE RUN ORPHANAGE IN NEBRASKA
I UNDERSTAND YOU HAVE TWO BOYS IN YOUR CARE WHO'VE HAD THE MISFORTUNE OF BEING RECENTLY ORPHANED.
I BELIEVE I CAN BE OF SOME ASSISTANCE...
THE SUNSET HOME FOR FOUNDLINGS...
HERE IT IS, GUYS-- WELCOME TO YOUR NEW HOME.
BUT I DON'T WANNA LIVE HERE! IT'S SCARY!
I WANNA LIVE IN OUR REAL HOME-- WITH OUR REAL MOMMY AND DADDY!
THIS PLACE KINDA CREEPS ME OUT TOO, 'LEX. BUT OUR MOMMY AND DADDY ARE GONE--
--AND UNTIL SOMEONE COMES TO ADOPT THE TWO OF US--
--I GUESS WE OUGHTA GET USED TO LIVING HERE.
my my my. LOOKS LIKE WE'VE GOT SOME NEW BLOOD...

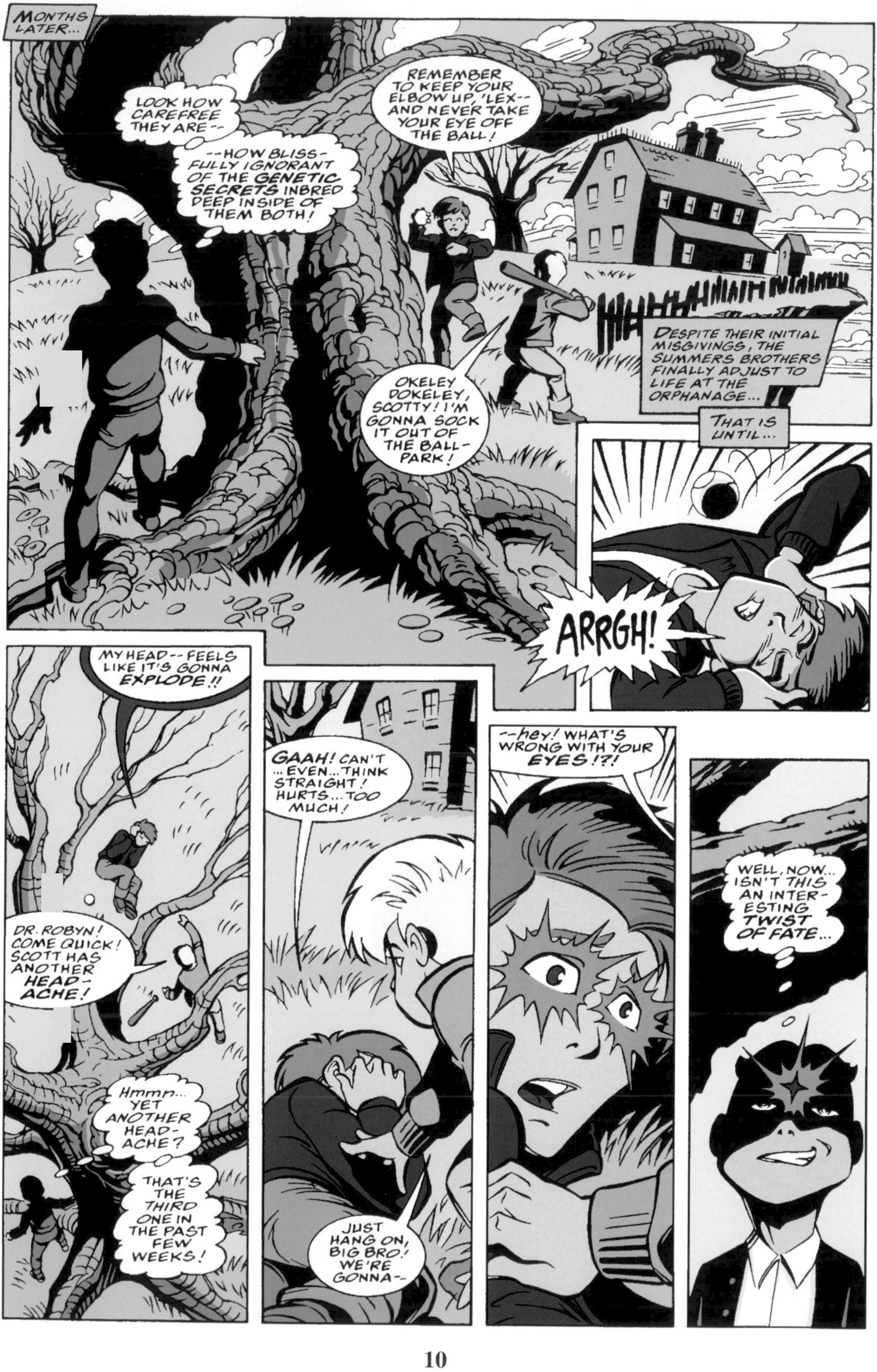
MONTHS LATER...
LOOK HOW CAREFREE THEY ARE--
--HOW BLISSFULLY IGNORANT OF THE GENETIC SECRETS INBRED DEEP INSIDE OF THEM BOTH!
REMEMBER TO KEEP YOUR ELBOW UP, 'LEX-- AND NEVER TAKE YOUR EYE OFF THE BALL!
OKELEY DOKELEY, SCOTTY! I'M GONNA SOCK IT OUT OF THE BALL-PARK!
DESPITE THEIR INITIAL MISGIVINGS, THE SUMMERS BROTHERS FINALLY ADJUST TO LIFE AT THE ORPHANAGE...
THAT IS UNTIL...
ARRGH!
MY HEAD--FEELS LIKE IT'S GONNA EXPLODE!!
DR. ROBYN! COME QUICK! SCOTT HAS ANOTHER HEAD-ACHE!
Hmmm... YET ANOTHER HEAD-ACHE?
THAT'S THE THIRD ONE IN THE PAST FEW WEEKS!
GAAH! CAN'T ...EVEN...THINK STRAIGHT! HURTS...TOO MUCH!
JUST HANG ON, BIG BRO! WE'RE GONNA--
--hey! WHAT'S WRONG WITH YOUR EYES!?!
WELL, NOW... ISN'T THIS AN INTER-ESTING TWIST OF FATE...

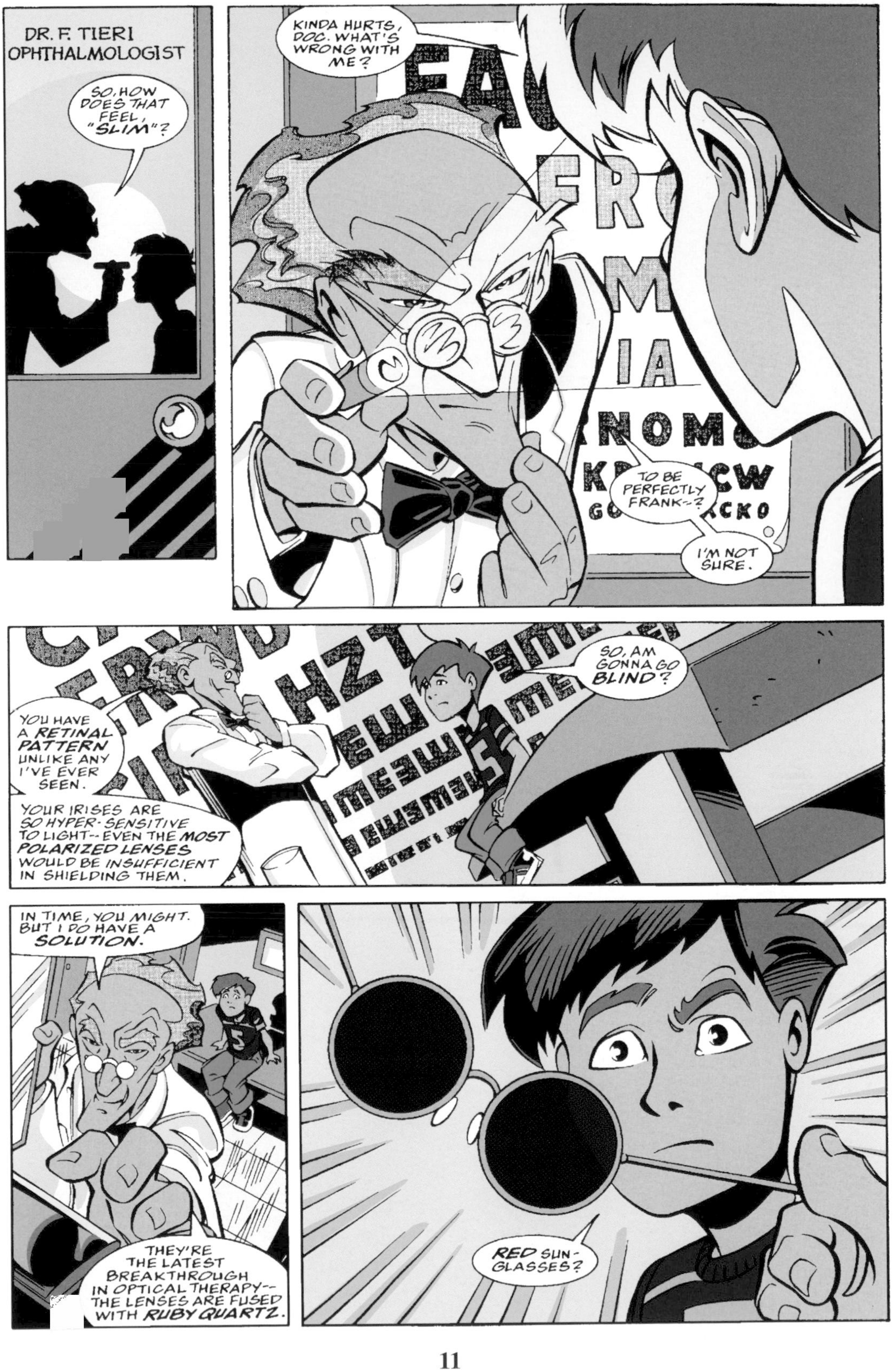
DR. F. TIERI
OPHTHALMOLOGIST
SO, HOW DOES THAT FEEL, "SLIM"?
KINDA HURTS, DOC. WHAT'S WRONG WITH ME?
TO BE PERFECTLY FRANK--?
I'M NOT SURE.
SO, AM I GONNA GO BLIND?
YOU HAVE A RETINAL PATTERN UNLIKE ANY I'VE EVER SEEN.
YOUR IRISES ARE SO HYPER-SENSITIVE TO LIGHT--EVEN THE MOST POLARIZED LENSES WOULD BE INSUFFICIENT IN SHIELDING THEM.
IN TIME, YOU MIGHT. BUT I DO HAVE A SOLUTION.
THEY'RE THE LATEST BREAKTHROUGH IN OPTICAL THERAPY--THE LENSES ARE FUSED WITH RUBY QUARTZ.
RED SUN-GLASSES?

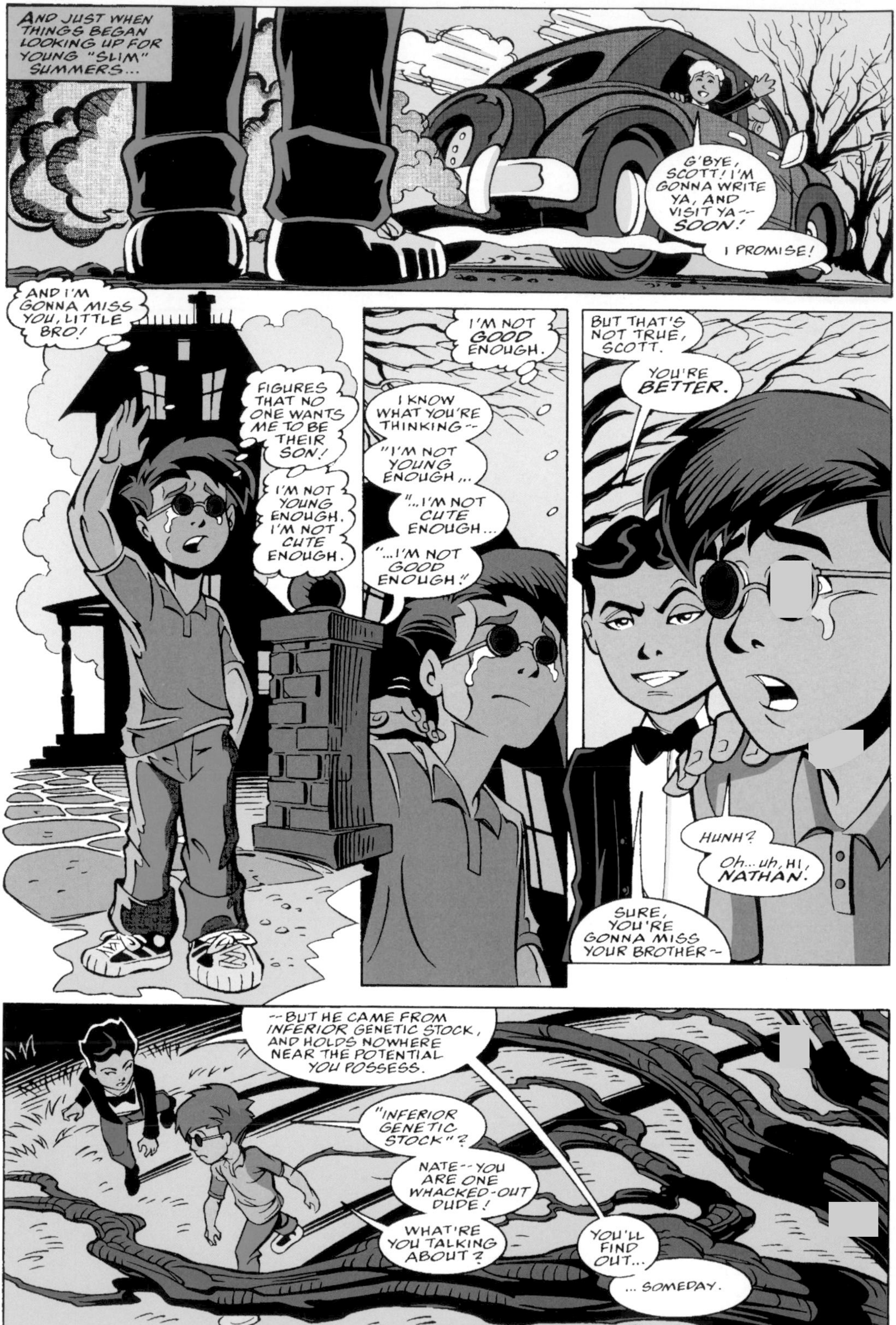
AND JUST WHEN THINGS BEGAN LOOKING UP FOR YOUNG "SLIM" SUMMERS...
G'BYE, SCOTT! I'M GONNA WRITE YA, AND VISIT YA-- SOON!
I PROMISE!
AND I'M GONNA MISS YOU, LITTLE BRO!
FIGURES THAT NO ONE WANTS ME TO BE THEIR SON!
I'M NOT YOUNG ENOUGH. I'M NOT CUTE ENOUGH.
I'M NOT GOOD ENOUGH.
I KNOW WHAT YOU'RE THINKING--
"I'M NOT YOUNG ENOUGH...
"...I'M NOT CUTE ENOUGH...
"...I'M NOT GOOD ENOUGH."
BUT THAT'S NOT TRUE, SCOTT.
YOU'RE BETTER.
HUNH?
Oh...uh, HI, NATHAN.
SURE, YOU'RE GONNA MISS YOUR BROTHER--
--BUT HE CAME FROM INFERIOR GENETIC STOCK, AND HOLDS NOWHERE NEAR THE POTENTIAL YOU POSSESS.
"INFERIOR GENETIC STOCK"?
NATE--YOU ARE ONE WHACKED-OUT DUDE!
WHAT'RE YOU TALKING ABOUT?
YOU'LL FIND OUT...
...SOMEDAY.

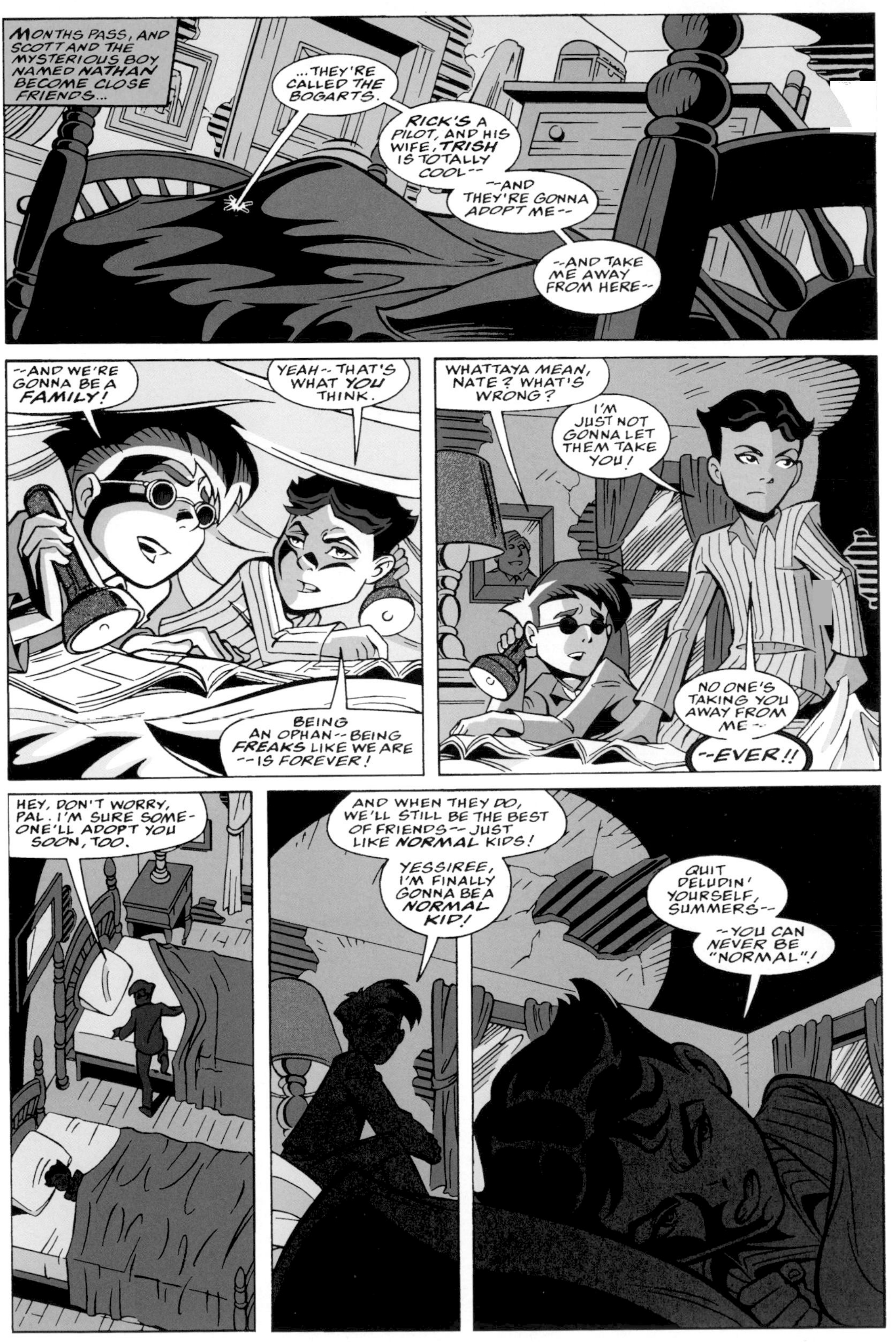

MONTHS PASS, AND SCOTT AND THE MYSTERIOUS BOY NAMED NATHAN BECOME CLOSE FRIENDS...
...THEY'RE CALLED THE BOGARTS.
RICK'S A PILOT, AND HIS WIFE, TRISH IS TOTALLY COOL--
--AND THEY'RE GONNA ADOPT ME--
--AND TAKE ME AWAY FROM HERE--
--AND WE'RE GONNA BE A FAMILY!
YEAH--THAT'S WHAT YOU THINK.
BEING AN OPHAN--BEING FREAKS LIKE WE ARE--IS FOREVER!
WHATTAYA MEAN, NATE? WHAT'S WRONG?
I'M JUST NOT GONNA LET THEM TAKE YOU!
NO ONE'S TAKING YOU AWAY FROM ME--
--EVER!!
HEY, DON'T WORRY, PAL. I'M SURE SOME-ONE'LL ADOPT YOU SOON, TOO.
AND WHEN THEY DO, WE'LL STILL BE THE BEST OF FRIENDS--JUST LIKE NORMAL KIDS!
YESSIREE, I'M FINALLY GONNA BE A NORMAL KID!
QUIT DELUDIN' YOURSELF, SUMMERS--
--YOU CAN NEVER BE "NORMAL"!

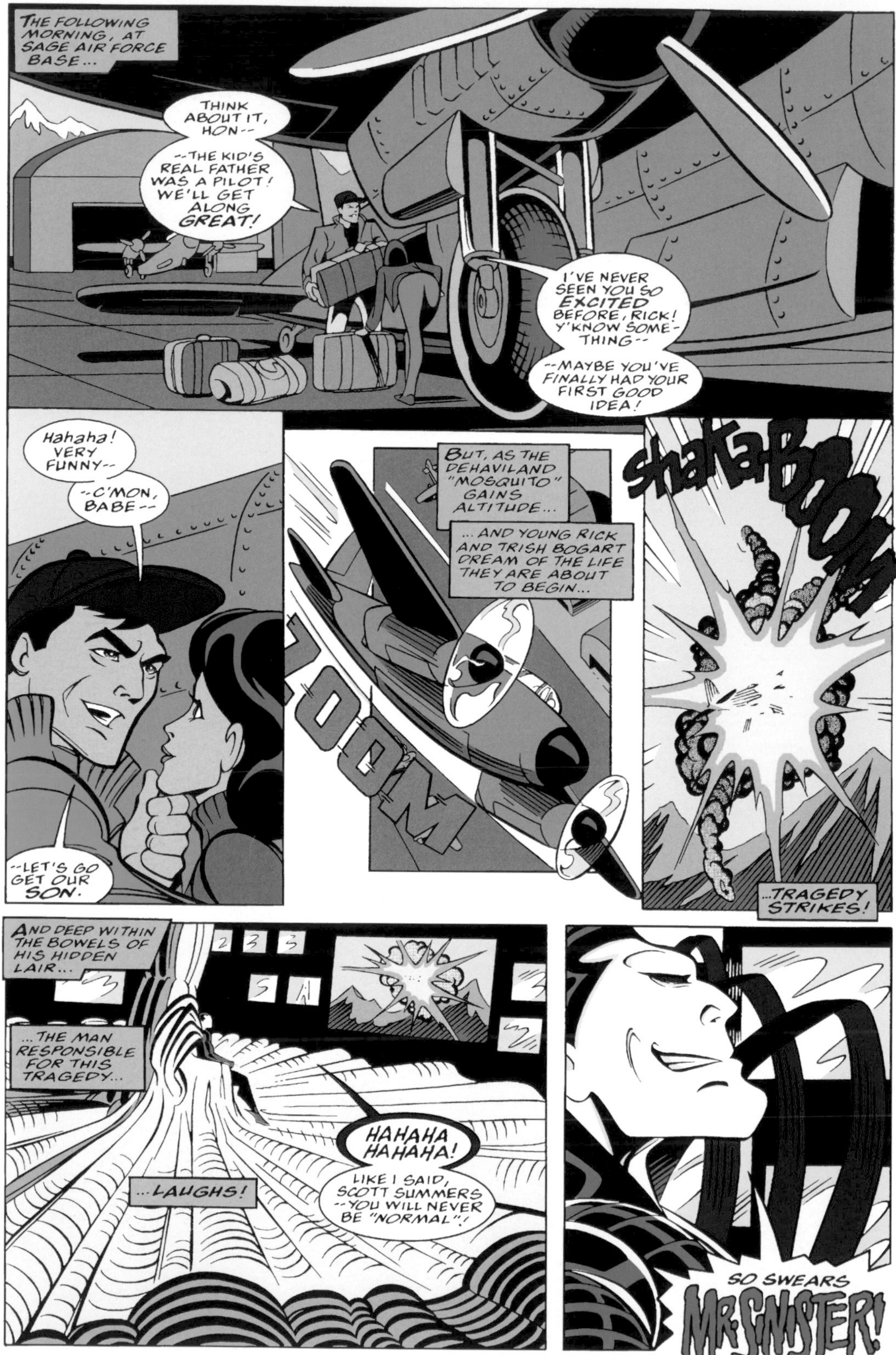

THE FOLLOWING MORNING, AT SAGE AIR FORCE BASE...
THINK ABOUT IT, HON--
--THE KID'S REAL FATHER WAS A PILOT! WE'LL GET ALONG GREAT!
I'VE NEVER SEEN YOU SO EXCITED BEFORE, RICK! Y'KNOW SOME-THING--
--MAYBE YOU'VE FINALLY HAD YOUR FIRST GOOD IDEA!
Hahaha! VERY FUNNY--
--C'MON, BABE--
--LET'S GO GET OUR SON.
BUT, AS THE DEHAVILAND "MOSQUITO" GAINS ALTITUDE...
...AND YOUNG RICK AND TRISH BOGART DREAM OF THE LIFE THEY ARE ABOUT TO BEGIN...
ZOOM
Shaka-BOOM
...TRAGEDY STRIKES!
AND DEEP WITHIN THE BOWELS OF HIS HIDDEN LAIR...
...THE MAN RESPONSIBLE FOR THIS TRAGEDY...
...LAUGHS!
HAHAHA HAHAHA!
LIKE I SAID, SCOTT SUMMERS --YOU WILL NEVER BE "NORMAL"!
SO SWEARS MR. SINISTER!

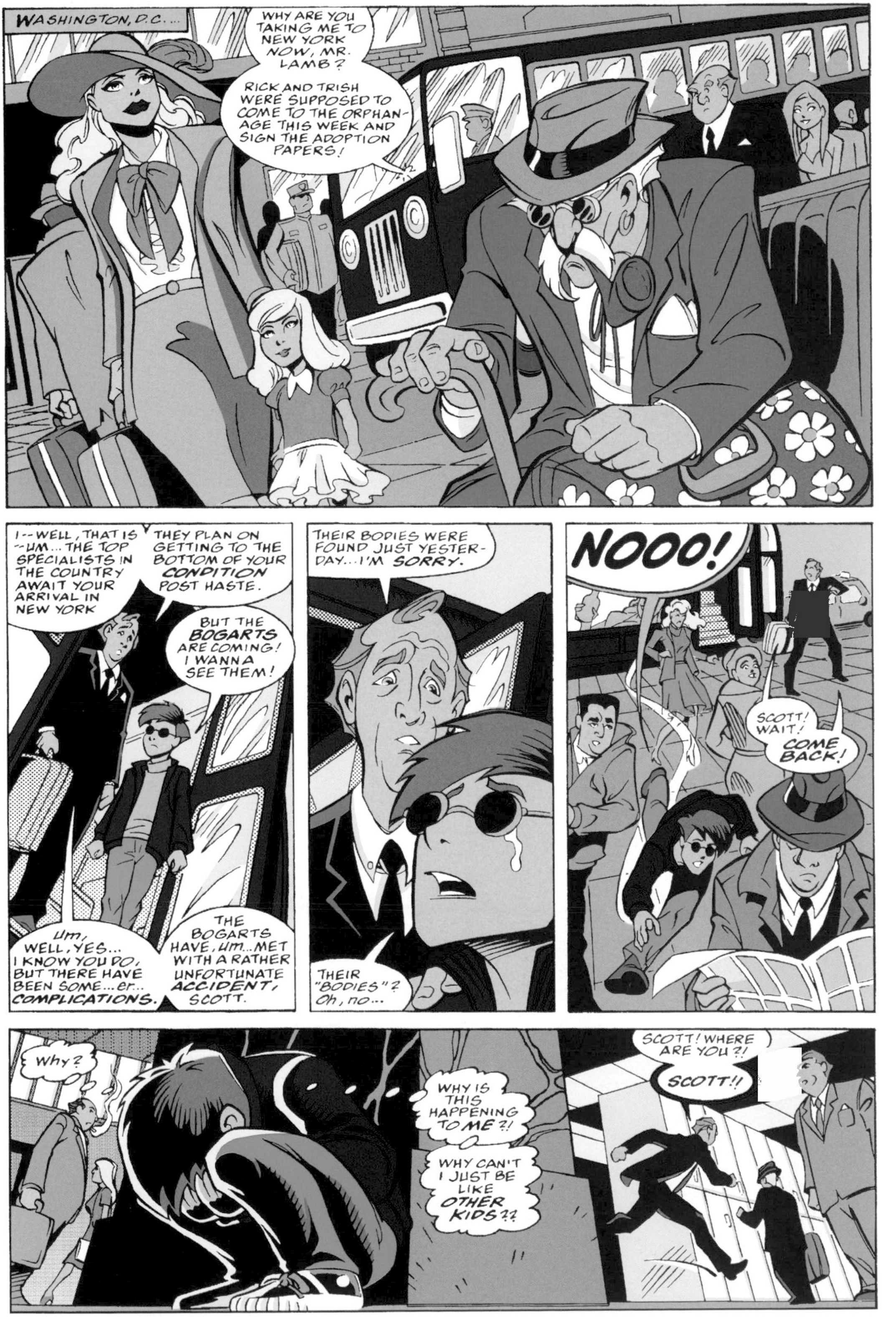
WASHINGTON, D.C. ...
WHY ARE YOU TAKING ME TO NEW YORK NOW, MR. LAMB?
RICK AND TRISH WERE SUPPOSED TO COME TO THE ORPHANAGE THIS WEEK AND SIGN THE ADOPTION PAPERS!
I--WELL, THAT IS --UM... THE TOP SPECIALISTS IN THE COUNTRY AWAIT YOUR ARRIVAL IN NEW YORK
THEY PLAN ON GETTING TO THE BOTTOM OF YOUR CONDITION POST HASTE.
BUT THE BOGARTS ARE COMING! I WANNA SEE THEM!
UM, WELL, YES... I KNOW YOU DO, BUT THERE HAVE BEEN SOME... ER... COMPLICATIONS.
THE BOGARTS HAVE, UM... MET WITH A RATHER UNFORTUNATE ACCIDENT, SCOTT.
THEIR BODIES WERE FOUND JUST YESTERDAY... I'M SORRY.
THEIR "BODIES"? OH, NO...
NOOO!
SCOTT! WAIT! COME BACK!
WHY?
WHY IS THIS HAPPENING TO ME?!
WHY CAN'T I JUST BE LIKE OTHER KIDS??
SCOTT! WHERE ARE YOU?!
SCOTT!!

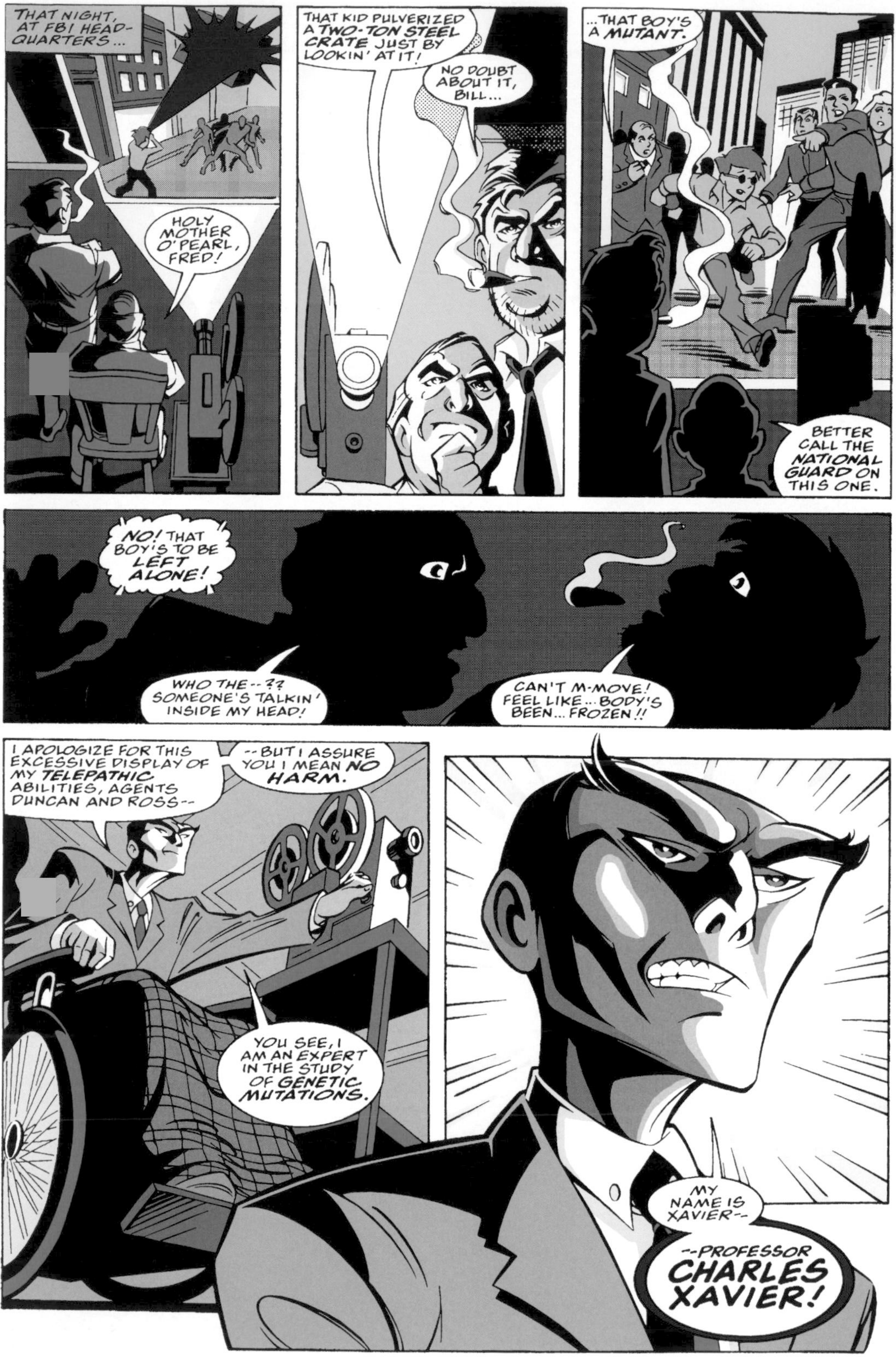
THAT NIGHT, AT FBI HEAD-QUARTERS...
HOLY MOTHER O'PEARL, FRED!
THAT KID PULVERIZED A TWO-TON STEEL CRATE JUST BY LOOKIN' AT IT!
NO DOUBT ABOUT IT, BILL...
...THAT BOY'S A MUTANT.
BETTER CALL THE NATIONAL GUARD ON THIS ONE.
NO! THAT BOY'S TO BE LEFT ALONE!
WHO THE--?? SOMEONE'S TALKIN' INSIDE MY HEAD!
CAN'T M-MOVE! FEEL LIKE... BODY'S BEEN... FROZEN!!
I APOLOGIZE FOR THIS EXCESSIVE DISPLAY OF MY TELEPATHIC ABILITIES, AGENTS DUNCAN AND ROSS--
--BUT I ASSURE YOU I MEAN NO HARM.
YOU SEE, I AM AN EXPERT IN THE STUDY OF GENETIC MUTATIONS.
MY NAME IS XAVIER--
--PROFESSOR CHARLES XAVIER!

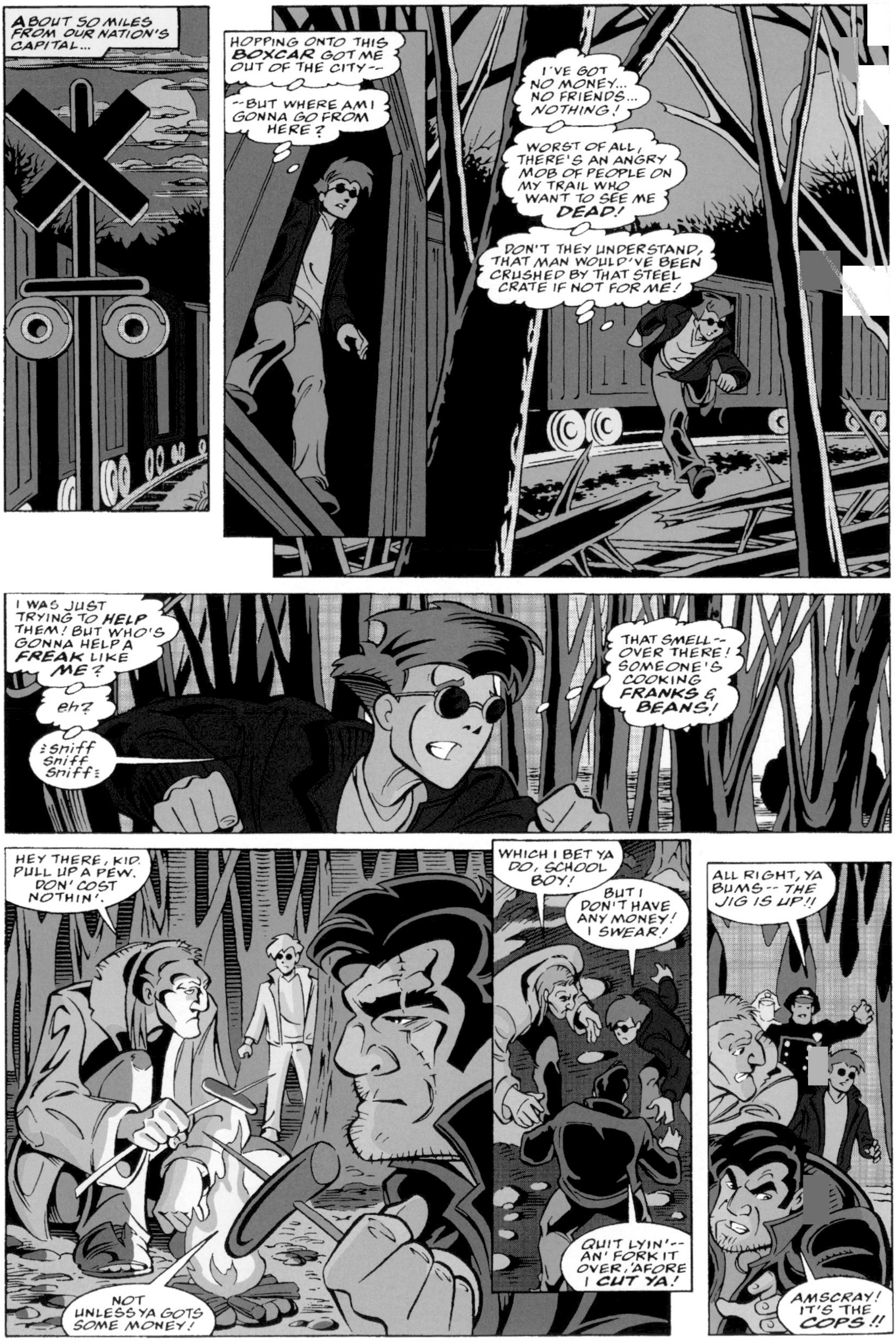
ABOUT 50 MILES FROM OUR NATION'S CAPITAL...
HOPPING ONTO THIS BOXCAR GOT ME OUT OF THE CITY--
--BUT WHERE AM I GONNA GO FROM HERE?
I'VE GOT NO MONEY... NO FRIENDS... NOTHING!
WORST OF ALL, THERE'S AN ANGRY MOB OF PEOPLE ON MY TRAIL WHO WANT TO SEE ME DEAD!
DON'T THEY UNDERSTAND, THAT MAN WOULD'VE BEEN CRUSHED BY THAT STEEL CRATE IF NOT FOR ME!
I WAS JUST TRYING TO HELP THEM! BUT WHO'S GONNA HELP A FREAK LIKE ME?
eh?
sniff sniff sniff
THAT SMELL-- OVER THERE! SOMEONE'S COOKING FRANKS & BEANS!
HEY THERE, KID. PULL UP A PEW. DON' COST NOTHIN'.
NOT UNLESS YA GOTS SOME MONEY!
WHICH I BET YA DO, SCHOOL BOY!
BUT I DON'T HAVE ANY MONEY! I SWEAR!
QUIT LYIN'-- AN' FORK IT OVER, 'AFORE I CUT YA!
ALL RIGHT, YA BUMS -- THE JIG IS UP!!
AMSCRAY! IT'S THE COPS!!

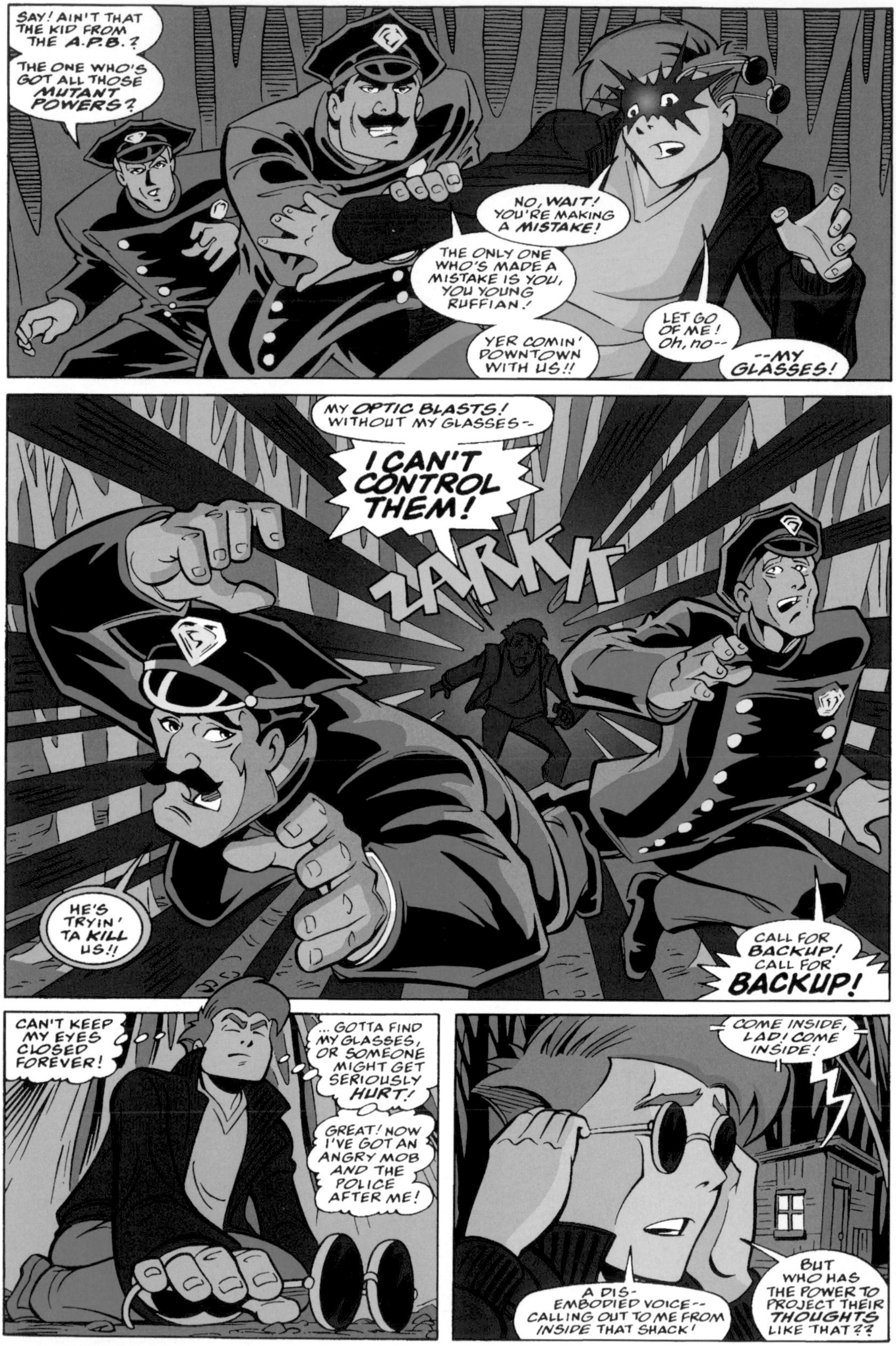
SAY! AIN'T THAT THE KID FROM THE A.P.B.?
THE ONE WHO'S GOT ALL THOSE MUTANT POWERS?
NO, WAIT! YOU'RE MAKING A MISTAKE!
THE ONLY ONE WHO'S MADE A MISTAKE IS YOU, YOU YOUNG RUFFIAN!
YER COMIN' DOWNTOWN WITH US!!
LET GO OF ME! Oh, no--
--MY GLASSES!
MY OPTIC BLASTS! WITHOUT MY GLASSES--
I CAN'T CONTROL THEM!
ZARKT
HE'S TRYIN' TA KILL US!!
CALL FOR BACKUP! CALL FOR BACKUP!
CAN'T KEEP MY EYES CLOSED FOREVER!
...GOTTA FIND MY GLASSES, OR SOMEONE MIGHT GET SERIOUSLY HURT!
GREAT! NOW I'VE GOT AN ANGRY MOB AND THE POLICE AFTER ME!
COME INSIDE, LAD! COME INSIDE!
A DIS-EMBODIED VOICE--CALLING OUT TO ME FROM INSIDE THAT SHACK!
BUT WHO HAS THE POWER TO PROJECT THEIR THOUGHTS LIKE THAT??

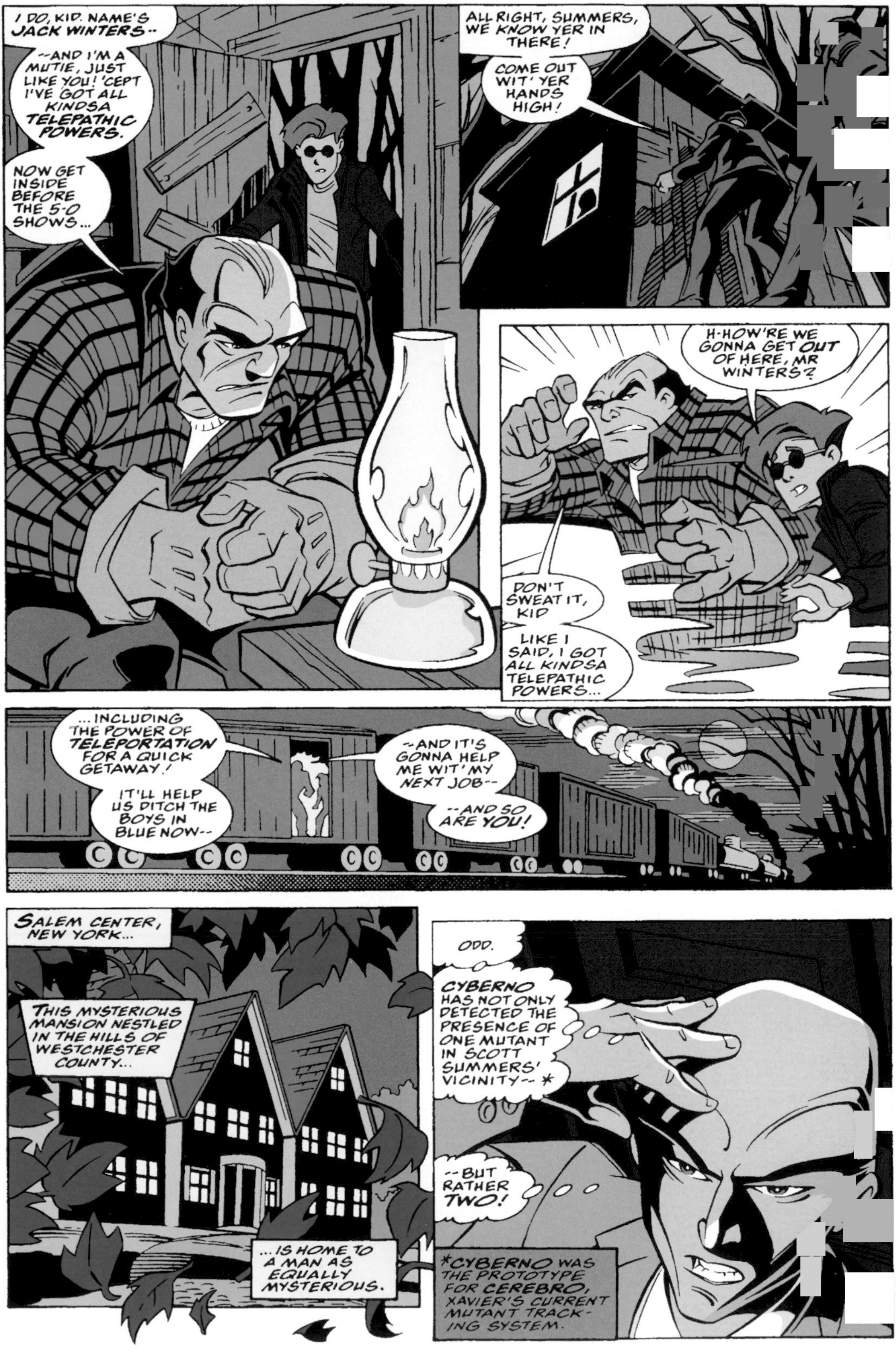
I DO, KID. NAME'S JACK WINTERS--
--AND I'M A MUTIE, JUST LIKE YOU! 'CEPT I'VE GOT ALL KINDSA TELEPATHIC POWERS.
NOW GET INSIDE BEFORE THE 5-0 SHOWS...
ALL RIGHT, SUMMERS, WE KNOW YER IN THERE!
COME OUT WIT' YER HANDS HIGH!
H-HOW'RE WE GONNA GET OUT OF HERE, MR WINTERS?
DON'T SWEAT IT, KID
LIKE I SAID, I GOT ALL KINDSA TELEPATHIC POWERS...
...INCLUDING THE POWER OF TELEPORTATION FOR A QUICK GETAWAY!
IT'LL HELP US DITCH THE BOYS IN BLUE NOW--
--AND IT'S GONNA HELP ME WIT' MY NEXT JOB--
--AND SO ARE YOU!
SALEM CENTER, NEW YORK...
THIS MYSTERIOUS MANSION NESTLED IN THE HILLS OF WESTCHESTER COUNTY...
...IS HOME TO A MAN AS EQUALLY MYSTERIOUS.
ODD.
CYBERNO HAS NOT ONLY DETECTED THE PRESENCE OF ONE MUTANT IN SCOTT SUMMERS' VICINITY-- *
--BUT RATHER TWO!
*CYBERNO WAS THE PROTOTYPE FOR CEREBRO, XAVIER'S CURRENT MUTANT TRACKING SYSTEM.

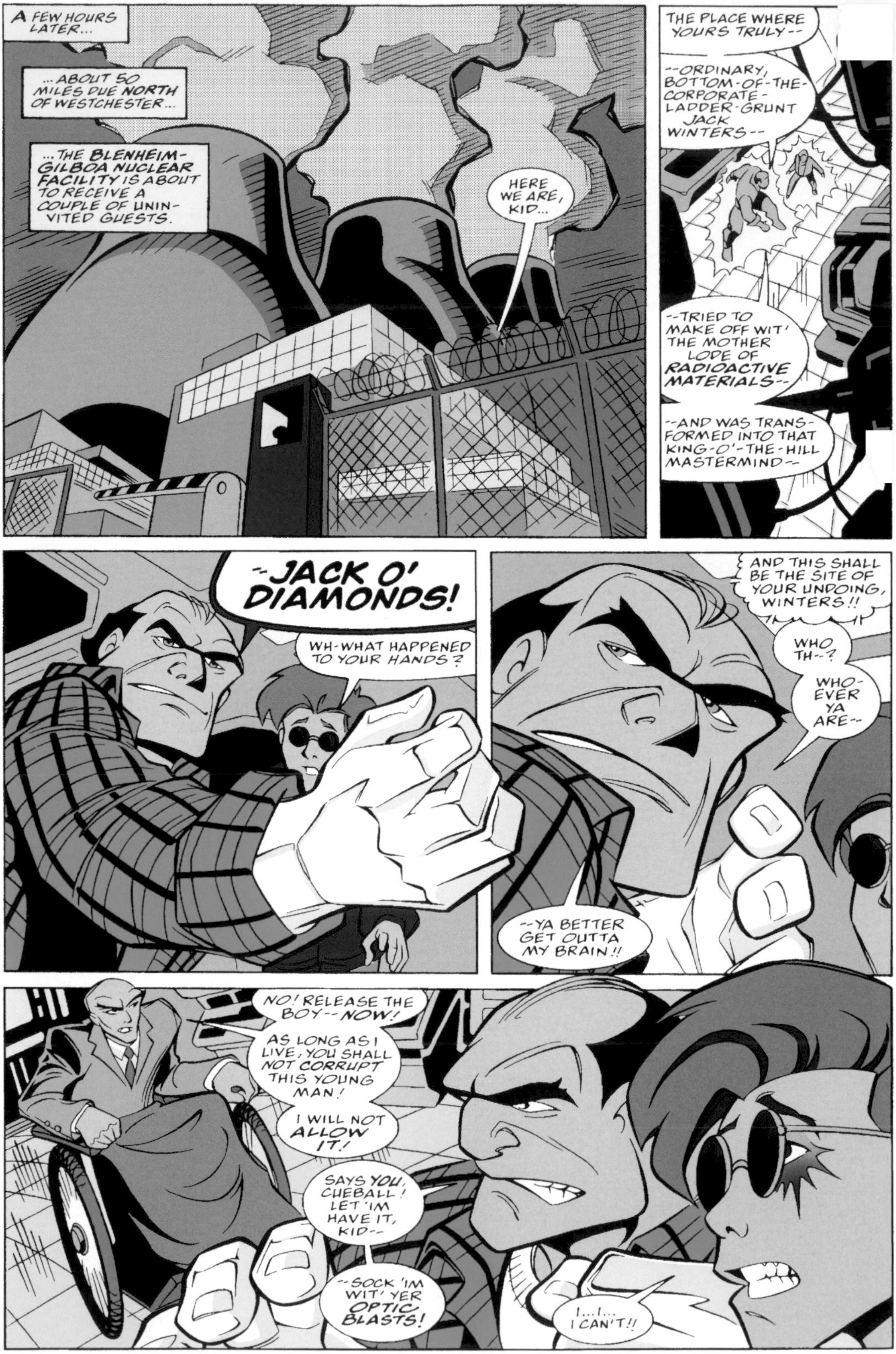
A FEW HOURS LATER...
...ABOUT 50 MILES DUE NORTH OF WESTCHESTER...
...THE BLENHEIM-GILBOA NUCLEAR FACILITY IS ABOUT TO RECEIVE A COUPLE OF UNINVITED GUESTS.
HERE WE ARE, KID...
THE PLACE WHERE YOURS TRULY--
--ORDINARY, BOTTOM-OF-THE-CORPORATE-LADDER-GRUNT JACK WINTERS--
--TRIED TO MAKE OFF WIT' THE MOTHER LODE OF RADIOACTIVE MATERIALS--
--AND WAS TRANSFORMED INTO THAT KING-O'-THE-HILL MASTERMIND--
--JACK O' DIAMONDS!
WH-WHAT HAPPENED TO YOUR HANDS?
AND THIS SHALL BE THE SITE OF YOUR UNDOING, WINTERS!!
WHO TH--?
WHO-EVER YA ARE--
--YA BETTER GET OUTTA MY BRAIN!!
NO! RELEASE THE BOY--NOW!
AS LONG AS I LIVE, YOU SHALL NOT CORRUPT THIS YOUNG MAN!
I WILL NOT ALLOW IT!
SAYS YOU, CUEBALL! LET 'IM HAVE IT, KID--
--SOCK 'IM WIT' YER OPTIC BLASTS!
I...I... I CAN'T!!

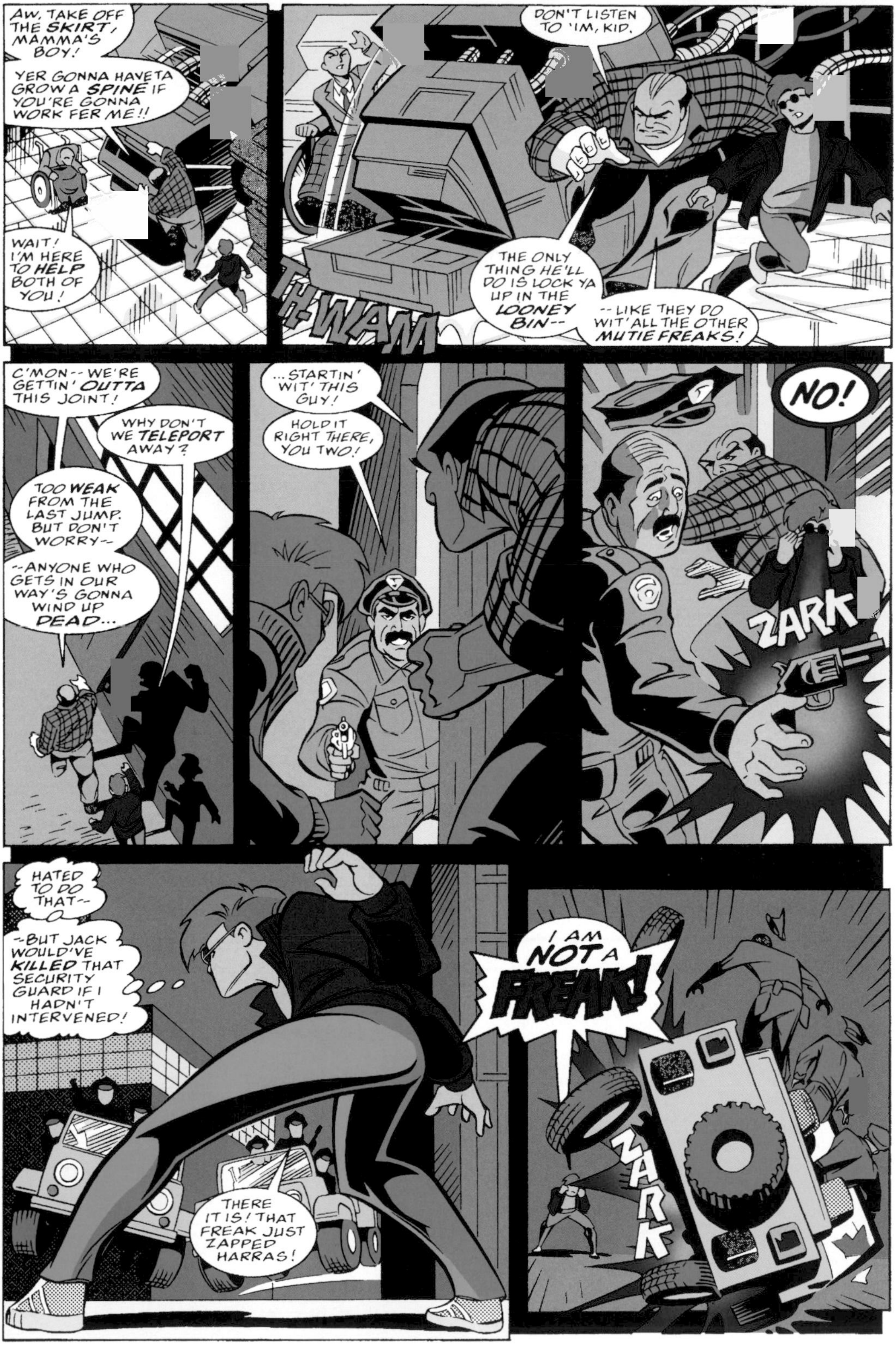
AW, TAKE OFF THE SKIRT, MAMMA'S BOY!
YER GONNA HAVETA GROW A SPINE IF YOU'RE GONNA WORK FER ME!!
WAIT! I'M HERE TO HELP BOTH OF YOU!
TH-WAM
DON'T LISTEN TO 'IM, KID.
THE ONLY THING HE'LL DO IS LOCK YA UP IN THE LOONEY BIN--
--LIKE THEY DO WIT' ALL THE OTHER MUTIE FREAKS!
C'MON-- WE'RE GETTIN' OUTTA THIS JOINT!
WHY DON'T WE TELEPORT AWAY?
TOO WEAK FROM THE LAST JUMP. BUT DON'T WORRY--
--ANYONE WHO GETS IN OUR WAY'S GONNA WIND UP DEAD...
...STARTIN' WIT' THIS GUY!
HOLD IT RIGHT THERE, YOU TWO!
NO!
ZARK
HATED TO DO THAT--
--BUT JACK WOULD'VE KILLED THAT SECURITY GUARD IF I HADN'T INTERVENED!
THERE IT IS! THAT FREAK JUST ZAPPED HARRAS!
I AM NOT A FREAK!
ZARK
ZARK

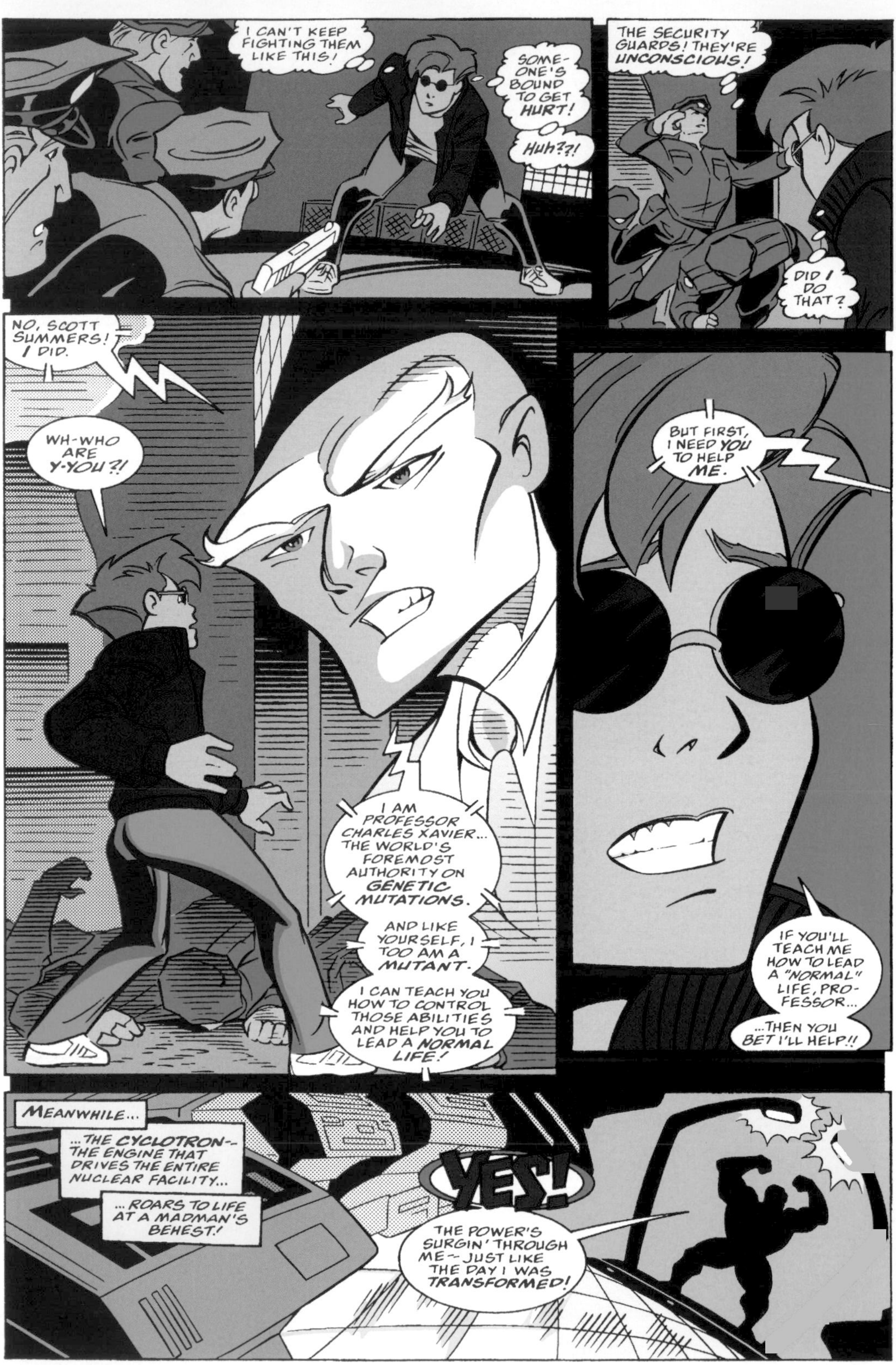
I CAN'T KEEP FIGHTING THEM LIKE THIS!
SOME-ONE'S BOUND TO GET HURT!
Huh??!
THE SECURITY GUARDS! THEY'RE UNCONSCIOUS!
DID I DO THAT?
NO, SCOTT SUMMERS! I DID.
WH-WHO ARE Y-YOU?!
BUT FIRST, I NEED YOU TO HELP ME.
I AM PROFESSOR CHARLES XAVIER... THE WORLD'S FOREMOST AUTHORITY ON GENETIC MUTATIONS.
AND LIKE YOURSELF, I TOO AM A MUTANT.
I CAN TEACH YOU HOW TO CONTROL THOSE ABILITIES AND HELP YOU TO LEAD A NORMAL LIFE!
IF YOU'LL TEACH ME HOW TO LEAD A "NORMAL" LIFE, PRO-FESSOR...
...THEN YOU BET I'LL HELP!!
MEANWHILE...
...THE CYCLOTRON-- THE ENGINE THAT DRIVES THE ENTIRE NUCLEAR FACILITY...
...ROARS TO LIFE AT A MADMAN'S BEHEST!
YES!
THE POWER'S SURGIN' THROUGH ME-- JUST LIKE THE DAY I WAS TRANSFORMED!

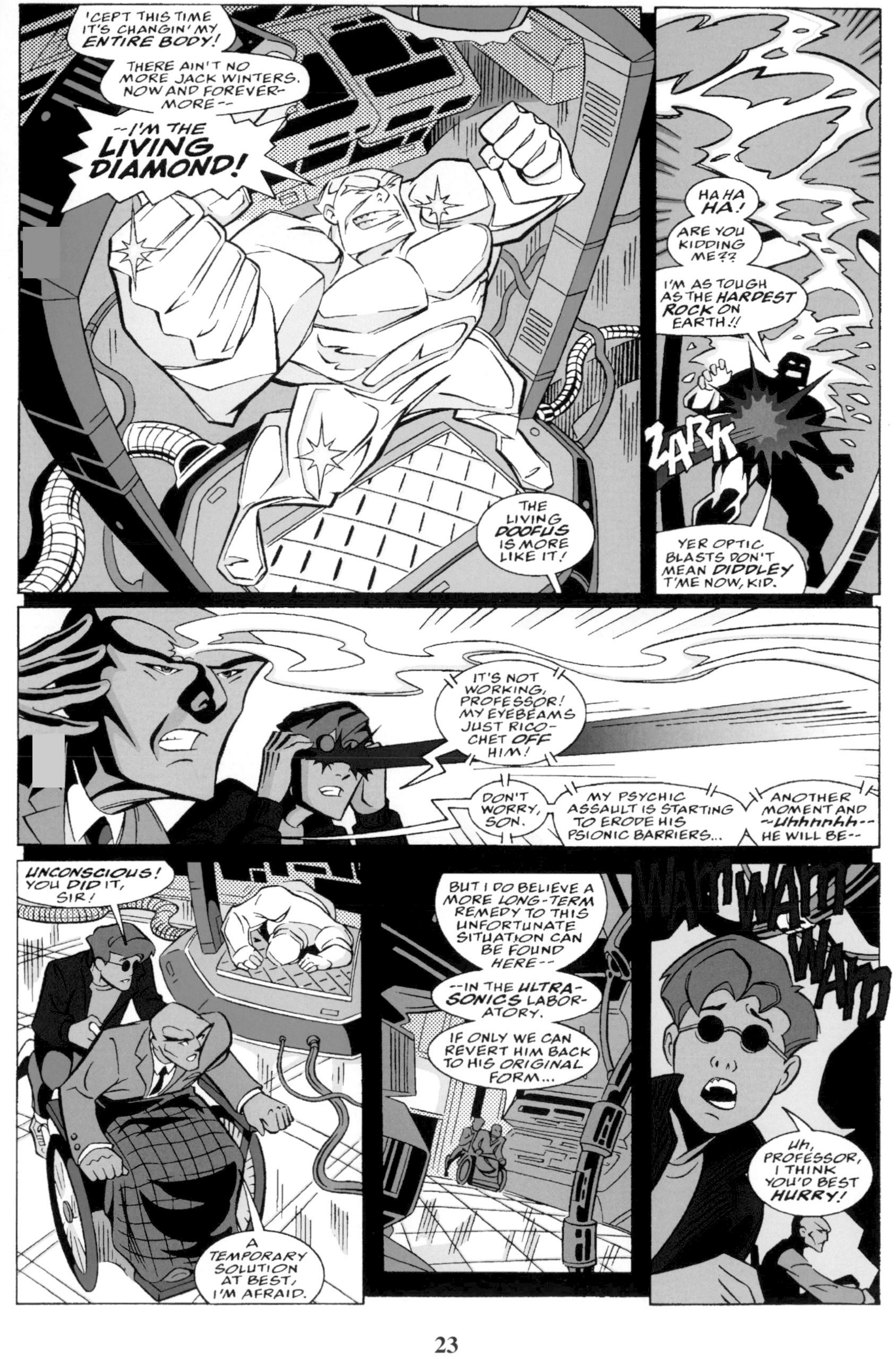
'CEPT THIS TIME IT'S CHANGIN' MY ENTIRE BODY!
THERE AIN'T NO MORE JACK WINTERS. NOW AND FOREVER-MORE--
--I'M THE LIVING DIAMOND!
THE LIVING DOOFUS IS MORE LIKE IT!
HA HA HA!
ARE YOU KIDDING ME??
I'M AS TOUGH AS THE HARDEST ROCK ON EARTH!!
ZARK
YER OPTIC BLASTS DON'T MEAN DIDDLEY T'ME NOW, KID.
IT'S NOT WORKING, PROFESSOR! MY EYEBEAMS JUST RICO-CHET OFF HIM!
DON'T WORRY, SON.
MY PSYCHIC ASSAULT IS STARTING TO ERODE HIS PSIONIC BARRIERS...
ANOTHER MOMENT AND --Uhhhhhh-- HE WILL BE--
UNCONSCIOUS! YOU DID IT, SIR!
A TEMPORARY SOLUTION AT BEST, I'M AFRAID.
BUT I DO BELIEVE A MORE LONG-TERM REMEDY TO THIS UNFORTUNATE SITUATION CAN BE FOUND HERE--
--IN THE ULTRA-SONICS LABOR-ATORY.
IF ONLY WE CAN REVERT HIM BACK TO HIS ORIGINAL FORM...
WAM WAM WAM
UH, PROFESSOR, I THINK YOU'D BEST HURRY!

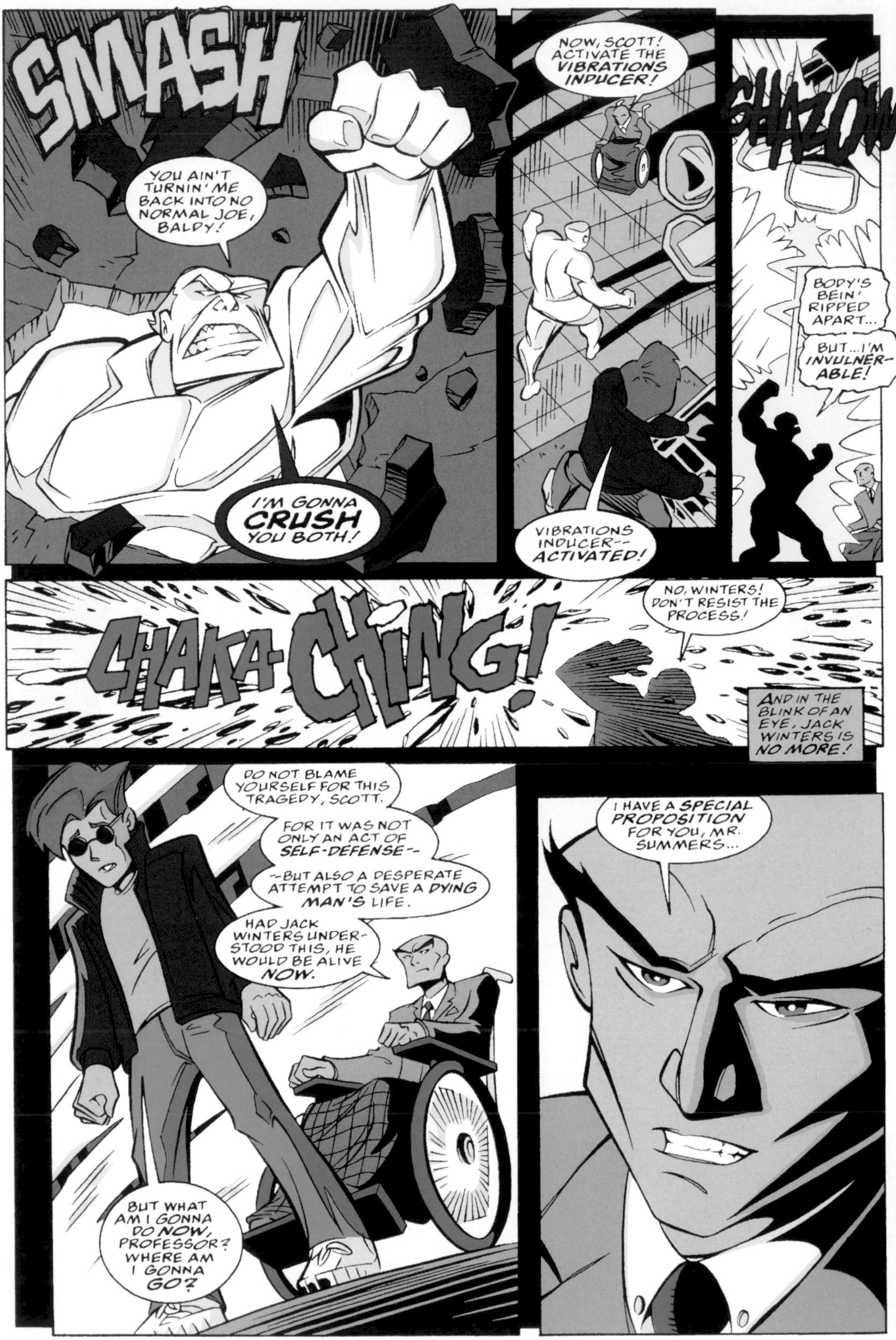
SMASH
YOU AIN'T TURNIN' ME BACK INTO NO NORMAL JOE, BALDY!
I'M GONNA CRUSH YOU BOTH!
NOW, SCOTT! ACTIVATE THE VIBRATIONS INDUCER!
VIBRATIONS INDUCER--ACTIVATED!
SHAZOW
BODY'S BEIN' RIPPED APART...
BUT...I'M INVULNERABLE!
CHAKA-CHING!
NO, WINTERS! DON'T RESIST THE PROCESS!
AND IN THE BLINK OF AN EYE, JACK WINTERS IS NO MORE!
DO NOT BLAME YOURSELF FOR THIS TRAGEDY, SCOTT.
FOR IT WAS NOT ONLY AN ACT OF SELF-DEFENSE--
--BUT ALSO A DESPERATE ATTEMPT TO SAVE A DYING MAN'S LIFE.
HAD JACK WINTERS UNDERSTOOD THIS, HE WOULD BE ALIVE NOW.
BUT WHAT AM I GONNA DO NOW, PROFESSOR? WHERE AM I GONNA GO?
I HAVE A SPECIAL PROPOSITION FOR YOU, MR. SUMMERS...

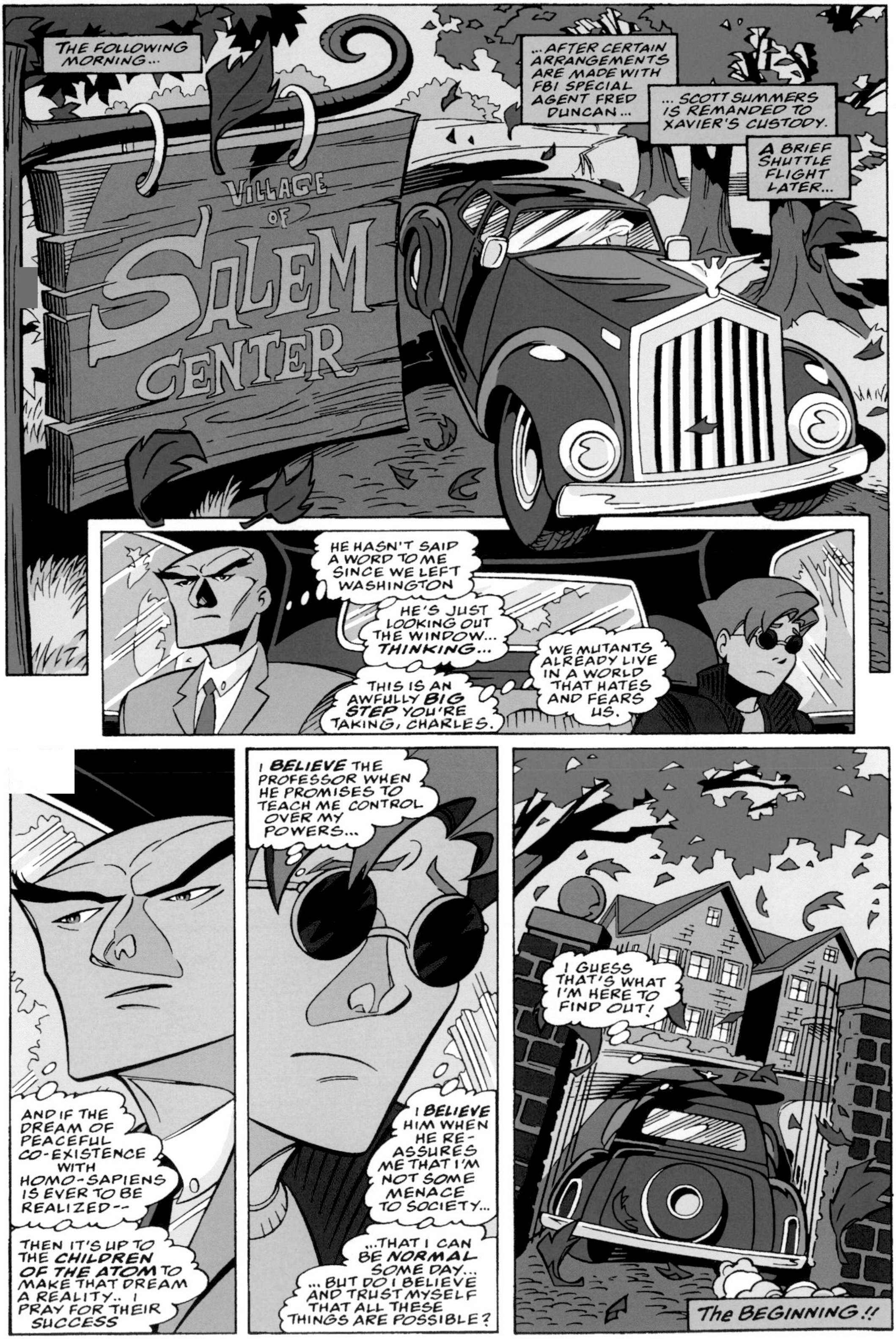
THE FOLLOWING MORNING...
...AFTER CERTAIN ARRANGEMENTS ARE MADE WITH FBI SPECIAL AGENT FRED DUNCAN...
...SCOTT SUMMERS IS REMANDED TO XAVIER'S CUSTODY.
A BRIEF SHUTTLE FLIGHT LATER...
VILLAGE OF SALEM CENTER
HE HASN'T SAID A WORD TO ME SINCE WE LEFT WASHINGTON
HE'S JUST LOOKING OUT THE WINDOW... THINKING...
THIS IS AN AWFULLY BIG STEP YOU'RE TAKING, CHARLES.
WE MUTANTS ALREADY LIVE IN A WORLD THAT HATES AND FEARS US.
AND IF THE DREAM OF PEACEFUL CO-EXISTENCE WITH HOMO-SAPIENS IS EVER TO BE REALIZED--
THEN IT'S UP TO THE CHILDREN OF THE ATOM TO MAKE THAT DREAM A REALITY.. I PRAY FOR THEIR SUCCESS
I BELIEVE THE PROFESSOR WHEN HE PROMISES TO TEACH ME CONTROL OVER MY POWERS...
I BELIEVE HIM WHEN HE RE-ASSURES ME THAT I'M NOT SOME MENACE TO SOCIETY...
...THAT I CAN BE NORMAL SOME DAY...
...BUT DO I BELIEVE AND TRUST MYSELF THAT ALL THESE THINGS ARE POSSIBLE?
I GUESS THAT'S WHAT I'M HERE TO FIND OUT!
The BEGINNING!!

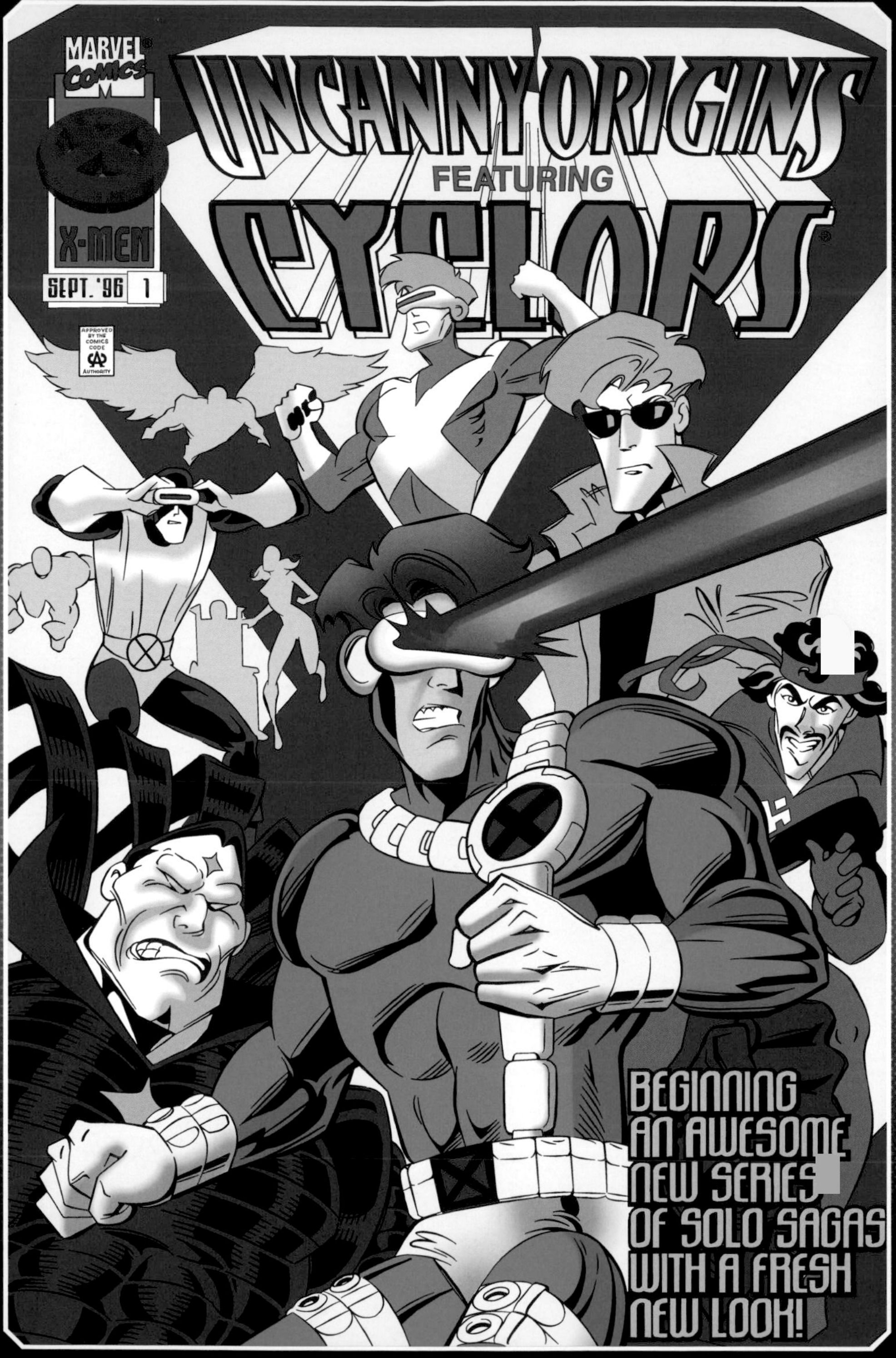
MARVEL COMICS
UNCANNY ORIGINS
FEATURING
CYCLOPS
X-MEN
SEPT. '96 1
APPROVED BY THE COMICS CODE AUTHORITY
BEGINNING AN AWESOME NEW SERIES OF SOLO SAGAS WITH A FRESH NEW LOOK!

UNCANNY ORIGINS #1 VARIANT BY DAVE HOOVER & BILL ANDERSON

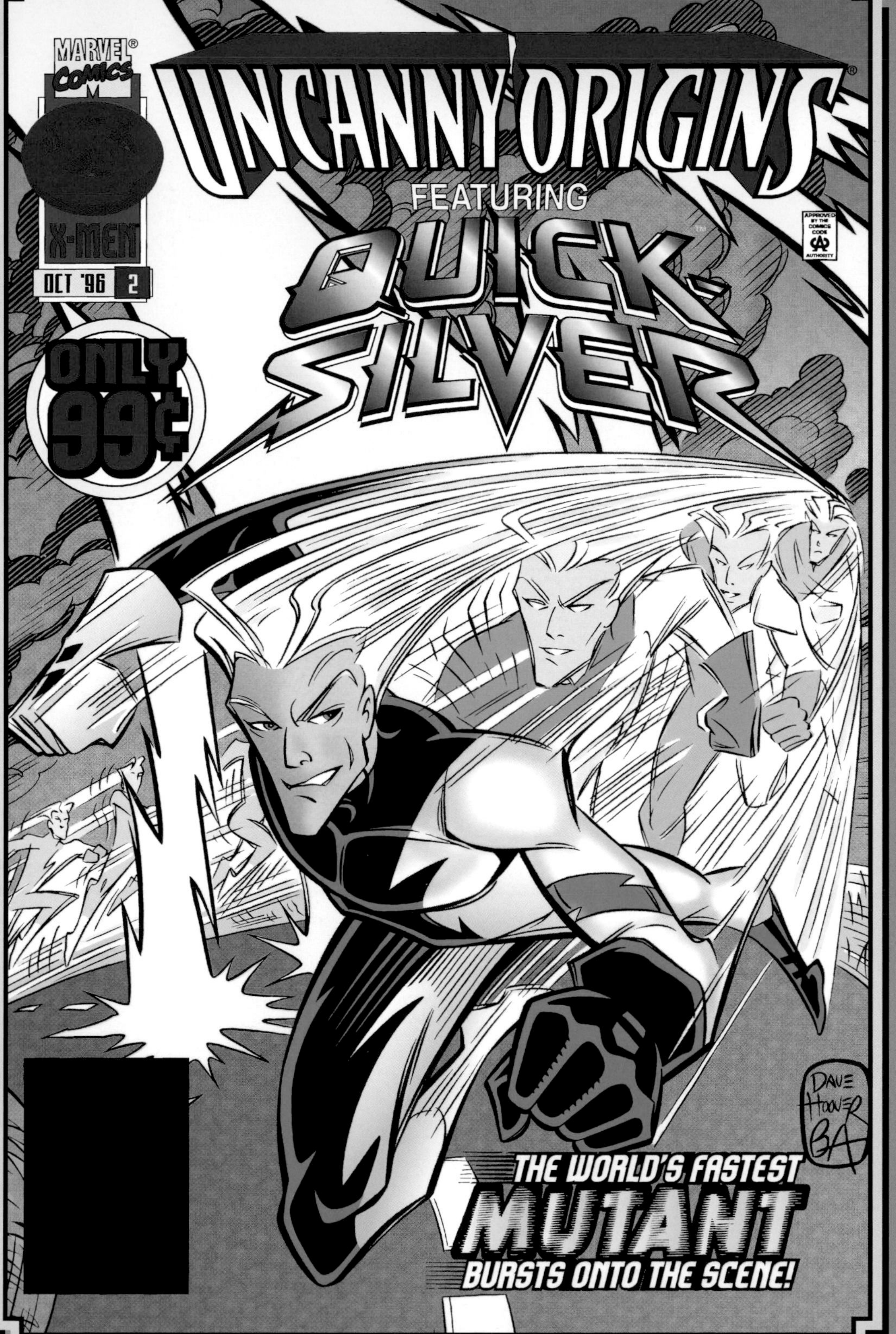
MARVEL COMICS
X-MEN
OCT '96 2
UNCANNY ORIGINS
FEATURING
QUICK-SILVER
ONLY 99¢
APPROVED BY THE COMICS CODE AUTHORITY
DAVE HOOVER BA
THE WORLD'S FASTEST
MUTANT
BURSTS ONTO THE SCENE!

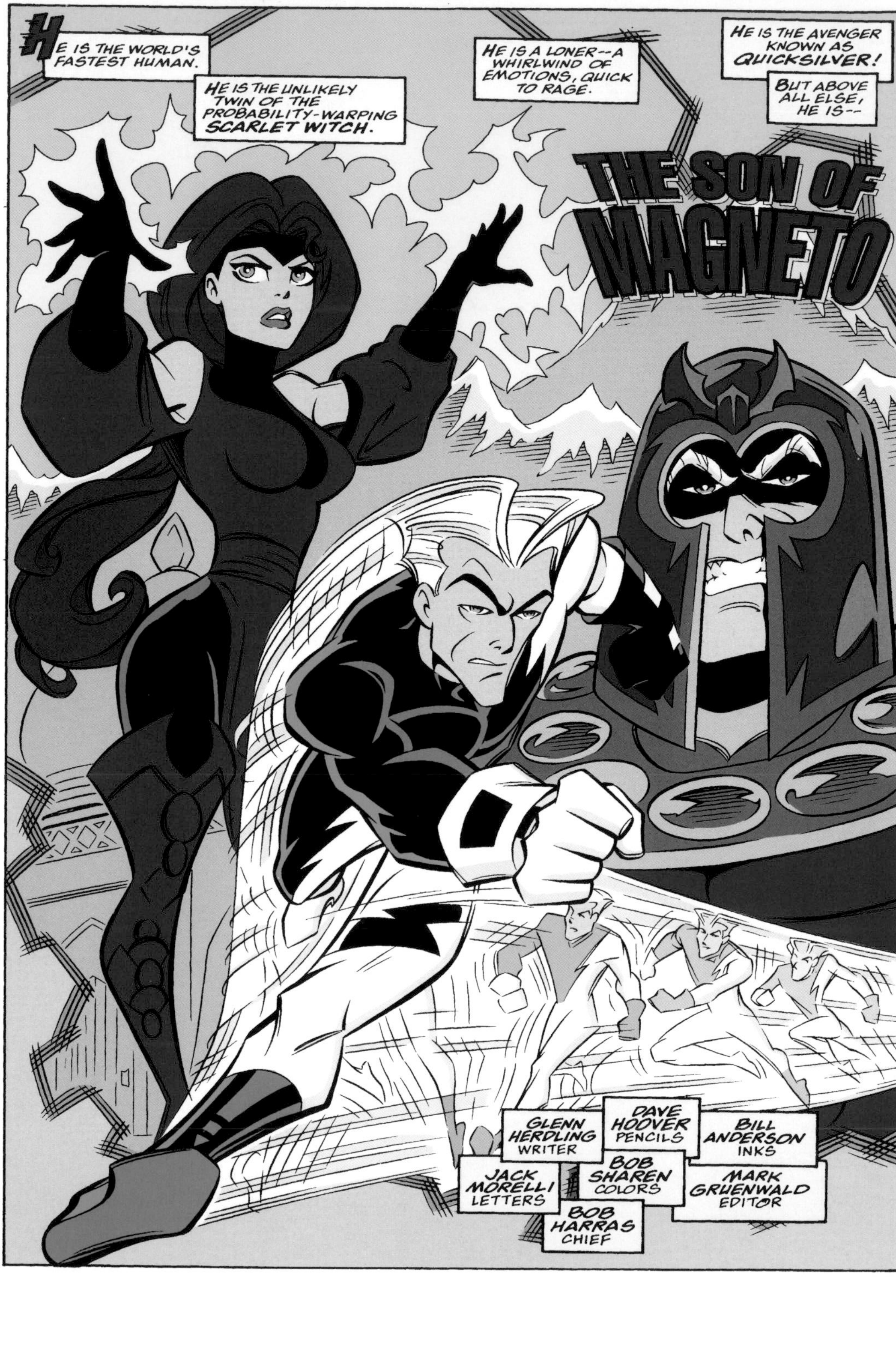
HE IS THE WORLD'S FASTEST HUMAN.
HE IS THE UNLIKELY TWIN OF THE PROBABILITY-WARPING SCARLET WITCH.
HE IS A LONER--A WHIRLWIND OF EMOTIONS, QUICK TO RAGE.
HE IS THE AVENGER KNOWN AS QUICKSILVER!
BUT ABOVE ALL ELSE, HE IS--
THE SON OF MAGNETO
GLENN HERDLING WRITER
DAVE HOOVER PENCILS
BILL ANDERSON INKS
JACK MORELLI LETTERS
BOB SHAREN COLORS
MARK GRUENWALD EDITOR
BOB HARRAS CHIEF

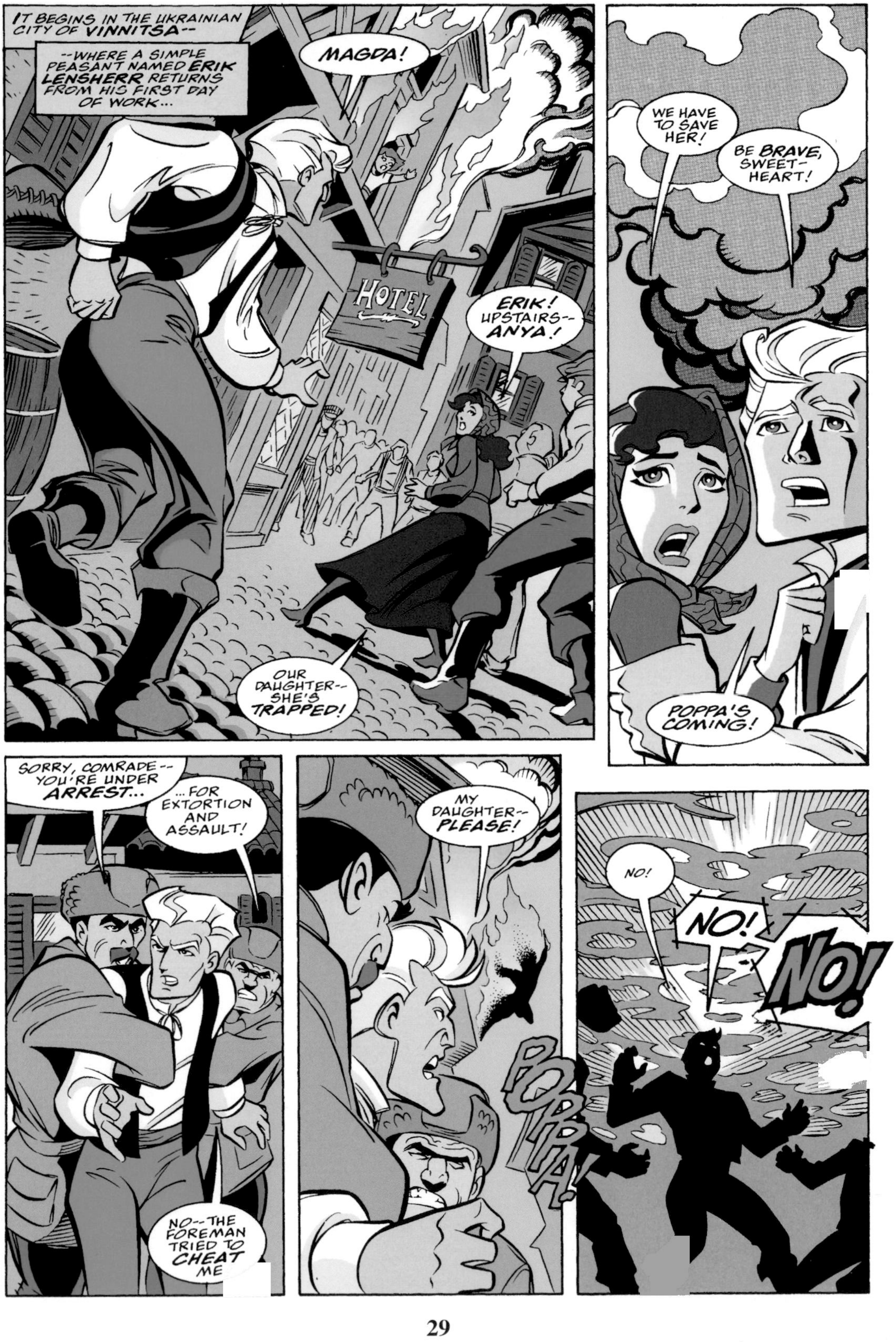
IT BEGINS IN THE UKRAINIAN CITY OF VINNITSA--
--WHERE A SIMPLE PEASANT NAMED ERIK LENSHERR RETURNS FROM HIS FIRST DAY OF WORK...
MAGDA!
HOTEL
ERIK! UPSTAIRS-- ANYA!
OUR DAUGHTER-- SHE'S TRAPPED!
WE HAVE TO SAVE HER!
BE BRAVE, SWEET-HEART!
POPPA'S COMING!
SORRY, COMRADE-- YOU'RE UNDER ARREST...
...FOR EXTORTION AND ASSAULT!
NO--THE FOREMAN TRIED TO CHEAT ME
MY DAUGHTER-- PLEASE!
POPPA!
NO!
NO!
NO!

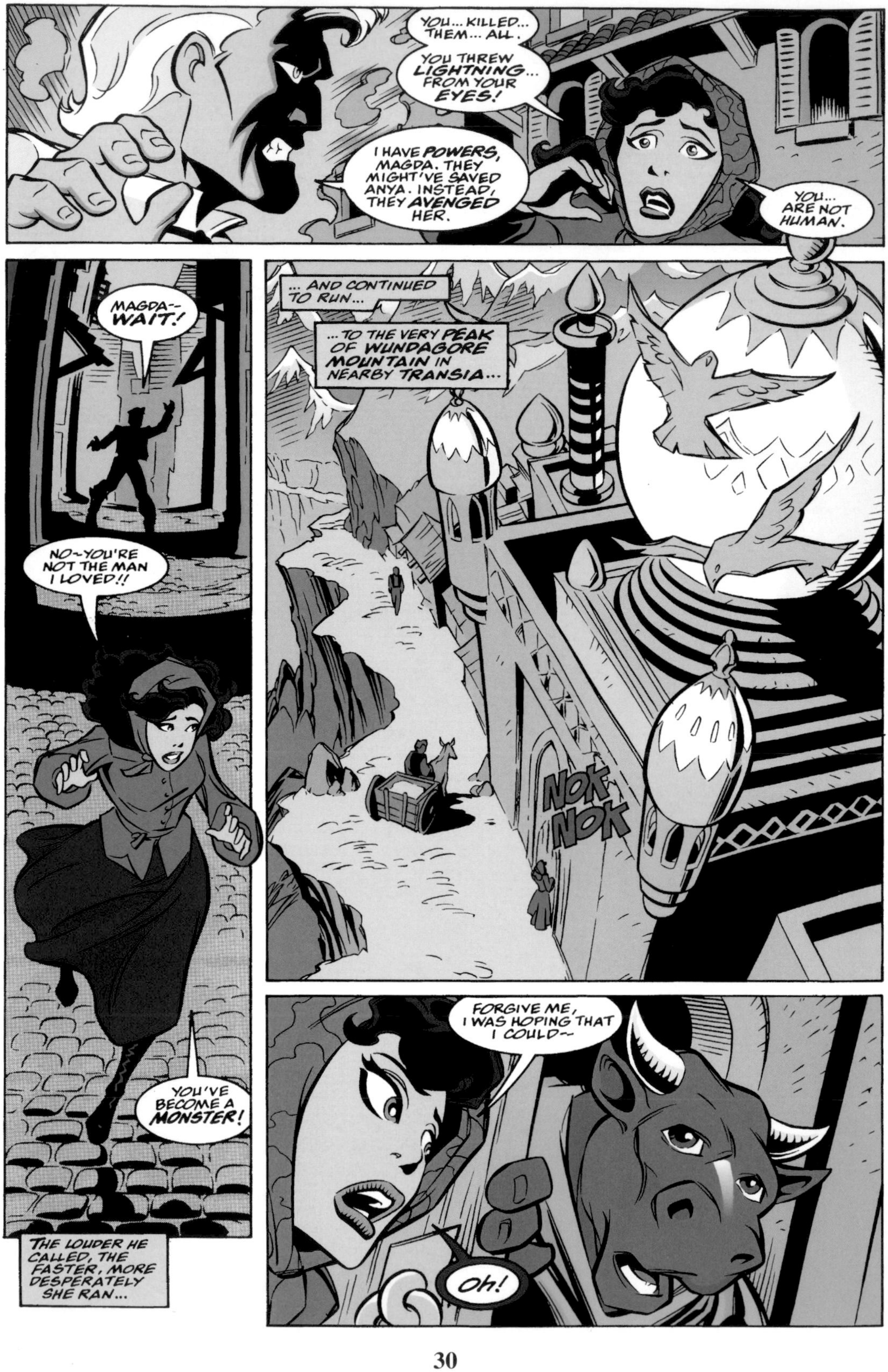
YOU... KILLED... THEM... ALL.
YOU THREW LIGHTNING... FROM YOUR EYES!
I HAVE POWERS, MAGDA. THEY MIGHT'VE SAVED ANYA. INSTEAD, THEY AVENGED HER.
YOU... ARE NOT HUMAN.
MAGDA-- WAIT!
NO-YOU'RE NOT THE MAN I LOVED!!
YOU'VE BECOME A MONSTER!
THE LOUDER HE CALLED, THE FASTER, MORE DESPERATELY SHE RAN...
... AND CONTINUED TO RUN...
...TO THE VERY PEAK OF WUNDAGORE MOUNTAIN IN NEARBY TRANSIA...
NOK NOK
FORGIVE ME, I WAS HOPING THAT I COULD--
Oh!

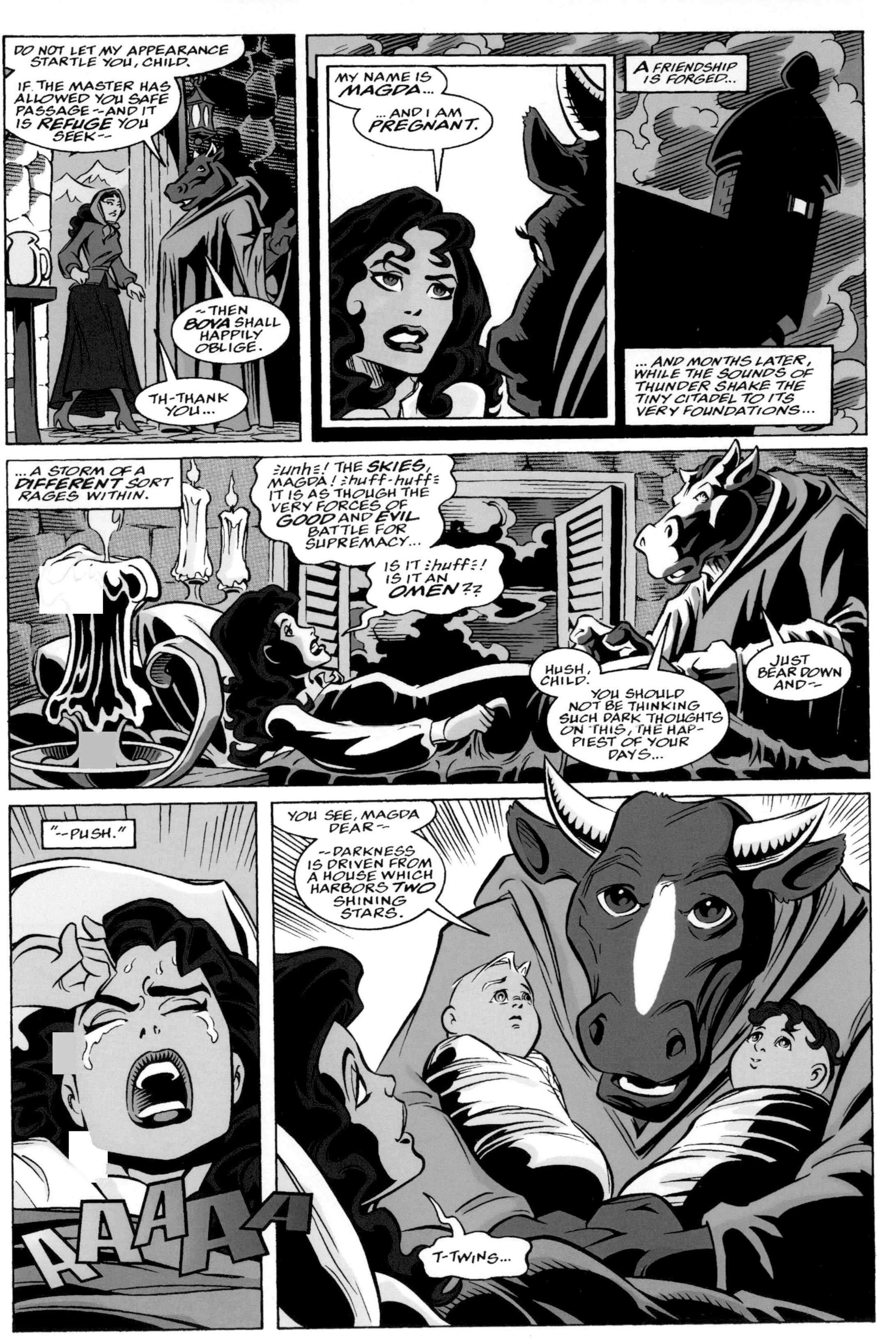

DO NOT LET MY APPEARANCE STARTLE YOU, CHILD.
IF THE MASTER HAS ALLOWED YOU SAFE PASSAGE--AND IT IS REFUGE YOU SEEK--
--THEN BOVA SHALL HAPPILY OBLIGE.
TH-THANK YOU...
MY NAME IS MAGDA...
...AND I AM PREGNANT.
A FRIENDSHIP IS FORGED...
...AND MONTHS LATER, WHILE THE SOUNDS OF THUNDER SHAKE THE TINY CITADEL TO ITS VERY FOUNDATIONS...
...A STORM OF A DIFFERENT SORT RAGES WITHIN.
:unh:! THE SKIES, MAGDA! :huff-huff: IT IS AS THOUGH THE VERY FORCES OF GOOD AND EVIL BATTLE FOR SUPREMACY...
IS IT :huff:! IS IT AN OMEN??
HUSH, CHILD.
YOU SHOULD NOT BE THINKING SUCH DARK THOUGHTS ON THIS, THE HAPPIEST OF YOUR DAYS...
JUST BEAR DOWN AND--
"--PUSH."
RAAAAA
YOU SEE, MAGDA DEAR--
--DARKNESS IS DRIVEN FROM A HOUSE WHICH HARBORS TWO SHINING STARS.
T-TWINS...

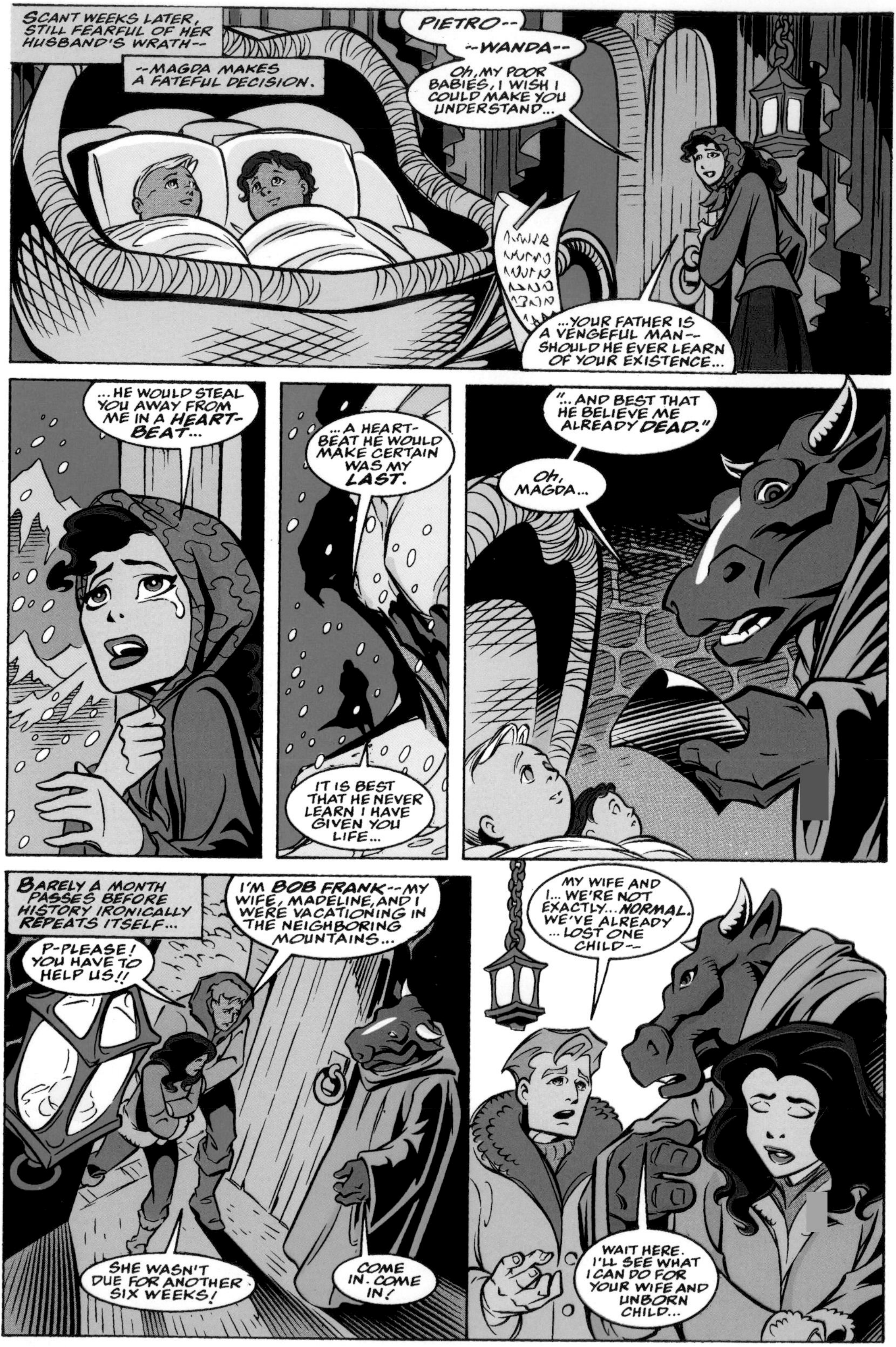
SCANT WEEKS LATER, STILL FEARFUL OF HER HUSBAND'S WRATH--
--MAGDA MAKES A FATEFUL DECISION.
PIETRO--
--WANDA--
OH, MY POOR BABIES, I WISH I COULD MAKE YOU UNDERSTAND...
...YOUR FATHER IS A VENGEFUL MAN--SHOULD HE EVER LEARN OF YOUR EXISTENCE...
...HE WOULD STEAL YOU AWAY FROM ME IN A HEART-BEAT...
...A HEART-BEAT HE WOULD MAKE CERTAIN WAS MY LAST.
IT IS BEST THAT HE NEVER LEARN I HAVE GIVEN YOU LIFE...
"...AND BEST THAT HE BELIEVE ME ALREADY DEAD."
OH, MAGDA...
BARELY A MONTH PASSES BEFORE HISTORY IRONICALLY REPEATS ITSELF...
P-PLEASE! YOU HAVE TO HELP US!!
I'M BOB FRANK--MY WIFE, MADELINE, AND I WERE VACATIONING IN THE NEIGHBORING MOUNTAINS...
SHE WASN'T DUE FOR ANOTHER SIX WEEKS!
COME IN. COME IN!
MY WIFE AND I... WE'RE NOT EXACTLY... NORMAL. WE'VE ALREADY ... LOST ONE CHILD--
WAIT HERE. I'LL SEE WHAT I CAN DO FOR YOUR WIFE AND UNBORN CHILD...

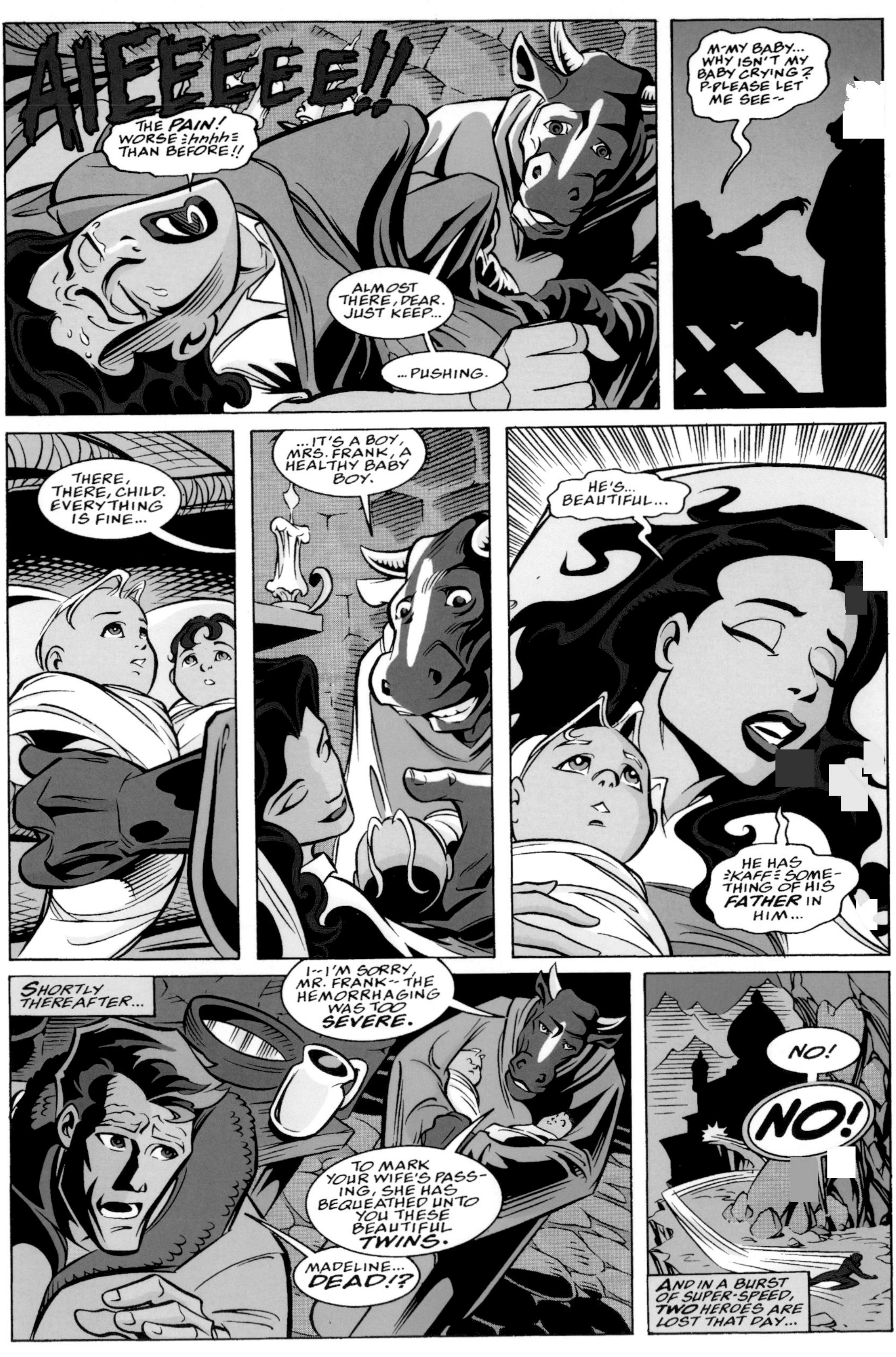
AIEEEEEE!!
THE PAIN! WORSE =hnhh= THAN BEFORE!!
ALMOST THERE, DEAR. JUST KEEP...
...PUSHING.
M-MY BABY... WHY ISN'T MY BABY CRYING? P-PLEASE LET ME SEE--
THERE, THERE, CHILD. EVERYTHING IS FINE...
...IT'S A BOY, MRS. FRANK, A HEALTHY BABY BOY.
HE'S... BEAUTIFUL...
HE HAS =KAFF= SOMETHING OF HIS FATHER IN HIM...
SHORTLY THEREAFTER...
I--I'M SORRY, MR. FRANK-- THE HEMORRHAGING WAS TOO SEVERE.
TO MARK YOUR WIFE'S PASSING, SHE HAS BEQUEATHED UNTO YOU THESE BEAUTIFUL TWINS.
MADELINE... DEAD!?
NO!
NO!
AND IN A BURST OF SUPER-SPEED, TWO HEROES ARE LOST THAT DAY...

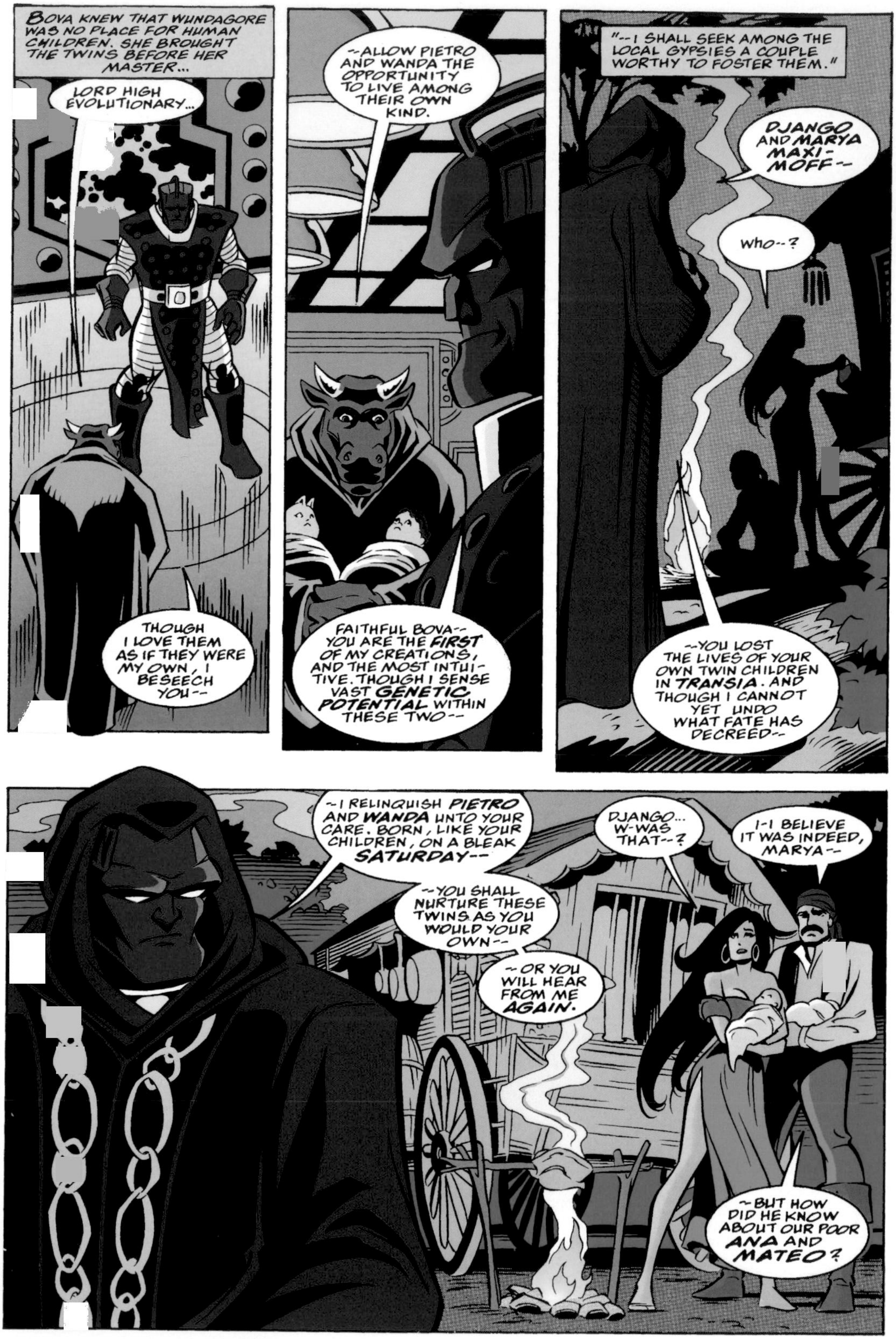
BOVA KNEW THAT WUNDAGORE WAS NO PLACE FOR HUMAN CHILDREN. SHE BROUGHT THE TWINS BEFORE HER MASTER...
LORD HIGH EVOLUTIONARY...
THOUGH I LOVE THEM AS IF THEY WERE MY OWN, I BESEECH YOU--
--ALLOW PIETRO AND WANDA THE OPPORTUNITY TO LIVE AMONG THEIR OWN KIND.
FAITHFUL BOVA-- YOU ARE THE FIRST OF MY CREATIONS, AND THE MOST INTUITIVE. THOUGH I SENSE VAST GENETIC POTENTIAL WITHIN THESE TWO--
"--I SHALL SEEK AMONG THE LOCAL GYPSIES A COUPLE WORTHY TO FOSTER THEM."
DJANGO AND MARYA MAXIMOFF--
Who--?
--YOU LOST THE LIVES OF YOUR OWN TWIN CHILDREN IN TRANSIA. AND THOUGH I CANNOT YET UNDO WHAT FATE HAS DECREED--
--I RELINQUISH PIETRO AND WANDA UNTO YOUR CARE. BORN, LIKE YOUR CHILDREN, ON A BLEAK SATURDAY--
--YOU SHALL NURTURE THESE TWINS AS YOU WOULD YOUR OWN--
--OR YOU WILL HEAR FROM ME AGAIN.
DJANGO... W-WAS THAT--?
I-I BELIEVE IT WAS INDEED, MARYA--
--BUT HOW DID HE KNOW ABOUT OUR POOR ANA AND MATEO?

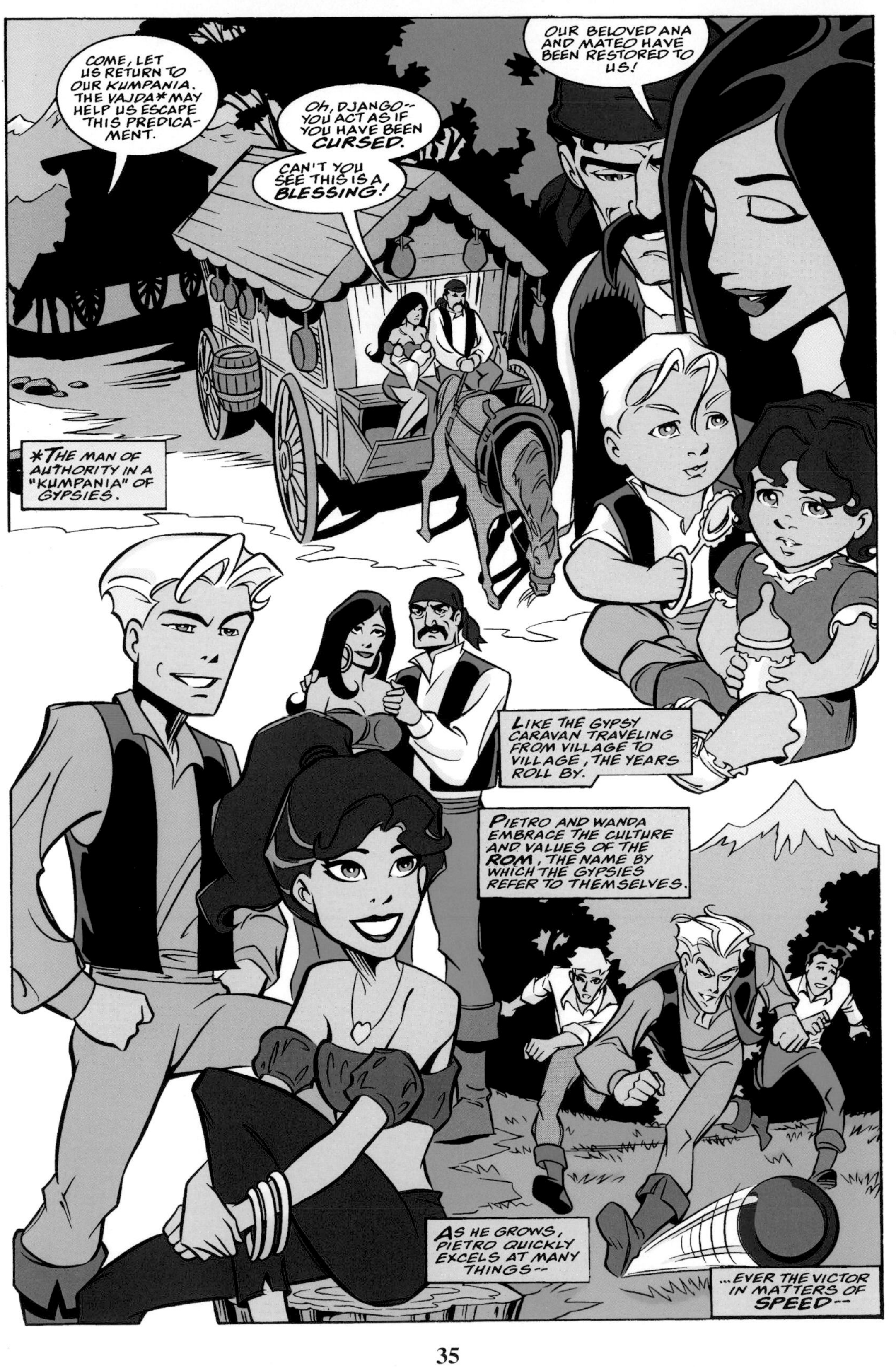

COME, LET US RETURN TO OUR KUMPANIA. THE VAJDA* MAY HELP US ESCAPE THIS PREDICAMENT.
Oh, DJANGO-- YOU ACT AS IF YOU HAVE BEEN CURSED.
CAN'T YOU SEE THIS IS A BLESSING!
OUR BELOVED ANA AND MATEO HAVE BEEN RESTORED TO US!
*THE MAN OF AUTHORITY IN A "KUMPANIA" OF GYPSIES.
LIKE THE GYPSY CARAVAN TRAVELING FROM VILLAGE TO VILLAGE, THE YEARS ROLL BY.
PIETRO AND WANDA EMBRACE THE CULTURE AND VALUES OF THE ROM, THE NAME BY WHICH THE GYPSIES REFER TO THEMSELVES.
AS HE GROWS, PIETRO QUICKLY EXCELS AT MANY THINGS--
...EVER THE VICTOR IN MATTERS OF SPEED--

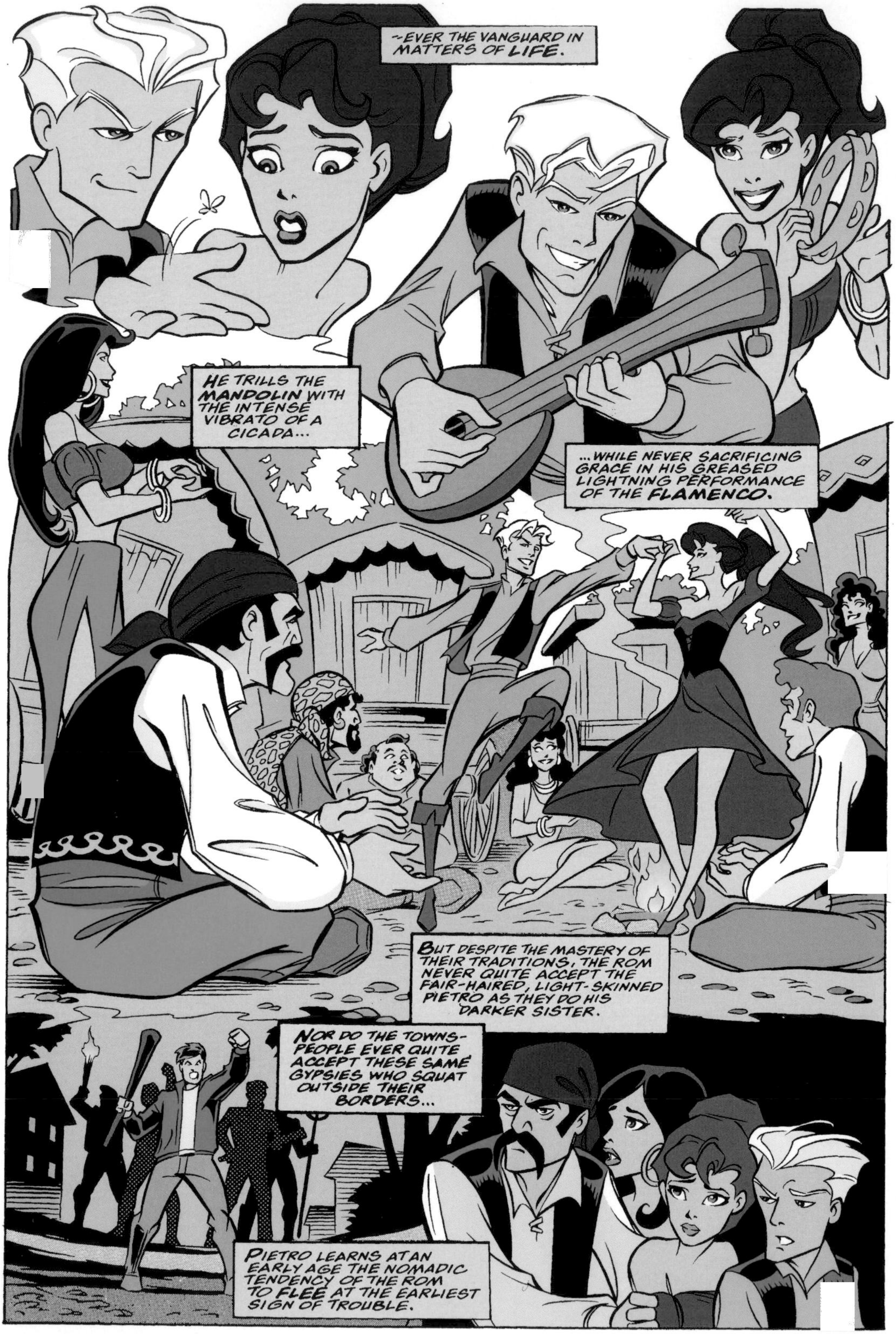
--EVER THE VANGUARD IN MATTERS OF LIFE.
HE TRILLS THE MANDOLIN WITH THE INTENSE VIBRATO OF A CICADA...
...WHILE NEVER SACRIFICING GRACE IN HIS GREASED LIGHTNING PERFORMANCE OF THE FLAMENCO.
BUT DESPITE THE MASTERY OF THEIR TRADITIONS, THE ROM NEVER QUITE ACCEPT THE FAIR-HAIRED, LIGHT-SKINNED PIETRO AS THEY DO HIS DARKER SISTER.
NOR DO THE TOWNSPEOPLE EVER QUITE ACCEPT THESE SAME GYPSIES WHO SQUAT OUTSIDE THEIR BORDERS...
PIETRO LEARNS AT AN EARLY AGE THE NOMADIC TENDENCY OF THE ROM TO FLEE AT THE EARLIEST SIGN OF TROUBLE.

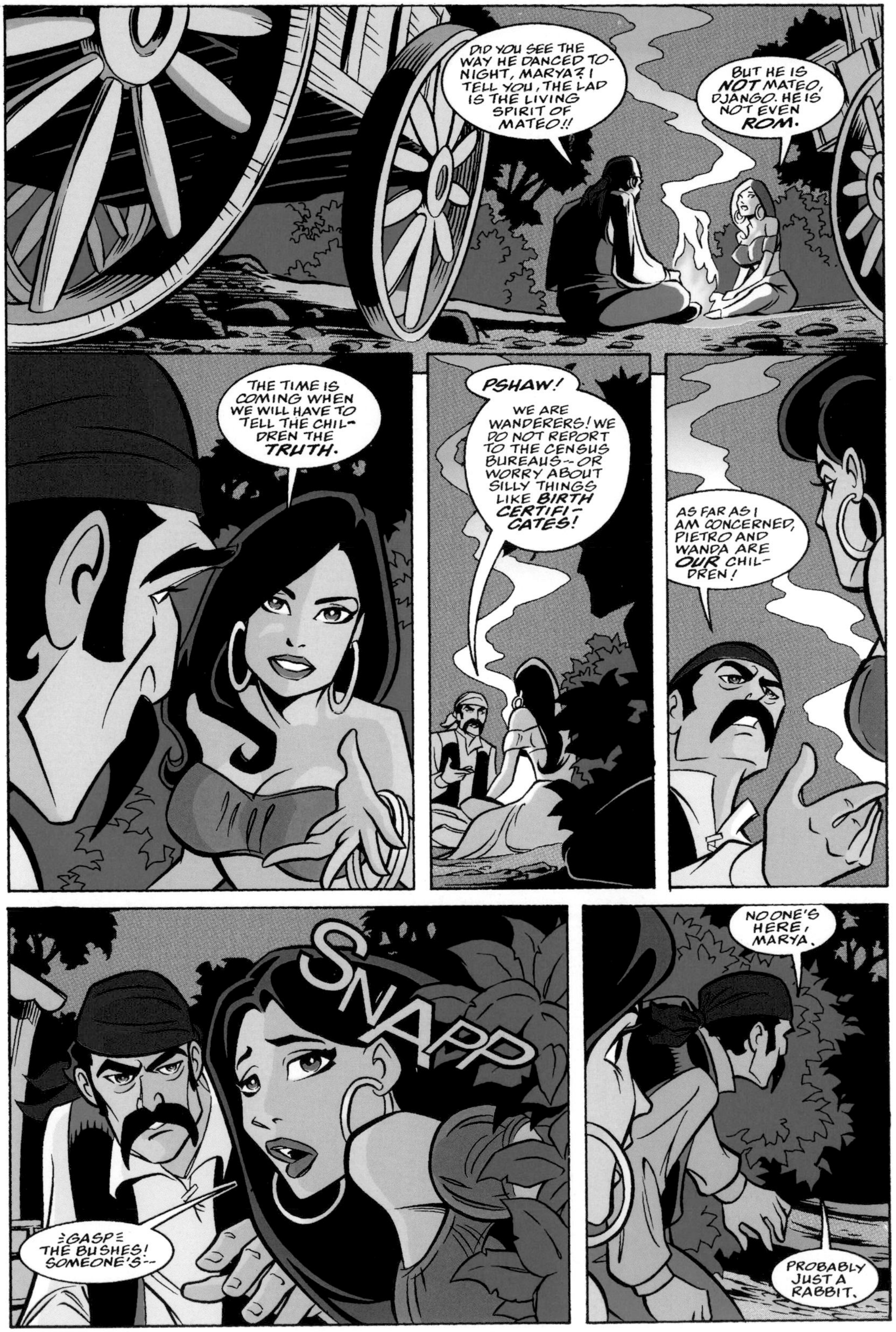
DID YOU SEE THE WAY HE DANCED TO-NIGHT, MARYA? I TELL YOU, THE LAD IS THE LIVING SPIRIT OF MATEO!!
BUT HE IS NOT MATEO, DJANGO. HE IS NOT EVEN ROM.
THE TIME IS COMING WHEN WE WILL HAVE TO TELL THE CHIL-DREN THE TRUTH.
PSHAW!
WE ARE WANDERERS! WE DO NOT REPORT TO THE CENSUS BUREAUS-- OR WORRY ABOUT SILLY THINGS LIKE BIRTH CERTIFI-CATES!
AS FAR AS I AM CONCERNED, PIETRO AND WANDA ARE OUR CHIL-DREN!
SNAPP
=GASP= THE BUSHES! SOMEONE'S--
NO ONE'S HERE, MARYA.
PROBABLY JUST A RABBIT.

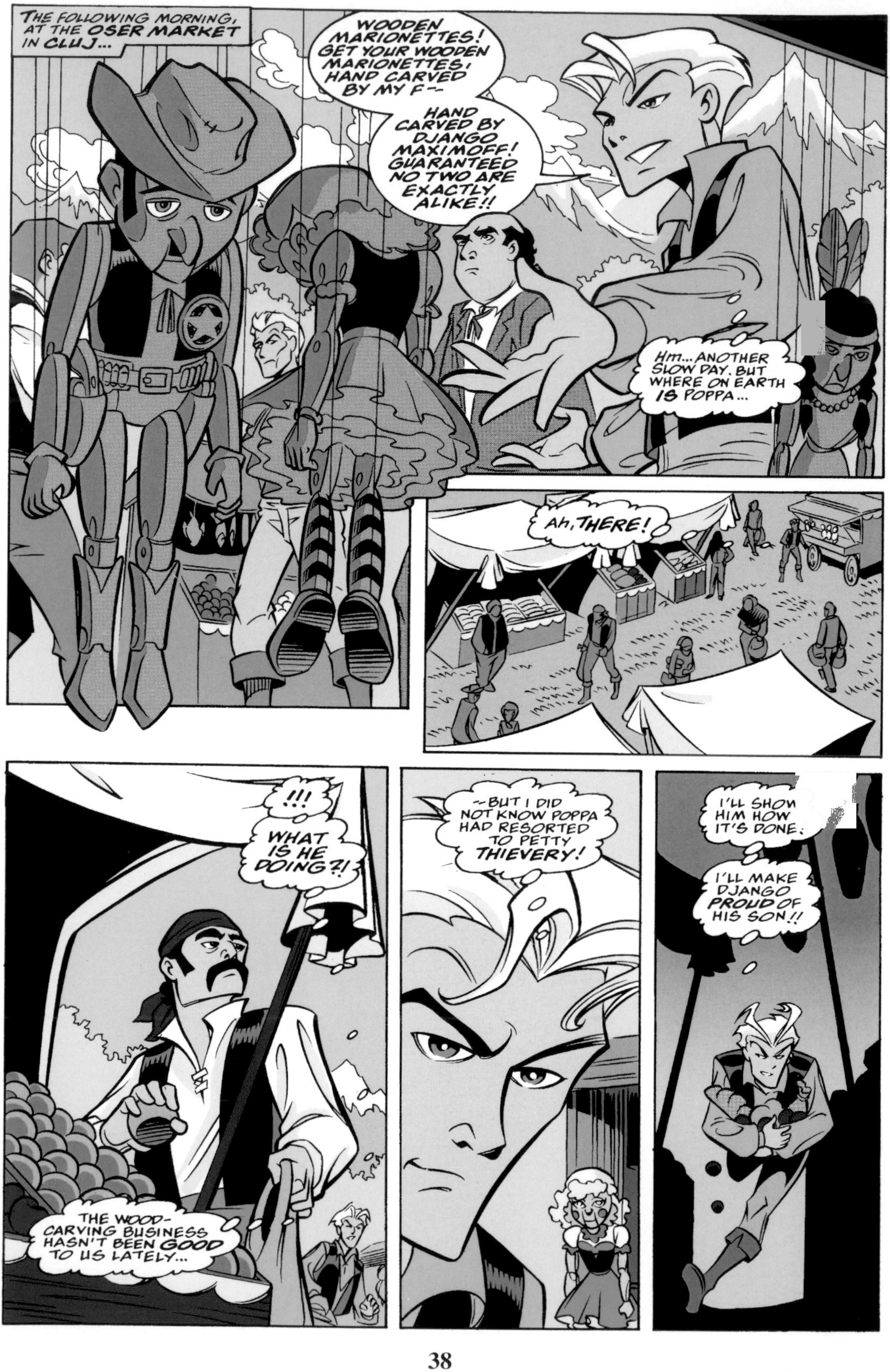
THE FOLLOWING MORNING, AT THE OSER MARKET IN CLUJ...
WOODEN MARIONETTES! GET YOUR WOODEN MARIONETTES, HAND CARVED BY MY F--
HAND CARVED BY DJANGO MAXIMOFF! GUARANTEED NO TWO ARE EXACTLY ALIKE!!
Hm... ANOTHER SLOW DAY. BUT WHERE ON EARTH IS POPPA...
Ah, THERE!
!!!
WHAT IS HE DOING?!
THE WOOD-CARVING BUSINESS HASN'T BEEN GOOD TO US LATELY...
--BUT I DID NOT KNOW POPPA HAD RESORTED TO PETTY THIEVERY!
I'LL SHOW HIM HOW IT'S DONE.
I'LL MAKE DJANGO PROUD OF HIS SON!!

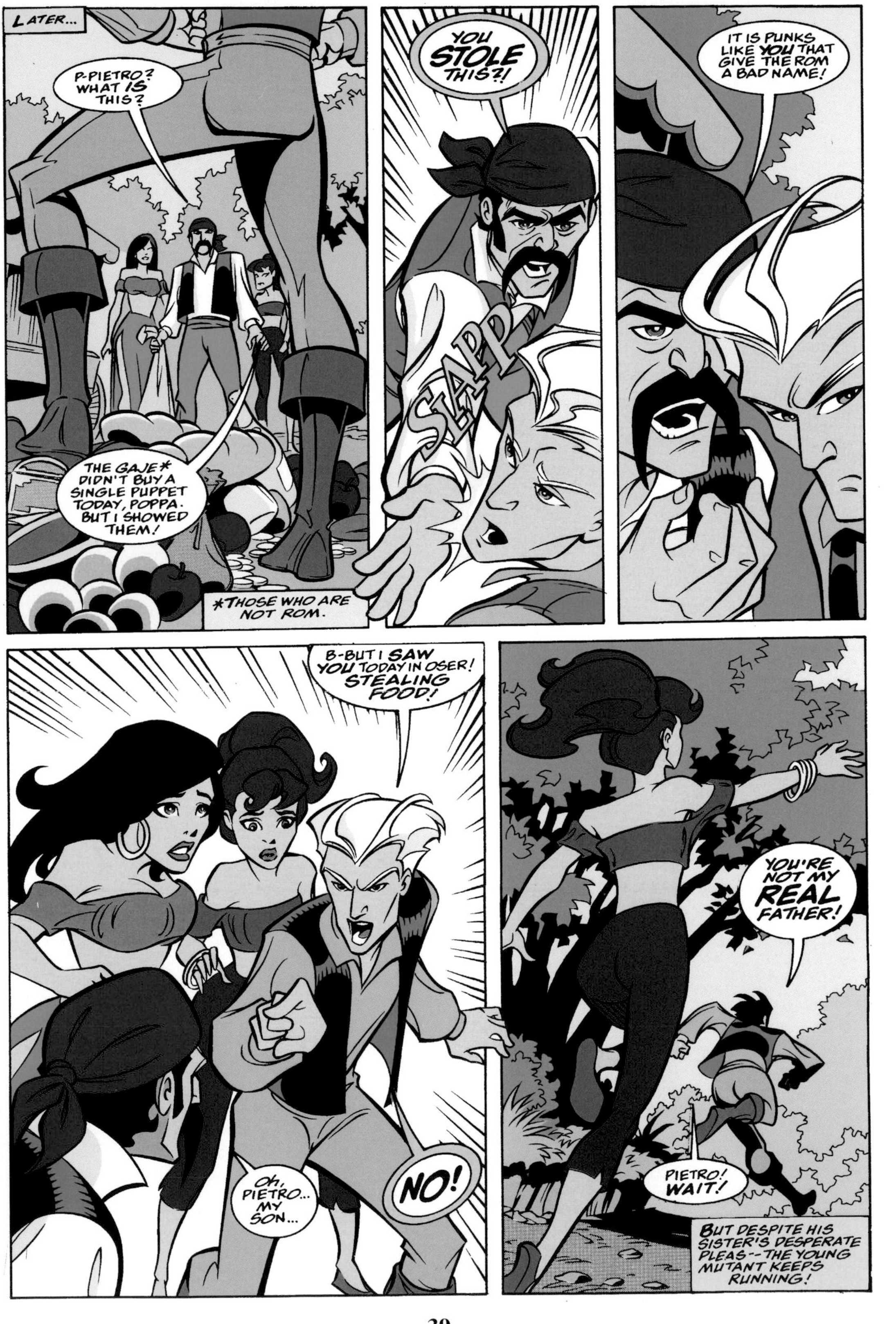
LATER...
P-PIETRO? WHAT IS THIS?
THE GAJE* DIDN'T BUY A SINGLE PUPPET TODAY, POPPA. BUT I SHOWED THEM!
*THOSE WHO ARE NOT ROM.
YOU STOLE THIS?!
SLAPP
IT IS PUNKS LIKE YOU THAT GIVE THE ROM A BAD NAME!
B-BUT I SAW YOU TODAY IN OSER! STEALING FOOD!
NO!
Oh, PIETRO... MY SON...
YOU'RE NOT MY REAL FATHER!
PIETRO! WAIT!
BUT DESPITE HIS SISTER'S DESPERATE PLEAS--THE YOUNG MUTANT KEEPS RUNNING!

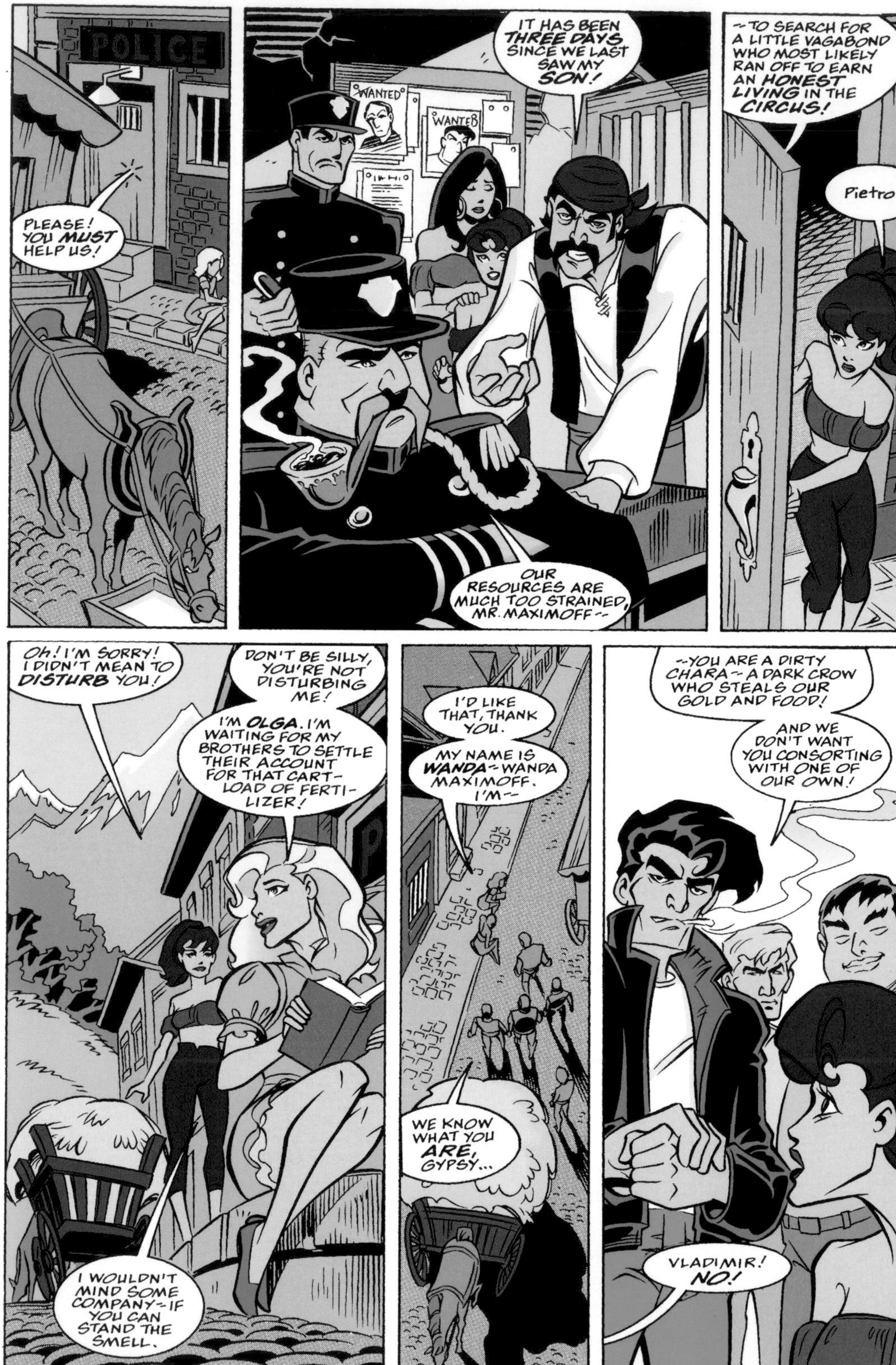
PLEASE! YOU MUST HELP US!
IT HAS BEEN THREE DAYS SINCE WE LAST SAW MY SON!
OUR RESOURCES ARE MUCH TOO STRAINED, MR. MAXIMOFF--
--TO SEARCH FOR A LITTLE VAGABOND WHO MOST LIKELY RAN OFF TO EARN AN HONEST LIVING IN THE CIRCUS!
Pietro...
Oh! I'M SORRY! I DIDN'T MEAN TO DISTURB YOU!
DON'T BE SILLY, YOU'RE NOT DISTURBING ME!
I'M OLGA. I'M WAITING FOR MY BROTHERS TO SETTLE THEIR ACCOUNT FOR THAT CART-LOAD OF FERTILIZER!
I WOULDN'T MIND SOME COMPANY--IF YOU CAN STAND THE SMELL.
I'D LIKE THAT, THANK YOU.
MY NAME IS WANDA--WANDA MAXIMOFF. I'M--
WE KNOW WHAT YOU ARE, GYPSY...
--YOU ARE A DIRTY CHARA--A DARK CROW WHO STEALS OUR GOLD AND FOOD!
AND WE DON'T WANT YOU CONSORTING WITH ONE OF OUR OWN!
VLADIMIR! NO!

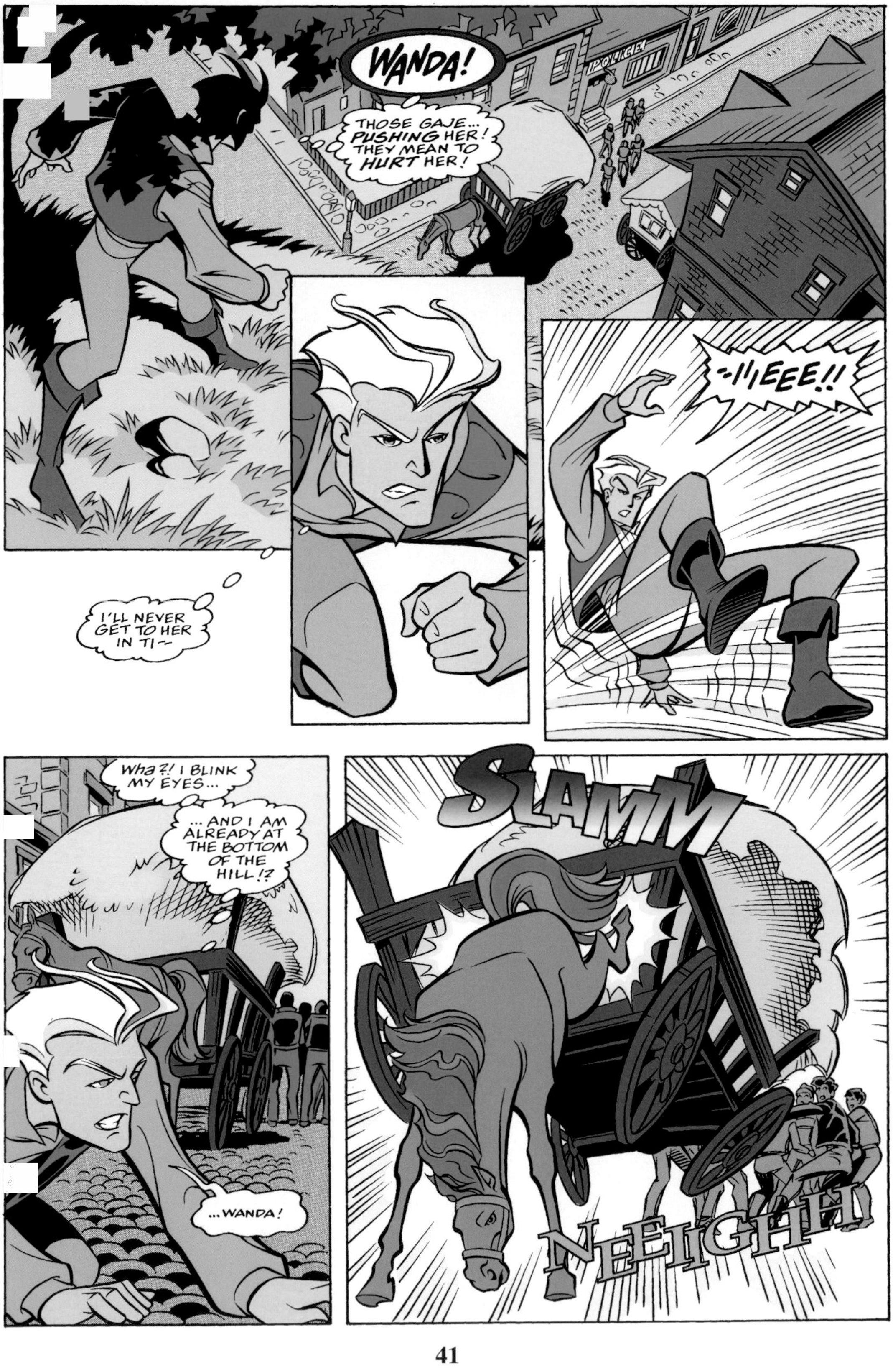
WANDA!
THOSE GAJE... PUSHING HER! THEY MEAN TO HURT HER!
POLICE
I'LL NEVER GET TO HER IN TI--
--IIEEE!!
Wha?! I BLINK MY EYES...
...AND I AM ALREADY AT THE BOTTOM OF THE HILL!?
...WANDA!
SLAMM
NEEIGHH

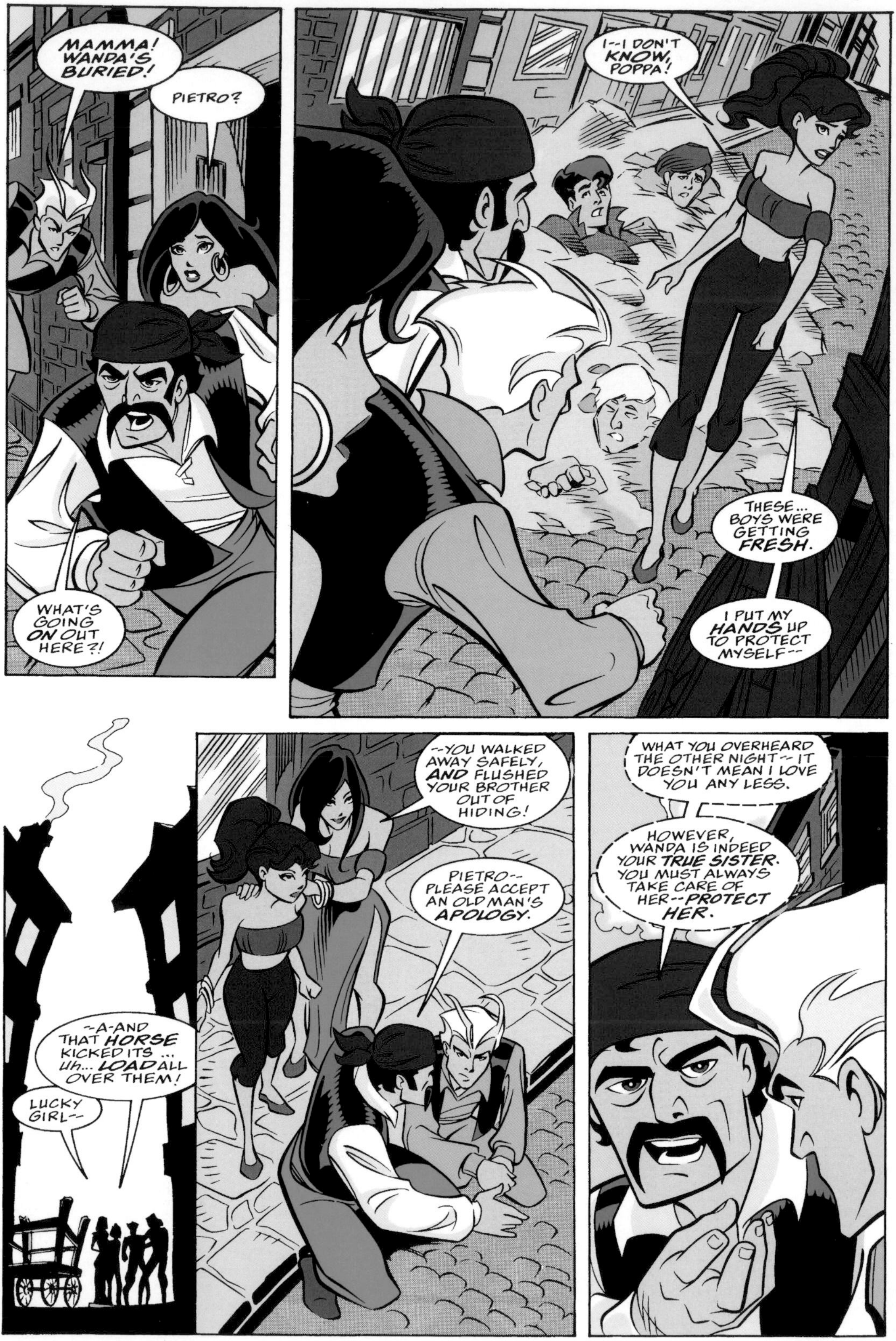
MAMMA! WANDA'S BURIED!
PIETRO?
WHAT'S GOING ON OUT HERE?!
I--I DON'T KNOW, POPPA!
THESE... BOYS WERE GETTING FRESH.
I PUT MY HANDS UP TO PROTECT MYSELF--
--A-AND THAT HORSE KICKED ITS ... uh... LOAD ALL OVER THEM!
LUCKY GIRL--
--YOU WALKED AWAY SAFELY, AND FLUSHED YOUR BROTHER OUT OF HIDING!
PIETRO-- PLEASE ACCEPT AN OLD MAN'S APOLOGY.
WHAT YOU OVERHEARD THE OTHER NIGHT-- IT DOESN'T MEAN I LOVE YOU ANY LESS.
HOWEVER, WANDA IS INDEED YOUR TRUE SISTER. YOU MUST ALWAYS TAKE CARE OF HER--PROTECT HER.

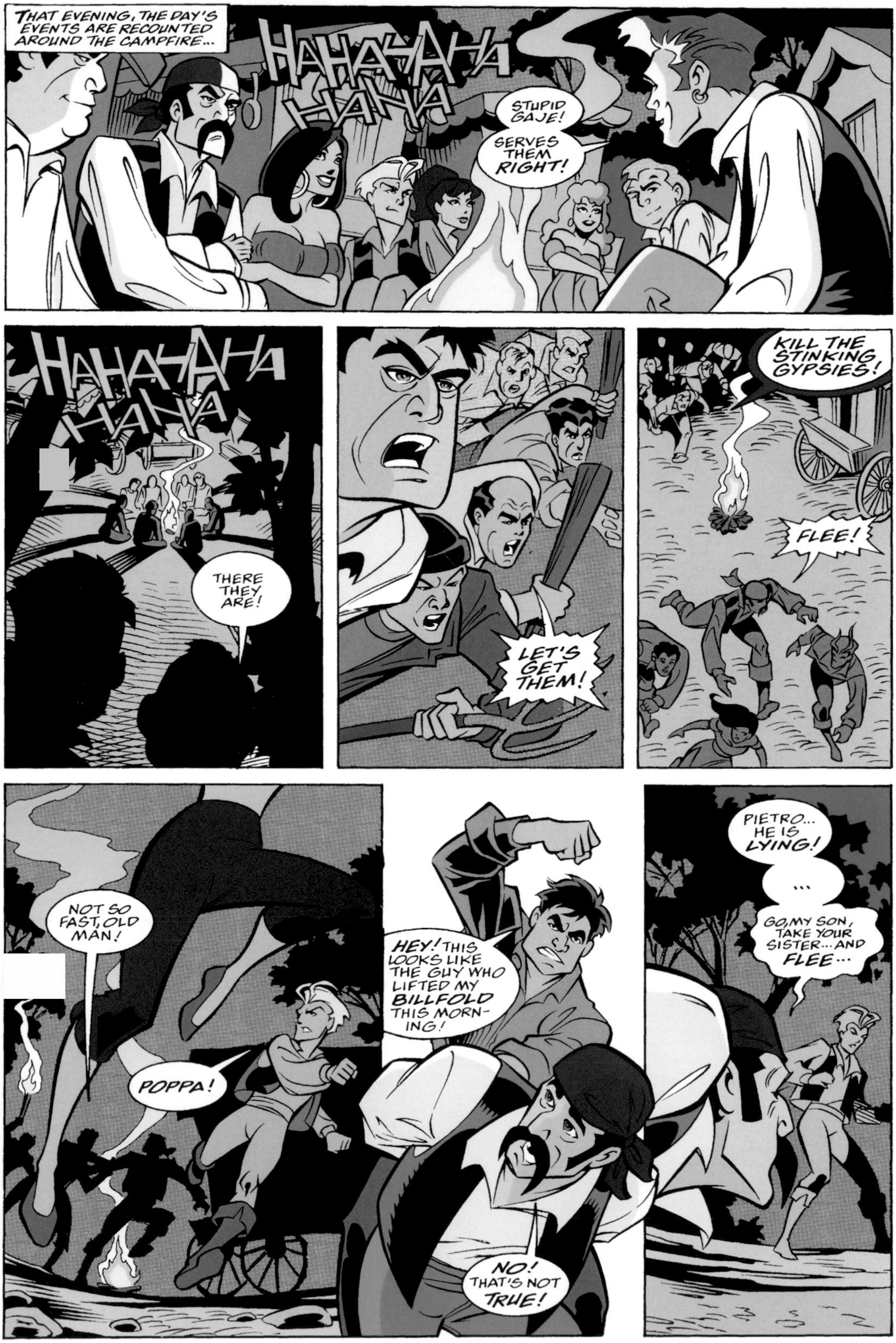
THAT EVENING, THE DAY'S EVENTS ARE RECOUNTED AROUND THE CAMPFIRE...
HAHAHAHA HAHA
STUPID GAJE!
SERVES THEM RIGHT!
HAHAHAHA HAHA
THERE THEY ARE!
LET'S GET THEM!
KILL THE STINKING GYPSIES!
FLEE!
NOT SO FAST, OLD MAN!
POPPA!
HEY! THIS LOOKS LIKE THE GUY WHO LIFTED MY BILLFOLD THIS MORNING!
NO! THAT'S NOT TRUE!
PIETRO... HE IS LYING!
...
GO, MY SON, TAKE YOUR SISTER... AND FLEE...

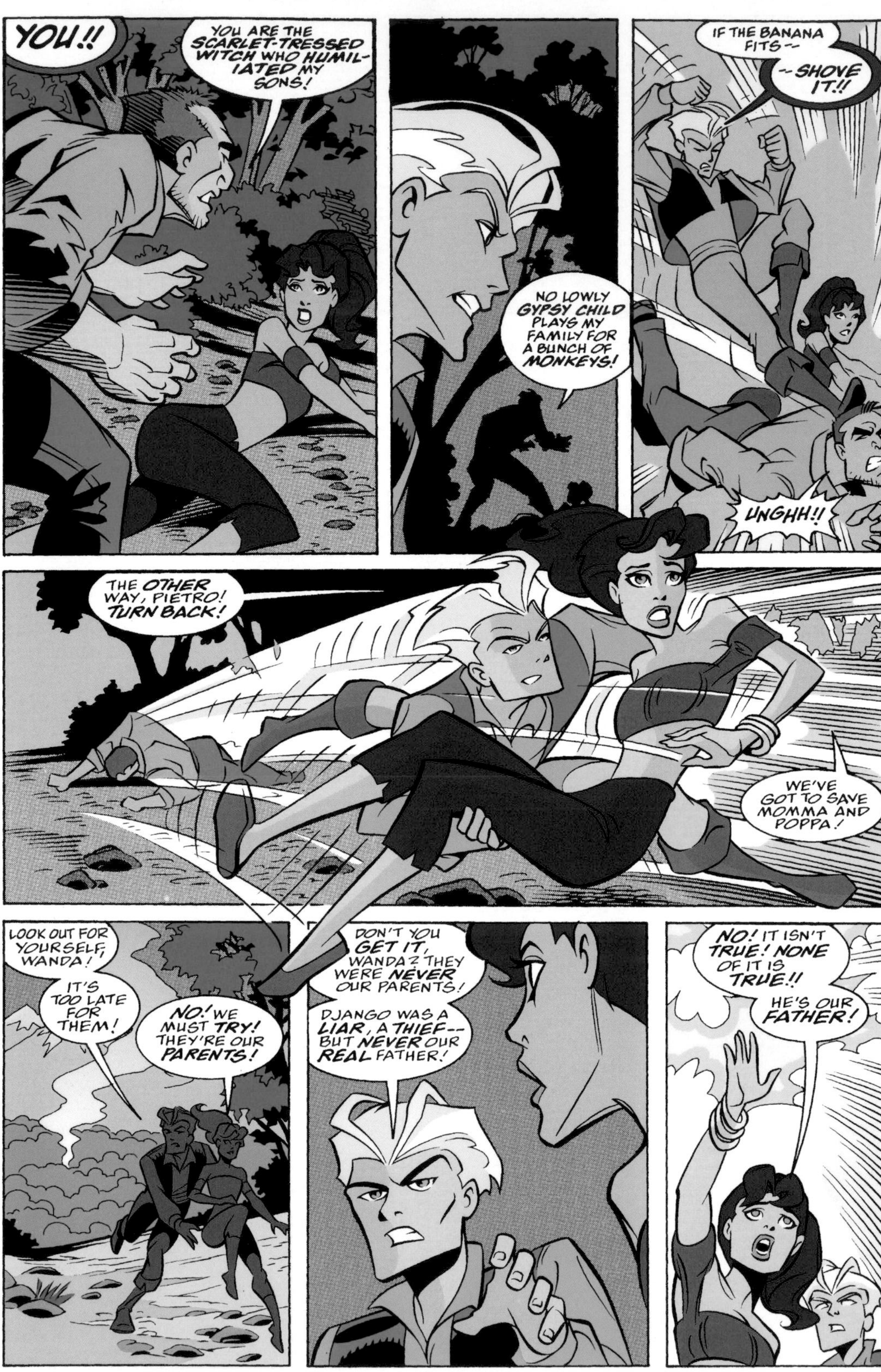
YOU!!
YOU ARE THE SCARLET-TRESSED WITCH WHO HUMILIATED MY SONS!
NO LOWLY GYPSY CHILD PLAYS MY FAMILY FOR A BUNCH OF MONKEYS!
IF THE BANANA FITS--
--SHOVE IT!!
UNGHH!!
THE OTHER WAY, PIETRO! TURN BACK!
WE'VE GOT TO SAVE MOMMA AND POPPA!
LOOK OUT FOR YOURSELF, WANDA!
IT'S TOO LATE FOR THEM!
NO! WE MUST TRY! THEY'RE OUR PARENTS!
DON'T YOU GET IT, WANDA? THEY WERE NEVER OUR PARENTS!
DJANGO WAS A LIAR, A THIEF--BUT NEVER OUR REAL FATHER!
NO! IT ISN'T TRUE! NONE OF IT IS TRUE!!
HE'S OUR FATHER!

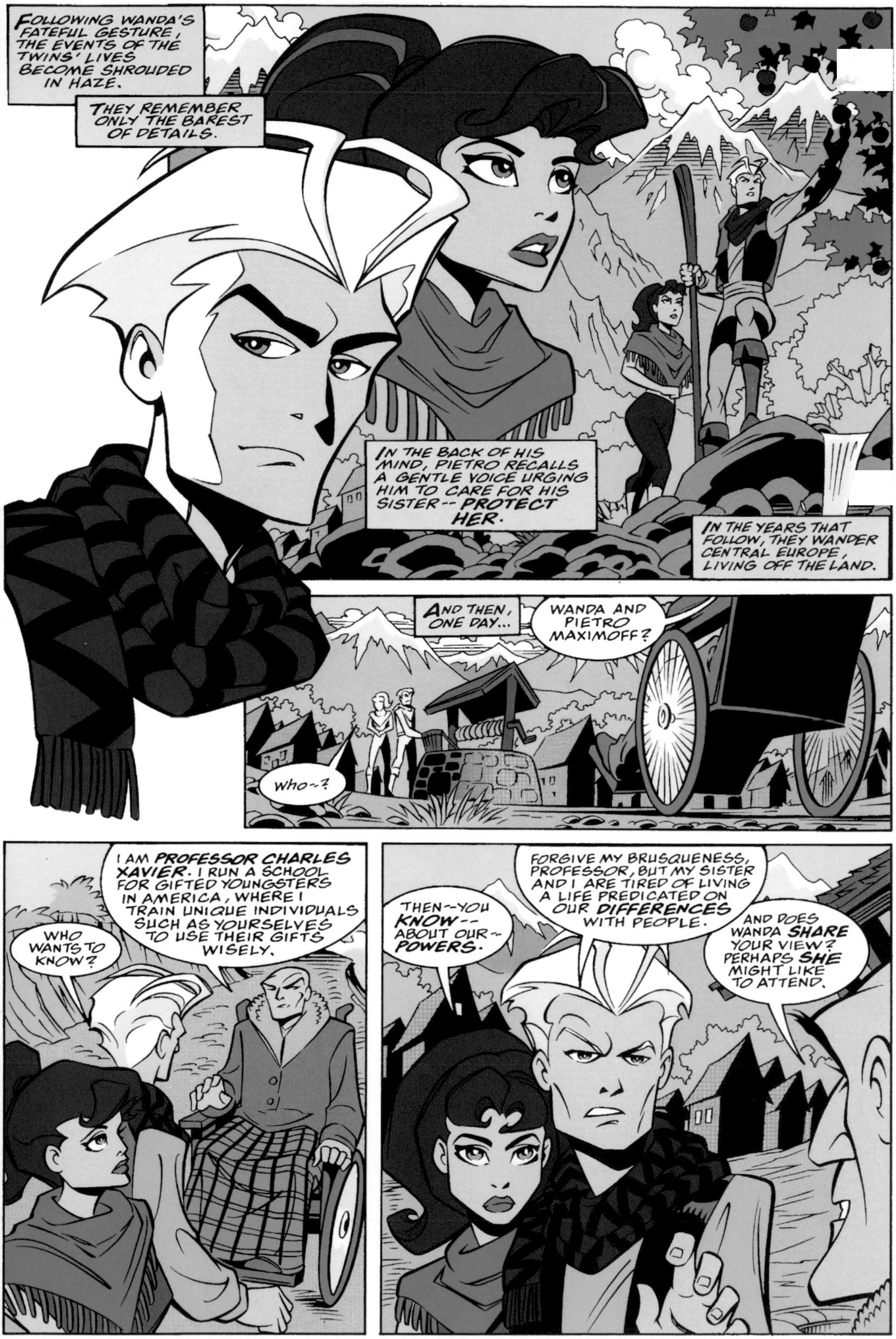

FOLLOWING WANDA'S FATEFUL GESTURE, THE EVENTS OF THE TWINS' LIVES BECOME SHROUDED IN HAZE.
THEY REMEMBER ONLY THE BAREST OF DETAILS.
IN THE BACK OF HIS MIND, PIETRO RECALLS A GENTLE VOICE URGING HIM TO CARE FOR HIS SISTER-- PROTECT HER.
IN THE YEARS THAT FOLLOW, THEY WANDER CENTRAL EUROPE, LIVING OFF THE LAND.
AND THEN, ONE DAY...
WANDA AND PIETRO MAXIMOFF?
WHO--?
WHO WANTS TO KNOW?
I AM PROFESSOR CHARLES XAVIER. I RUN A SCHOOL FOR GIFTED YOUNGSTERS IN AMERICA, WHERE I TRAIN UNIQUE INDIVIDUALS SUCH AS YOURSELVES TO USE THEIR GIFTS WISELY.
THEN--YOU KNOW-- ABOUT OUR-- POWERS.
FORGIVE MY BRUSQUENESS, PROFESSOR, BUT MY SISTER AND I ARE TIRED OF LIVING A LIFE PREDICATED ON OUR DIFFERENCES WITH PEOPLE.
AND DOES WANDA SHARE YOUR VIEW? PERHAPS SHE MIGHT LIKE TO ATTEND.

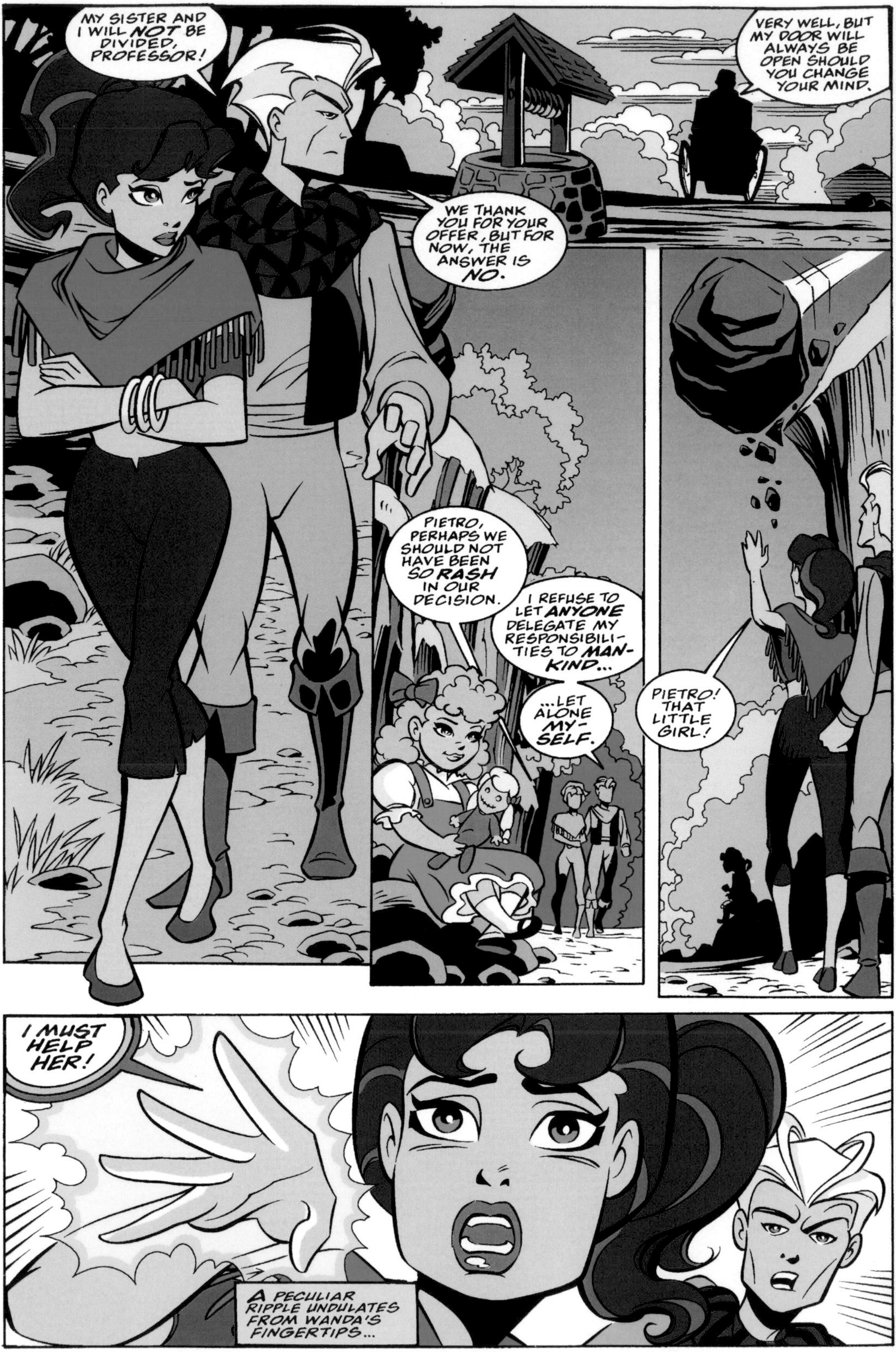
MY SISTER AND I WILL NOT BE DIVIDED, PROFESSOR!
VERY WELL, BUT MY DOOR WILL ALWAYS BE OPEN SHOULD YOU CHANGE YOUR MIND.
WE THANK YOU FOR YOUR OFFER, BUT FOR NOW, THE ANSWER IS NO.
PIETRO, PERHAPS WE SHOULD NOT HAVE BEEN SO RASH IN OUR DECISION.
I REFUSE TO LET ANYONE DELEGATE MY RESPONSIBILITIES TO MANKIND...
...LET ALONE MYSELF.
PIETRO! THAT LITTLE GIRL!
I MUST HELP HER!
A PECULIAR RIPPLE UNDULATES FROM WANDA'S FINGERTIPS...

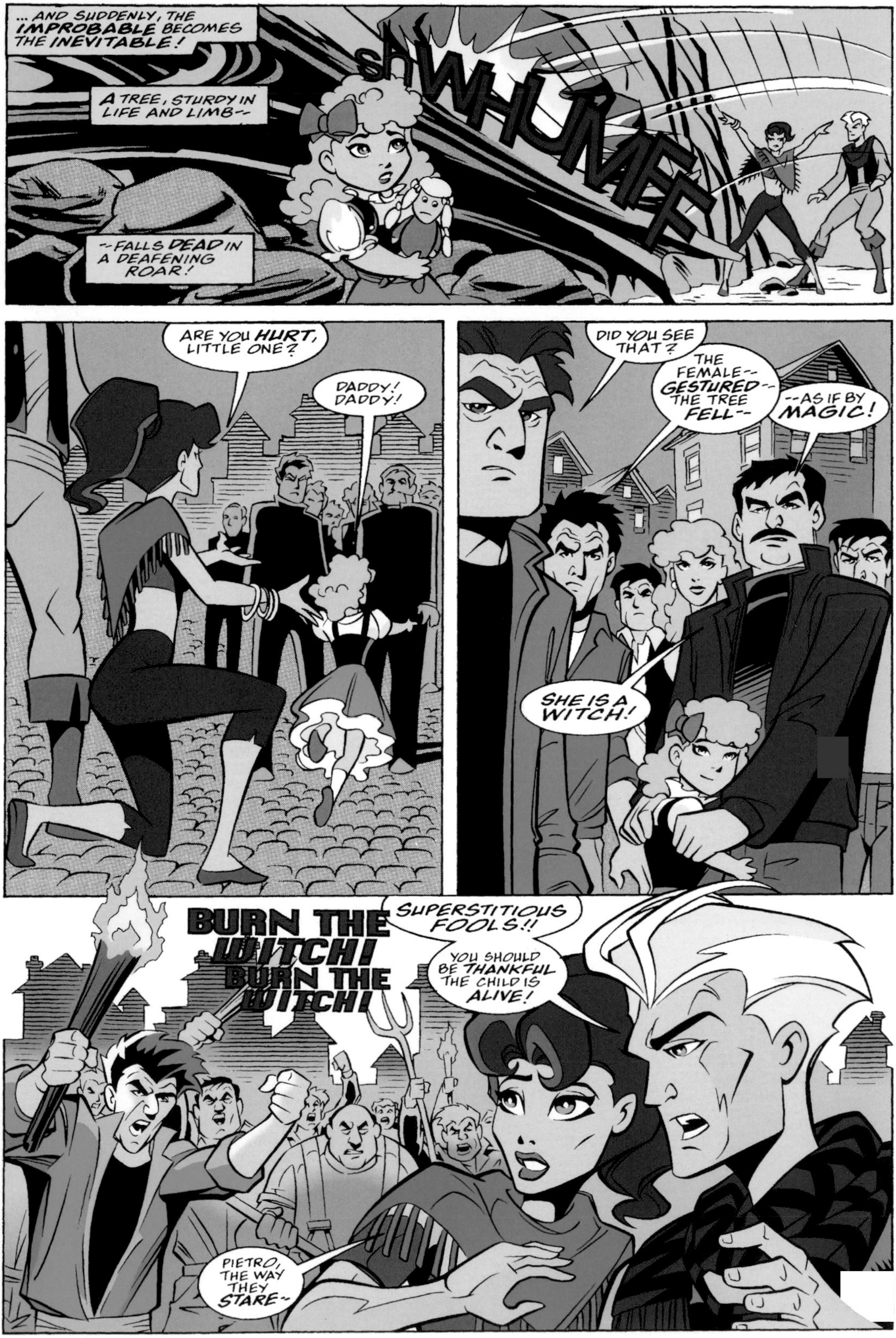
...AND SUDDENLY, THE IMPROBABLE BECOMES THE INEVITABLE!
A TREE, STURDY IN LIFE AND LIMB--
SHWHUMFF
--FALLS DEAD IN A DEAFENING ROAR!
ARE YOU HURT, LITTLE ONE?
DADDY! DADDY!
DID YOU SEE THAT?
THE FEMALE-- GESTURED-- THE TREE FELL--
--AS IF BY MAGIC!
SHE IS A WITCH!
BURN THE WITCH! BURN THE WITCH!
SUPERSTITIOUS FOOLS!!
YOU SHOULD BE THANKFUL THE CHILD IS ALIVE!
PIETRO, THE WAY THEY STARE--

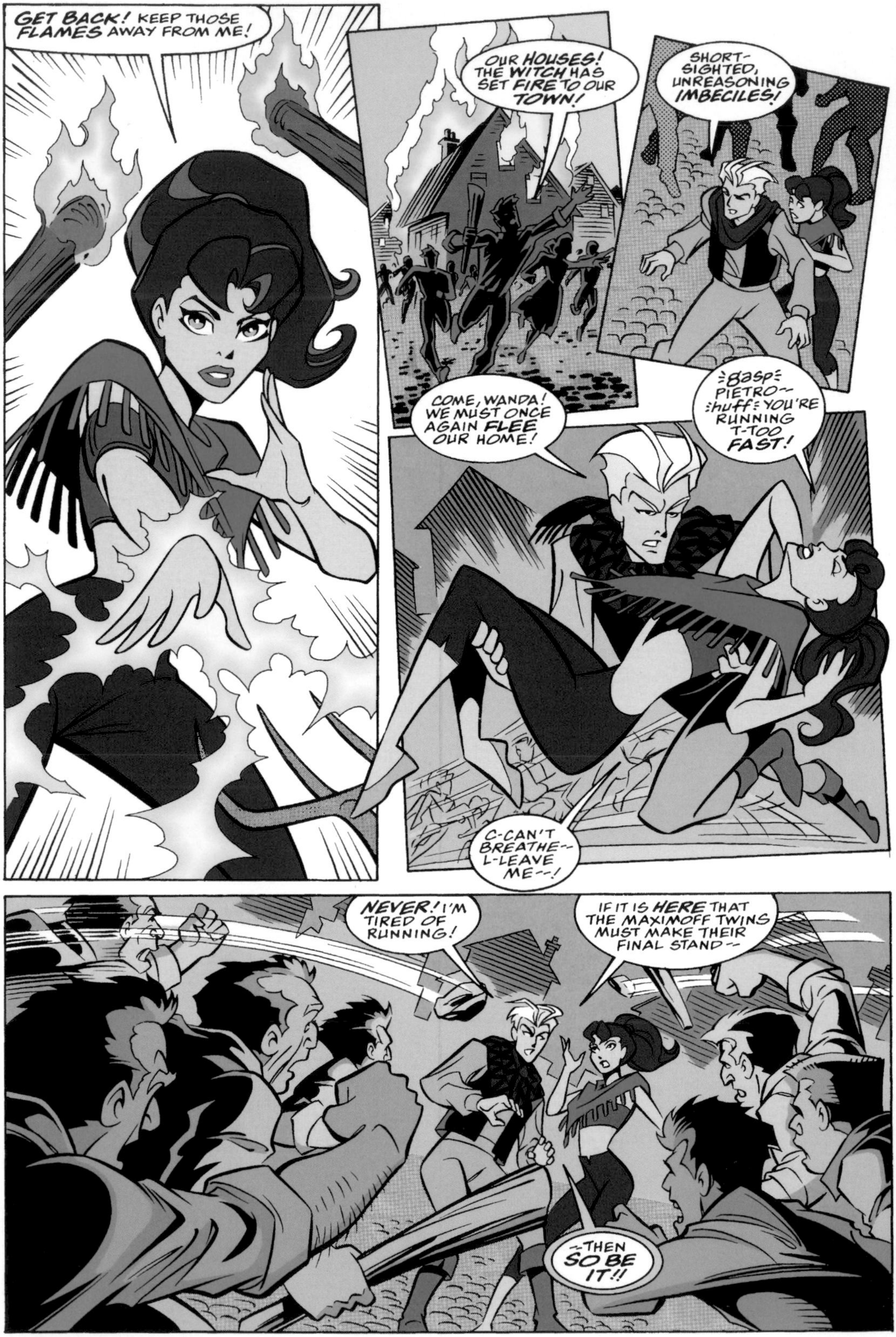
GET BACK! KEEP THOSE FLAMES AWAY FROM ME!
OUR HOUSES! THE WITCH HAS SET FIRE TO OUR TOWN!
SHORT-SIGHTED, UNREASONING IMBECILES!
COME, WANDA! WE MUST ONCE AGAIN FLEE OUR HOME!
gasp PIETRO-- huff YOU'RE RUNNING T-TOO FAST!
C-CAN'T BREATHE-- L-LEAVE ME--!
NEVER! I'M TIRED OF RUNNING!
IF IT IS HERE THAT THE MAXIMOFF TWINS MUST MAKE THEIR FINAL STAND--
--THEN SO BE IT!!

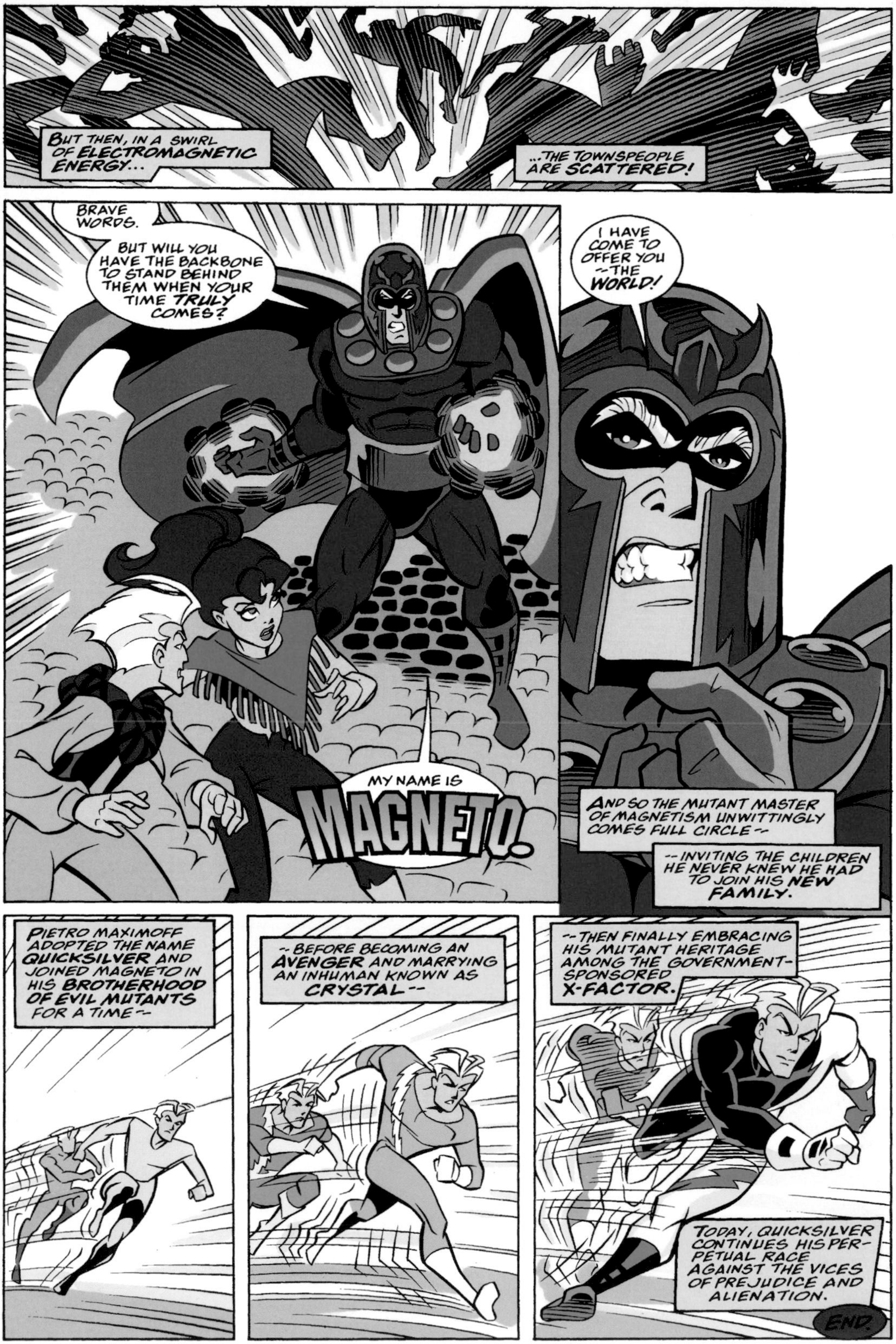
BUT THEN, IN A SWIRL OF ELECTROMAGNETIC ENERGY...
...THE TOWNSPEOPLE ARE SCATTERED!
BRAVE WORDS.
BUT WILL YOU HAVE THE BACKBONE TO STAND BEHIND THEM WHEN YOUR TIME TRULY COMES?
MY NAME IS
MAGNETO.
I HAVE COME TO OFFER YOU --THE WORLD!
AND SO THE MUTANT MASTER OF MAGNETISM UNWITTINGLY COMES FULL CIRCLE--
--INVITING THE CHILDREN HE NEVER KNEW HE HAD TO JOIN HIS NEW FAMILY.
PIETRO MAXIMOFF ADOPTED THE NAME QUICKSILVER AND JOINED MAGNETO IN HIS BROTHERHOOD OF EVIL MUTANTS FOR A TIME--
--BEFORE BECOMING AN AVENGER AND MARRYING AN INHUMAN KNOWN AS CRYSTAL--
--THEN FINALLY EMBRACING HIS MUTANT HERITAGE AMONG THE GOVERNMENT-SPONSORED X-FACTOR.
TODAY, QUICKSILVER CONTINUES HIS PERPETUAL RACE AGAINST THE VICES OF PREJUDICE AND ALIENATION.
END.

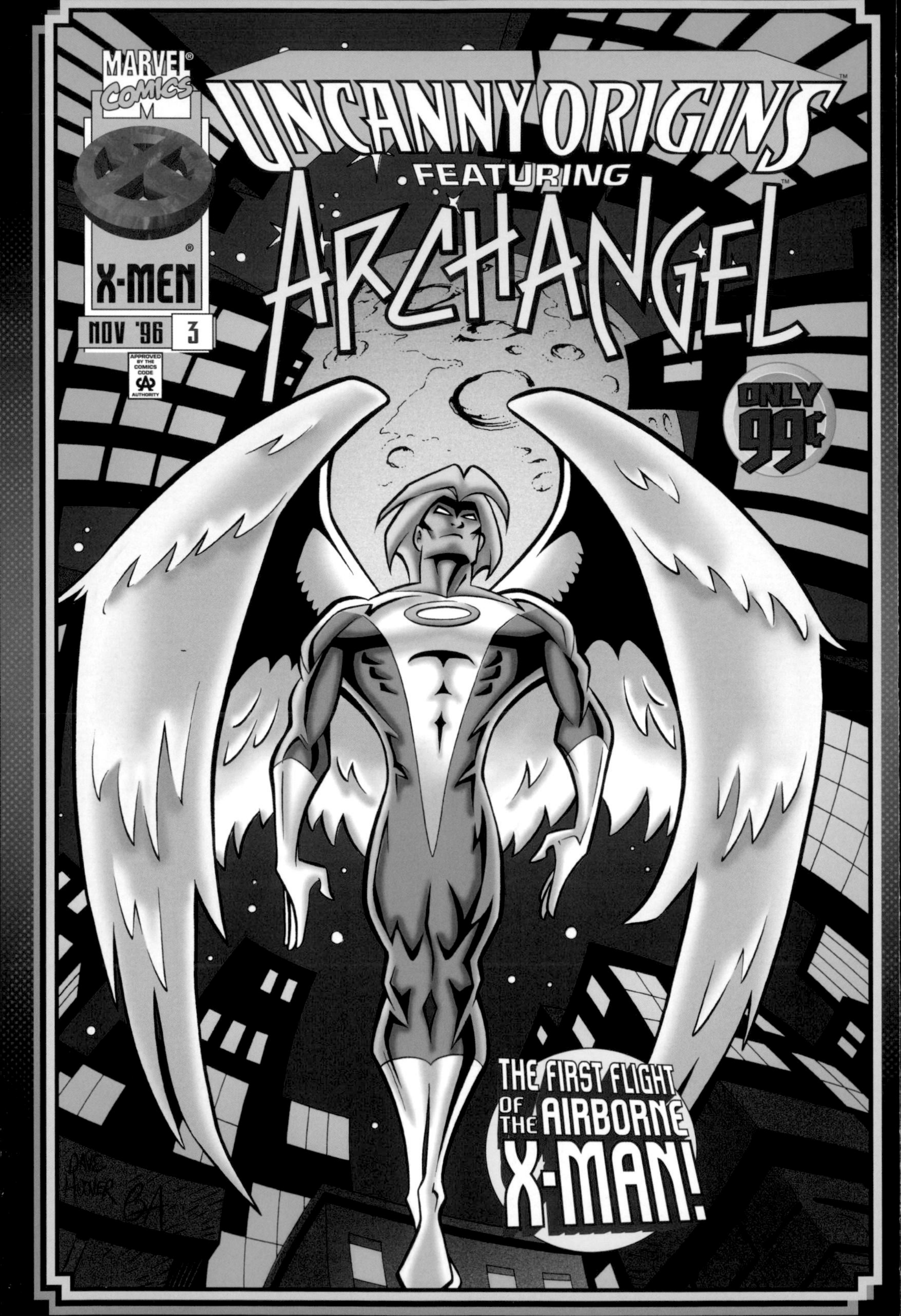
MARVEL COMICS
UNCANNY ORIGINS
FEATURING
ARCHANGEL
X-MEN
NOV '96
3
APPROVED BY THE COMICS CODE AUTHORITY
ONLY 99¢
THE FIRST FLIGHT OF THE AIRBORNE X-MAN!

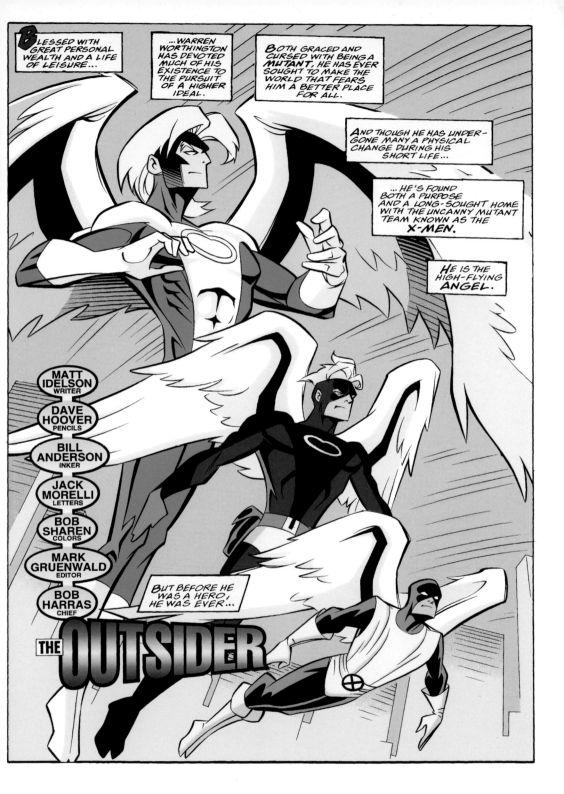

BLESSED WITH GREAT PERSONAL WEALTH AND A LIFE OF LEISURE...

...WARREN WORTHINGTON HAS DEVOTED MUCH OF HIS EXISTENCE TO THE PURSUIT OF A HIGHER IDEAL.

BOTH GRACED AND CURSED WITH BEING A *MUTANT*, HE HAS EVER SOUGHT TO MAKE THE WORLD THAT FEARS HIM A BETTER PLACE FOR ALL.

AND THOUGH HE HAS UNDER-GONE MANY A PHYSICAL CHANGE DURING HIS SHORT LIFE...

...HE'S FOUND BOTH A PURPOSE AND A LONG-SOUGHT HOME WITH THE UNCANNY MUTANT TEAM KNOWN AS THE **X-MEN**.

HE IS THE HIGH-FLYING **ANGEL**.

MATT **IDELSON**
WRITER

DAVE **HOOVER**
PENCILS

BILL **ANDERSON**
INKER

JACK **MORELLI**
LETTERS

BOB **SHAREN**
COLORS

MARK **GRUENWALD**
EDITOR

BOB **HARRAS**
CHIEF

BUT BEFORE HE WAS A HERO, HE WAS EVER...

THE OUTSIDER

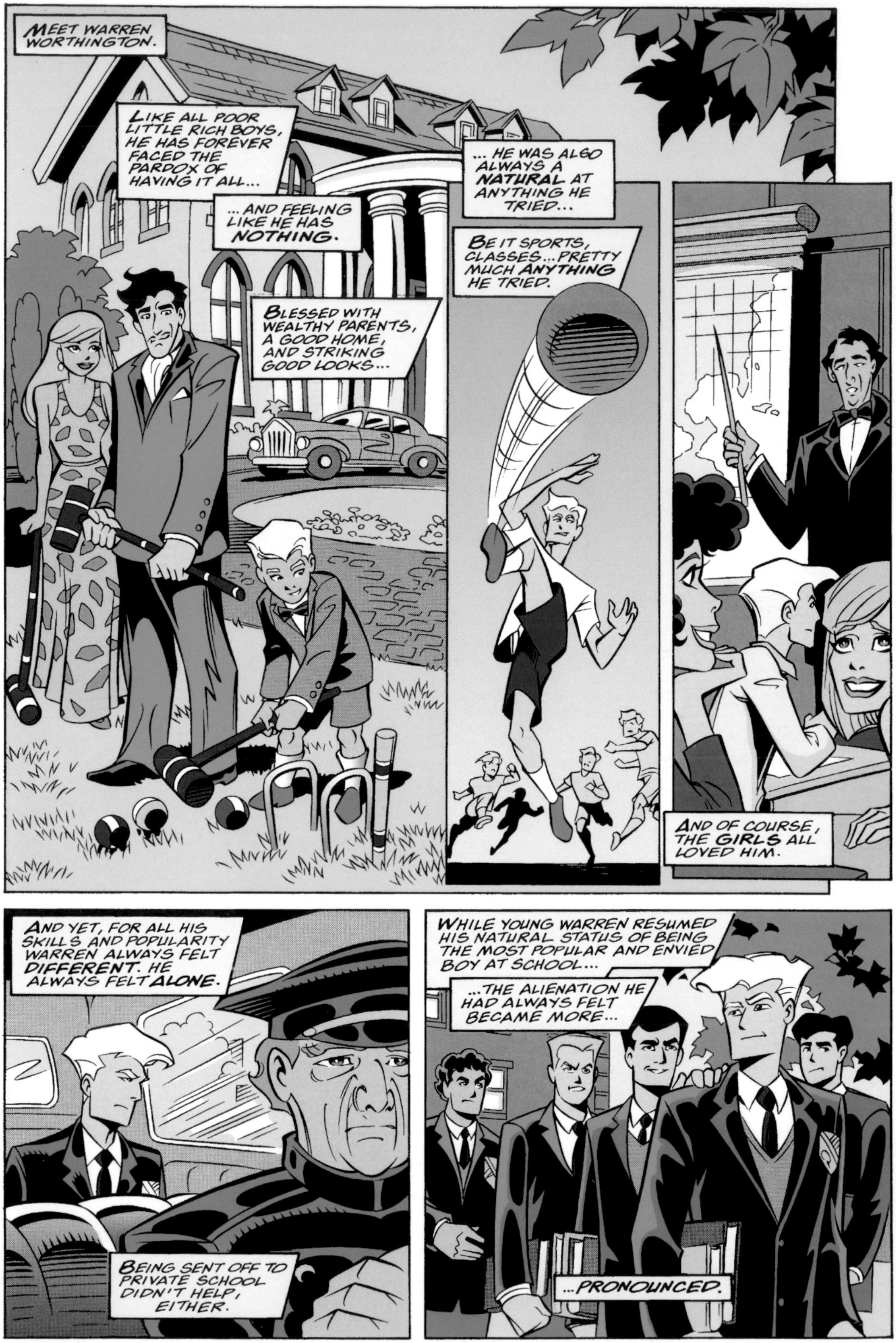
MEET WARREN WORTHINGTON.
LIKE ALL POOR LITTLE RICH BOYS, HE HAS FOREVER FACED THE PARDOX OF HAVING IT ALL...
...AND FEELING LIKE HE HAS NOTHING.
BLESSED WITH WEALTHY PARENTS, A GOOD HOME, AND STRIKING GOOD LOOKS...
...HE WAS ALSO ALWAYS A NATURAL AT ANYTHING HE TRIED...
BE IT SPORTS, CLASSES...PRETTY MUCH ANYTHING HE TRIED.
AND OF COURSE, THE GIRLS ALL LOVED HIM.
AND YET, FOR ALL HIS SKILLS AND POPULARITY WARREN ALWAYS FELT DIFFERENT. HE ALWAYS FELT ALONE.
BEING SENT OFF TO PRIVATE SCHOOL DIDN'T HELP, EITHER.
WHILE YOUNG WARREN RESUMED HIS NATURAL STATUS OF BEING THE MOST POPULAR AND ENVIED BOY AT SCHOOL...
...THE ALIENATION HE HAD ALWAYS FELT BECAME MORE...
...PRONOUNCED.

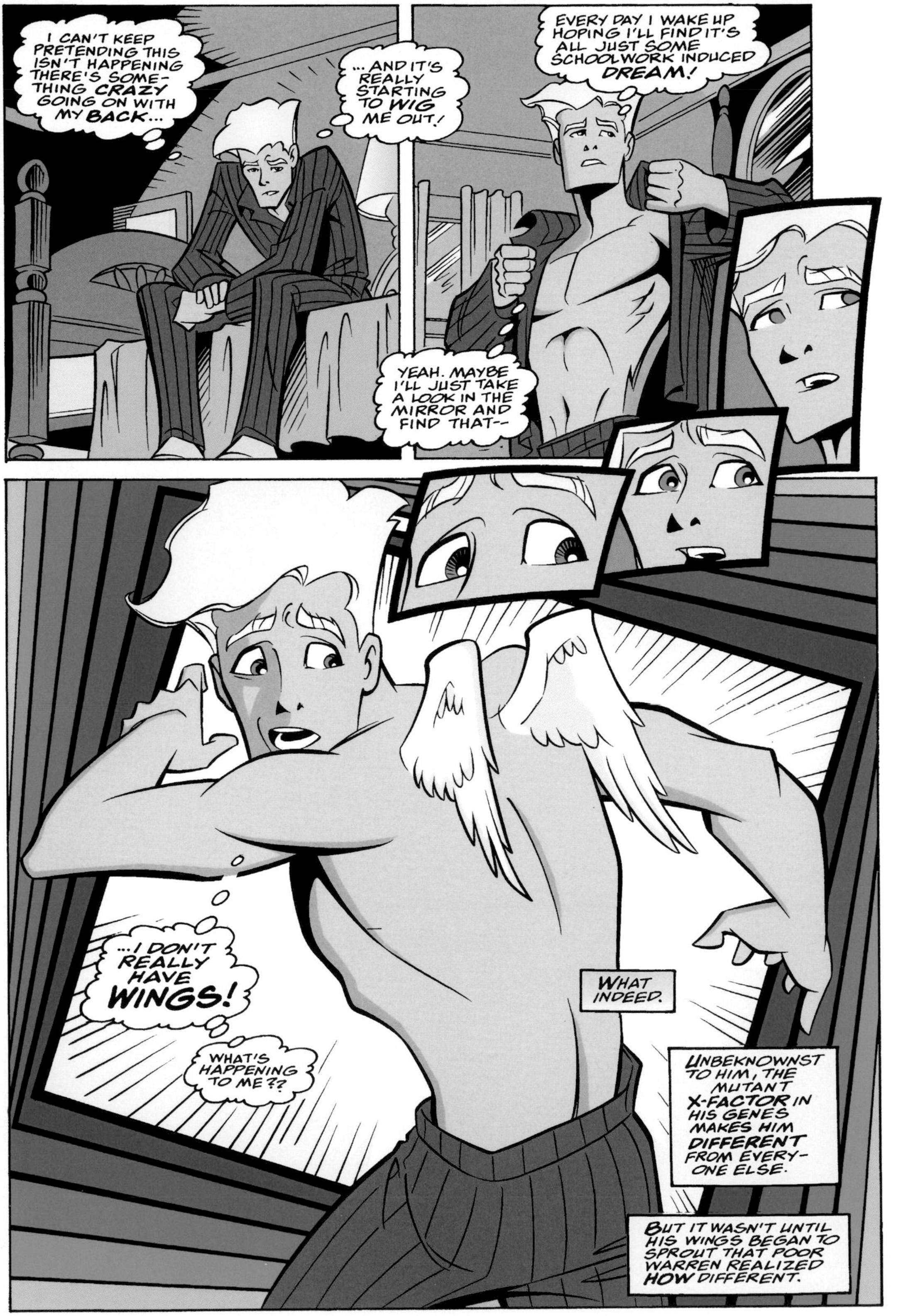
I CAN'T KEEP PRETENDING THIS ISN'T HAPPENING THERE'S SOME-THING CRAZY GOING ON WITH MY BACK...
...AND IT'S REALLY STARTING TO WIG ME OUT!
EVERY DAY I WAKE UP HOPING I'LL FIND IT'S ALL JUST SOME SCHOOLWORK INDUCED DREAM!
YEAH. MAYBE I'LL JUST TAKE A LOOK IN THE MIRROR AND FIND THAT--
...I DON'T REALLY HAVE WINGS!
WHAT'S HAPPENING TO ME??
WHAT INDEED.
UNBEKNOWNST TO HIM, THE MUTANT X-FACTOR IN HIS GENES MAKES HIM DIFFERENT FROM EVERY-ONE ELSE.
BUT IT WASN'T UNTIL HIS WINGS BEGAN TO SPROUT THAT POOR WARREN REALIZED HOW DIFFERENT.

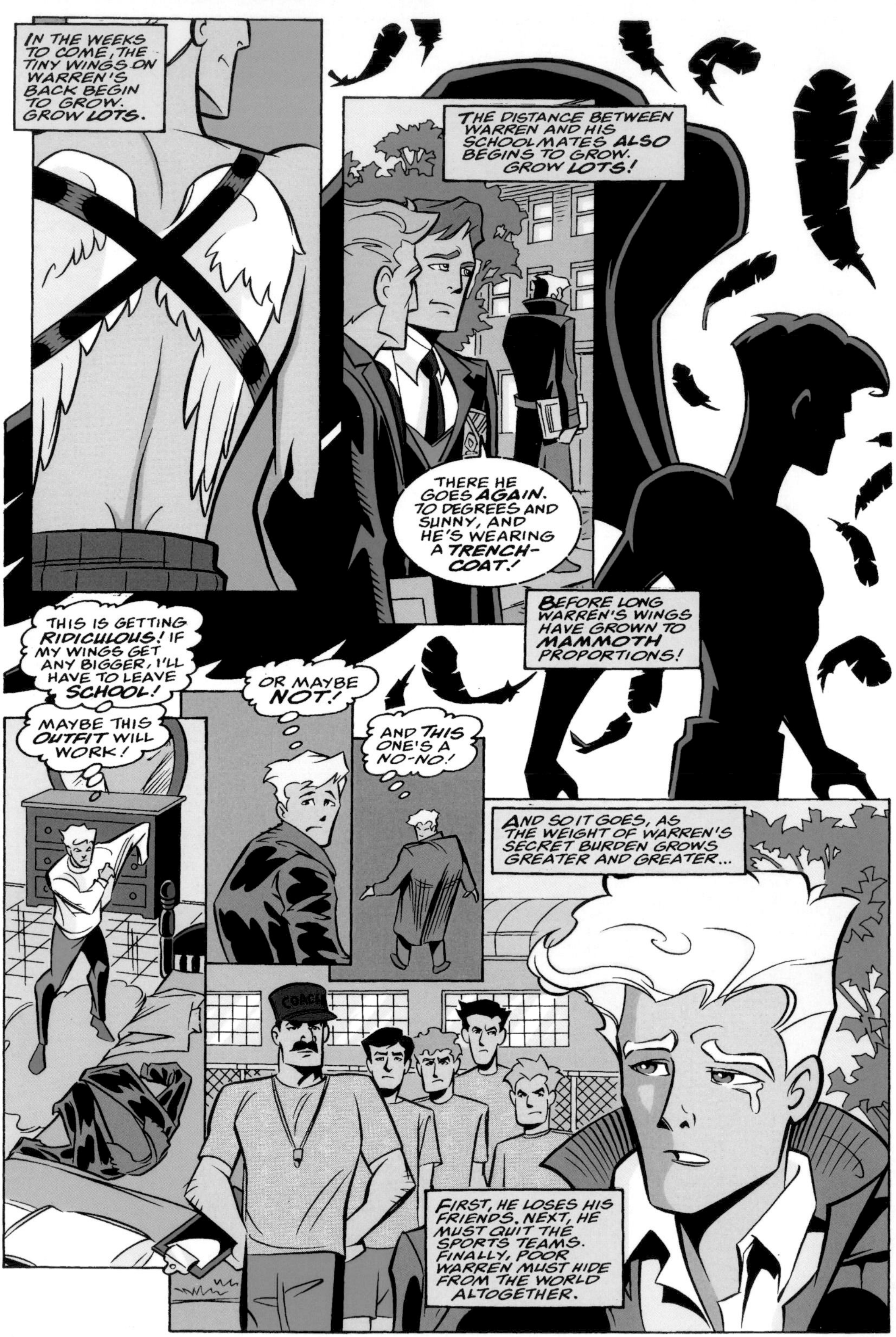
IN THE WEEKS TO COME, THE TINY WINGS ON WARREN'S BACK BEGIN TO GROW. GROW LOTS.
THE DISTANCE BETWEEN WARREN AND HIS SCHOOLMATES ALSO BEGINS TO GROW. GROW LOTS!
THERE HE GOES AGAIN. 70 DEGREES AND SUNNY, AND HE'S WEARING A TRENCH-COAT!
BEFORE LONG WARREN'S WINGS HAVE GROWN TO MAMMOTH PROPORTIONS!
THIS IS GETTING RIDICULOUS! IF MY WINGS GET ANY BIGGER, I'LL HAVE TO LEAVE SCHOOL!
MAYBE THIS OUTFIT WILL WORK!
OR MAYBE NOT!
AND THIS ONE'S A NO-NO!
AND SO IT GOES, AS THE WEIGHT OF WARREN'S SECRET BURDEN GROWS GREATER AND GREATER...
COACH
FIRST, HE LOSES HIS FRIENDS. NEXT, HE MUST QUIT THE SPORTS TEAMS. FINALLY, POOR WARREN MUST HIDE FROM THE WORLD ALTOGETHER.

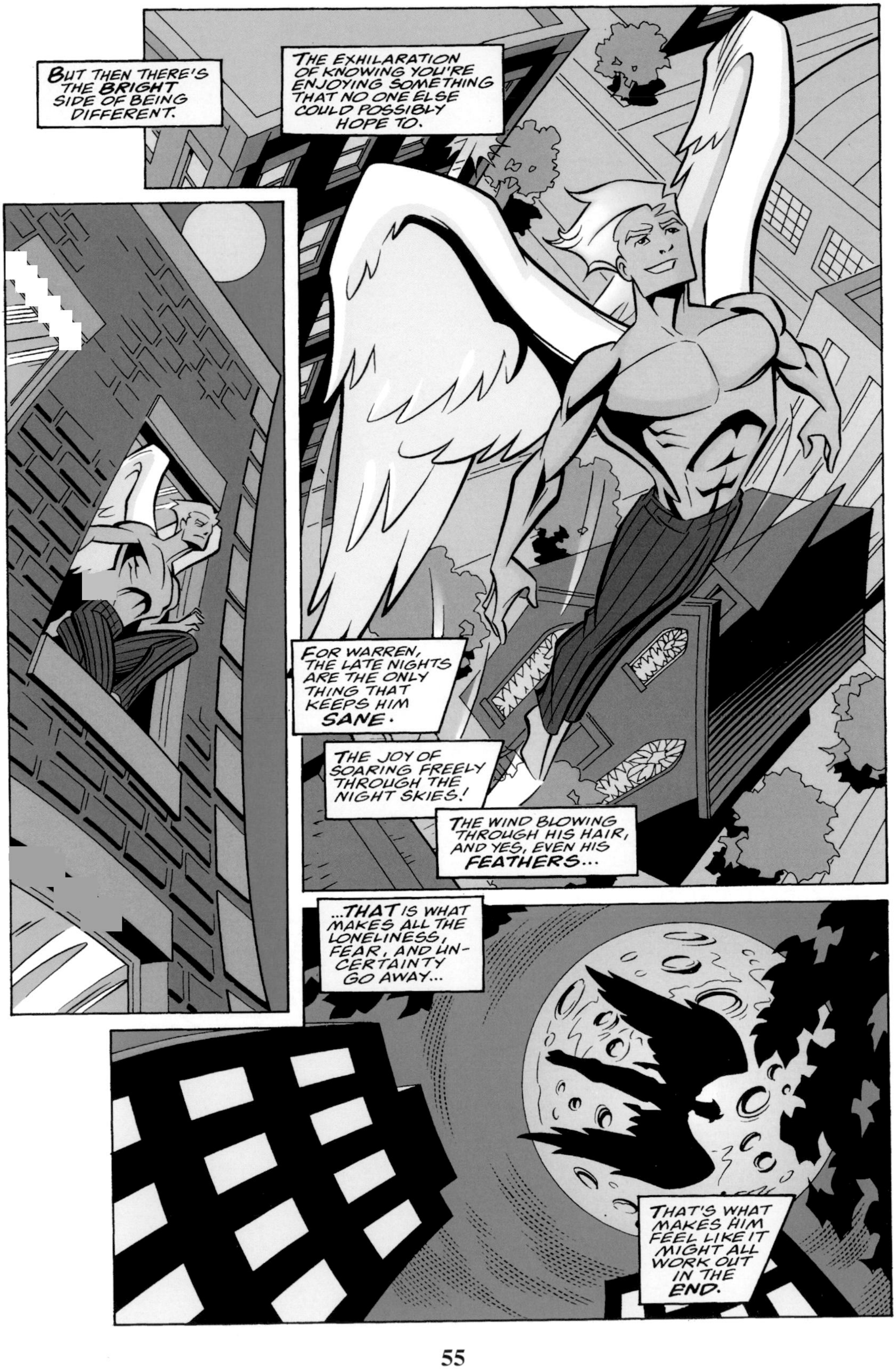
BUT THEN THERE'S THE BRIGHT SIDE OF BEING DIFFERENT.
THE EXHILARATION OF KNOWING YOU'RE ENJOYING SOMETHING THAT NO ONE ELSE COULD POSSIBLY HOPE TO.
FOR WARREN, THE LATE NIGHTS ARE THE ONLY THING THAT KEEPS HIM SANE.
THE JOY OF SOARING FREELY THROUGH THE NIGHT SKIES!
THE WIND BLOWING THROUGH HIS HAIR, AND YES, EVEN HIS FEATHERS...
...THAT IS WHAT MAKES ALL THE LONELINESS, FEAR, AND UNCERTAINTY GO AWAY...
THAT'S WHAT MAKES HIM FEEL LIKE IT MIGHT ALL WORK OUT IN THE END.

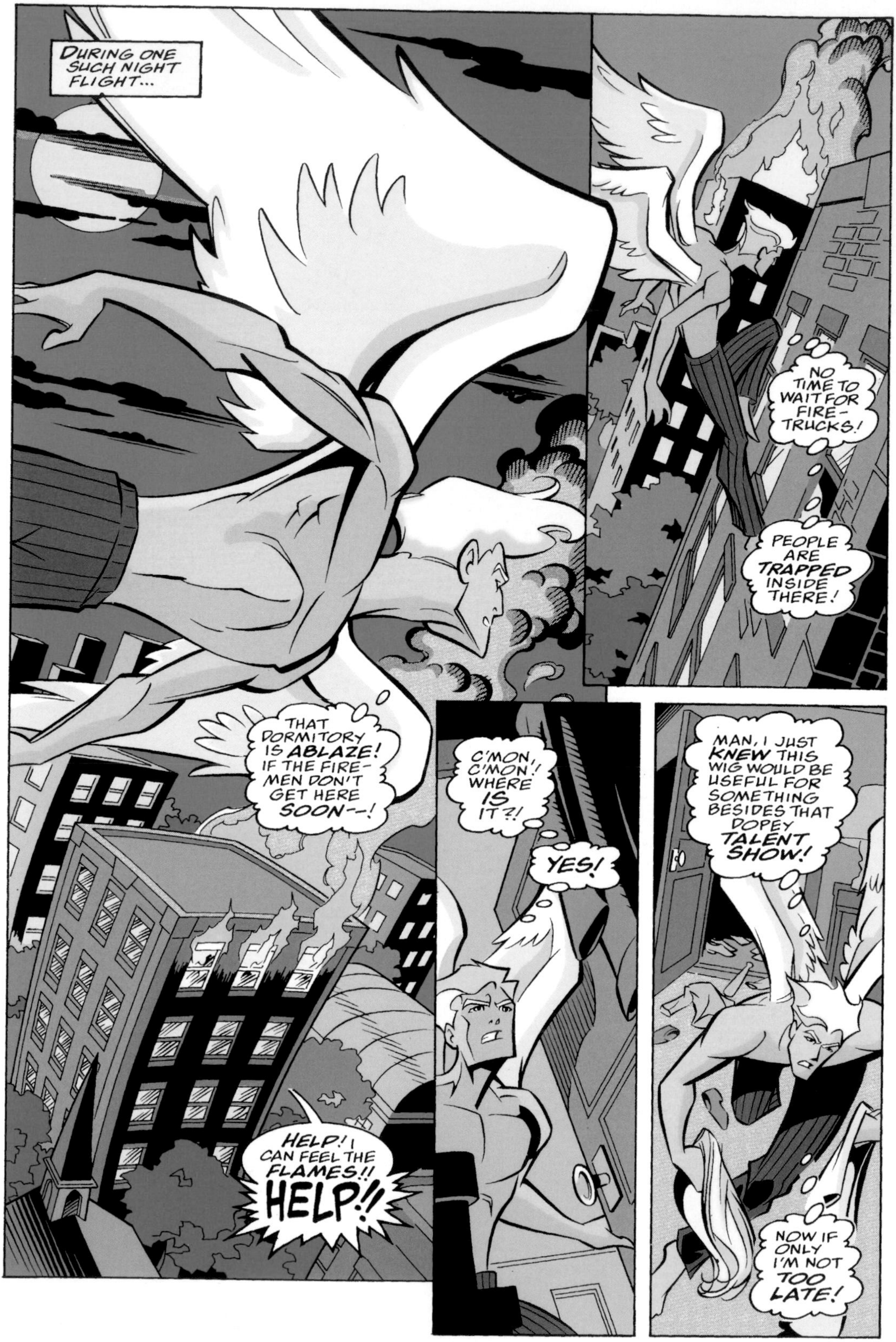
DURING ONE SUCH NIGHT FLIGHT...
NO TIME TO WAIT FOR FIRE-TRUCKS!
PEOPLE ARE TRAPPED INSIDE THERE!
THAT DORMITORY IS ABLAZE! IF THE FIRE-MEN DON'T GET HERE SOON--!
HELP! I CAN FEEL THE FLAMES!! HELP!!
C'MON, C'MON! WHERE IS IT?!
YES!
MAN, I JUST KNEW THIS WIG WOULD BE USEFUL FOR SOMETHING BESIDES THAT DOPEY TALENT SHOW!
NOW IF ONLY I'M NOT TOO LATE!

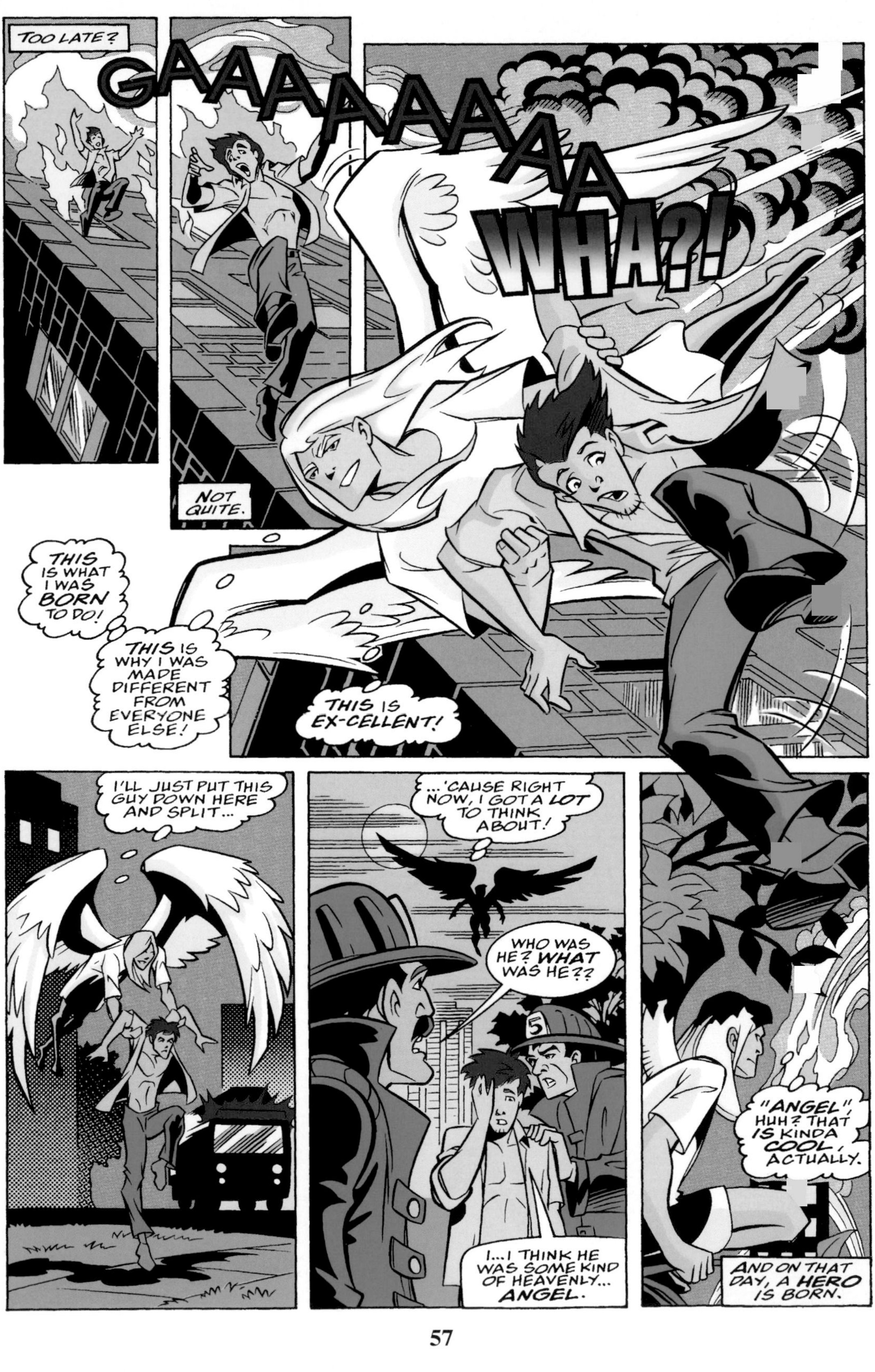
TOO LATE?
GAAAAAAAAA
NOT QUITE.
WHA?!
THIS IS WHAT I WAS BORN TO DO!
THIS IS WHY I WAS MADE DIFFERENT FROM EVERYONE ELSE!
THIS IS EX-CELLENT!
I'LL JUST PUT THIS GUY DOWN HERE AND SPLIT...
...'CAUSE RIGHT NOW, I GOT A LOT TO THINK ABOUT!
WHO WAS HE? WHAT WAS HE??
I...I THINK HE WAS SOME KIND OF HEAVENLY... ANGEL.
"ANGEL", HUH? THAT IS KINDA COOL, ACTUALLY.
AND ON THAT DAY, A HERO IS BORN.

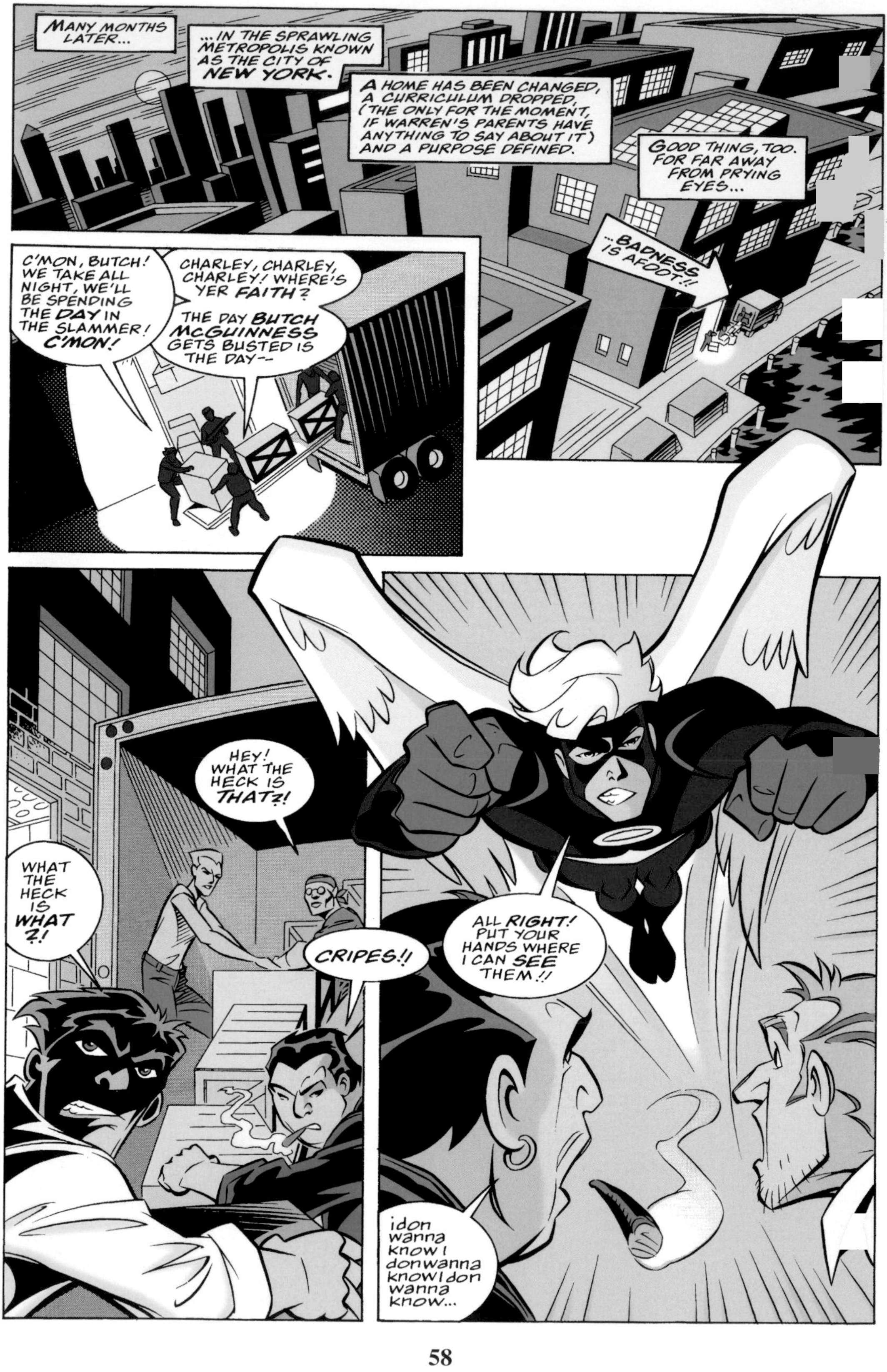

MANY MONTHS LATER...
...IN THE SPRAWLING METROPOLIS KNOWN AS THE CITY OF NEW YORK.
A HOME HAS BEEN CHANGED, A CURRICULUM DROPPED, (THE ONLY FOR THE MOMENT, IF WARREN'S PARENTS HAVE ANYTHING TO SAY ABOUT IT) AND A PURPOSE DEFINED.
GOOD THING, TOO. FOR FAR AWAY FROM PRYING EYES...
...BADNESS IS AFOOT!!
C'MON, BUTCH! WE TAKE ALL NIGHT, WE'LL BE SPENDING THE DAY IN THE SLAMMER! C'MON!
CHARLEY, CHARLEY, CHARLEY! WHERE'S YER FAITH?
THE DAY BUTCH McGUINNESS GETS BUSTED IS THE DAY--
HEY! WHAT THE HECK IS THAT?!
WHAT THE HECK IS WHAT?!
CRIPES!!
ALL RIGHT! PUT YOUR HANDS WHERE I CAN SEE THEM!!
idon wanna know I donwanna know I don wanna know...

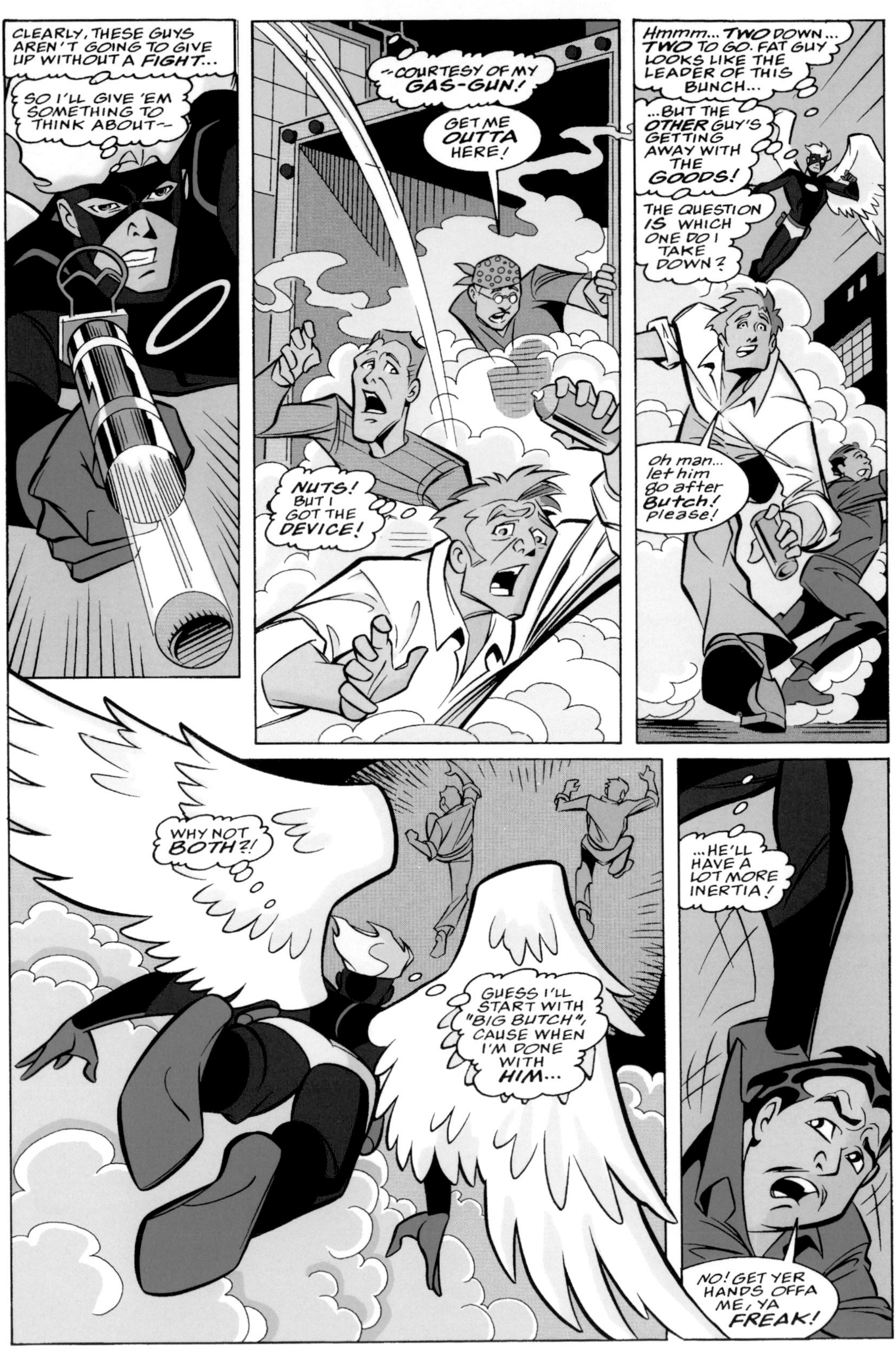

CLEARLY, THESE GUYS AREN'T GOING TO GIVE UP WITHOUT A FIGHT...
SO I'LL GIVE 'EM SOMETHING TO THINK ABOUT--
--COURTESY OF MY GAS-GUN!
GET ME OUTTA HERE!
NUTS! BUT I GOT THE DEVICE!
Hmmm... TWO DOWN... TWO TO GO. FAT GUY LOOKS LIKE THE LEADER OF THIS BUNCH...
...BUT THE OTHER GUY'S GETTING AWAY WITH THE GOODS!
THE QUESTION IS WHICH ONE DO I TAKE DOWN?
oh man... let him go after Butch! please!
WHY NOT BOTH?!
GUESS I'LL START WITH "BIG BUTCH", CAUSE WHEN I'M DONE WITH HIM...
...HE'LL HAVE A LOT MORE INERTIA!
NO! GET YER HANDS OFFA ME, YA FREAK!

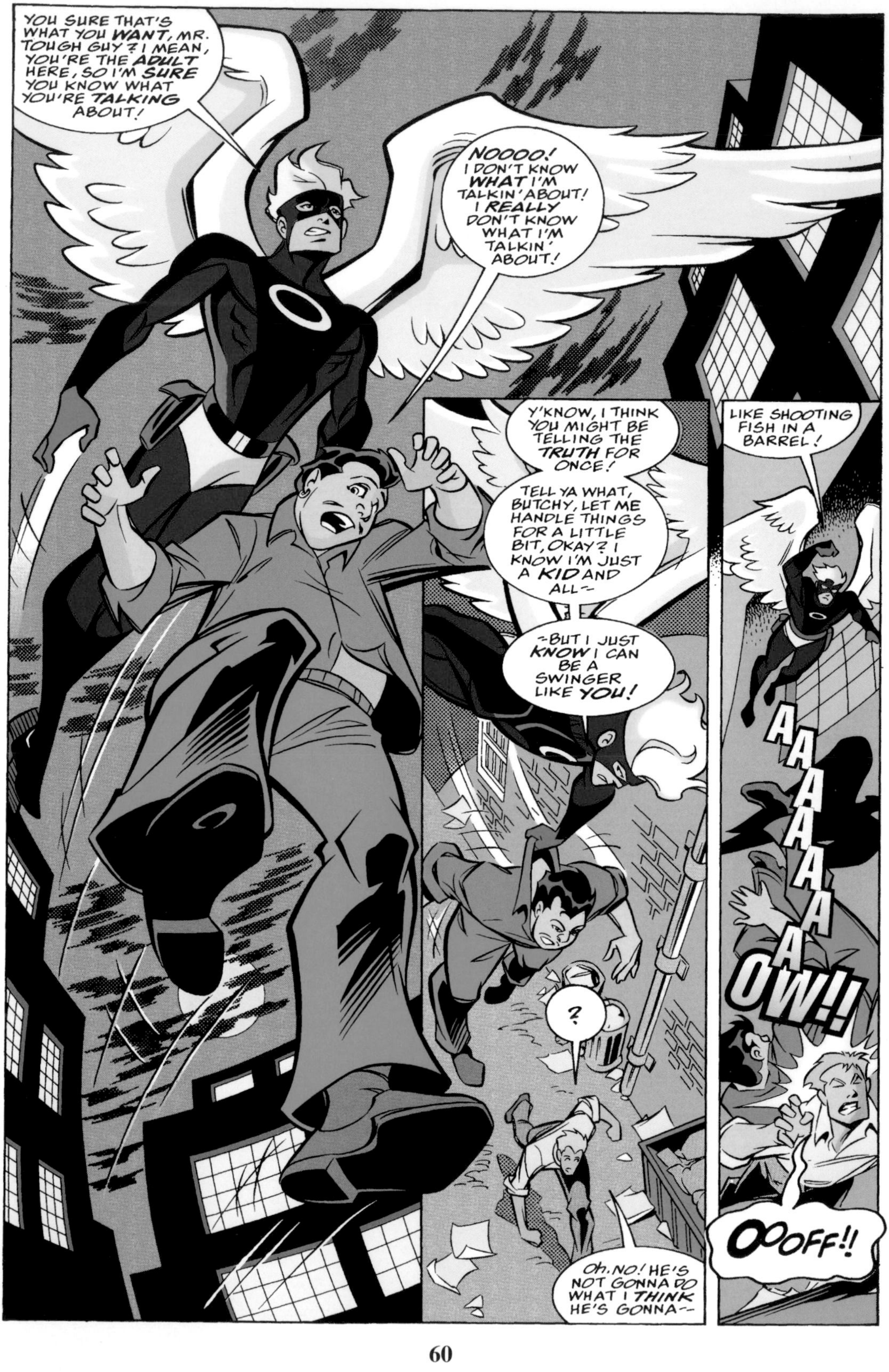
YOU SURE THAT'S WHAT YOU WANT, MR. TOUGH GUY? I MEAN, YOU'RE THE ADULT HERE, SO I'M SURE YOU KNOW WHAT YOU'RE TALKING ABOUT!
NOOOO! I DON'T KNOW WHAT I'M TALKIN' ABOUT! I REALLY DON'T KNOW WHAT I'M TALKIN' ABOUT!
Y'KNOW, I THINK YOU MIGHT BE TELLING THE TRUTH FOR ONCE!
TELL YA WHAT, BUTCHY, LET ME HANDLE THINGS FOR A LITTLE BIT, OKAY? I KNOW I'M JUST A KID AND ALL--
--BUT I JUST KNOW I CAN BE A SWINGER LIKE YOU!
?
Oh, NO! HE'S NOT GONNA DO WHAT I THINK HE'S GONNA--
LIKE SHOOTING FISH IN A BARREL!
AAAAAAAOW!!
OOOFF!!

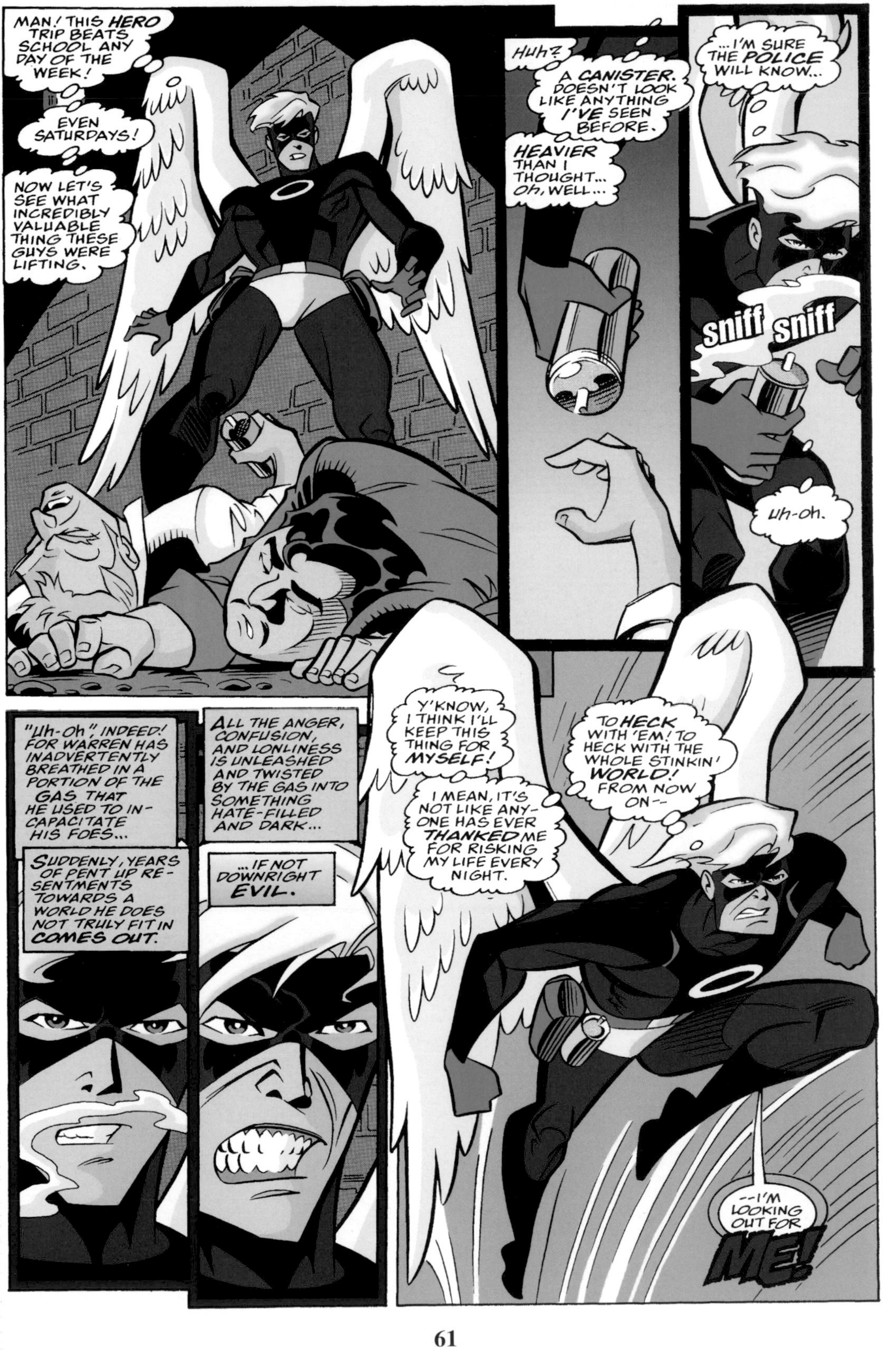
MAN! THIS HERO TRIP BEATS SCHOOL ANY DAY OF THE WEEK!
EVEN SATURDAYS!
NOW LET'S SEE WHAT INCREDIBLY VALUABLE THING THESE GUYS WERE LIFTING.
Huh?
A CANISTER. DOESN'T LOOK LIKE ANYTHING I'VE SEEN BEFORE.
HEAVIER THAN I THOUGHT... Oh, WELL...
...I'M SURE THE POLICE WILL KNOW...
Sniff Sniff
uh-oh.
"uh-oh," INDEED! FOR WARREN HAS INADVERTENTLY BREATHED IN A PORTION OF THE GAS THAT HE USED TO INCAPACITATE HIS FOES...
SUDDENLY, YEARS OF PENT UP RESENTMENTS TOWARDS A WORLD HE DOES NOT TRULY FIT IN COMES OUT.
ALL THE ANGER, CONFUSION, AND LONLINESS IS UNLEASHED AND TWISTED BY THE GAS INTO SOMETHING HATE-FILLED AND DARK...
...IF NOT DOWNRIGHT EVIL.
Y'KNOW, I THINK I'LL KEEP THIS THING FOR MYSELF!
I MEAN, IT'S NOT LIKE ANYONE HAS EVER THANKED ME FOR RISKING MY LIFE EVERY NIGHT.
TO HECK WITH 'EM! TO HECK WITH THE WHOLE STINKIN' WORLD! FROM NOW ON--
--I'M LOOKING OUT FOR ME!

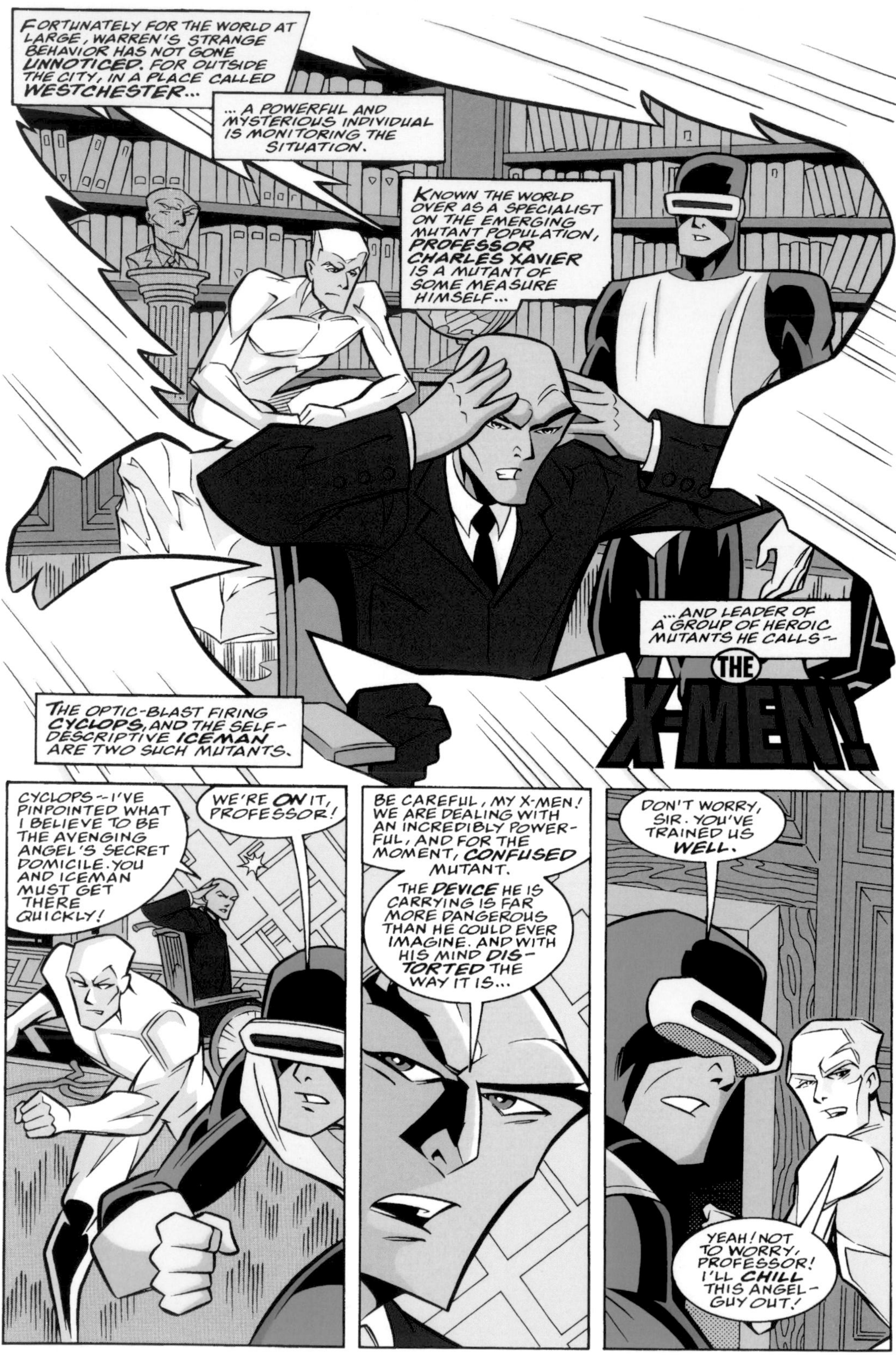
FORTUNATELY FOR THE WORLD AT LARGE, WARREN'S STRANGE BEHAVIOR HAS NOT GONE UNNOTICED. FOR OUTSIDE THE CITY, IN A PLACE CALLED WESTCHESTER...
... A POWERFUL AND MYSTERIOUS INDIVIDUAL IS MONITORING THE SITUATION.
KNOWN THE WORLD OVER AS A SPECIALIST ON THE EMERGING MUTANT POPULATION, PROFESSOR CHARLES XAVIER IS A MUTANT OF SOME MEASURE HIMSELF...
...AND LEADER OF A GROUP OF HEROIC MUTANTS HE CALLS--
THE X-MEN!
THE OPTIC-BLAST FIRING CYCLOPS, AND THE SELF-DESCRIPTIVE ICEMAN ARE TWO SUCH MUTANTS.
CYCLOPS--I'VE PINPOINTED WHAT I BELIEVE TO BE THE AVENGING ANGEL'S SECRET DOMICILE. YOU AND ICEMAN MUST GET THERE QUICKLY!
WE'RE ON IT, PROFESSOR!
BE CAREFUL, MY X-MEN! WE ARE DEALING WITH AN INCREDIBLY POWERFUL, AND FOR THE MOMENT, CONFUSED MUTANT.
THE DEVICE HE IS CARRYING IS FAR MORE DANGEROUS THAN HE COULD EVER IMAGINE. AND WITH HIS MIND DISTORTED THE WAY IT IS...
DON'T WORRY, SIR. YOU'VE TRAINED US WELL.
YEAH! NOT TO WORRY, PROFESSOR! I'LL CHILL THIS ANGEL-GUY OUT!

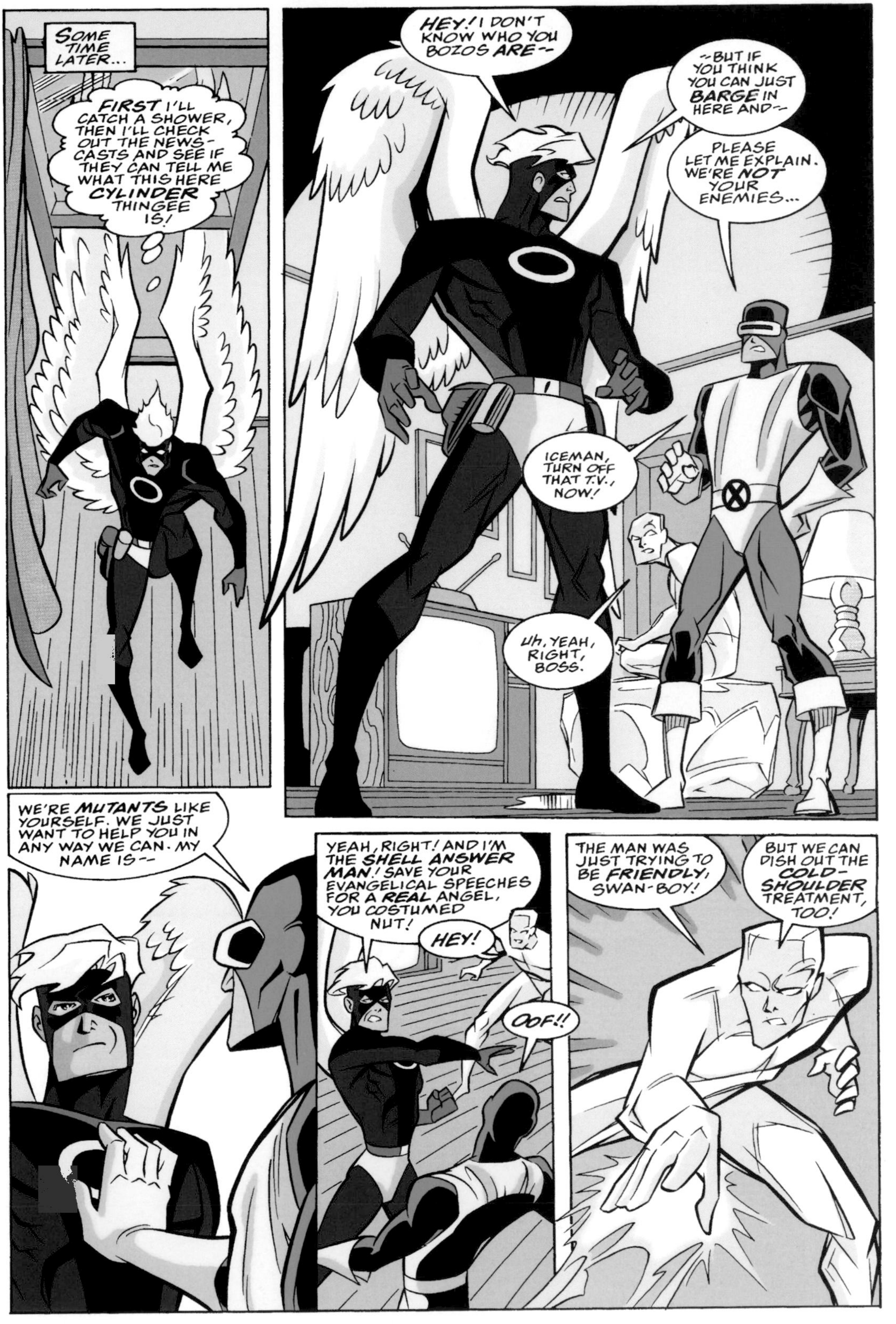
SOME TIME LATER...
FIRST I'LL CATCH A SHOWER, THEN I'LL CHECK OUT THE NEWSCASTS AND SEE IF THEY CAN TELL ME WHAT THIS HERE CYLINDER THINGEE IS!
HEY! I DON'T KNOW WHO YOU BOZOS ARE--
--BUT IF YOU THINK YOU CAN JUST BARGE IN HERE AND--
PLEASE LET ME EXPLAIN. WE'RE NOT YOUR ENEMIES...
ICEMAN, TURN OFF THAT T.V., NOW!
UH, YEAH, RIGHT, BOSS.
WE'RE MUTANTS LIKE YOURSELF. WE JUST WANT TO HELP YOU IN ANY WAY WE CAN. MY NAME IS--
YEAH, RIGHT! AND I'M THE SHELL ANSWER MAN! SAVE YOUR EVANGELICAL SPEECHES FOR A REAL ANGEL, YOU COSTUMED NUT!
HEY!
OOF!!
THE MAN WAS JUST TRYING TO BE FRIENDLY, SWAN-BOY!
BUT WE CAN DISH OUT THE COLD-SHOULDER TREATMENT, TOO!

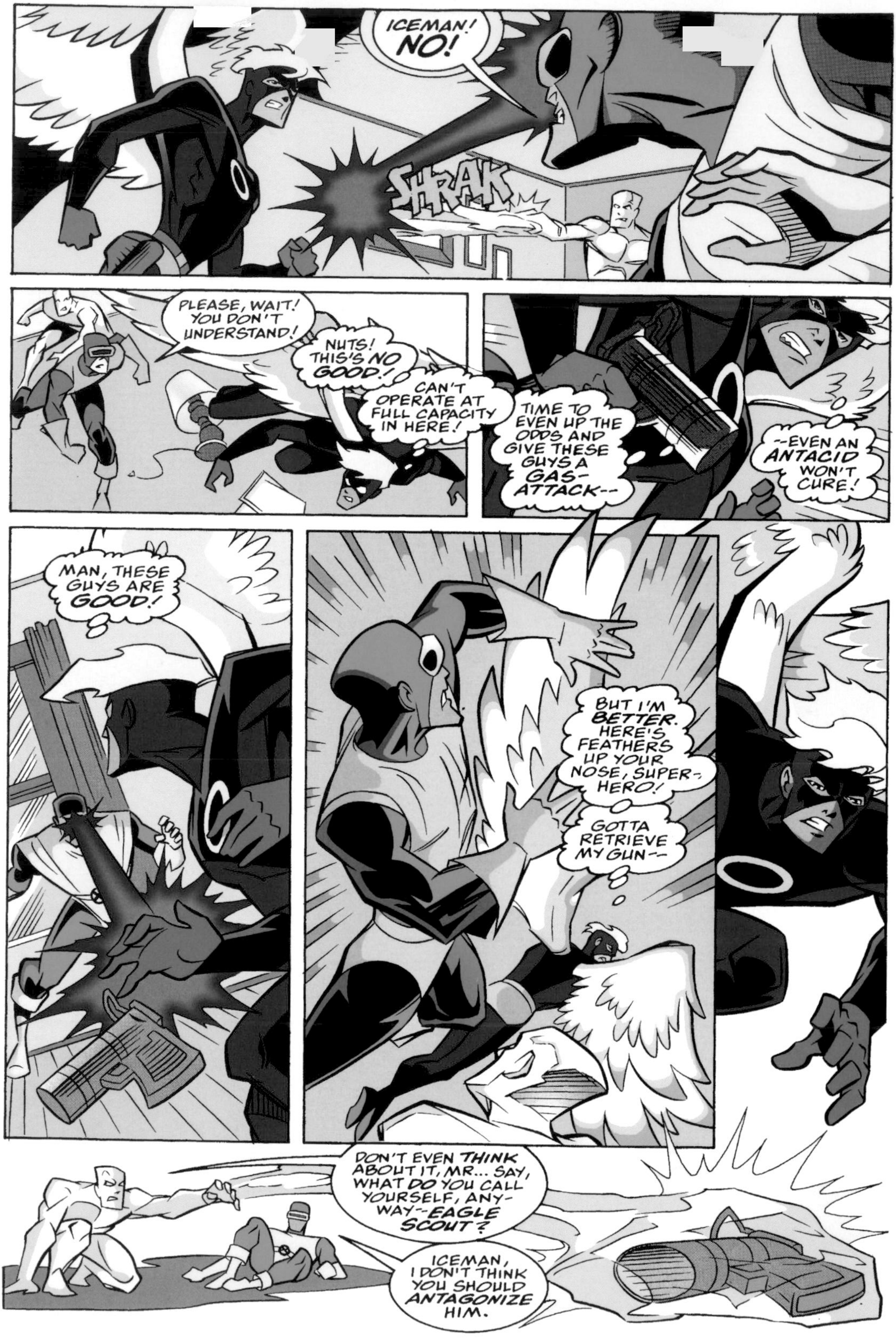
ICEMAN! NO!
SHRAK
PLEASE, WAIT! YOU DON'T UNDERSTAND!
NUTS! THIS'S NO GOOD.!
CAN'T OPERATE AT FULL CAPACITY IN HERE.!
TIME TO EVEN UP THE ODDS AND GIVE THESE GUYS A GAS-ATTACK--
--EVEN AN ANTACID WON'T CURE.!
MAN, THESE GUYS ARE GOOD.!
BUT I'M BETTER. HERE'S FEATHERS UP YOUR NOSE, SUPER-HERO!
GOTTA RETRIEVE MY GUN--
DON'T EVEN THINK ABOUT IT, MR... SAY, WHAT DO YOU CALL YOURSELF, ANYWAY--EAGLE SCOUT?
ICEMAN, I DON'T THINK YOU SHOULD ANTAGONIZE HIM.

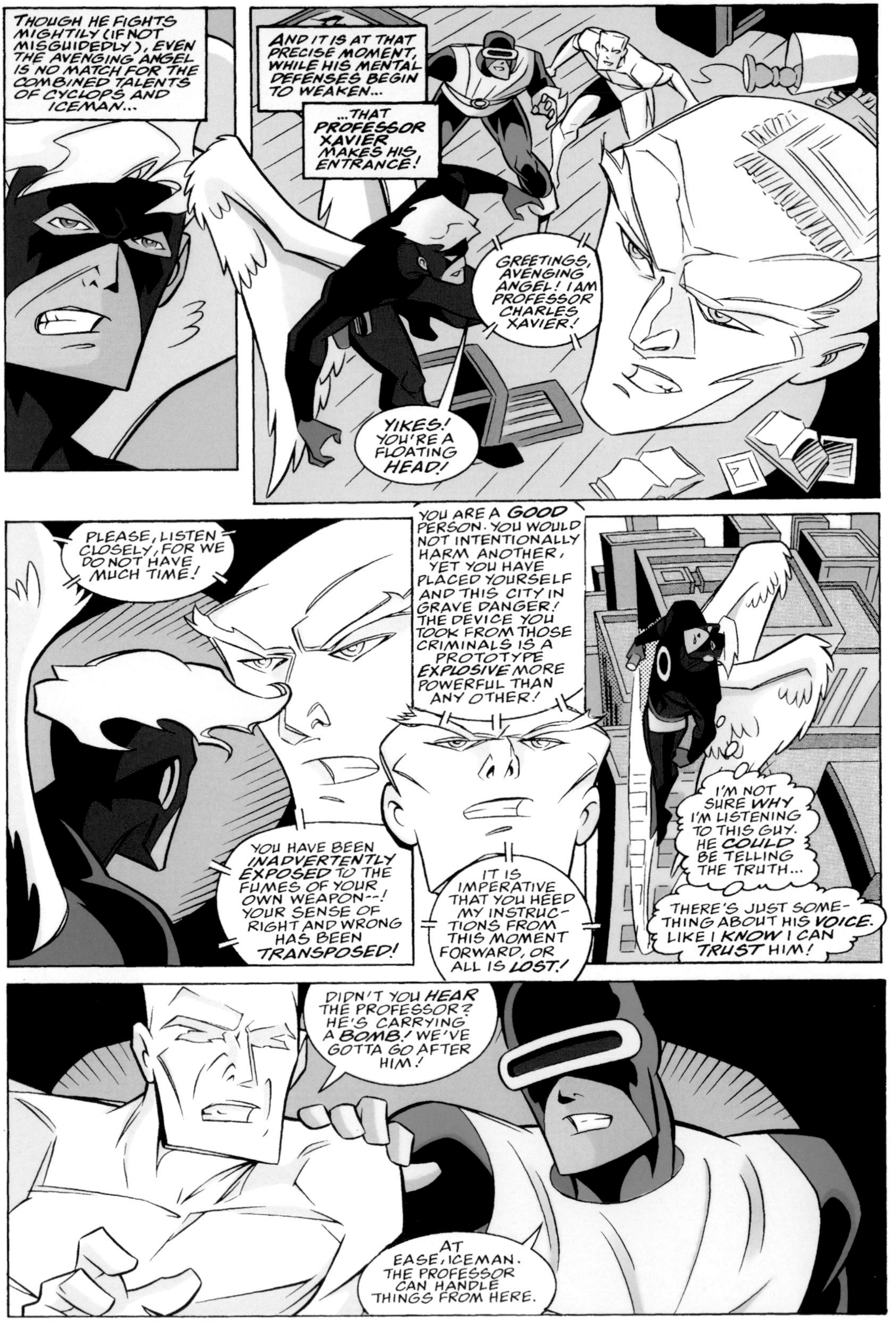
THOUGH HE FIGHTS MIGHTILY (IF NOT MISGUIDEDLY), EVEN THE AVENGING ANGEL IS NO MATCH FOR THE COMBINED TALENTS OF CYCLOPS AND ICEMAN...
AND IT IS AT THAT PRECISE MOMENT, WHILE HIS MENTAL DEFENSES BEGIN TO WEAKEN...
...THAT PROFESSOR XAVIER MAKES HIS ENTRANCE!
GREETINGS, AVENGING ANGEL! I AM PROFESSOR CHARLES XAVIER!
YIKES! YOU'RE A FLOATING HEAD!
PLEASE, LISTEN CLOSELY, FOR WE DO NOT HAVE MUCH TIME!
YOU HAVE BEEN INADVERTENTLY EXPOSED TO THE FUMES OF YOUR OWN WEAPON--! YOUR SENSE OF RIGHT AND WRONG HAS BEEN TRANSPOSED!
YOU ARE A GOOD PERSON. YOU WOULD NOT INTENTIONALLY HARM ANOTHER, YET YOU HAVE PLACED YOURSELF AND THIS CITY IN GRAVE DANGER! THE DEVICE YOU TOOK FROM THOSE CRIMINALS IS A PROTOTYPE EXPLOSIVE MORE POWERFUL THAN ANY OTHER!
IT IS IMPERATIVE THAT YOU HEED MY INSTRUCTIONS FROM THIS MOMENT FORWARD, OR ALL IS LOST!
I'M NOT SURE WHY I'M LISTENING TO THIS GUY. HE COULD BE TELLING THE TRUTH...
THERE'S JUST SOMETHING ABOUT HIS VOICE. LIKE I KNOW I CAN TRUST HIM!
DIDN'T YOU HEAR THE PROFESSOR? HE'S CARRYING A BOMB! WE'VE GOTTA GO AFTER HIM!
AT EASE, ICEMAN. THE PROFESSOR CAN HANDLE THINGS FROM HERE.

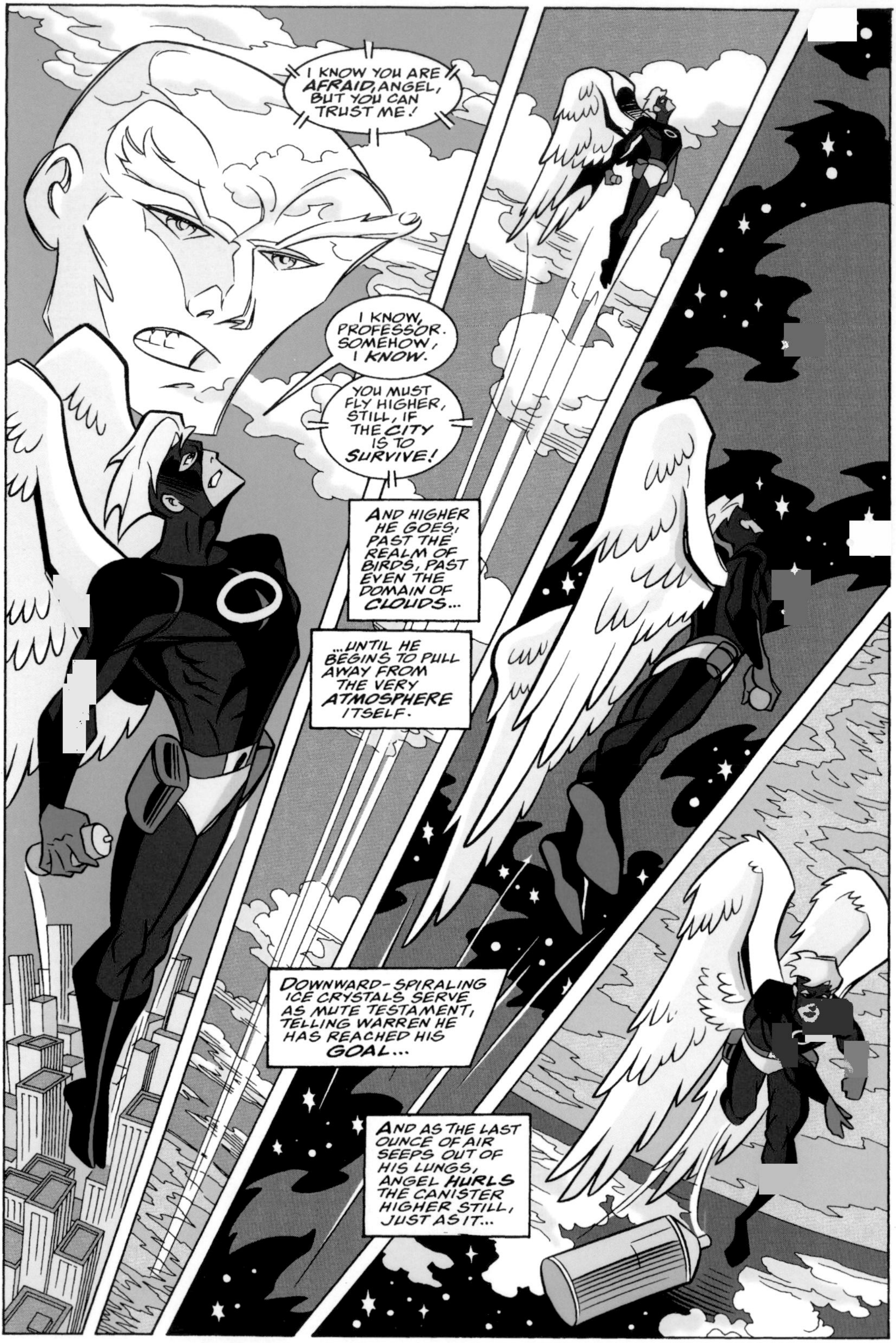

I KNOW YOU ARE AFRAID, ANGEL, BUT YOU CAN TRUST ME!
I KNOW, PROFESSOR. SOMEHOW, I KNOW.
YOU MUST FLY HIGHER, STILL, IF THE CITY IS TO SURVIVE!
AND HIGHER HE GOES, PAST THE REALM OF BIRDS, PAST EVEN THE DOMAIN OF CLOUDS...
...UNTIL HE BEGINS TO PULL AWAY FROM THE VERY ATMOSPHERE ITSELF.
DOWNWARD-SPIRALING ICE CRYSTALS SERVE AS MUTE TESTAMENT, TELLING WARREN HE HAS REACHED HIS GOAL...
AND AS THE LAST OUNCE OF AIR SEEPS OUT OF HIS LUNGS, ANGEL HURLS THE CANISTER HIGHER STILL, JUST AS IT...

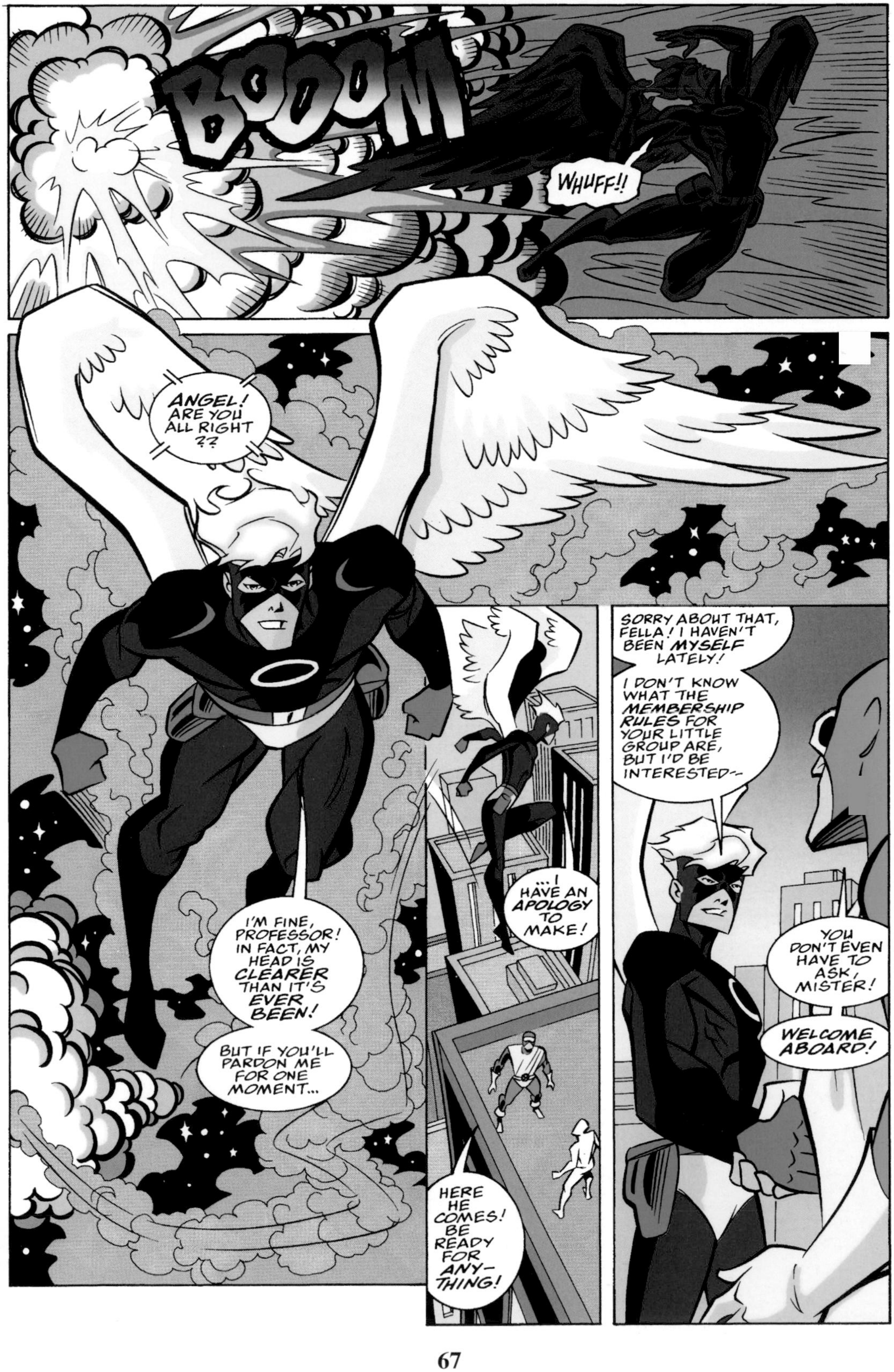
BOOOM
WHUFF!!
ANGEL! ARE YOU ALL RIGHT ??
I'M FINE, PROFESSOR! IN FACT, MY HEAD IS CLEARER THAN IT'S EVER BEEN!
BUT IF YOU'LL PARDON ME FOR ONE MOMENT...
...I HAVE AN APOLOGY TO MAKE!
HERE HE COMES! BE READY FOR ANY-THING!
SORRY ABOUT THAT, FELLA! I HAVEN'T BEEN MYSELF LATELY!
I DON'T KNOW WHAT THE MEMBERSHIP RULES FOR YOUR LITTLE GROUP ARE, BUT I'D BE INTERESTED--
YOU DON'T EVEN HAVE TO ASK, MISTER!
WELCOME ABOARD!

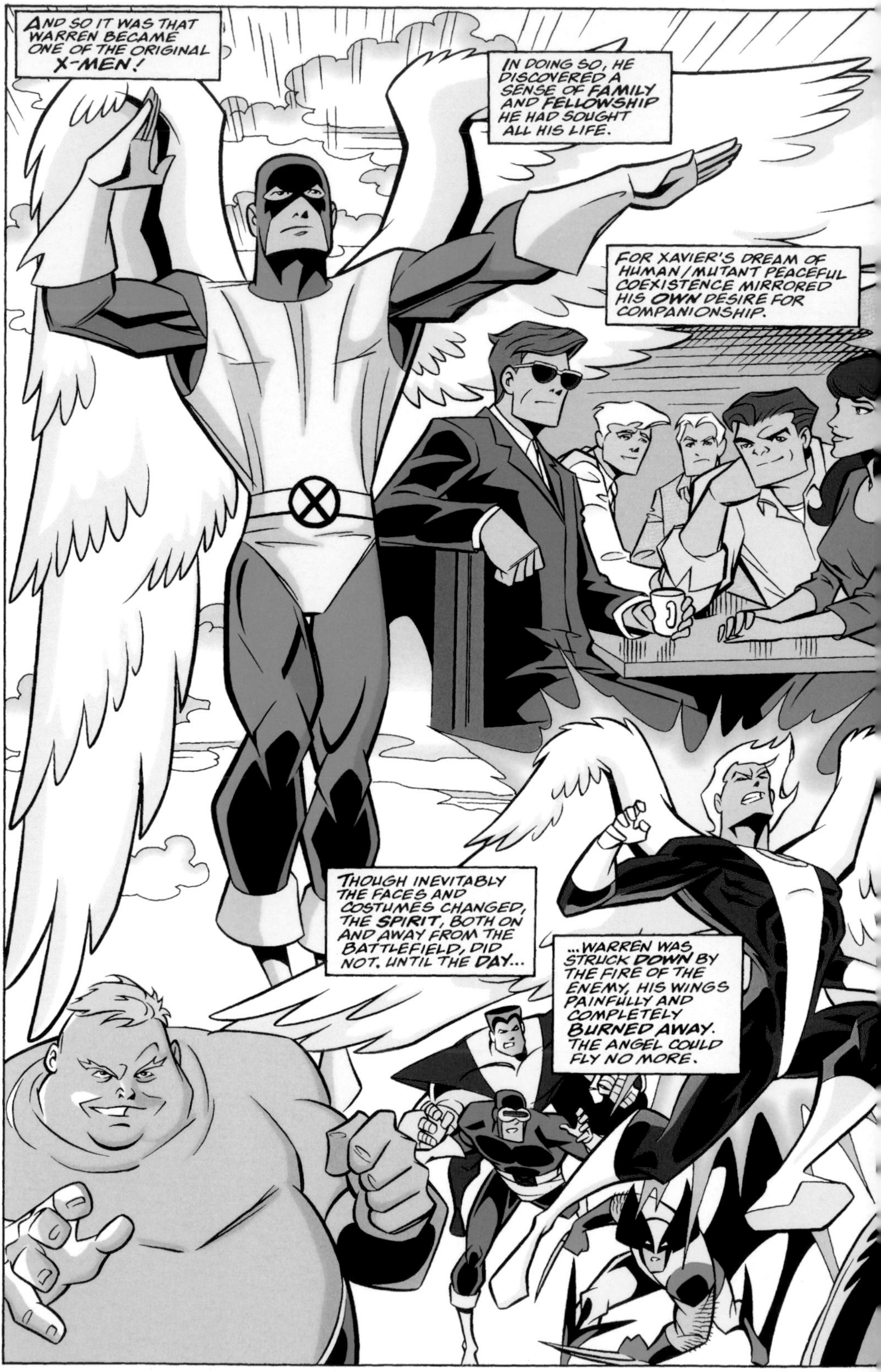
AND SO IT WAS THAT WARREN BECAME ONE OF THE ORIGINAL X-MEN!
IN DOING SO, HE DISCOVERED A SENSE OF FAMILY AND FELLOWSHIP HE HAD SOUGHT ALL HIS LIFE.
FOR XAVIER'S DREAM OF HUMAN/MUTANT PEACEFUL COEXISTENCE MIRRORED HIS OWN DESIRE FOR COMPANIONSHIP.
THOUGH INEVITABLY THE FACES AND COSTUMES CHANGED, THE SPIRIT, BOTH ON AND AWAY FROM THE BATTLEFIELD, DID NOT. UNTIL THE DAY...
...WARREN WAS STRUCK DOWN BY THE FIRE OF THE ENEMY, HIS WINGS PAINFULLY AND COMPLETELY BURNED AWAY. THE ANGEL COULD FLY NO MORE.

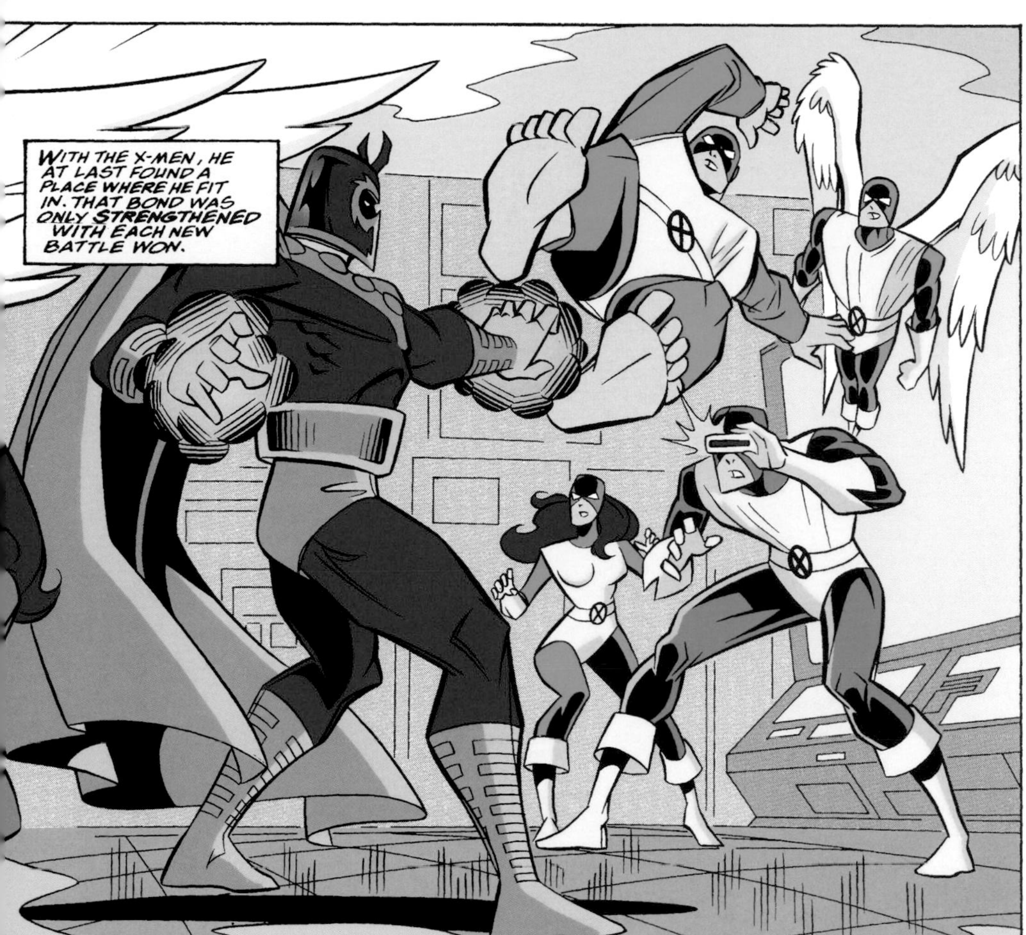
WITH THE X-MEN, HE AT LAST FOUND A PLACE WHERE HE FIT IN. THAT BOND WAS ONLY STRENGTHENED WITH EACH NEW BATTLE WON.

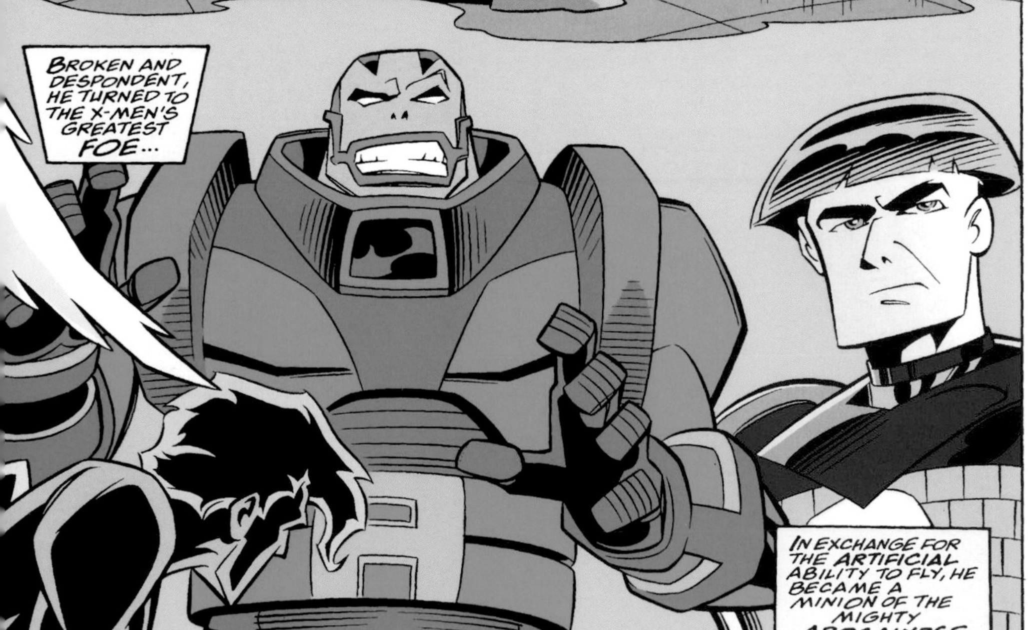
BROKEN AND DESPONDENT, HE TURNED TO THE X-MEN'S GREATEST FOE...
IN EXCHANGE FOR THE ARTIFICIAL ABILITY TO FLY, HE BECAME A MINION OF THE MIGHTY APOCALYPSE.

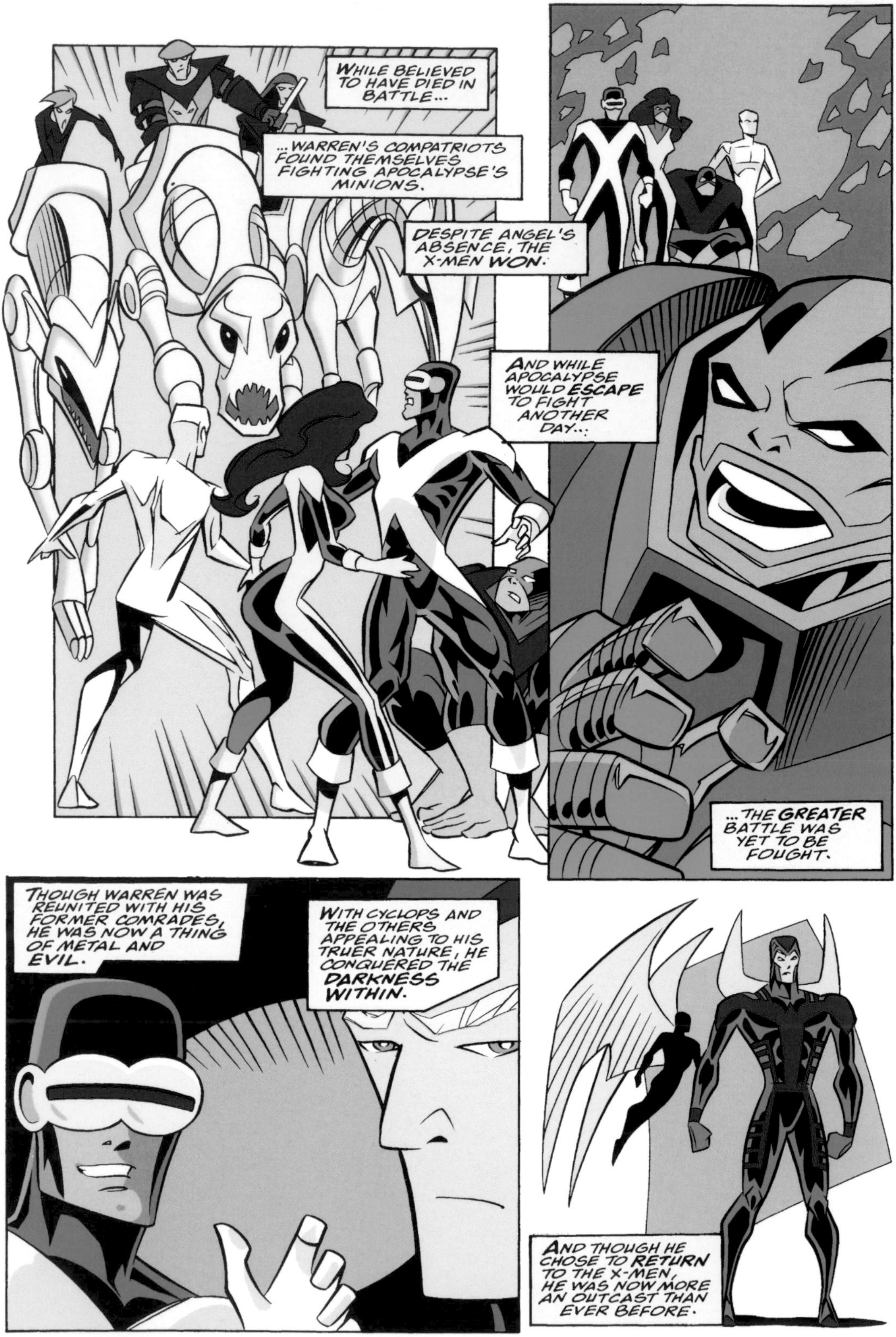
WHILE BELIEVED TO HAVE DIED IN BATTLE...
...WARREN'S COMPATRIOTS FOUND THEMSELVES FIGHTING APOCALYPSE'S MINIONS.
DESPITE ANGEL'S ABSENCE, THE X-MEN WON.
AND WHILE APOCALYPSE WOULD ESCAPE TO FIGHT ANOTHER DAY...
...THE GREATER BATTLE WAS YET TO BE FOUGHT.
THOUGH WARREN WAS REUNITED WITH HIS FORMER COMRADES, HE WAS NOW A THING OF METAL AND EVIL.
WITH CYCLOPS AND THE OTHERS APPEALING TO HIS TRUER NATURE, HE CONQUERED THE DARKNESS WITHIN.
AND THOUGH HE CHOSE TO RETURN TO THE X-MEN, HE WAS NOW MORE AN OUTCAST THAN EVER BEFORE.

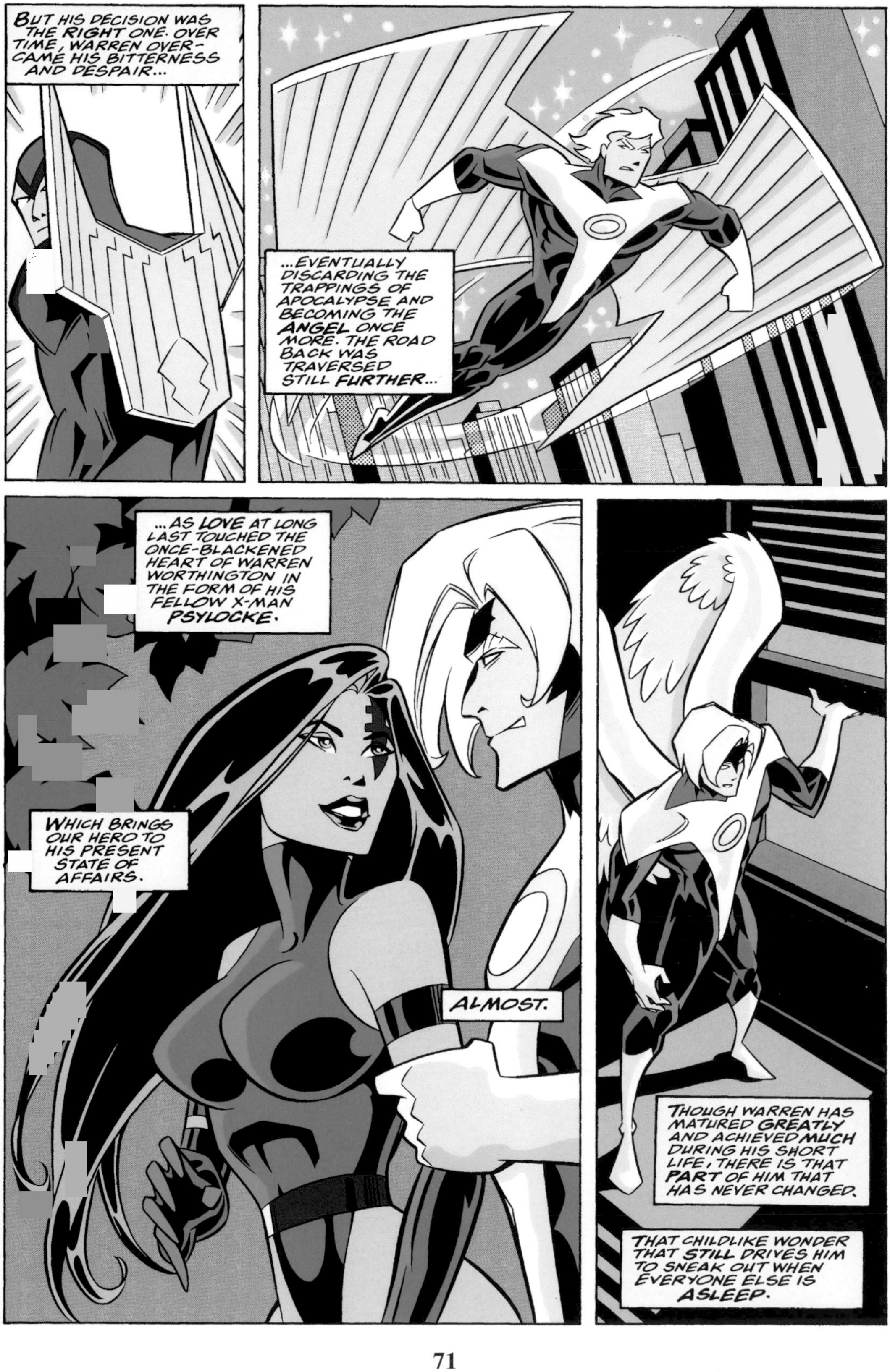
BUT HIS DECISION WAS THE RIGHT ONE. OVER TIME, WARREN OVERCAME HIS BITTERNESS AND DESPAIR...
...EVENTUALLY DISCARDING THE TRAPPINGS OF APOCALYPSE AND BECOMING THE ANGEL ONCE MORE. THE ROAD BACK WAS TRAVERSED STILL FURTHER...
...AS LOVE AT LONG LAST TOUCHED THE ONCE-BLACKENED HEART OF WARREN WORTHINGTON IN THE FORM OF HIS FELLOW X-MAN PSYLOCKE.
WHICH BRINGS OUR HERO TO HIS PRESENT STATE OF AFFAIRS.
ALMOST.
THOUGH WARREN HAS MATURED GREATLY AND ACHIEVED MUCH DURING HIS SHORT LIFE, THERE IS THAT PART OF HIM THAT HAS NEVER CHANGED.
THAT CHILDLIKE WONDER THAT STILL DRIVES HIM TO SNEAK OUT WHEN EVERYONE ELSE IS ASLEEP.

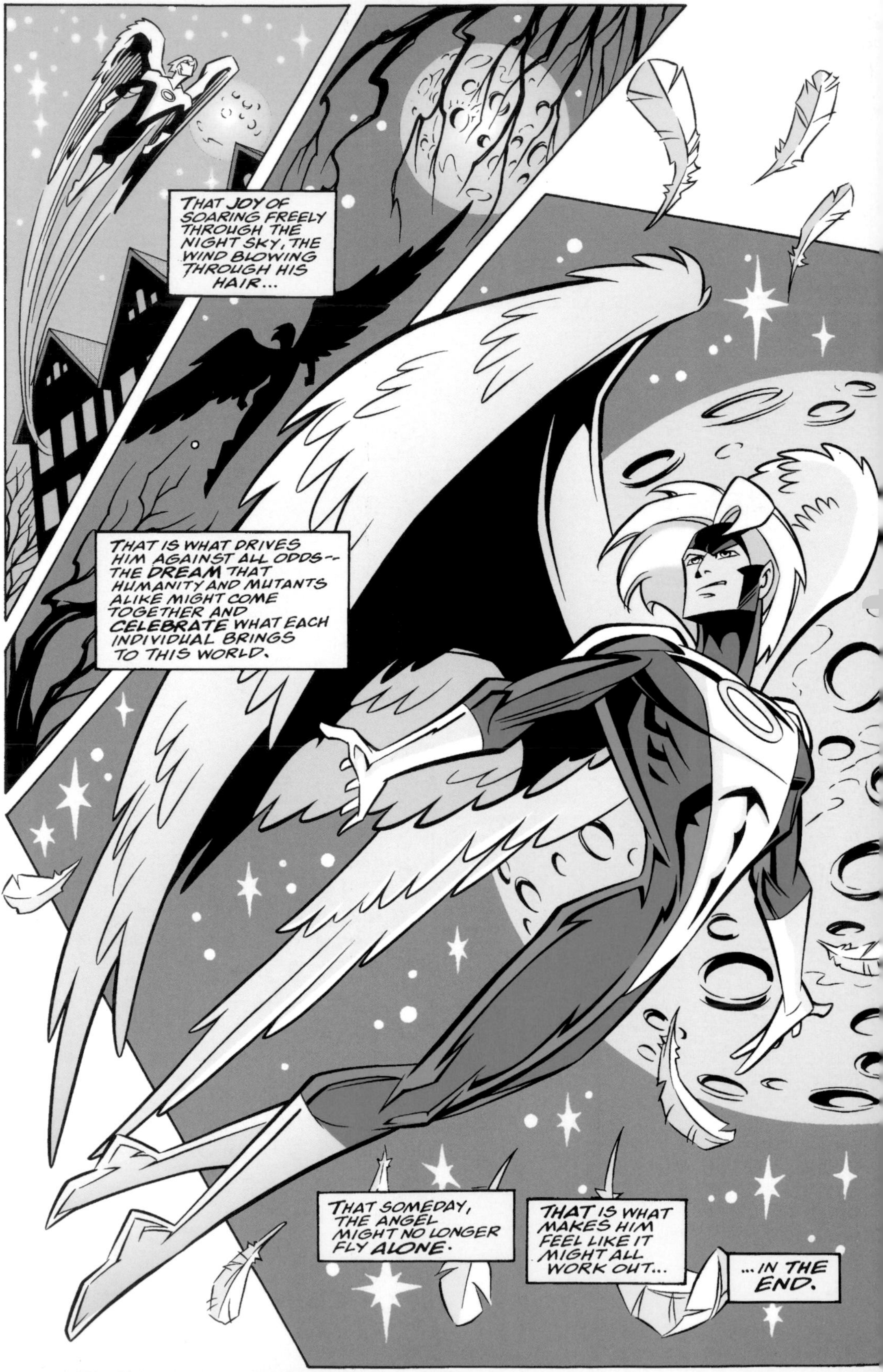
THAT JOY OF SOARING FREELY THROUGH THE NIGHT SKY, THE WIND BLOWING THROUGH HIS HAIR...
THAT IS WHAT DRIVES HIM AGAINST ALL ODDS-- THE DREAM THAT HUMANITY AND MUTANTS ALIKE MIGHT COME TOGETHER AND CELEBRATE WHAT EACH INDIVIDUAL BRINGS TO THIS WORLD.
THAT SOMEDAY, THE ANGEL MIGHT NO LONGER FLY ALONE.
THAT IS WHAT MAKES HIM FEEL LIKE IT MIGHT ALL WORK OUT...
...IN THE END.

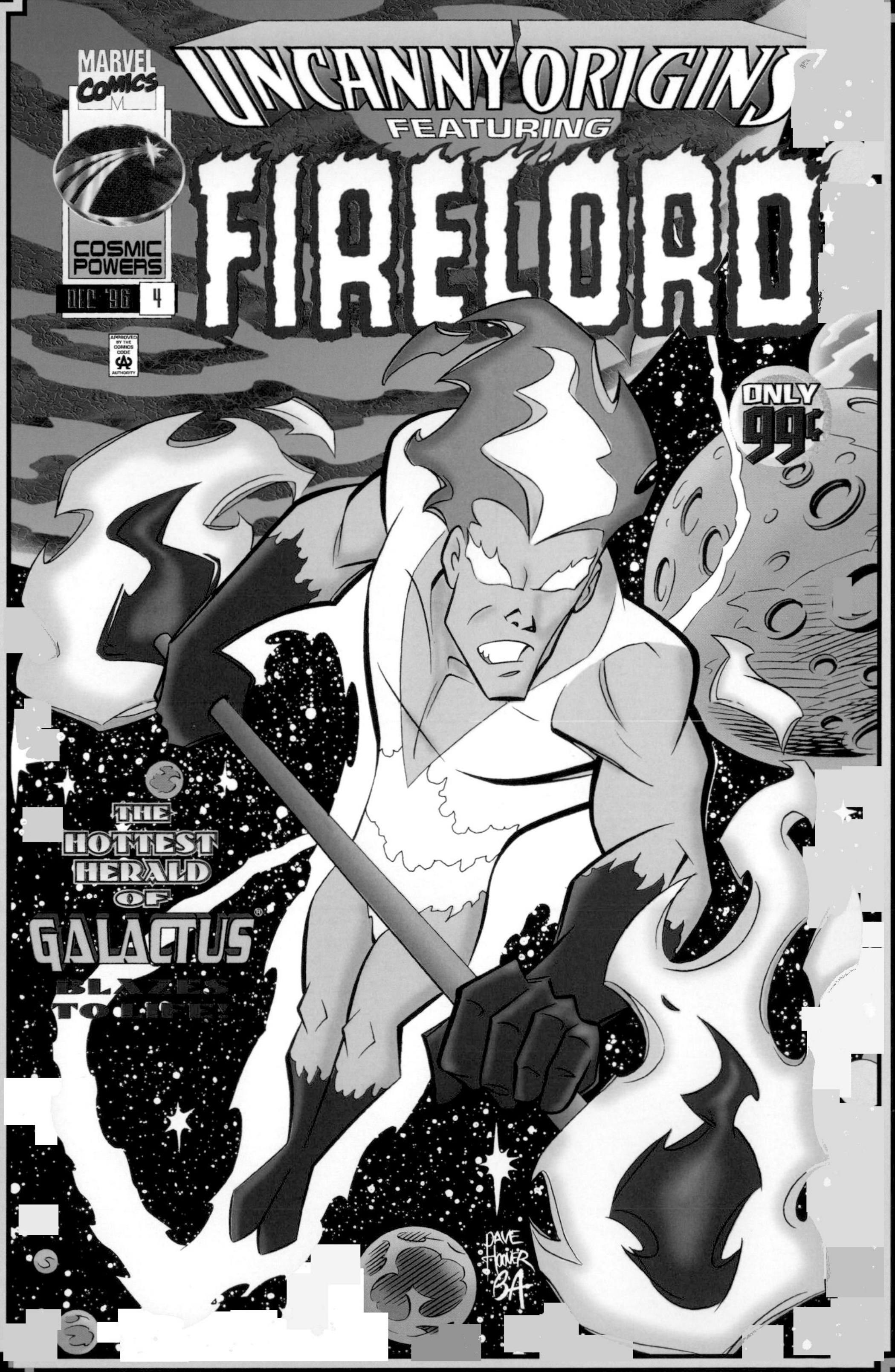

MARVEL COMICS
UNCANNY ORIGINS
FEATURING
FIRELORD
COSMIC POWERS
DEC '96 4
APPROVED BY THE COMICS CODE AUTHORITY
ONLY 99¢
THE HOTTEST HERALD OF GALACTUS®
BLAZES TO LIFE!
DAVE HOOVER BA

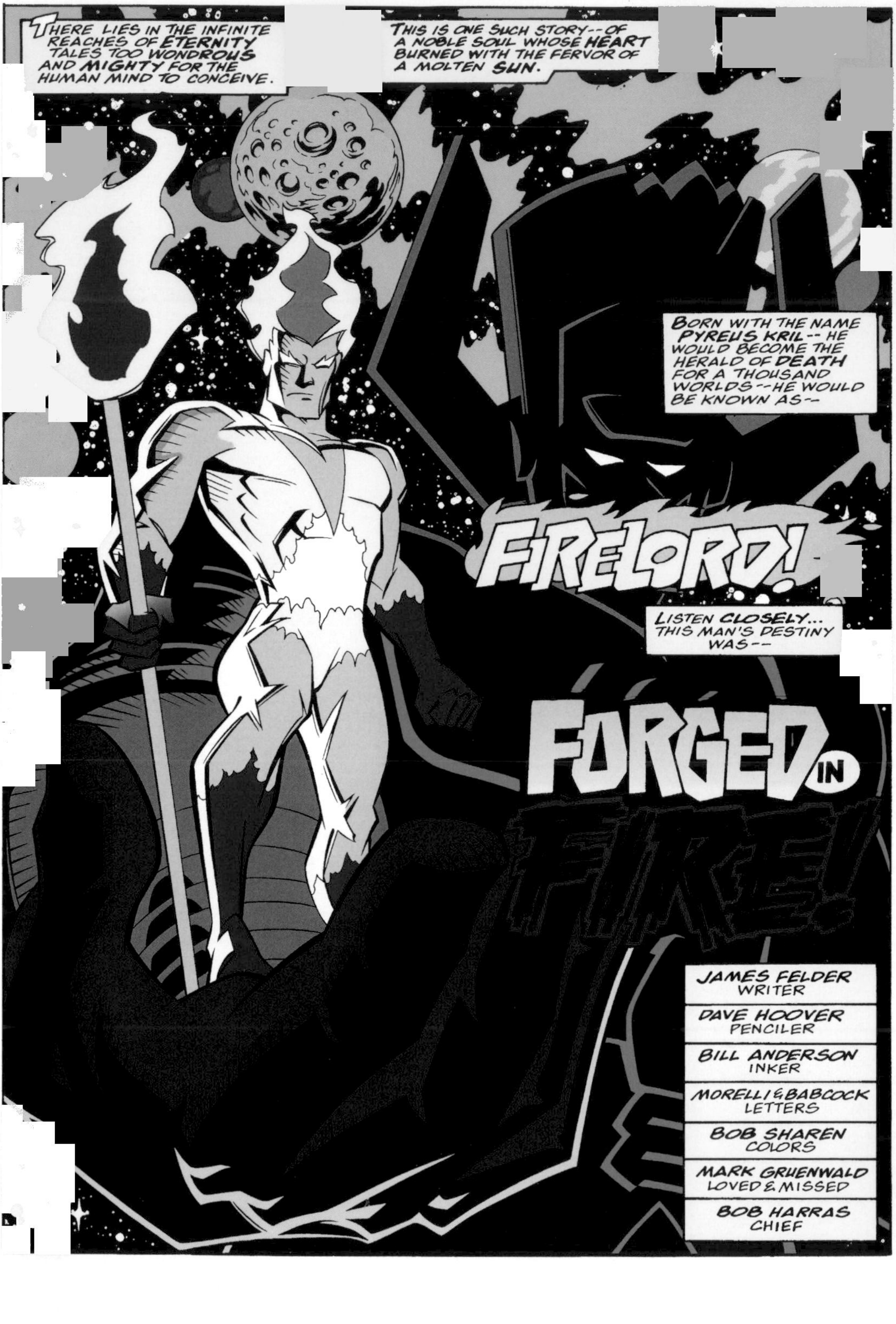

THERE LIES IN THE INFINITE REACHES OF ETERNITY TALES TOO WONDROUS AND MIGHTY FOR THE HUMAN MIND TO CONCEIVE.
THIS IS ONE SUCH STORY--OF A NOBLE SOUL WHOSE HEART BURNED WITH THE FERVOR OF A MOLTEN SUN.
BORN WITH THE NAME PYREUS KRIL--HE WOULD BECOME THE HERALD OF DEATH FOR A THOUSAND WORLDS--HE WOULD BE KNOWN AS--
FIRELORD!
LISTEN CLOSELY... THIS MAN'S DESTINY WAS--
FORGED IN FIRE!
JAMES FELDER WRITER
DAVE HOOVER PENCILER
BILL ANDERSON INKER
MORELLI & BABCOCK LETTERS
BOB SHAREN COLORS
MARK GRUENWALD LOVED & MISSED
BOB HARRAS CHIEF

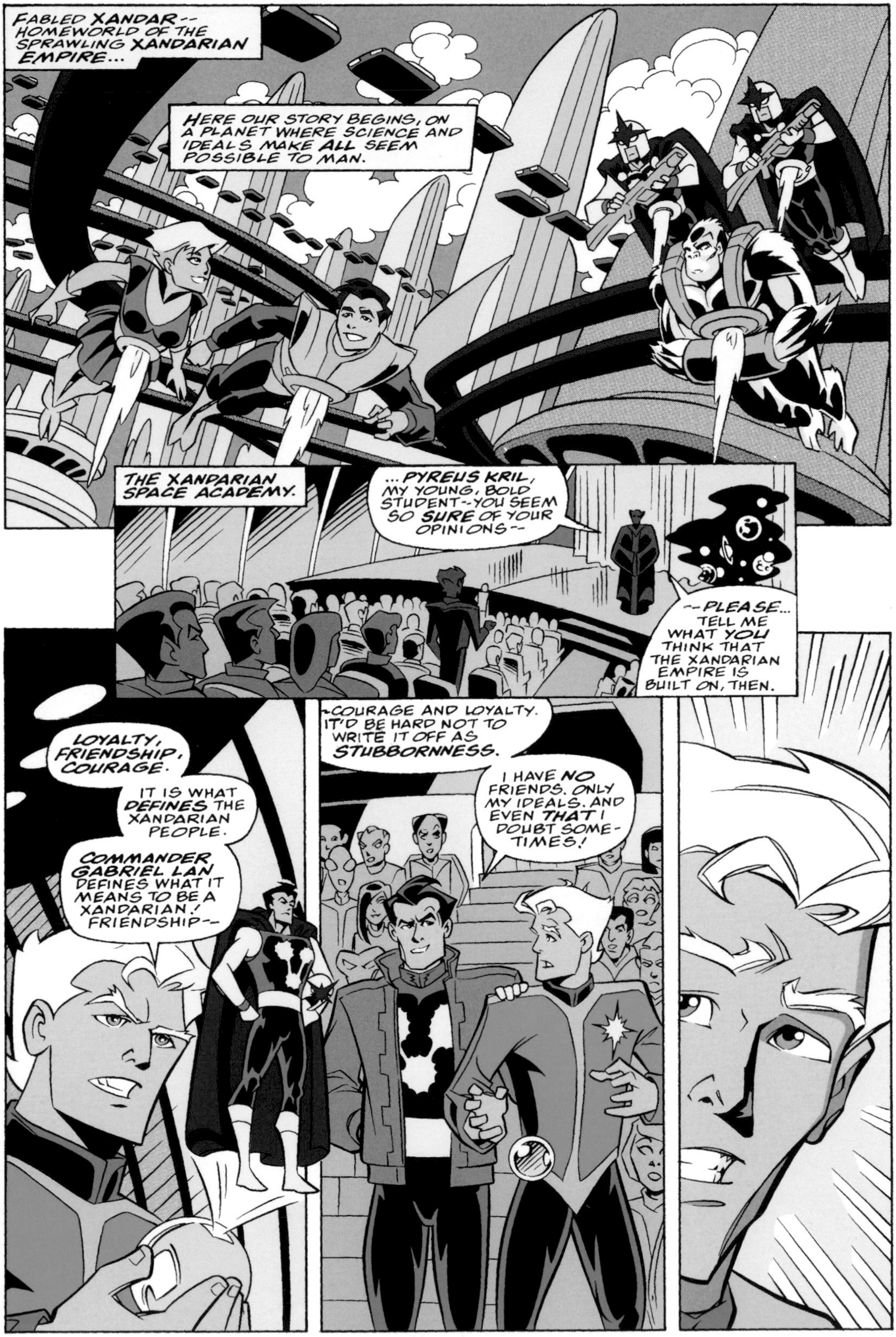

FABLED XANDAR-- HOMEWORLD OF THE SPRAWLING XANDARIAN EMPIRE...
HERE OUR STORY BEGINS, ON A PLANET WHERE SCIENCE AND IDEALS MAKE ALL SEEM POSSIBLE TO MAN.
THE XANDARIAN SPACE ACADEMY.
...PYREUS KRIL, MY YOUNG, BOLD STUDENT--YOU SEEM SO SURE OF YOUR OPINIONS--
--PLEASE... TELL ME WHAT YOU THINK THAT THE XANDARIAN EMPIRE IS BUILT ON, THEN.
LOYALTY, FRIENDSHIP, COURAGE.
IT IS WHAT DEFINES THE XANDARIAN PEOPLE.
COMMANDER GABRIEL LAN DEFINES WHAT IT MEANS TO BE A XANDARIAN! FRIENDSHIP--
--COURAGE AND LOYALTY. IT'D BE HARD NOT TO WRITE IT OFF AS STUBBORNNESS.
I HAVE NO FRIENDS. ONLY MY IDEALS. AND EVEN THAT I DOUBT SOME-TIMES!

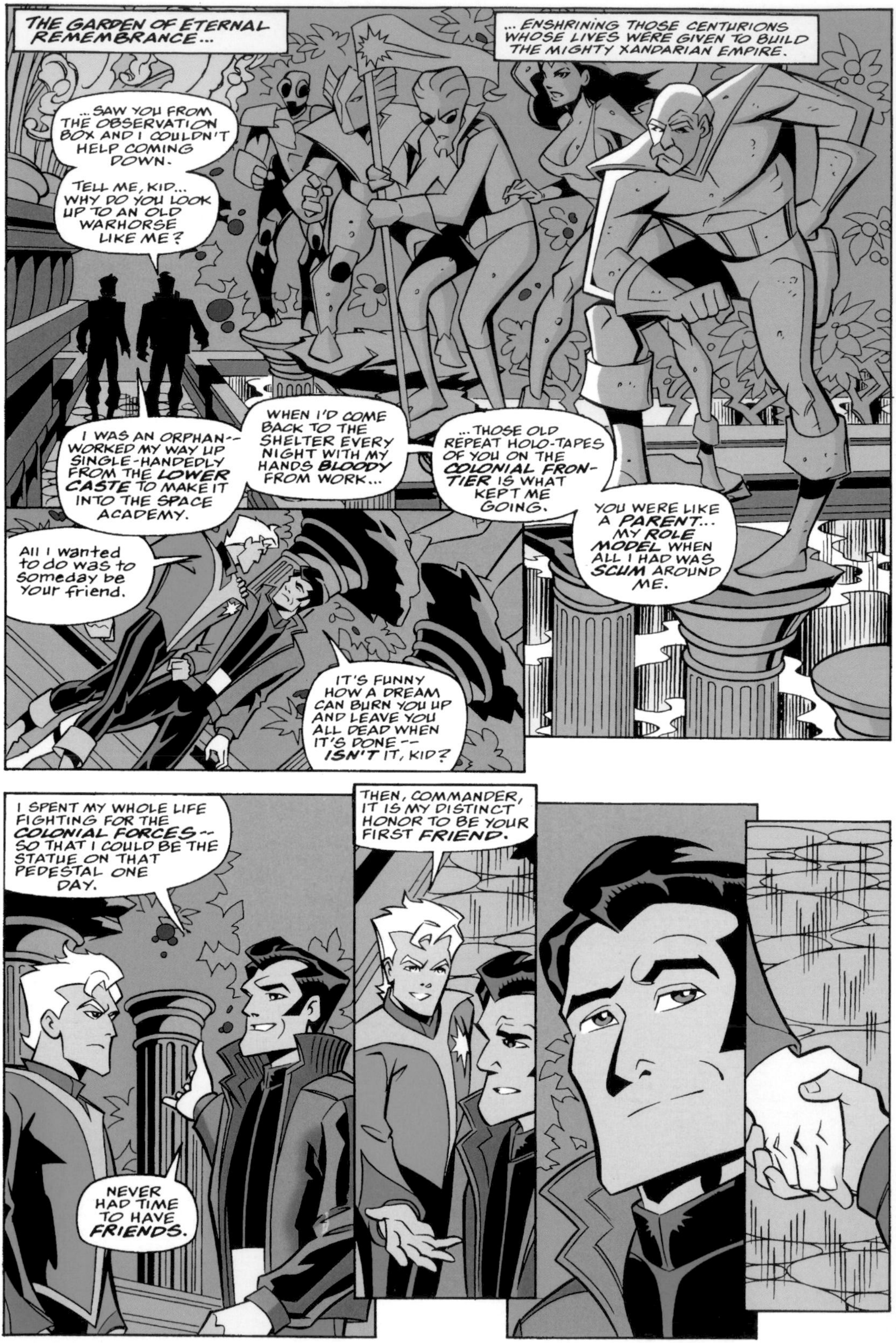
THE GARDEN OF ETERNAL REMEMBRANCE...
...ENSHRINING THOSE CENTURIONS WHOSE LIVES WERE GIVEN TO BUILD THE MIGHTY XANDARIAN EMPIRE.
...SAW YOU FROM THE OBSERVATION BOX AND I COULDN'T HELP COMING DOWN.
TELL ME, KID... WHY DO YOU LOOK UP TO AN OLD WARHORSE LIKE ME?
I WAS AN ORPHAN--WORKED MY WAY UP SINGLE-HANDEDLY FROM THE LOWER CASTE TO MAKE IT INTO THE SPACE ACADEMY.
WHEN I'D COME BACK TO THE SHELTER EVERY NIGHT WITH MY HANDS BLOODY FROM WORK...
...THOSE OLD REPEAT HOLO-TAPES OF YOU ON THE COLONIAL FRONTIER IS WHAT KEPT ME GOING.
YOU WERE LIKE A PARENT... MY ROLE MODEL WHEN ALL I HAD WAS SCUM AROUND ME.
All I wanted to do was to someday be your friend.
IT'S FUNNY HOW A DREAM CAN BURN YOU UP AND LEAVE YOU ALL DEAD WHEN IT'S DONE--ISN'T IT, KID?
I SPENT MY WHOLE LIFE FIGHTING FOR THE COLONIAL FORCES--SO THAT I COULD BE THE STATUE ON THAT PEDESTAL ONE DAY.
NEVER HAD TIME TO HAVE FRIENDS.
THEN, COMMANDER, IT IS MY DISTINCT HONOR TO BE YOUR FIRST FRIEND.

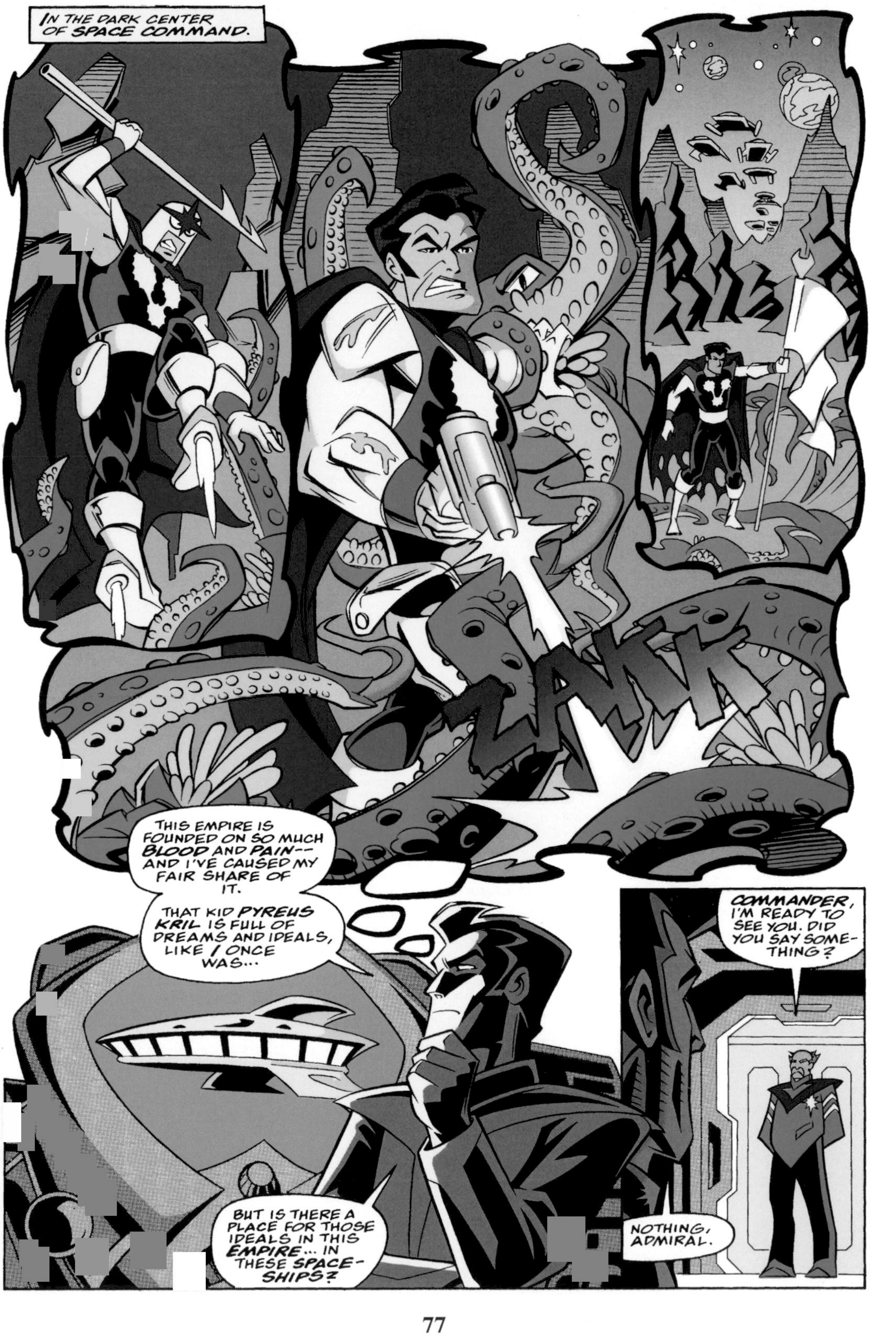
IN THE DARK CENTER OF SPACE COMMAND.
ZAKK
THIS EMPIRE IS FOUNDED ON SO MUCH BLOOD AND PAIN-- AND I'VE CAUSED MY FAIR SHARE OF IT.
THAT KID PYREUS KRIL IS FULL OF DREAMS AND IDEALS, LIKE I ONCE WAS...
BUT IS THERE A PLACE FOR THOSE IDEALS IN THIS EMPIRE... IN THESE SPACE-SHIPS?
COMMANDER, I'M READY TO SEE YOU. DID YOU SAY SOMETHING?
NOTHING, ADMIRAL.

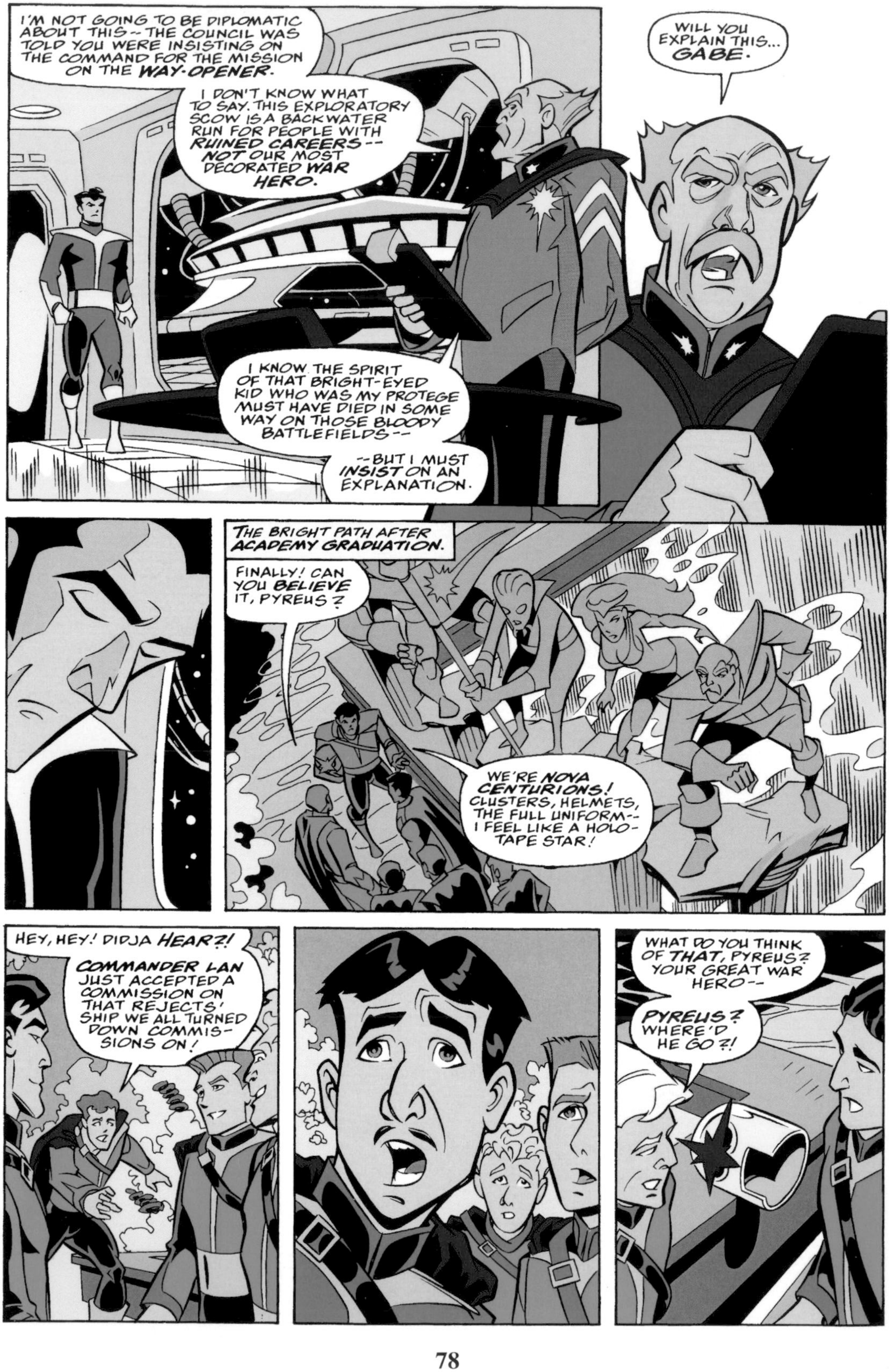

I'M NOT GOING TO BE DIPLOMATIC ABOUT THIS -- THE COUNCIL WAS TOLD YOU WERE INSISTING ON THE COMMAND FOR THE MISSION ON THE WAY-OPENER.
I DON'T KNOW WHAT TO SAY. THIS EXPLORATORY SCOW IS A BACKWATER RUN FOR PEOPLE WITH RUINED CAREERS -- NOT OUR MOST DECORATED WAR HERO.
WILL YOU EXPLAIN THIS... GABE.
I KNOW THE SPIRIT OF THAT BRIGHT-EYED KID WHO WAS MY PROTEGE MUST HAVE DIED IN SOME WAY ON THOSE BLOODY BATTLEFIELDS--
--BUT I MUST INSIST ON AN EXPLANATION.
THE BRIGHT PATH AFTER ACADEMY GRADUATION.
FINALLY! CAN YOU BELIEVE IT, PYREUS?
WE'RE NOVA CENTURIONS! CLUSTERS, HELMETS, THE FULL UNIFORM-- I FEEL LIKE A HOLO-TAPE STAR!
HEY, HEY! DIDJA HEAR?!
COMMANDER LAN JUST ACCEPTED A COMMISSION ON THAT REJECTS' SHIP WE ALL TURNED DOWN COMMISSIONS ON!
WHAT DO YOU THINK OF THAT, PYREUS? YOUR GREAT WAR HERO--
PYREUS? WHERE'D HE GO?!

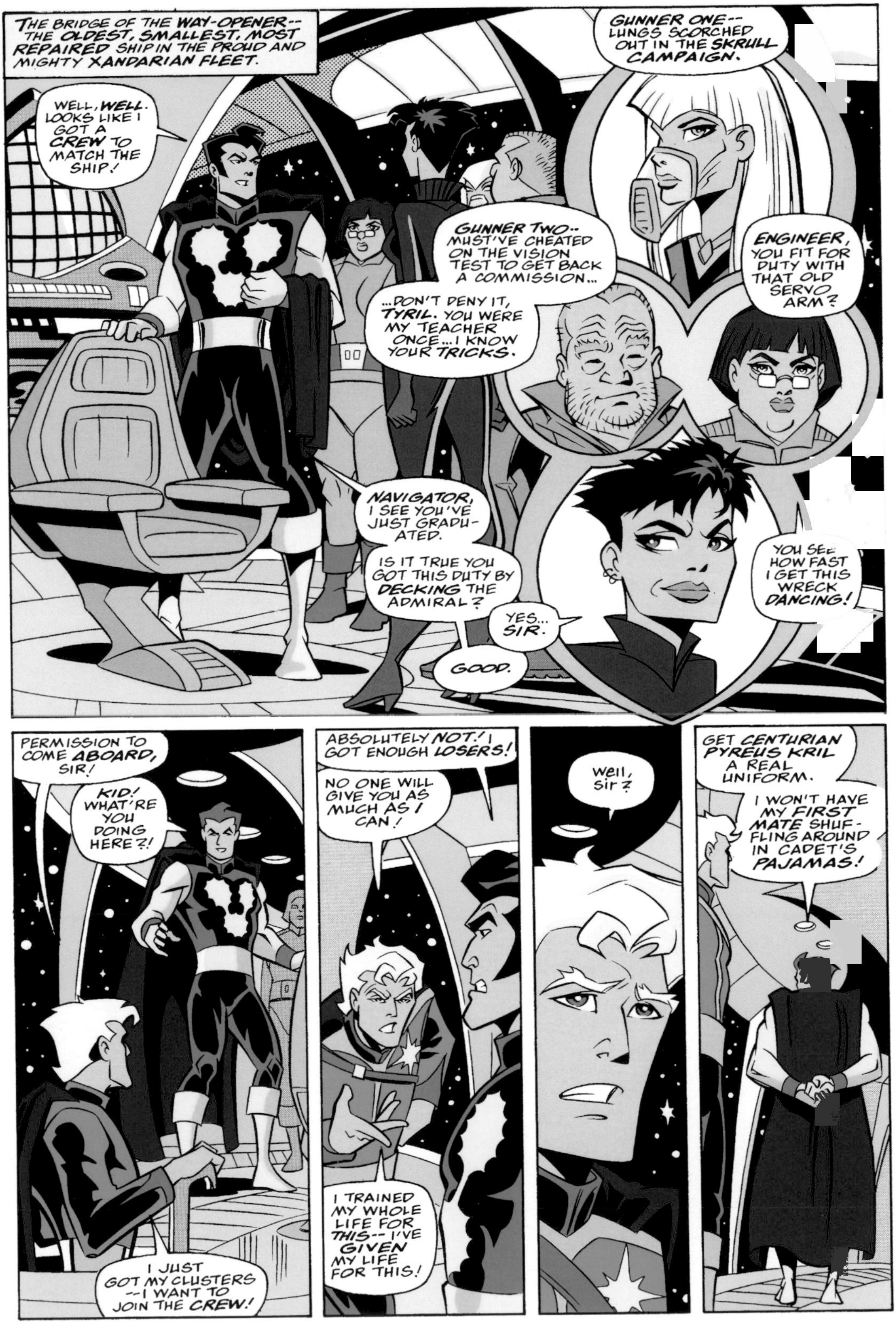
THE BRIDGE OF THE WAY-OPENER-- THE OLDEST, SMALLEST, MOST REPAIRED SHIP IN THE PROUD AND MIGHTY XANDARIAN FLEET.
WELL, WELL. LOOKS LIKE I GOT A CREW TO MATCH THE SHIP!
GUNNER ONE-- LUNGS SCORCHED OUT IN THE SKRULL CAMPAIGN.
GUNNER TWO-- MUST'VE CHEATED ON THE VISION TEST TO GET BACK A COMMISSION...
...DON'T DENY IT, TYRIL. YOU WERE MY TEACHER ONCE...I KNOW YOUR TRICKS.
ENGINEER, YOU FIT FOR DUTY WITH THAT OLD SERVO ARM?
YOU SEE HOW FAST I GET THIS WRECK DANCING!
NAVIGATOR, I SEE YOU'VE JUST GRADUATED.
IS IT TRUE YOU GOT THIS DUTY BY DECKING THE ADMIRAL?
YES... SIR.
GOOD.
PERMISSION TO COME ABOARD, SIR!
KID! WHAT'RE YOU DOING HERE?!
I JUST GOT MY CLUSTERS --I WANT TO JOIN THE CREW!
ABSOLUTELY NOT! I GOT ENOUGH LOSERS!
NO ONE WILL GIVE YOU AS MUCH AS I CAN!
I TRAINED MY WHOLE LIFE FOR THIS-- I'VE GIVEN MY LIFE FOR THIS!
Well, Sir?
GET CENTURIAN PYREUS KRIL A REAL UNIFORM.
I WON'T HAVE MY FIRST MATE SHUFFLING AROUND IN CADET'S PAJAMAS!

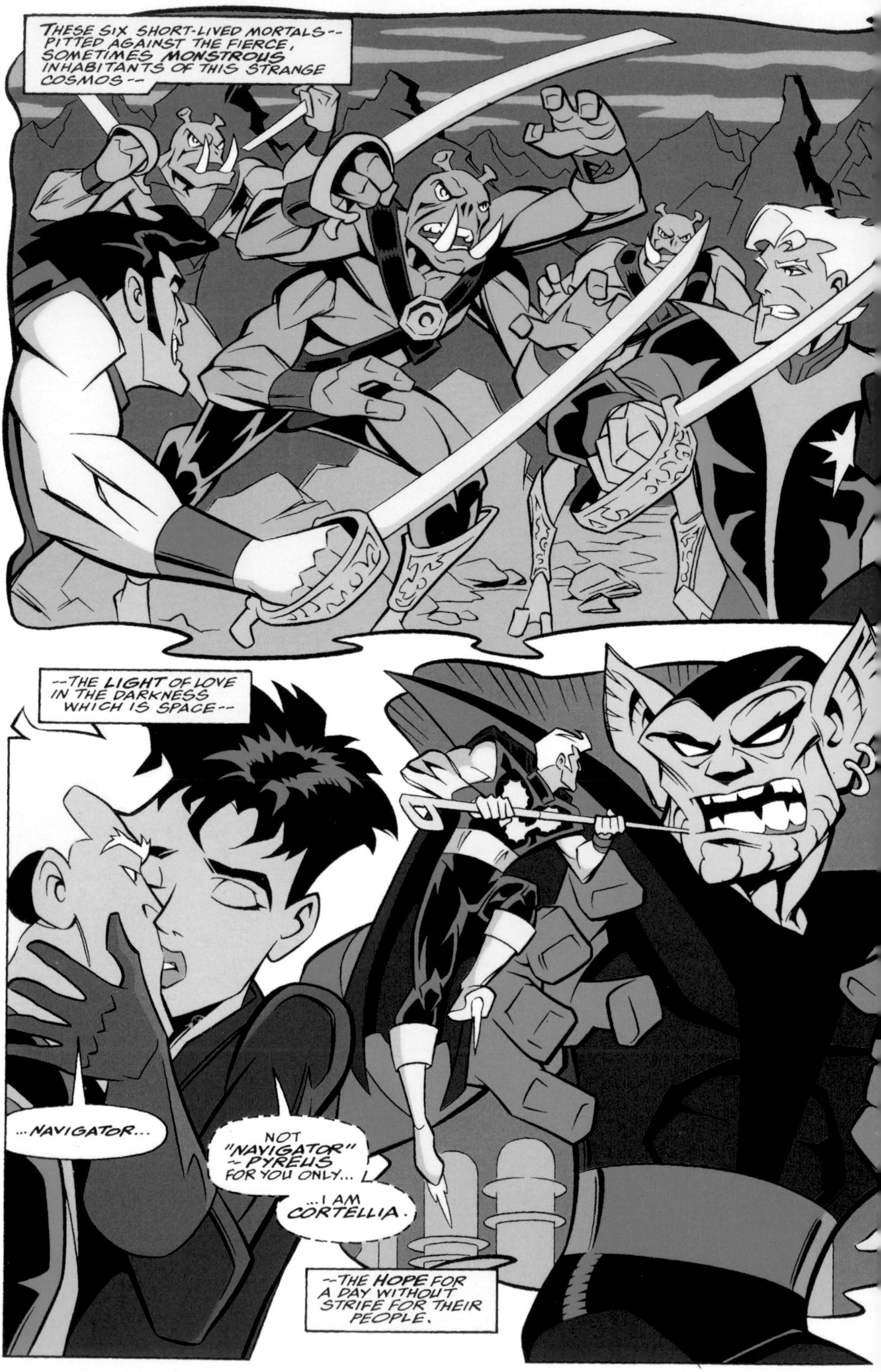
THESE SIX SHORT-LIVED MORTALS-- PITTED AGAINST THE FIERCE, SOMETIMES MONSTROUS INHABITANTS OF THIS STRANGE COSMOS--
--THE LIGHT OF LOVE IN THE DARKNESS WHICH IS SPACE--
...NAVIGATOR...
NOT "NAVIGATOR" -- PYREUS FOR YOU ONLY...
...I AM CORTELLIA.
--THE HOPE FOR A DAY WITHOUT STRIFE FOR THEIR PEOPLE.

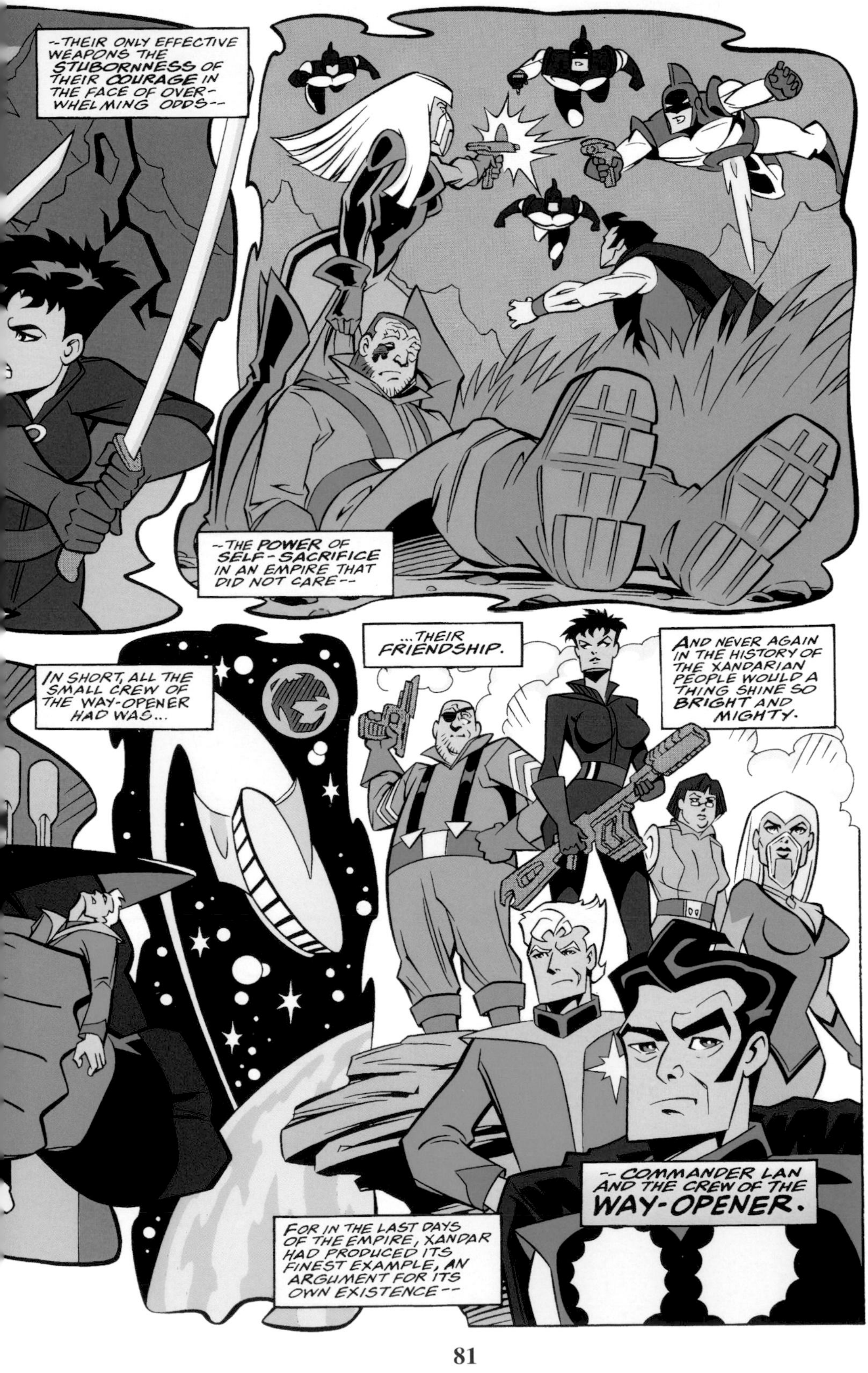
--THEIR ONLY EFFECTIVE WEAPONS THE STUBBORNNESS OF THEIR COURAGE IN THE FACE OF OVER-WHELMING ODDS--
--THE POWER OF SELF-SACRIFICE IN AN EMPIRE THAT DID NOT CARE--
IN SHORT, ALL THE SMALL CREW OF THE WAY-OPENER HAD WAS...
...THEIR FRIENDSHIP.
AND NEVER AGAIN IN THE HISTORY OF THE XANDARIAN PEOPLE WOULD A THING SHINE SO BRIGHT AND MIGHTY.
FOR IN THE LAST DAYS OF THE EMPIRE, XANDAR HAD PRODUCED ITS FINEST EXAMPLE, AN ARGUMENT FOR ITS OWN EXISTENCE--
--COMMANDER LAN AND THE CREW OF THE WAY-OPENER.

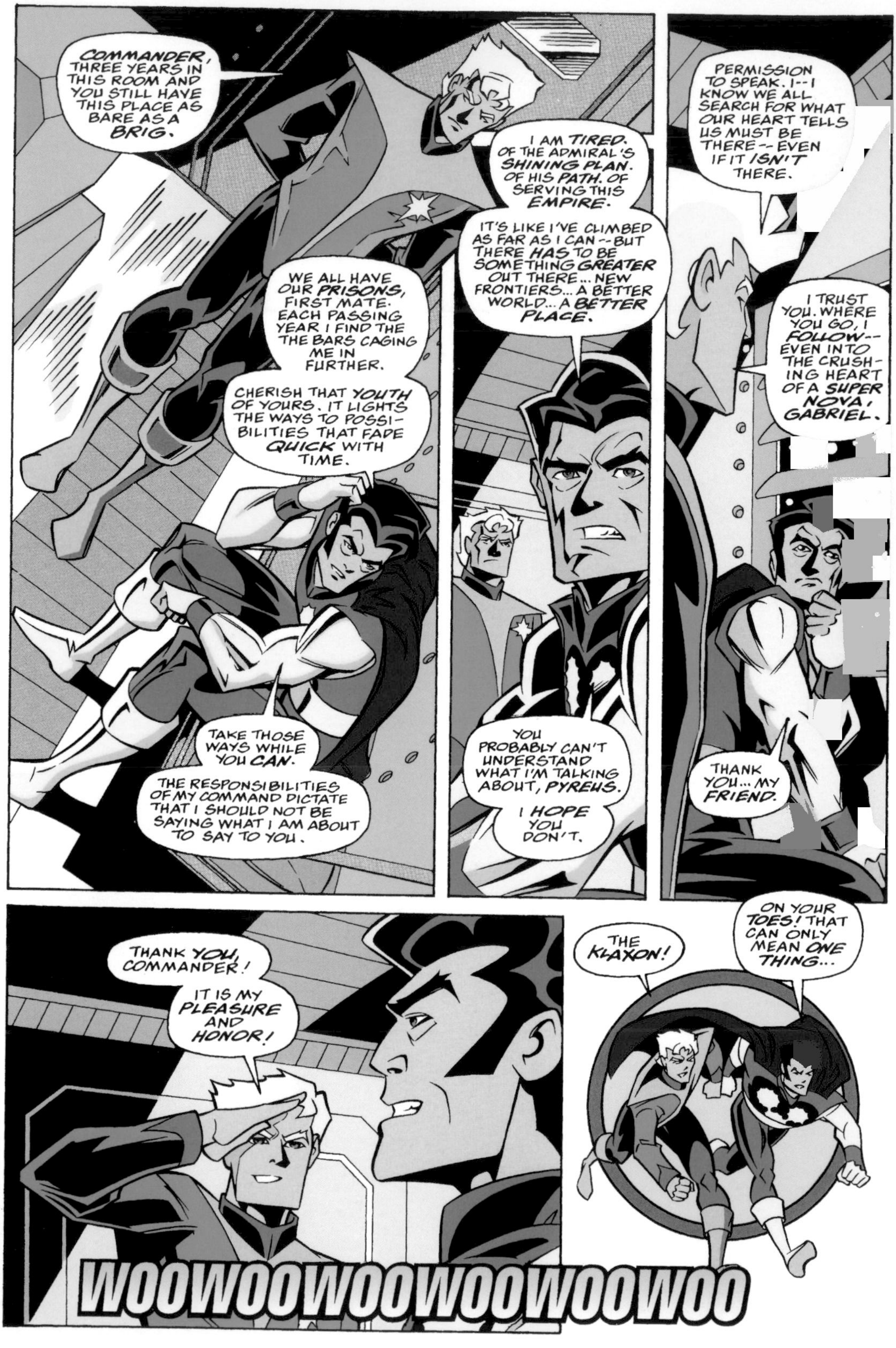
COMMANDER, THREE YEARS IN THIS ROOM AND YOU STILL HAVE THIS PLACE AS BARE AS A BRIG.
WE ALL HAVE OUR PRISONS, FIRST MATE. EACH PASSING YEAR I FIND THE THE BARS CAGING ME IN FURTHER.
CHERISH THAT YOUTH OF YOURS. IT LIGHTS THE WAYS TO POSSIBILITIES THAT FADE QUICK WITH TIME.
TAKE THOSE WAYS WHILE YOU CAN.
THE RESPONSIBILITIES OF MY COMMAND DICTATE THAT I SHOULD NOT BE SAYING WHAT I AM ABOUT TO SAY TO YOU.
I AM TIRED. OF THE ADMIRAL'S SHINING PLAN. OF HIS PATH. OF SERVING THIS EMPIRE.
IT'S LIKE I'VE CLIMBED AS FAR AS I CAN -- BUT THERE HAS TO BE SOMETHING GREATER OUT THERE... NEW FRONTIERS... A BETTER WORLD... A BETTER PLACE.
YOU PROBABLY CAN'T UNDERSTAND WHAT I'M TALKING ABOUT, PYREUS.
I HOPE YOU DON'T.
PERMISSION TO SPEAK. I-- I KNOW WE ALL SEARCH FOR WHAT OUR HEART TELLS US MUST BE THERE -- EVEN IF IT ISN'T THERE.
I TRUST YOU. WHERE YOU GO, I FOLLOW -- EVEN INTO THE CRUSHING HEART OF A SUPER NOVA, GABRIEL.
THANK YOU... MY FRIEND.
THANK YOU, COMMANDER!
IT IS MY PLEASURE AND HONOR!
WOOWOOWOOWOOWOOWOO
THE KLAXON!
ON YOUR TOES! THAT CAN ONLY MEAN ONE THING...

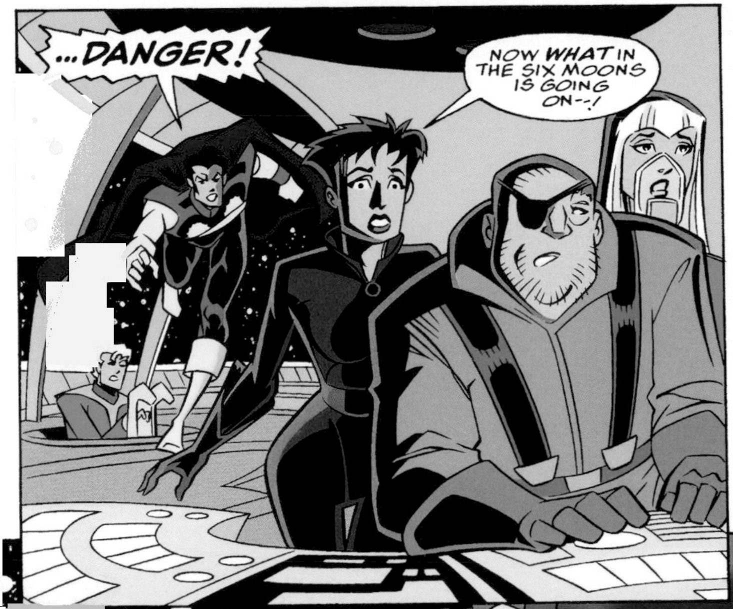
...DANGER!
NOW WHAT IN THE SIX MOONS IS GOING ON--!

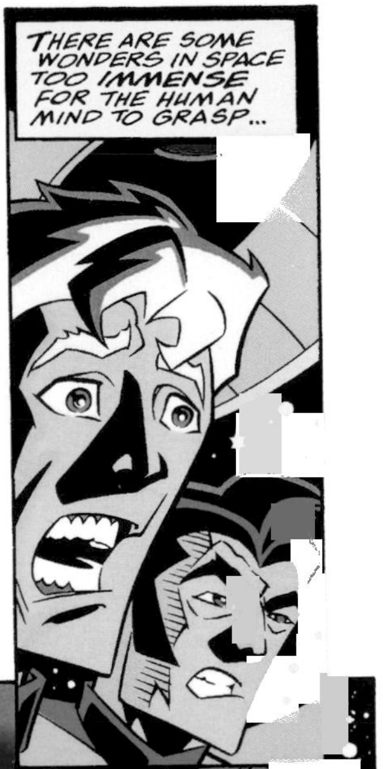
THERE ARE SOME WONDERS IN SPACE TOO IMMENSE FOR THE HUMAN MIND TO GRASP...

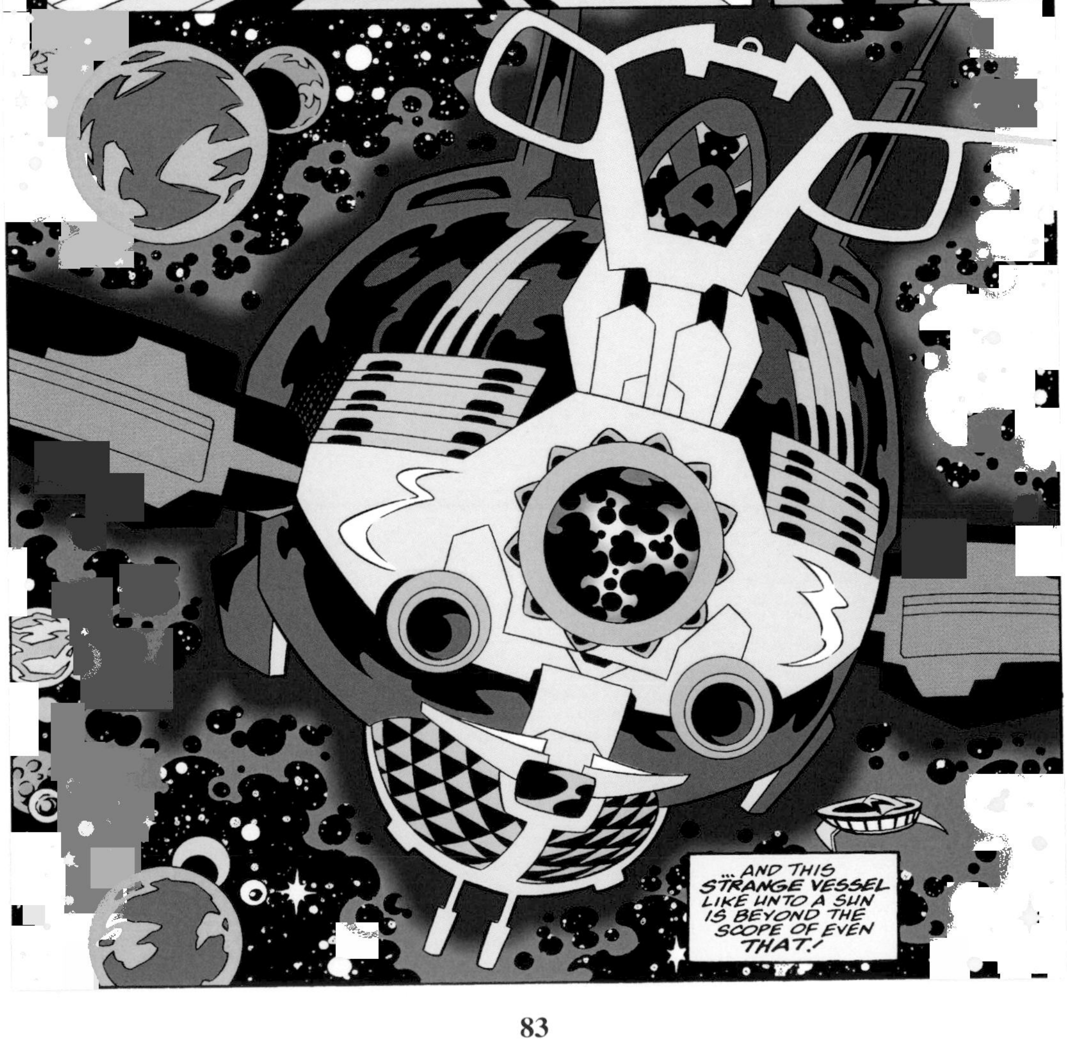
...AND THIS STRANGE VESSEL LIKE UNTO A SUN IS BEYOND THE SCOPE OF EVEN THAT!

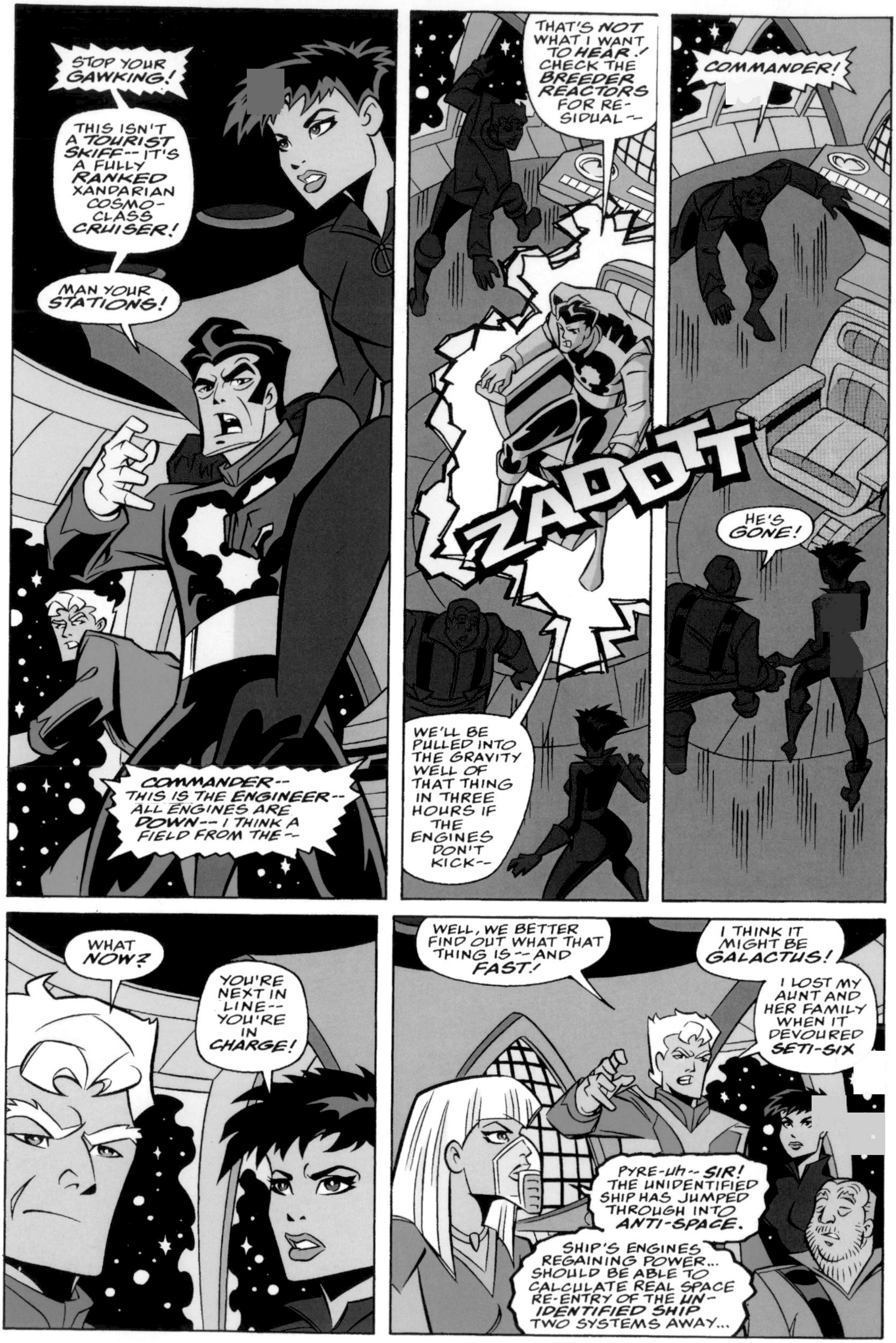
STOP YOUR GAWKING!
THIS ISN'T A TOURIST SKIFF--IT'S A FULLY RANKED XANDARIAN COSMO-CLASS CRUISER!
MAN YOUR STATIONS!
COMMANDER-- THIS IS THE ENGINEER-- ALL ENGINES ARE DOWN-- I THINK A FIELD FROM THE--
THAT'S NOT WHAT I WANT TO HEAR! CHECK THE BREEDER REACTORS FOR RE-SIDUAL--
ZADOTT
WE'LL BE PULLED INTO THE GRAVITY WELL OF THAT THING IN THREE HOURS IF THE ENGINES DON'T KICK--
COMMANDER!
HE'S GONE!
WHAT NOW?
YOU'RE NEXT IN LINE-- YOU'RE IN CHARGE!
WELL, WE BETTER FIND OUT WHAT THAT THING IS--AND FAST!
I THINK IT MIGHT BE GALACTUS!
I LOST MY AUNT AND HER FAMILY WHEN IT DEVOURED SETI-SIX
PYRE-uh-- SIR! THE UNIDENTIFIED SHIP HAS JUMPED THROUGH INTO ANTI-SPACE.
SHIP'S ENGINES REGAINING POWER... SHOULD BE ABLE TO CALCULATE REAL SPACE RE-ENTRY OF THE UNIDENTIFIED SHIP TWO SYSTEMS AWAY...

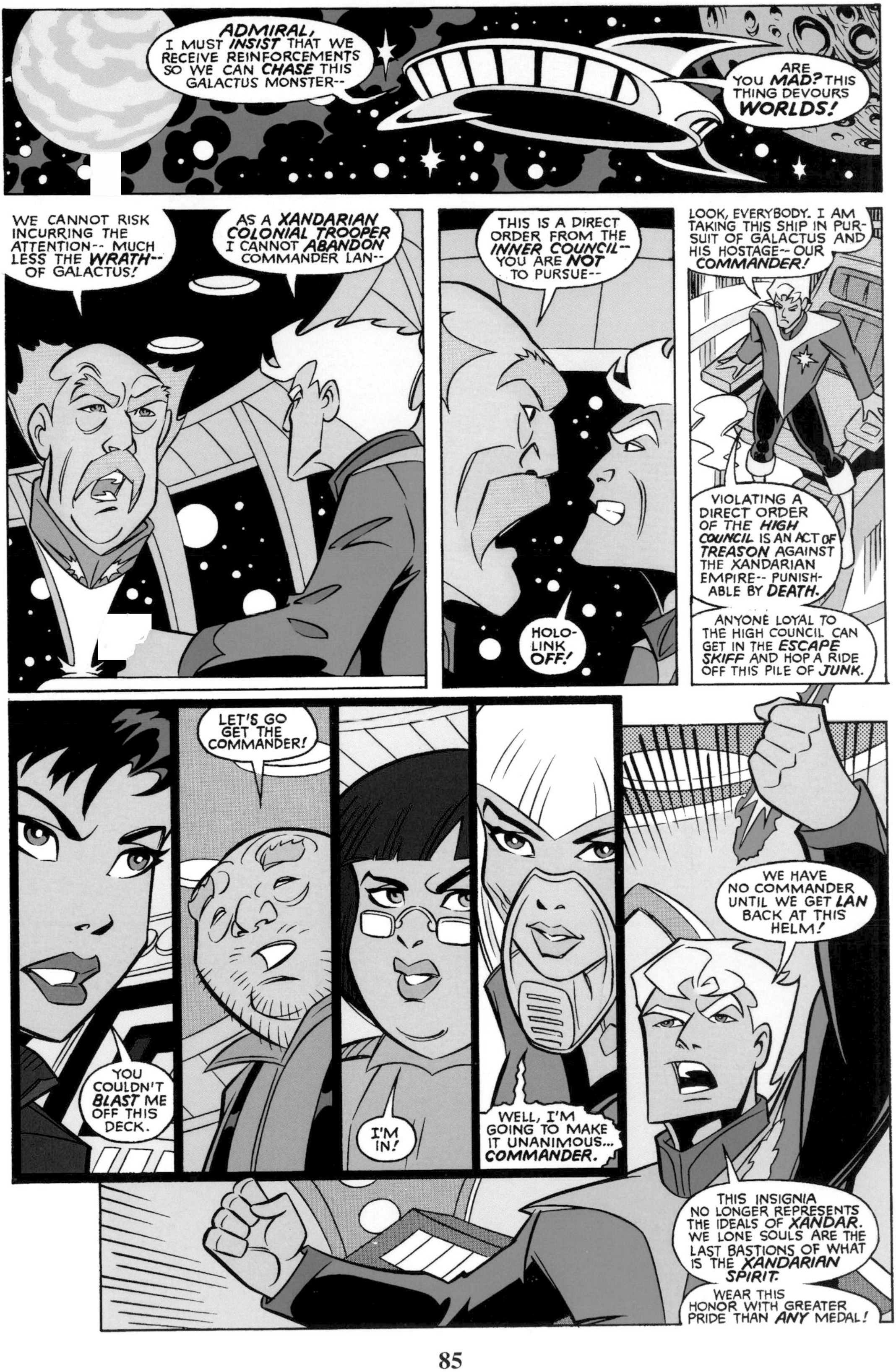
ADMIRAL, I MUST INSIST THAT WE RECEIVE REINFORCEMENTS SO WE CAN CHASE THIS GALACTUS MONSTER--
ARE YOU MAD? THIS THING DEVOURS WORLDS!
WE CANNOT RISK INCURRING THE ATTENTION-- MUCH LESS THE WRATH-- OF GALACTUS!
AS A XANDARIAN COLONIAL TROOPER I CANNOT ABANDON COMMANDER LAN--
THIS IS A DIRECT ORDER FROM THE INNER COUNCIL-- YOU ARE NOT TO PURSUE--
HOLO-LINK OFF!
LOOK, EVERYBODY. I AM TAKING THIS SHIP IN PURSUIT OF GALACTUS AND HIS HOSTAGE-- OUR COMMANDER!
VIOLATING A DIRECT ORDER OF THE HIGH COUNCIL IS AN ACT OF TREASON AGAINST THE XANDARIAN EMPIRE-- PUNISHABLE BY DEATH.
ANYONE LOYAL TO THE HIGH COUNCIL CAN GET IN THE ESCAPE SKIFF AND HOP A RIDE OFF THIS PILE OF JUNK.
YOU COULDN'T BLAST ME OFF THIS DECK.
LET'S GO GET THE COMMANDER!
I'M IN!
WELL, I'M GOING TO MAKE IT UNANIMOUS... COMMANDER.
WE HAVE NO COMMANDER UNTIL WE GET LAN BACK AT THIS HELM!
THIS INSIGNIA NO LONGER REPRESENTS THE IDEALS OF XANDAR. WE LONE SOULS ARE THE LAST BASTIONS OF WHAT IS THE XANDARIAN SPIRIT.
WEAR THIS HONOR WITH GREATER PRIDE THAN ANY MEDAL!

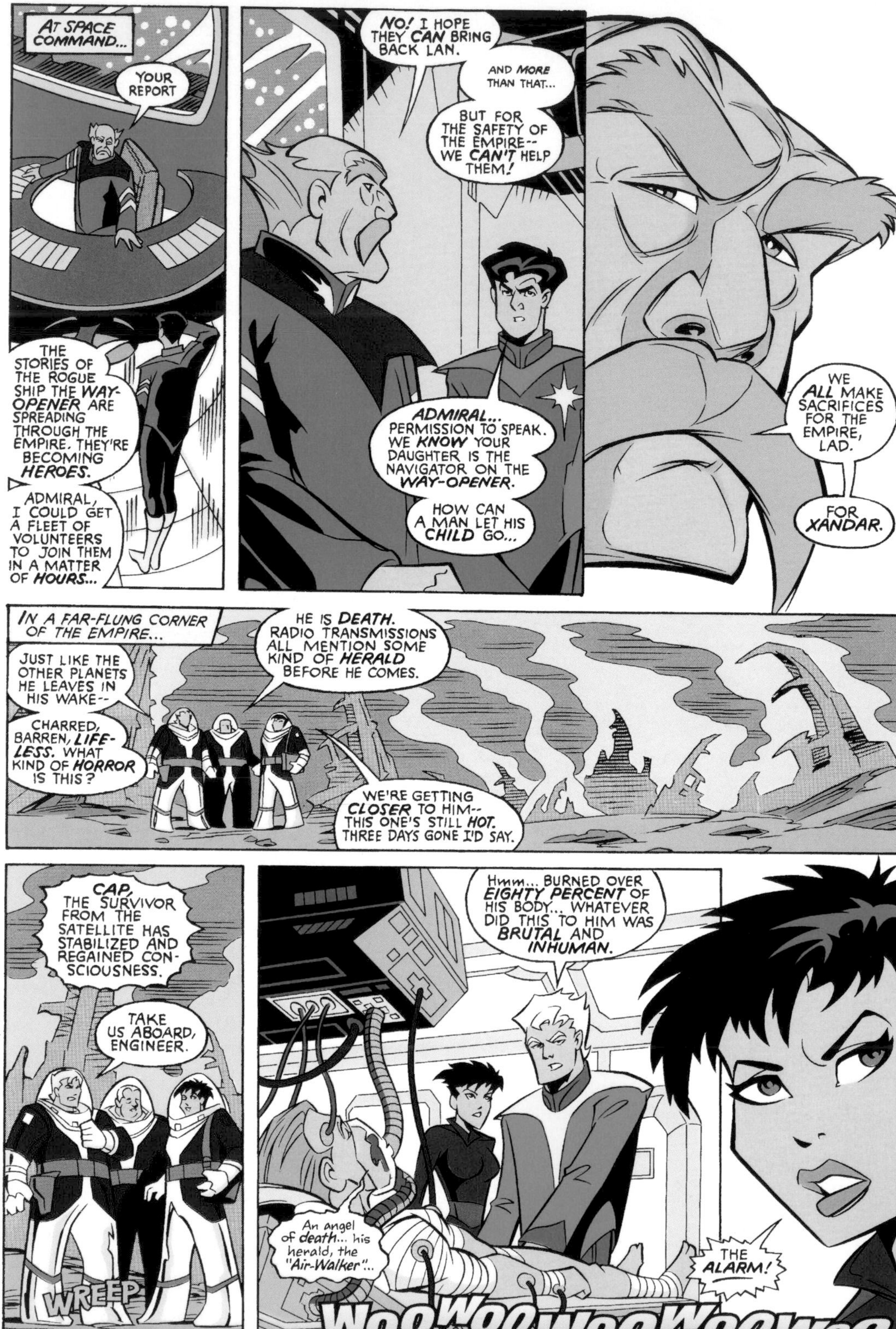
AT SPACE COMMAND...
YOUR REPORT
THE STORIES OF THE ROGUE SHIP THE WAY-OPENER ARE SPREADING THROUGH THE EMPIRE. THEY'RE BECOMING HEROES.
ADMIRAL, I COULD GET A FLEET OF VOLUNTEERS TO JOIN THEM IN A MATTER OF HOURS...
NO! I HOPE THEY CAN BRING BACK LAN.
AND MORE THAN THAT...
BUT FOR THE SAFETY OF THE EMPIRE-- WE CAN'T HELP THEM!
ADMIRAL... PERMISSION TO SPEAK. WE KNOW YOUR DAUGHTER IS THE NAVIGATOR ON THE WAY-OPENER.
HOW CAN A MAN LET HIS CHILD GO...
WE ALL MAKE SACRIFICES FOR THE EMPIRE, LAD.
FOR XANDAR.
IN A FAR-FLUNG CORNER OF THE EMPIRE...
JUST LIKE THE OTHER PLANETS HE LEAVES IN HIS WAKE--
CHARRED, BARREN, LIFE-LESS. WHAT KIND OF HORROR IS THIS?
HE IS DEATH. RADIO TRANSMISSIONS ALL MENTION SOME KIND OF HERALD BEFORE HE COMES.
WE'RE GETTING CLOSER TO HIM-- THIS ONE'S STILL HOT. THREE DAYS GONE I'D SAY.
CAP, THE SURVIVOR FROM THE SATELLITE HAS STABILIZED AND REGAINED CON-SCIOUSNESS.
TAKE US ABOARD, ENGINEER.
WREEP
Hmm... BURNED OVER EIGHTY PERCENT OF HIS BODY... WHATEVER DID THIS TO HIM WAS BRUTAL AND INHUMAN.
An angel of death... his herald, the "Air-Walker"...
THE ALARM!
WOOWOOWOOWOOWOO

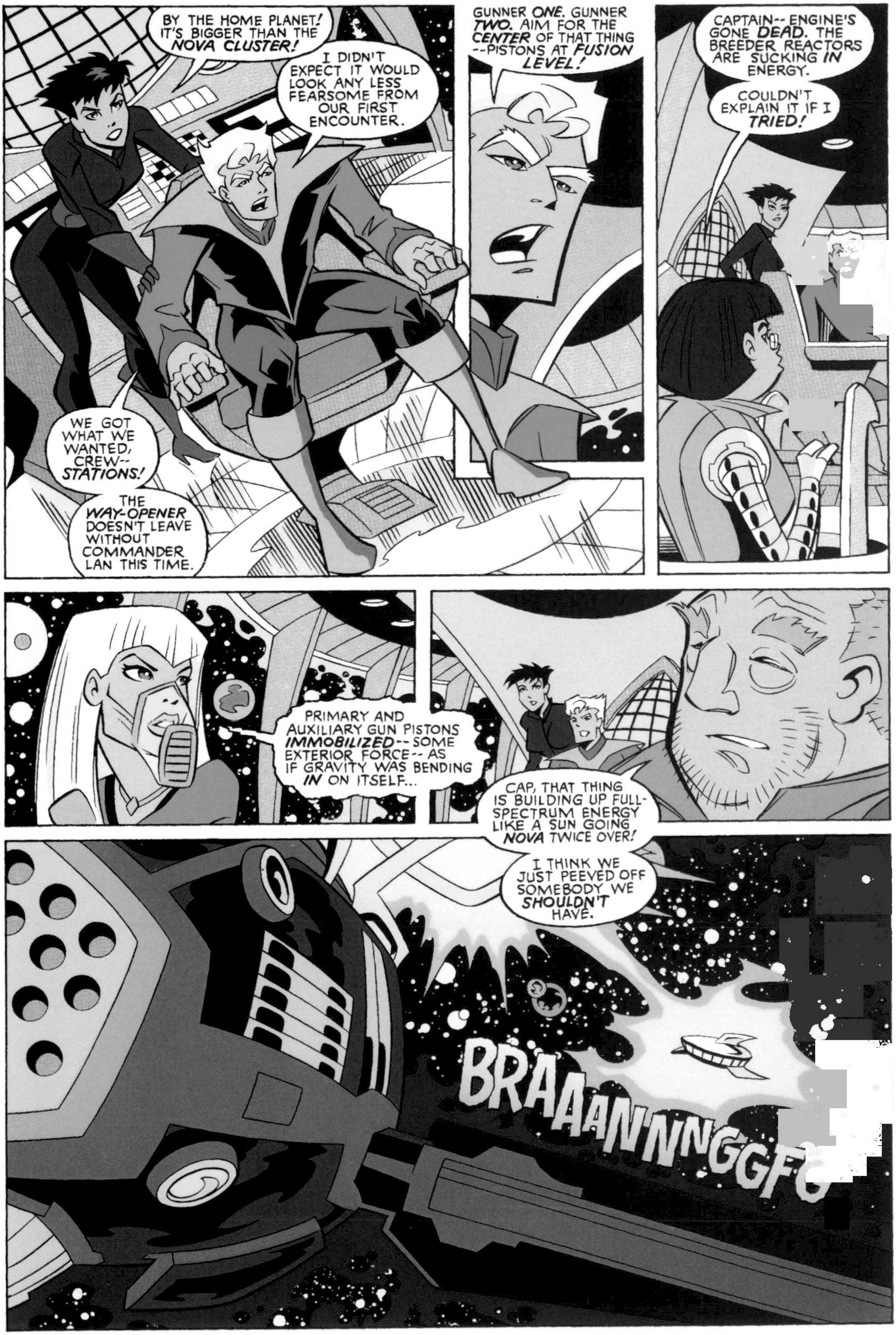
BY THE HOME PLANET! IT'S BIGGER THAN THE NOVA CLUSTER!
I DIDN'T EXPECT IT WOULD LOOK ANY LESS FEARSOME FROM OUR FIRST ENCOUNTER.
WE GOT WHAT WE WANTED, CREW-- STATIONS!
THE WAY-OPENER DOESN'T LEAVE WITHOUT COMMANDER LAN THIS TIME.
GUNNER ONE. GUNNER TWO. AIM FOR THE CENTER OF THAT THING --PISTONS AT FUSION LEVEL!
CAPTAIN-- ENGINE'S GONE DEAD. THE BREEDER REACTORS ARE SUCKING IN ENERGY.
COULDN'T EXPLAIN IT IF I TRIED!
PRIMARY AND AUXILIARY GUN PISTONS IMMOBILIZED-- SOME EXTERIOR FORCE-- AS IF GRAVITY WAS BENDING IN ON ITSELF...
CAP, THAT THING IS BUILDING UP FULL-SPECTRUM ENERGY LIKE A SUN GOING NOVA TWICE OVER!
I THINK WE JUST PEEVED OFF SOMEBODY WE SHOULDN'T HAVE.
BRAAANNNGGFO

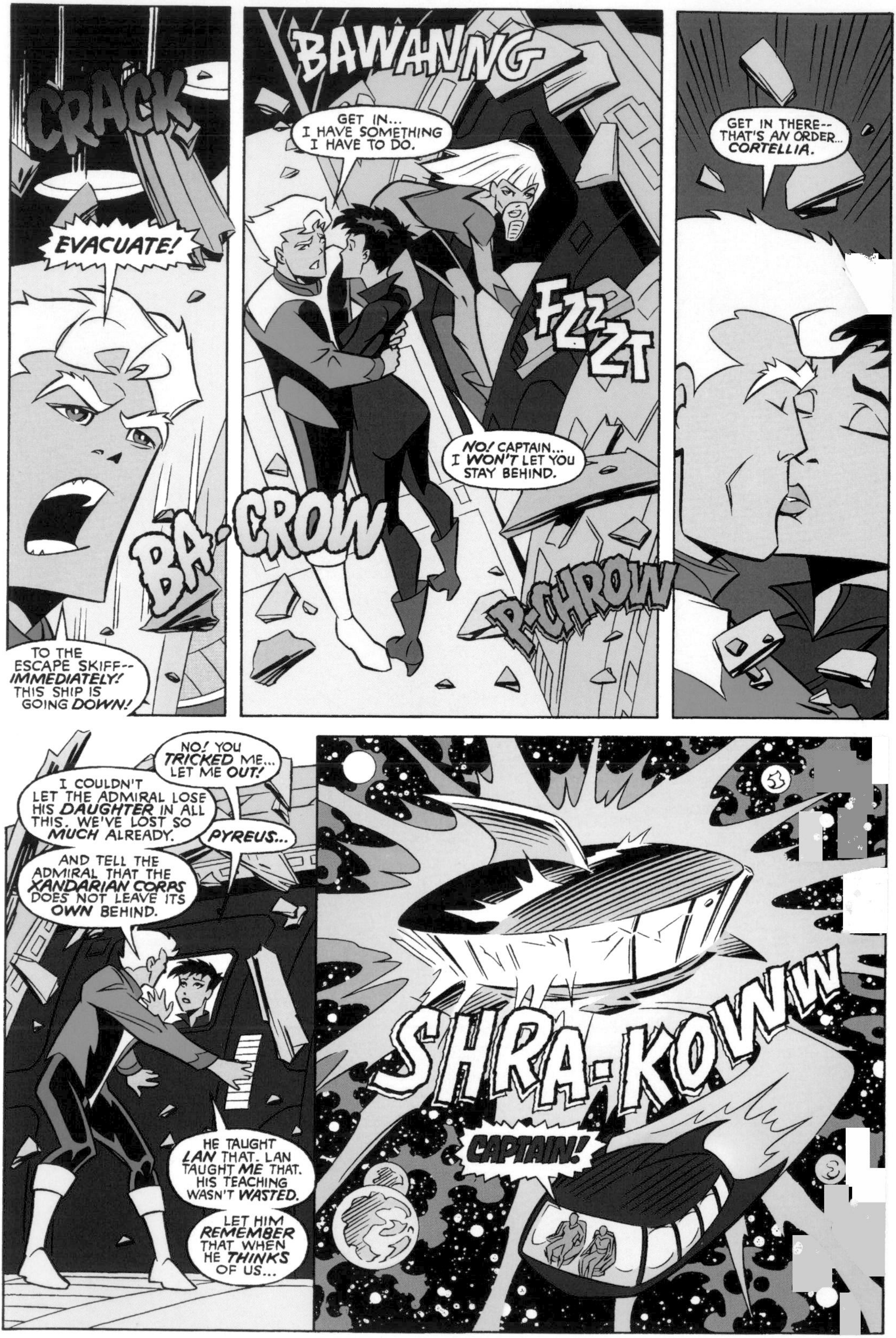
CRACK
EVACUATE!
TO THE ESCAPE SKIFF-- IMMEDIATELY! THIS SHIP IS GOING DOWN!
BA-CROW
BAWANNG
GET IN... I HAVE SOMETHING I HAVE TO DO.
FZZZT
NO! CAPTAIN... I WON'T LET YOU STAY BEHIND.
P-CHROW
GET IN THERE-- THAT'S AN ORDER... CORTELLIA.
I COULDN'T LET THE ADMIRAL LOSE HIS DAUGHTER IN ALL THIS. WE'VE LOST SO MUCH ALREADY.
NO! YOU TRICKED ME... LET ME OUT!
PYREUS...
AND TELL THE ADMIRAL THAT THE XANDARIAN CORPS DOES NOT LEAVE ITS OWN BEHIND.
HE TAUGHT LAN THAT. LAN TAUGHT ME THAT. HIS TEACHING WASN'T WASTED.
LET HIM REMEMBER THAT WHEN HE THINKS OF US...
SHRA-KOWW
CAPTAIN!

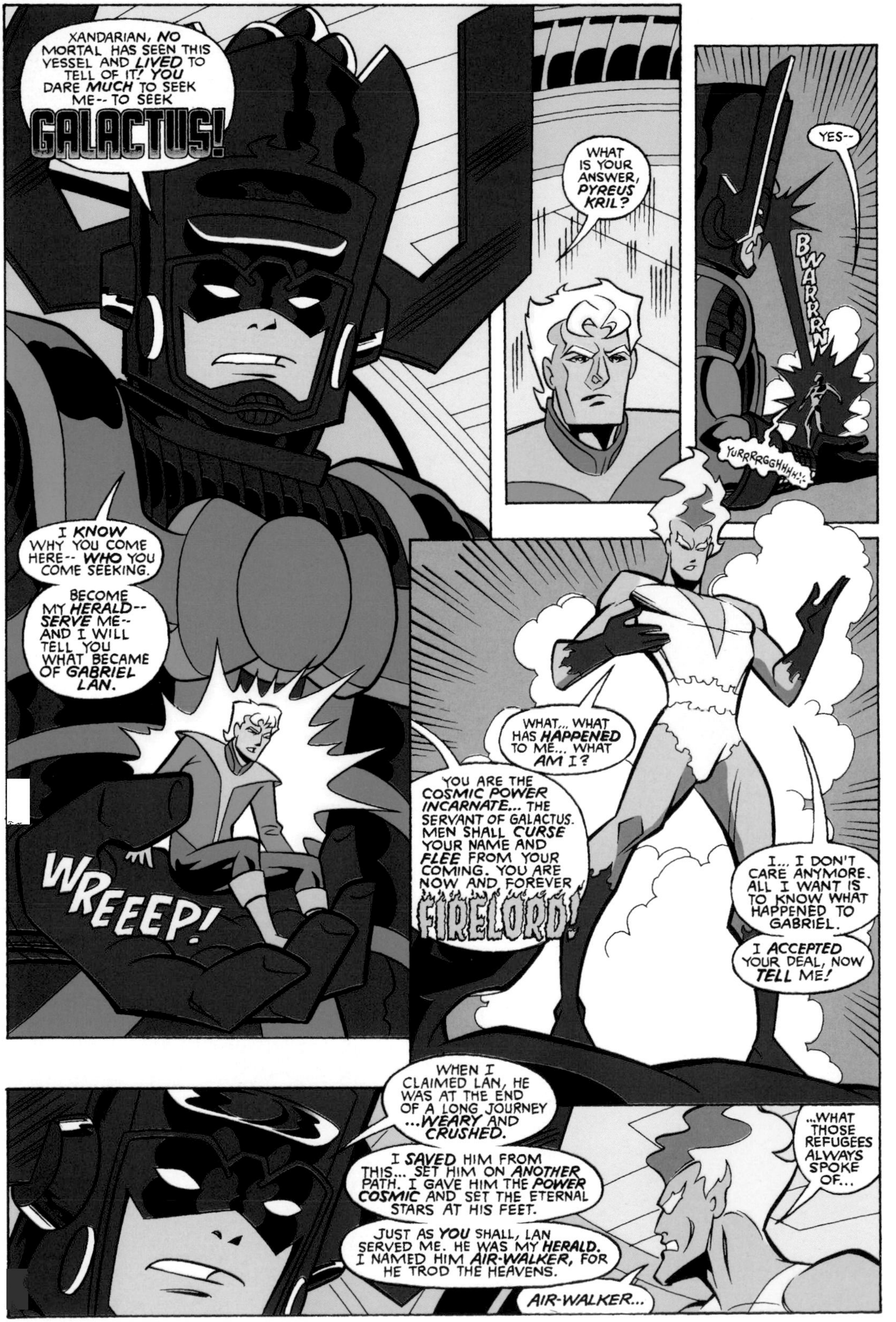

XANDARIAN, NO MORTAL HAS SEEN THIS VESSEL AND LIVED TO TELL OF IT! YOU DARE MUCH TO SEEK ME-- TO SEEK GALACTUS!
WHAT IS YOUR ANSWER, PYREUS KRIL?
YES--
BWARRRN
YURRRRGGHHHH!!
I KNOW WHY YOU COME HERE-- WHO YOU COME SEEKING.
BECOME MY HERALD-- SERVE ME-- AND I WILL TELL YOU WHAT BECAME OF GABRIEL LAN.
WREEEP!
WHAT... WHAT HAS HAPPENED TO ME... WHAT AM I?
YOU ARE THE COSMIC POWER INCARNATE... THE SERVANT OF GALACTUS. MEN SHALL CURSE YOUR NAME AND FLEE FROM YOUR COMING. YOU ARE NOW AND FOREVER FIRELORD!
I... I DON'T CARE ANYMORE. ALL I WANT IS TO KNOW WHAT HAPPENED TO GABRIEL.
I ACCEPTED YOUR DEAL, NOW TELL ME!
WHEN I CLAIMED LAN, HE WAS AT THE END OF A LONG JOURNEY ...WEARY AND CRUSHED.
I SAVED HIM FROM THIS... SET HIM ON ANOTHER PATH. I GAVE HIM THE POWER COSMIC AND SET THE ETERNAL STARS AT HIS FEET.
JUST AS YOU SHALL, LAN SERVED ME. HE WAS MY HERALD. I NAMED HIM AIR-WALKER, FOR HE TROD THE HEAVENS.
AIR-WALKER...
...WHAT THOSE REFUGEES ALWAYS SPOKE OF...

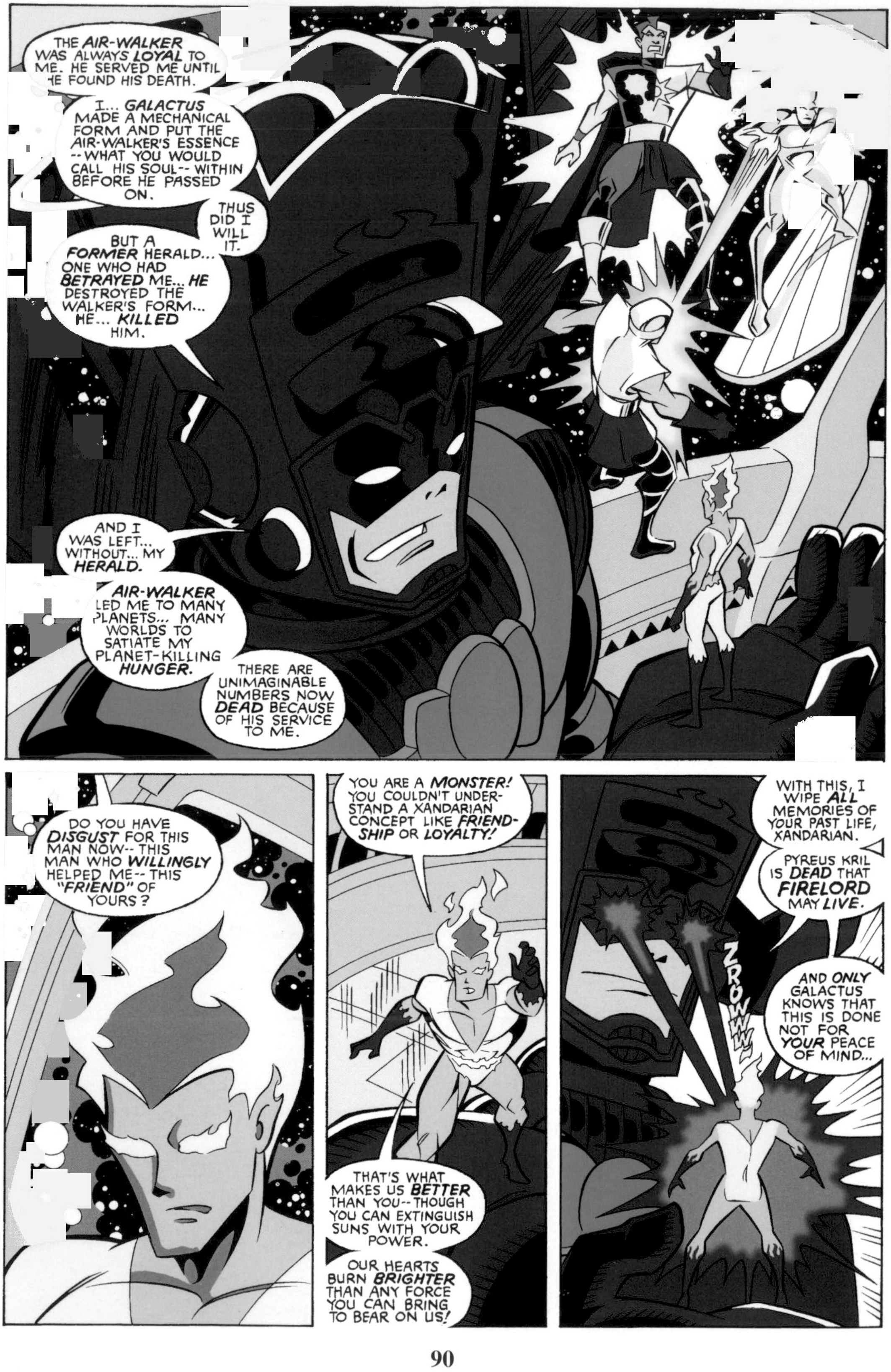
THE AIR-WALKER WAS ALWAYS LOYAL TO ME. HE SERVED ME UNTIL HE FOUND HIS DEATH.
I... GALACTUS MADE A MECHANICAL FORM AND PUT THE AIR-WALKER'S ESSENCE --WHAT YOU WOULD CALL HIS SOUL-- WITHIN BEFORE HE PASSED ON.
THUS DID I WILL IT.
BUT A FORMER HERALD... ONE WHO HAD BETRAYED ME... HE DESTROYED THE WALKER'S FORM... HE... KILLED HIM.
AND I WAS LEFT... WITHOUT... MY HERALD.
AIR-WALKER LED ME TO MANY PLANETS... MANY WORLDS TO SATIATE MY PLANET-KILLING HUNGER.
THERE ARE UNIMAGINABLE NUMBERS NOW DEAD BECAUSE OF HIS SERVICE TO ME.
DO YOU HAVE DISGUST FOR THIS MAN NOW-- THIS MAN WHO WILLINGLY HELPED ME-- THIS "FRIEND" OF YOURS?
YOU ARE A MONSTER! YOU COULDN'T UNDER-STAND A XANDARIAN CONCEPT LIKE FRIEND-SHIP OR LOYALTY!
THAT'S WHAT MAKES US BETTER THAN YOU-- THOUGH YOU CAN EXTINGUISH SUNS WITH YOUR POWER.
OUR HEARTS BURN BRIGHTER THAN ANY FORCE YOU CAN BRING TO BEAR ON US!
WITH THIS, I WIPE ALL MEMORIES OF YOUR PAST LIFE, XANDARIAN.
PYREUS KRIL IS DEAD THAT FIRELORD MAY LIVE.
ZROWWW
AND ONLY GALACTUS KNOWS THAT THIS IS DONE NOT FOR YOUR PEACE OF MIND...

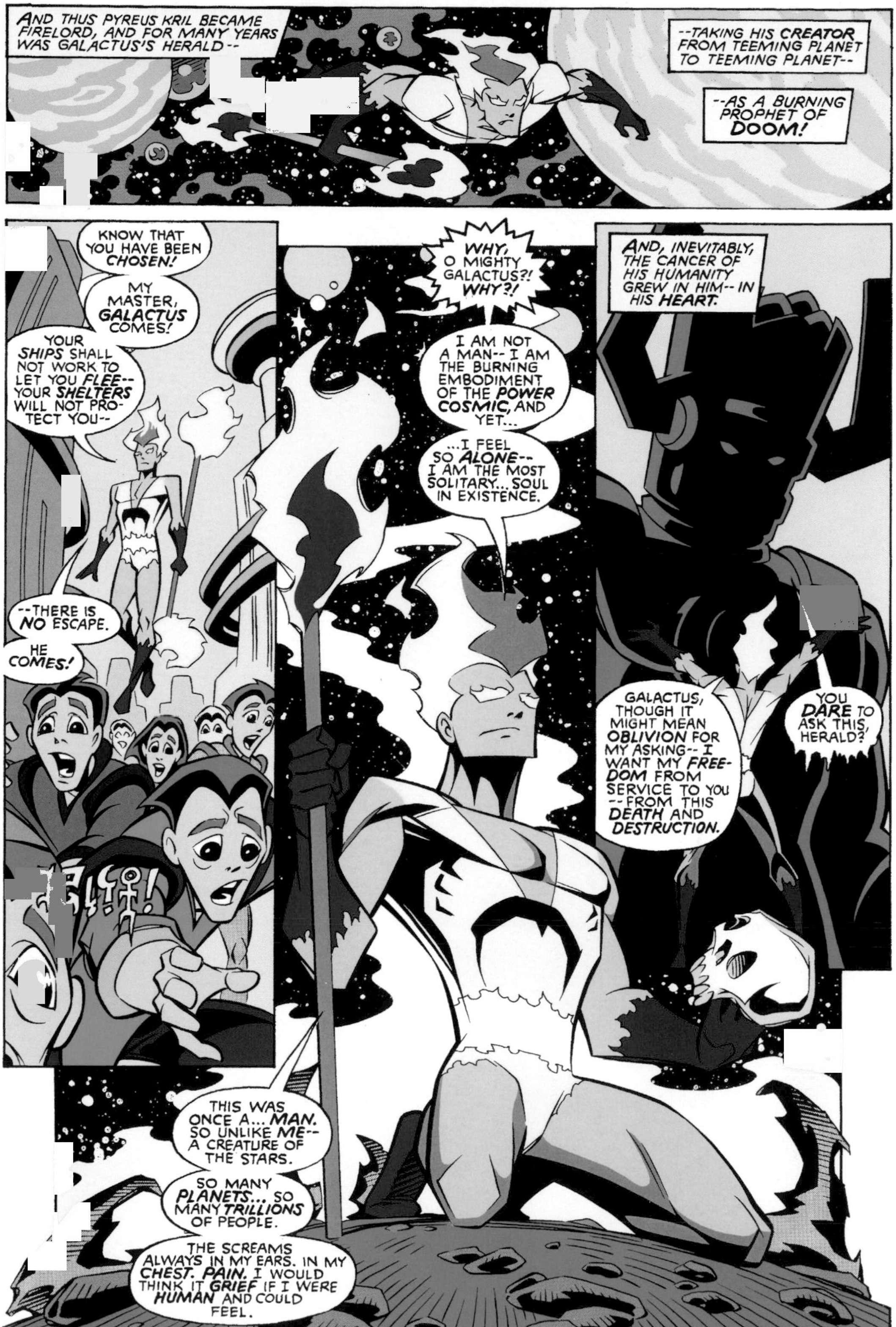

AND THUS PYREUS KRIL BECAME FIRELORD, AND FOR MANY YEARS WAS GALACTUS'S HERALD--
--TAKING HIS CREATOR FROM TEEMING PLANET TO TEEMING PLANET--
--AS A BURNING PROPHET OF DOOM!
KNOW THAT YOU HAVE BEEN CHOSEN!
MY MASTER, GALACTUS COMES!
YOUR SHIPS SHALL NOT WORK TO LET YOU FLEE-- YOUR SHELTERS WILL NOT PROTECT YOU--
--THERE IS NO ESCAPE.
HE COMES!
WHY, O MIGHTY GALACTUS?! WHY?!
I AM NOT A MAN-- I AM THE BURNING EMBODIMENT OF THE POWER COSMIC, AND YET...
...I FEEL SO ALONE-- I AM THE MOST SOLITARY... SOUL IN EXISTENCE.
AND, INEVITABLY, THE CANCER OF HIS HUMANITY GREW IN HIM-- IN HIS HEART.
GALACTUS, THOUGH IT MIGHT MEAN OBLIVION FOR MY ASKING-- I WANT MY FREEDOM FROM SERVICE TO YOU --FROM THIS DEATH AND DESTRUCTION.
YOU DARE TO ASK THIS, HERALD?
THIS WAS ONCE A... MAN. SO UNLIKE ME-- A CREATURE OF THE STARS.
SO MANY PLANETS... SO MANY TRILLIONS OF PEOPLE.
THE SCREAMS ALWAYS IN MY EARS. IN MY CHEST. PAIN. I WOULD THINK IT GRIEF IF I WERE HUMAN AND COULD FEEL.

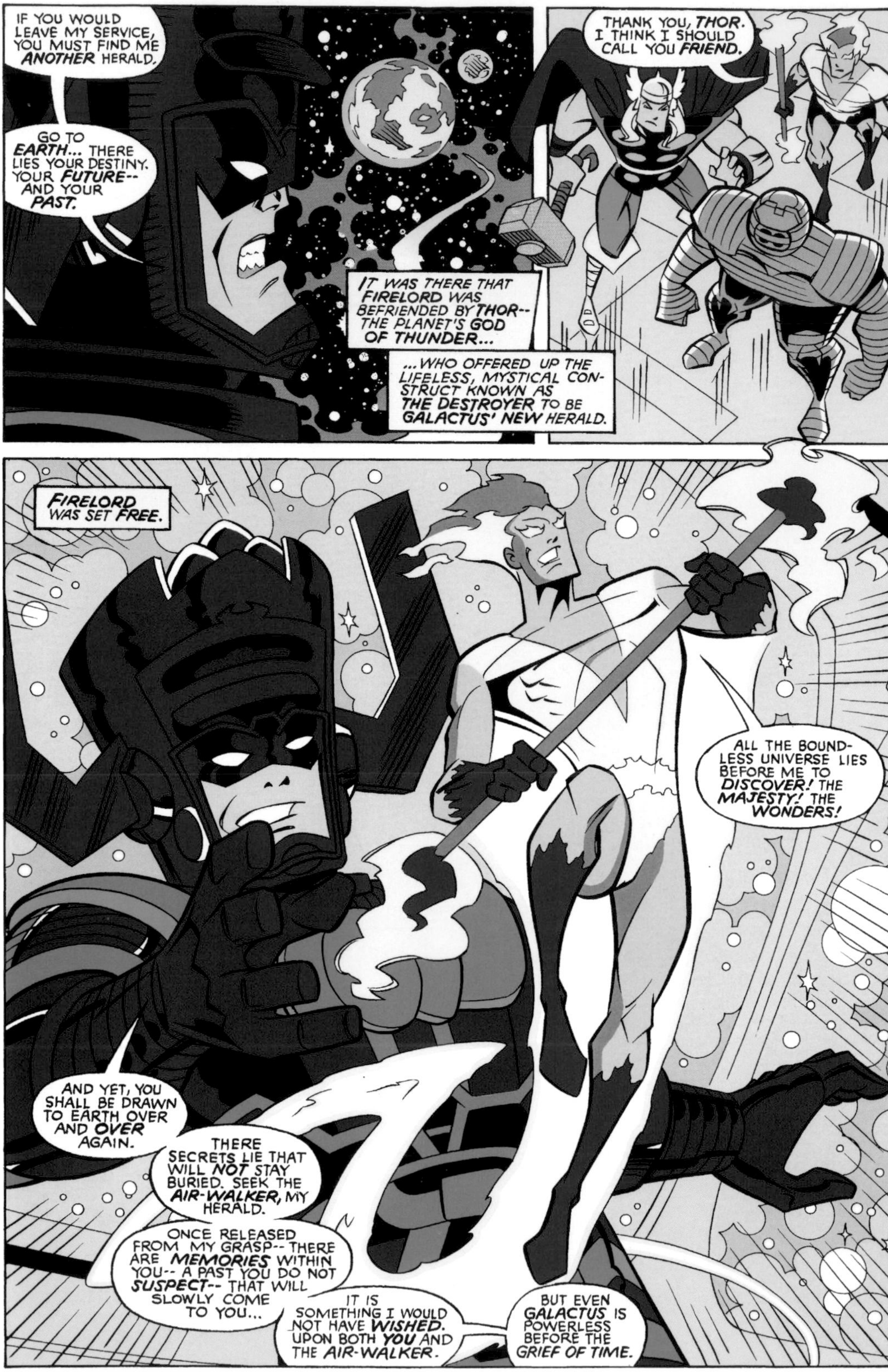
IF YOU WOULD LEAVE MY SERVICE, YOU MUST FIND ME ANOTHER HERALD.
GO TO EARTH... THERE LIES YOUR DESTINY. YOUR FUTURE-- AND YOUR PAST.
IT WAS THERE THAT FIRELORD WAS BEFRIENDED BY THOR-- THE PLANET'S GOD OF THUNDER...
...WHO OFFERED UP THE LIFELESS, MYSTICAL CONSTRUCT KNOWN AS THE DESTROYER TO BE GALACTUS' NEW HERALD.
THANK YOU, THOR. I THINK I SHOULD CALL YOU FRIEND.
FIRELORD WAS SET FREE.
ALL THE BOUNDLESS UNIVERSE LIES BEFORE ME TO DISCOVER! THE MAJESTY! THE WONDERS!
AND YET, YOU SHALL BE DRAWN TO EARTH OVER AND OVER AGAIN.
THERE SECRETS LIE THAT WILL NOT STAY BURIED. SEEK THE AIR-WALKER, MY HERALD.
ONCE RELEASED FROM MY GRASP-- THERE ARE MEMORIES WITHIN YOU-- A PAST YOU DO NOT SUSPECT-- THAT WILL SLOWLY COME TO YOU...
IT IS SOMETHING I WOULD NOT HAVE WISHED. UPON BOTH YOU AND THE AIR-WALKER.
BUT EVEN GALACTUS IS POWERLESS BEFORE THE GRIEF OF TIME.

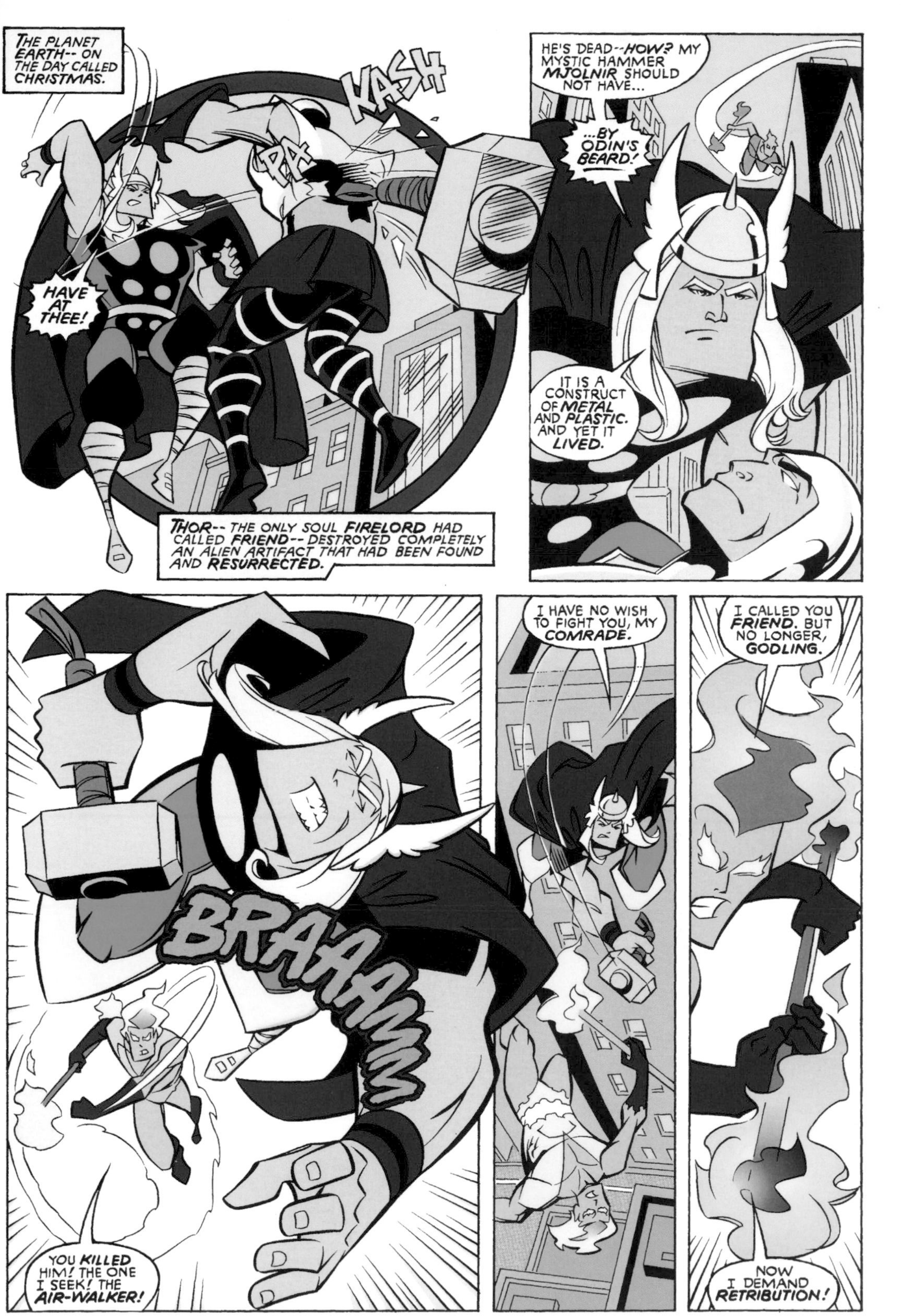

THE PLANET EARTH-- ON THE DAY CALLED CHRISTMAS.
KASH
PA
HAVE AT THEE!
THOR-- THE ONLY SOUL FIRELORD HAD CALLED FRIEND-- DESTROYED COMPLETELY AN ALIEN ARTIFACT THAT HAD BEEN FOUND AND RESURRECTED.
HE'S DEAD--HOW? MY MYSTIC HAMMER MJOLNIR SHOULD NOT HAVE...
...BY ODIN'S BEARD!
IT IS A CONSTRUCT OF METAL AND PLASTIC. AND YET IT LIVED.
BRAAAAMM
YOU KILLED HIM! THE ONE I SEEK! THE AIR-WALKER!
I HAVE NO WISH TO FIGHT YOU, MY COMRADE.
I CALLED YOU FRIEND. BUT NO LONGER, GODLING.
NOW I DEMAND RETRIBUTION!

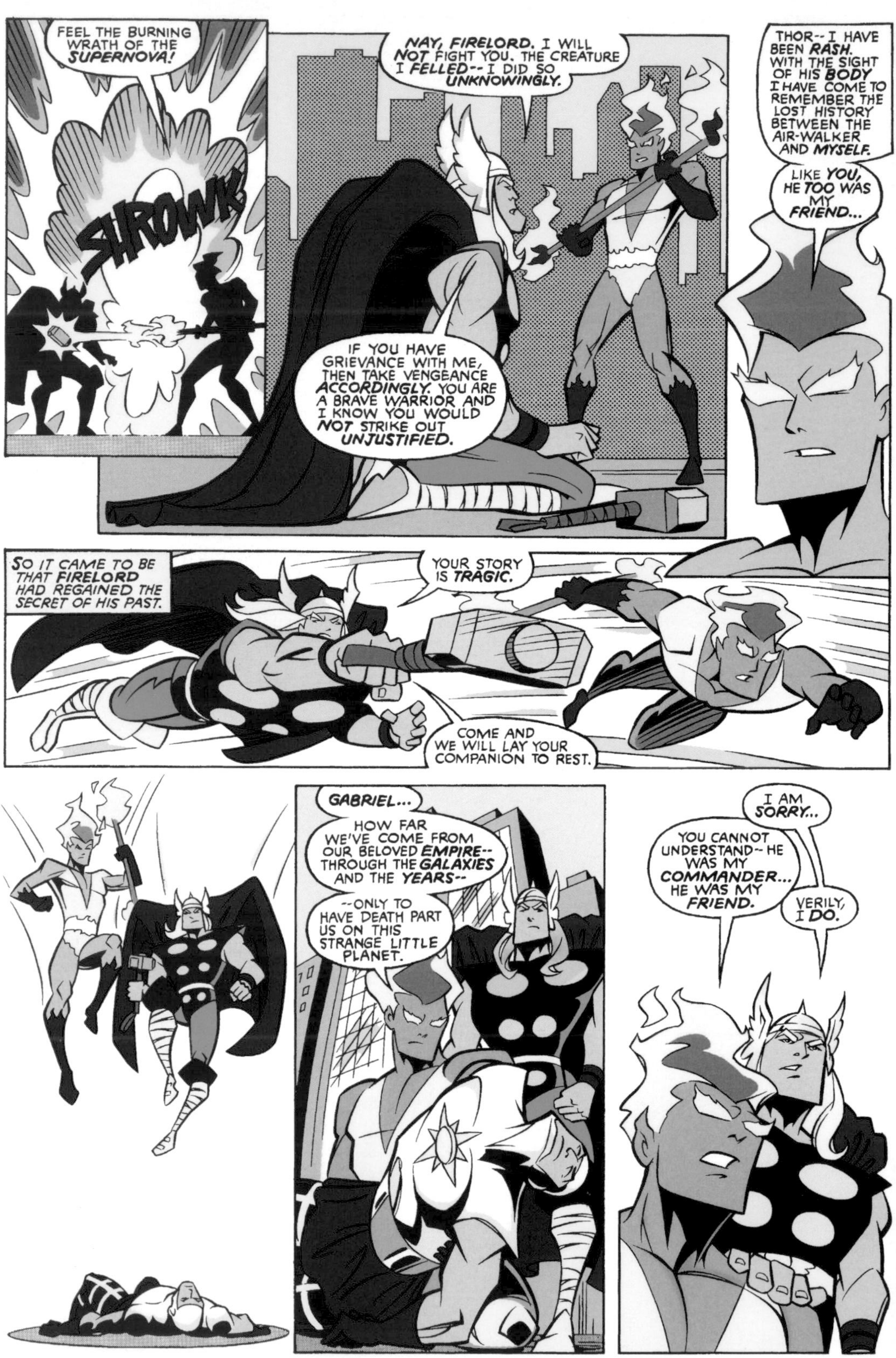
FEEL THE BURNING WRATH OF THE SUPERNOVA!
SHROWK
NAY, FIRELORD. I WILL NOT FIGHT YOU. THE CREATURE I FELLED-- I DID SO UNKNOWINGLY.
IF YOU HAVE GRIEVANCE WITH ME, THEN TAKE VENGEANCE ACCORDINGLY. YOU ARE A BRAVE WARRIOR AND I KNOW YOU WOULD NOT STRIKE OUT UNJUSTIFIED.
THOR-- I HAVE BEEN RASH. WITH THE SIGHT OF HIS BODY I HAVE COME TO REMEMBER THE LOST HISTORY BETWEEN THE AIR-WALKER AND MYSELF.
LIKE YOU, HE TOO WAS MY FRIEND...
SO IT CAME TO BE THAT FIRELORD HAD REGAINED THE SECRET OF HIS PAST.
YOUR STORY IS TRAGIC.
COME AND WE WILL LAY YOUR COMPANION TO REST.
GABRIEL...
HOW FAR WE'VE COME FROM OUR BELOVED EMPIRE-- THROUGH THE GALAXIES AND THE YEARS--
--ONLY TO HAVE DEATH PART US ON THIS STRANGE LITTLE PLANET.
I AM SORRY...
YOU CANNOT UNDERSTAND-- HE WAS MY COMMANDER... HE WAS MY FRIEND.
VERILY, I DO.

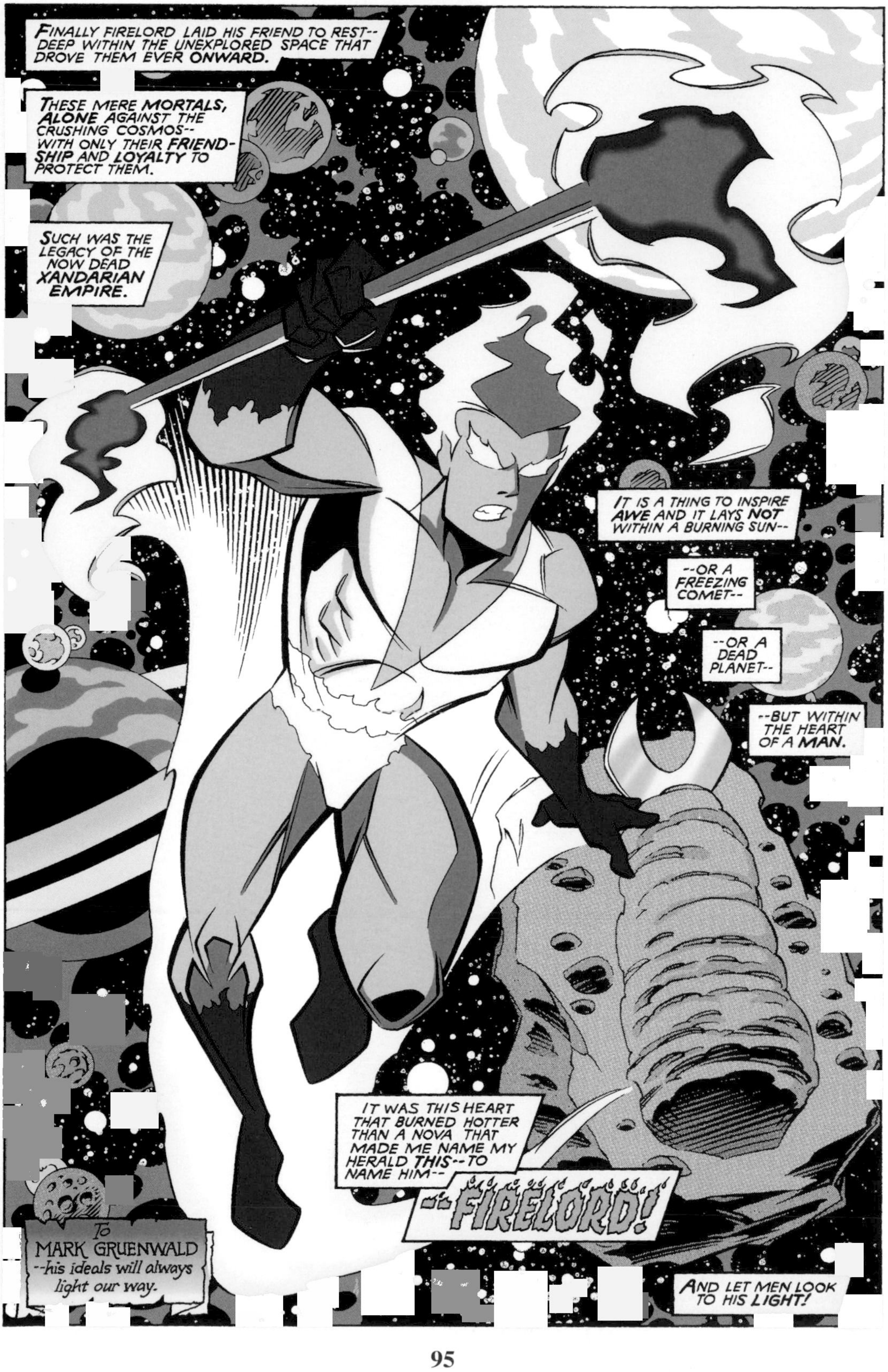
FINALLY FIRELORD LAID HIS FRIEND TO REST--DEEP WITHIN THE UNEXPLORED SPACE THAT DROVE THEM EVER ONWARD.
THESE MERE MORTALS, ALONE AGAINST THE CRUSHING COSMOS--WITH ONLY THEIR FRIENDSHIP AND LOYALTY TO PROTECT THEM.
SUCH WAS THE LEGACY OF THE NOW DEAD XANDARIAN EMPIRE.
IT IS A THING TO INSPIRE AWE AND IT LAYS NOT WITHIN A BURNING SUN--
--OR A FREEZING COMET--
--OR A DEAD PLANET--
--BUT WITHIN THE HEART OF A MAN.
IT WAS THIS HEART THAT BURNED HOTTER THAN A NOVA THAT MADE ME NAME MY HERALD THIS--TO NAME HIM--
--FIRELORD!
AND LET MEN LOOK TO HIS LIGHT!
To MARK GRUENWALD --his ideals will always light our way.

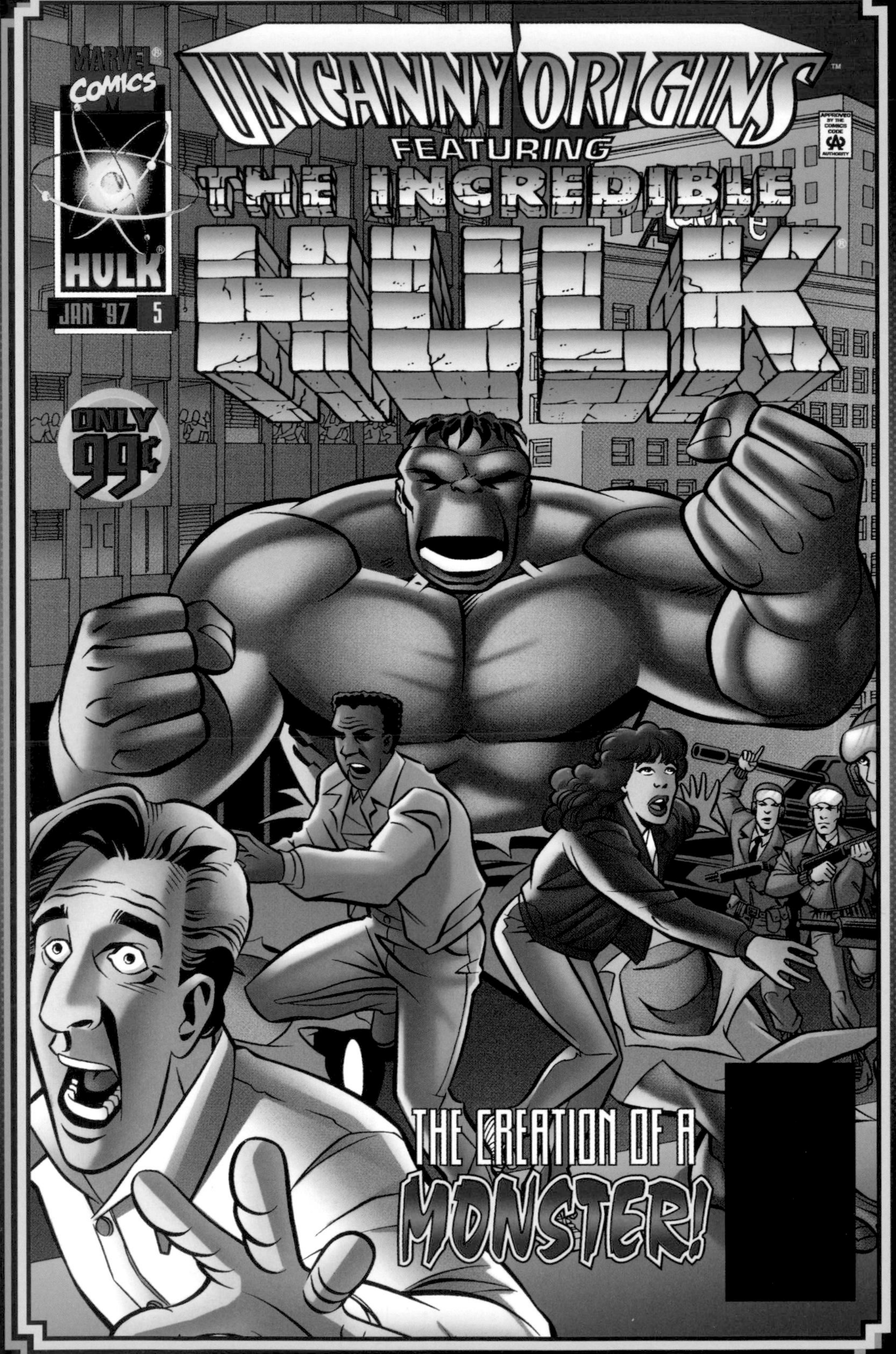

MARVEL COMICS
HULK
JAN '97
5
UNCANNY ORIGINS
FEATURING
THE INCREDIBLE
HULK
ONLY 99¢
THE CREATION OF A
MONSTER!

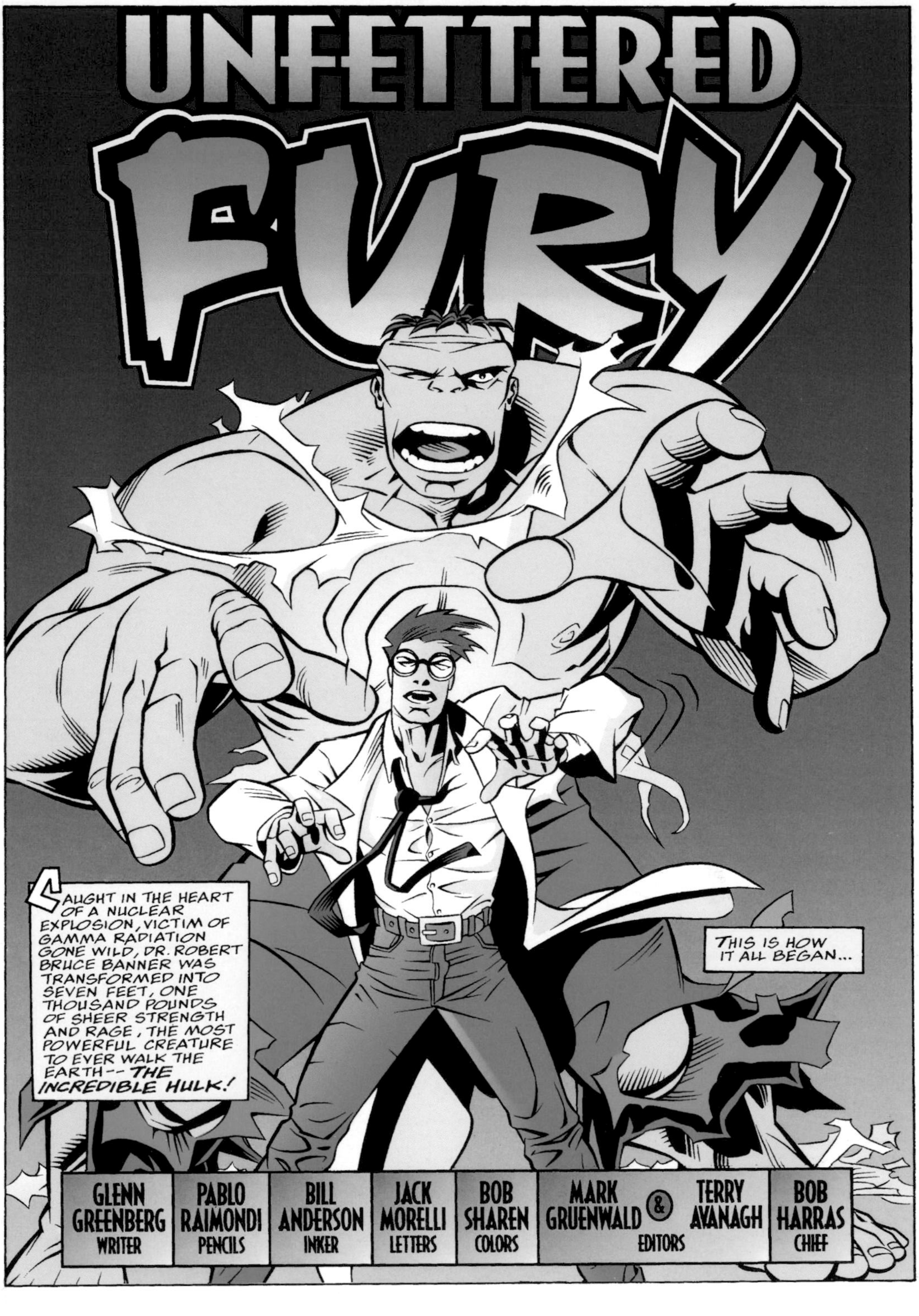
UNFETTERED FURY
CAUGHT IN THE HEART OF A NUCLEAR EXPLOSION, VICTIM OF GAMMA RADIATION GONE WILD, DR. ROBERT BRUCE BANNER WAS TRANSFORMED INTO SEVEN FEET, ONE THOUSAND POUNDS OF SHEER STRENGTH AND RAGE, THE MOST POWERFUL CREATURE TO EVER WALK THE EARTH-- THE INCREDIBLE HULK!
THIS IS HOW IT ALL BEGAN...
GLENN GREENBERG WRITER
PABLO RAIMONDI PENCILS
BILL ANDERSON INKER
JACK MORELLI LETTERS
BOB SHAREN COLORS
MARK GRUENWALD & TERRY AVANAGH EDITORS
BOB HARRAS CHIEF

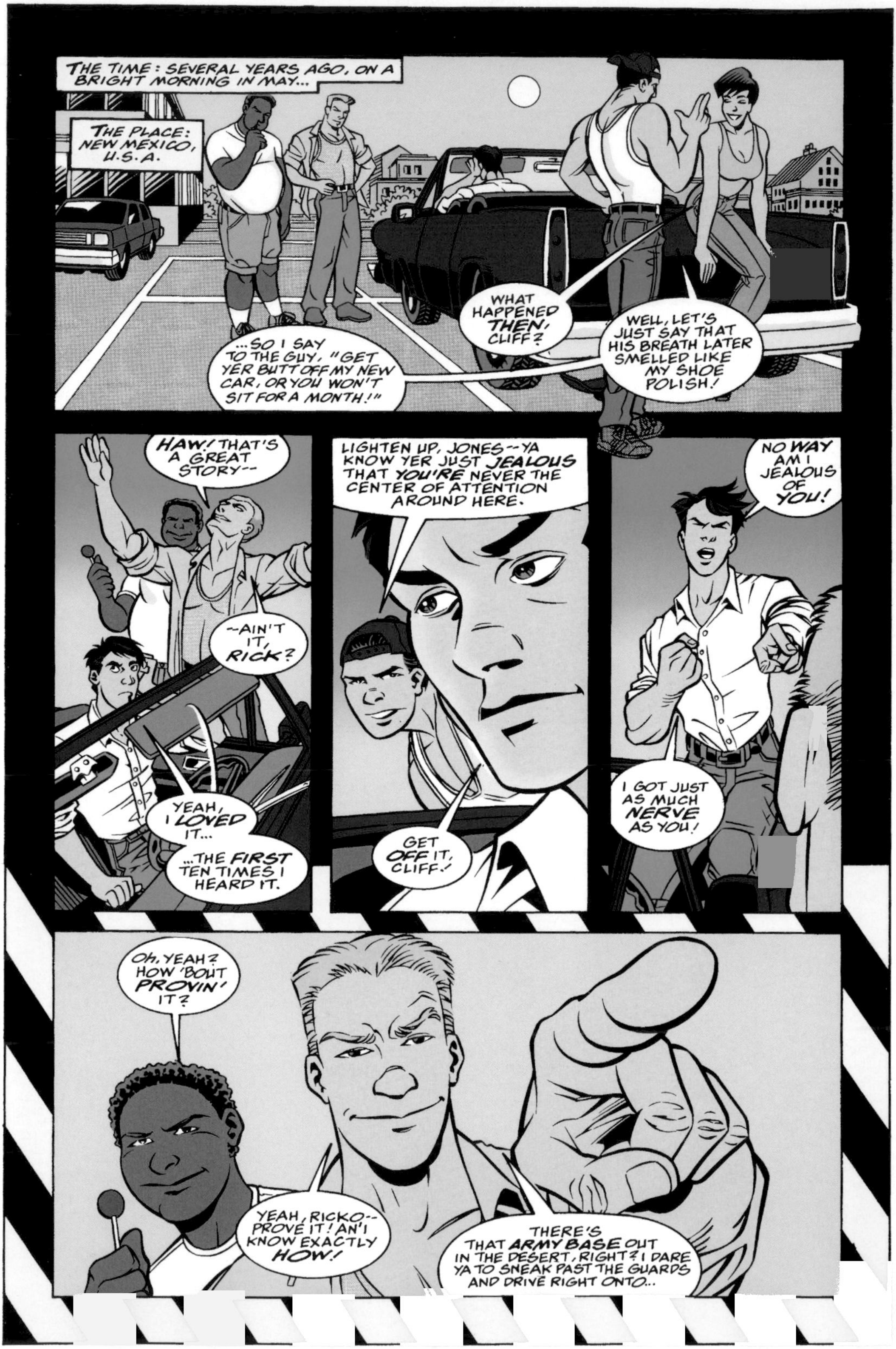
THE TIME: SEVERAL YEARS AGO, ON A BRIGHT MORNING IN MAY...
THE PLACE: NEW MEXICO, U.S.A.
...SO I SAY TO THE GUY, "GET YER BUTT OFF MY NEW CAR, OR YOU WON'T SIT FOR A MONTH!"
WHAT HAPPENED THEN, CLIFF?
WELL, LET'S JUST SAY THAT HIS BREATH LATER SMELLED LIKE MY SHOE POLISH!
HAW! THAT'S A GREAT STORY--
--AIN'T IT, RICK?
YEAH, I LOVED IT...
...THE FIRST TEN TIMES I HEARD IT.
LIGHTEN UP, JONES--YA KNOW YER JUST JEALOUS THAT YOU'RE NEVER THE CENTER OF ATTENTION AROUND HERE.
GET OFF IT, CLIFF.
NO WAY AM I JEALOUS OF YOU!
I GOT JUST AS MUCH NERVE AS YOU!
OH, YEAH? HOW 'BOUT PROVIN' IT?
YEAH, RICKO-- PROVE IT! AN' I KNOW EXACTLY HOW!
THERE'S THAT ARMY BASE OUT IN THE DESERT, RIGHT? I DARE YA TO SNEAK PAST THE GUARDS AND DRIVE RIGHT ONTO...

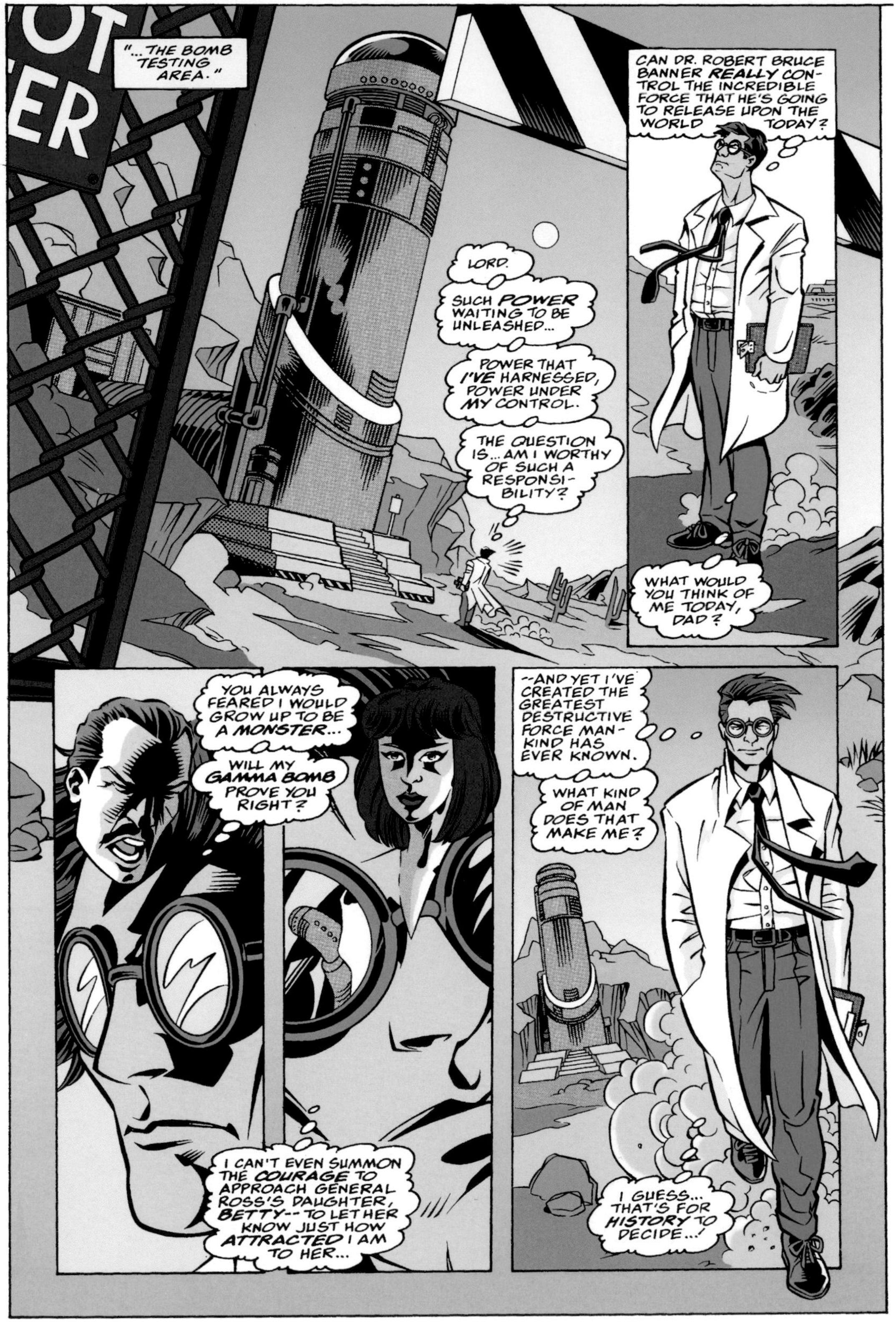
"...THE BOMB TESTING AREA."
CAN DR. ROBERT BRUCE BANNER REALLY CONTROL THE INCREDIBLE FORCE THAT HE'S GOING TO RELEASE UPON THE WORLD TODAY?
LORD.
SUCH POWER WAITING TO BE UNLEASHED...
POWER THAT I'VE HARNESSED, POWER UNDER MY CONTROL.
THE QUESTION IS... AM I WORTHY OF SUCH A RESPONSIBILITY?
WHAT WOULD YOU THINK OF ME TODAY, DAD?
YOU ALWAYS FEARED I WOULD GROW UP TO BE A MONSTER...
WILL MY GAMMA BOMB PROVE YOU RIGHT?
I CAN'T EVEN SUMMON THE COURAGE TO APPROACH GENERAL ROSS'S DAUGHTER, BETTY-- TO LET HER KNOW JUST HOW ATTRACTED I AM TO HER...
--AND YET I'VE CREATED THE GREATEST DESTRUCTIVE FORCE MANKIND HAS EVER KNOWN.
WHAT KIND OF MAN DOES THAT MAKE ME?
I GUESS... THAT'S FOR HISTORY TO DECIDE...!

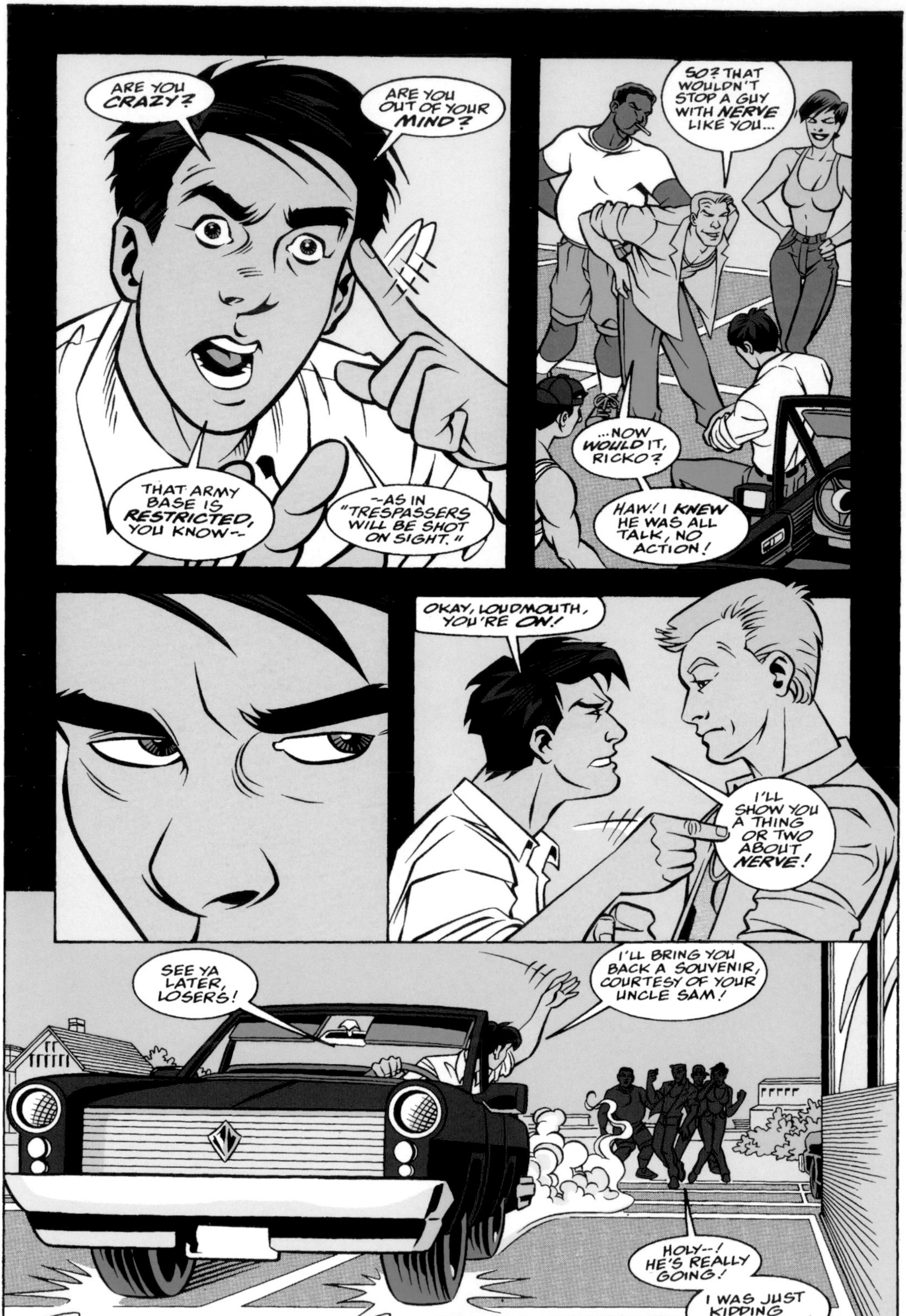
ARE YOU CRAZY?
ARE YOU OUT OF YOUR MIND?
THAT ARMY BASE IS RESTRICTED, YOU KNOW--
--AS IN "TRESPASSERS WILL BE SHOT ON SIGHT."
SO? THAT WOULDN'T STOP A GUY WITH NERVE LIKE YOU...
...NOW WOULD IT, RICKO?
HAW! I KNEW HE WAS ALL TALK, NO ACTION!
OKAY, LOUDMOUTH, YOU'RE ON!
I'LL SHOW YOU A THING OR TWO ABOUT NERVE!
SEE YA LATER, LOSERS!
I'LL BRING YOU BACK A SOUVENIR, COURTESY OF YOUR UNCLE SAM!
HOLY--! HE'S REALLY GOING!
I WAS JUST KIDDING AROUND--!

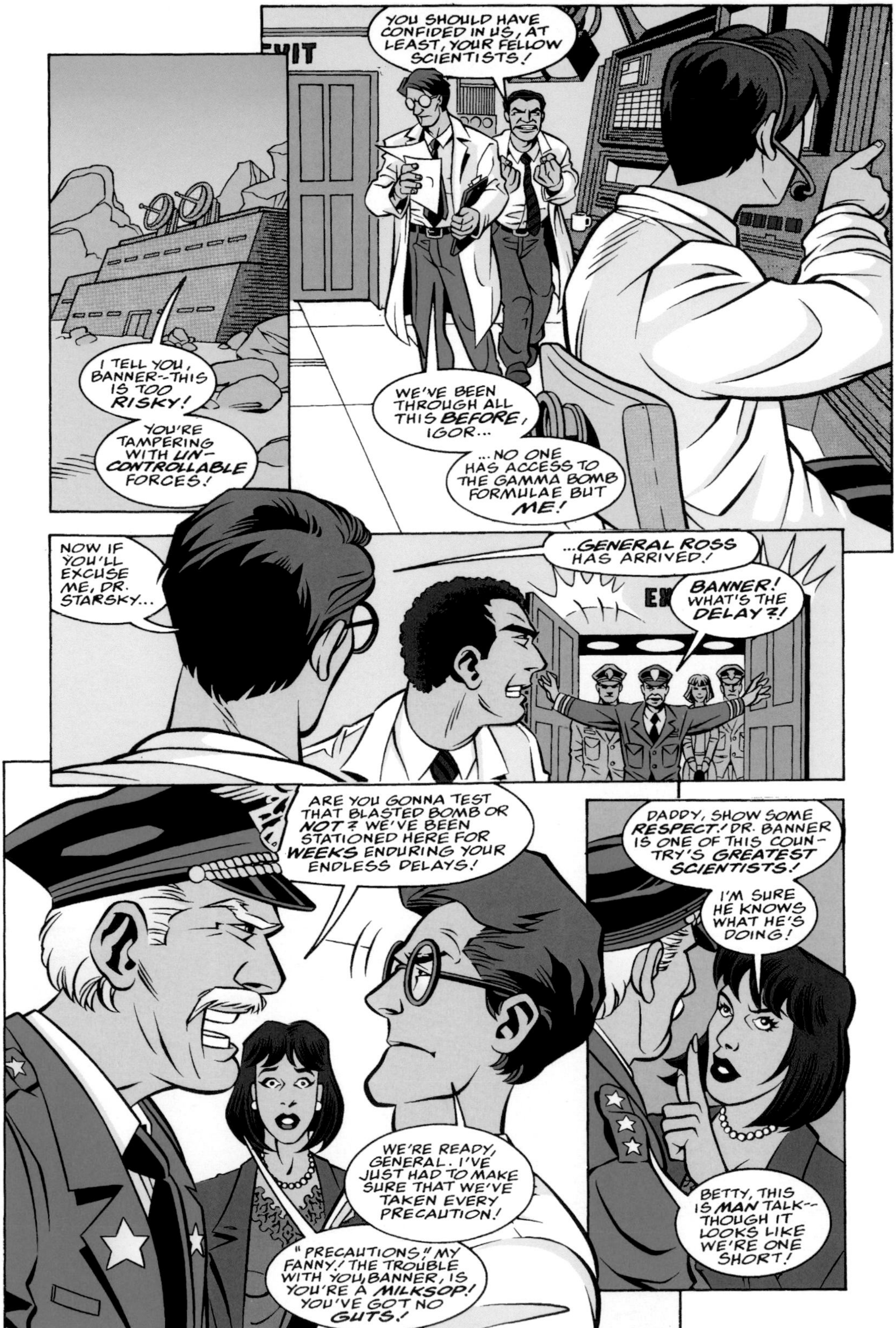

EXIT
YOU SHOULD HAVE CONFIDED IN US, AT LEAST, YOUR FELLOW SCIENTISTS!
I TELL YOU, BANNER--THIS IS TOO RISKY!
YOU'RE TAMPERING WITH UNCONTROLLABLE FORCES!
WE'VE BEEN THROUGH ALL THIS BEFORE, IGOR...
...NO ONE HAS ACCESS TO THE GAMMA BOMB FORMULAE BUT ME!
NOW IF YOU'LL EXCUSE ME, DR. STARSKY...
...GENERAL ROSS HAS ARRIVED!
BANNER! WHAT'S THE DELAY?!
ARE YOU GONNA TEST THAT BLASTED BOMB OR NOT? WE'VE BEEN STATIONED HERE FOR WEEKS ENDURING YOUR ENDLESS DELAYS!
WE'RE READY, GENERAL. I'VE JUST HAD TO MAKE SURE THAT WE'VE TAKEN EVERY PRECAUTION!
"PRECAUTIONS," MY FANNY! THE TROUBLE WITH YOU, BANNER, IS YOU'RE A MILKSOP! YOU'VE GOT NO GUTS!
DADDY, SHOW SOME RESPECT! DR. BANNER IS ONE OF THIS COUNTRY'S GREATEST SCIENTISTS!
I'M SURE HE KNOWS WHAT HE'S DOING!
BETTY, THIS IS MAN TALK--THOUGH IT LOOKS LIKE WE'RE ONE SHORT!

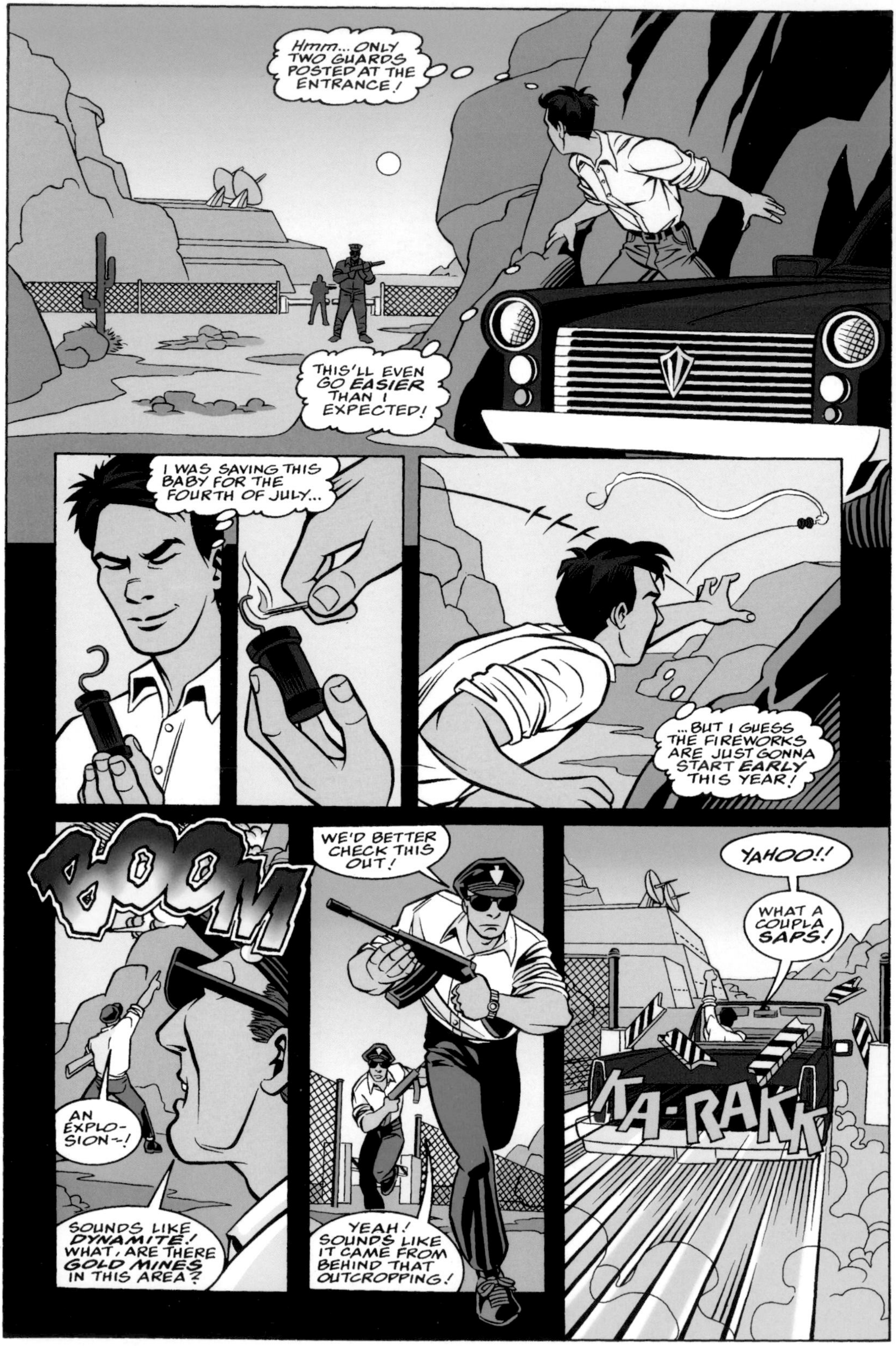
Hmm... ONLY TWO GUARDS POSTED AT THE ENTRANCE!
THIS'LL EVEN GO EASIER THAN I EXPECTED!
I WAS SAVING THIS BABY FOR THE FOURTH OF JULY...
...BUT I GUESS THE FIREWORKS ARE JUST GONNA START EARLY THIS YEAR!
BOOM
AN EXPLOSION--!
SOUNDS LIKE DYNAMITE! WHAT, ARE THERE GOLD MINES IN THIS AREA?
WE'D BETTER CHECK THIS OUT!
YEAH! SOUNDS LIKE IT CAME FROM BEHIND THAT OUTCROPPING!
YAHOO!!
WHAT A COUPLA SAPS!
KA-RAKK

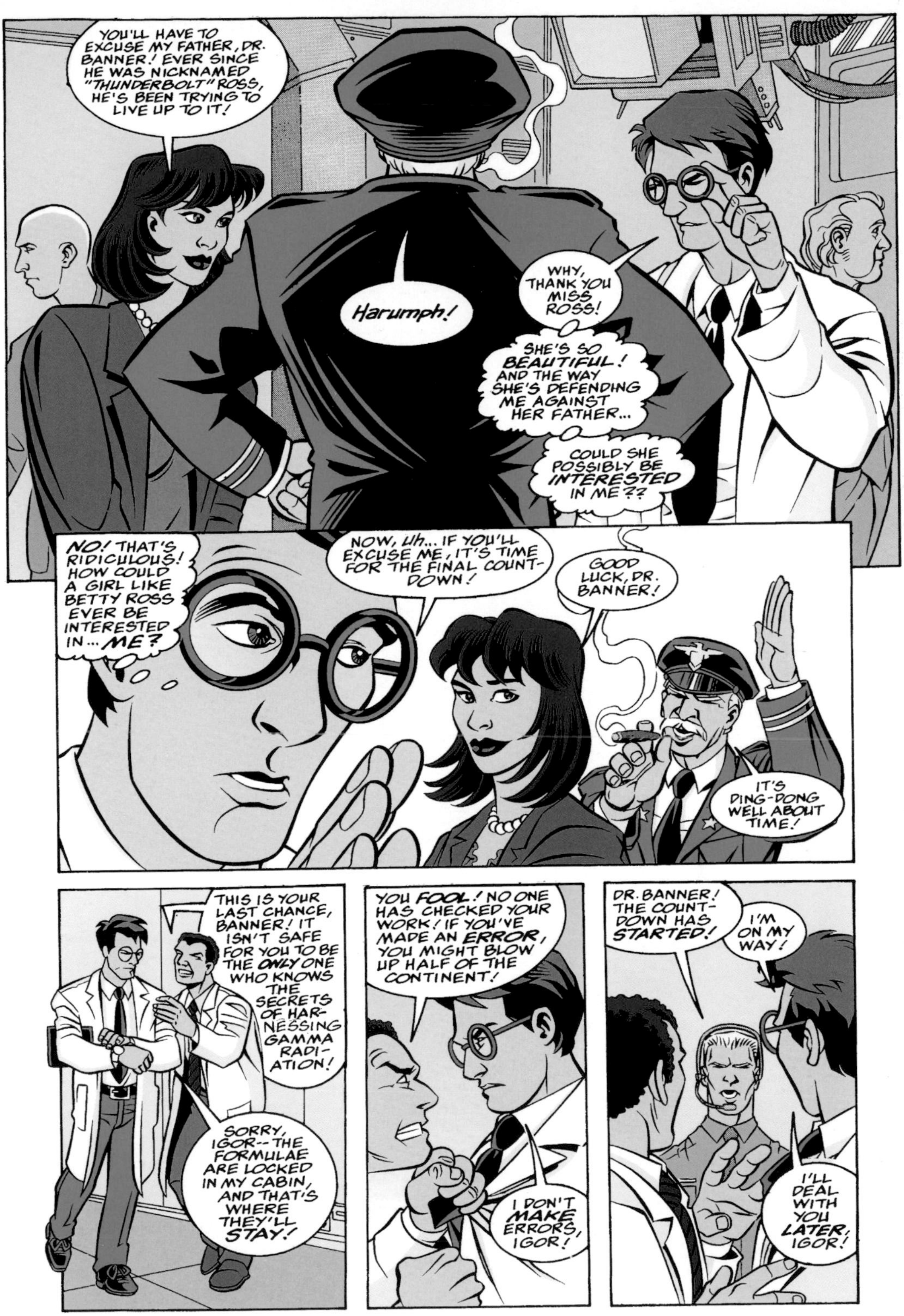
YOU'LL HAVE TO EXCUSE MY FATHER, DR. BANNER! EVER SINCE HE WAS NICKNAMED "THUNDERBOLT" ROSS, HE'S BEEN TRYING TO LIVE UP TO IT!
Harumph!
WHY, THANK YOU MISS ROSS!
SHE'S SO BEAUTIFUL! AND THE WAY SHE'S DEFENDING ME AGAINST HER FATHER...
COULD SHE POSSIBLY BE INTERESTED IN ME??
NO! THAT'S RIDICULOUS! HOW COULD A GIRL LIKE BETTY ROSS EVER BE INTERESTED IN... ME?
NOW, UH... IF YOU'LL EXCUSE ME, IT'S TIME FOR THE FINAL COUNT-DOWN!
GOOD LUCK, DR. BANNER!
IT'S DING-DONG WELL ABOUT TIME!
THIS IS YOUR LAST CHANCE, BANNER! IT ISN'T SAFE FOR YOU TO BE THE ONLY ONE WHO KNOWS THE SECRETS OF HAR-NESSING GAMMA RADI-ATION!
SORRY, IGOR-- THE FORMULAE ARE LOCKED IN MY CABIN, AND THAT'S WHERE THEY'LL STAY!
YOU FOOL! NO ONE HAS CHECKED YOUR WORK! IF YOU'VE MADE AN ERROR, YOU MIGHT BLOW UP HALF OF THE CONTINENT!
I DON'T MAKE ERRORS, IGOR!
DR. BANNER! THE COUNT-DOWN HAS STARTED!
I'M ON MY WAY!
I'LL DEAL WITH YOU LATER, IGOR!

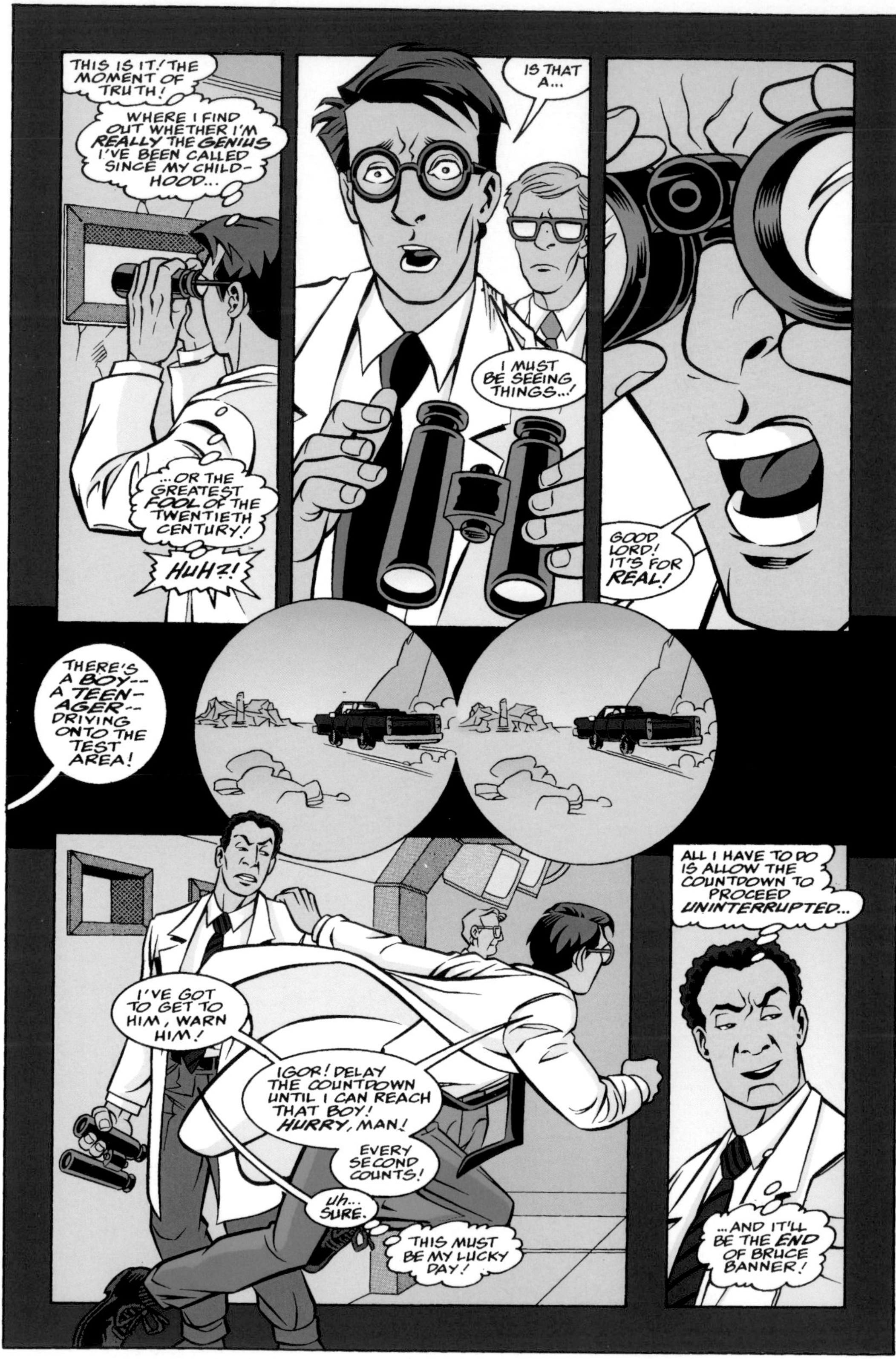
THIS IS IT! THE MOMENT OF TRUTH!
WHERE I FIND OUT WHETHER I'M REALLY THE GENIUS I'VE BEEN CALLED SINCE MY CHILD-HOOD...
...OR THE GREATEST FOOL OF THE TWENTIETH CENTURY!
HUH?!
IS THAT A...
I MUST BE SEEING THINGS...!
GOOD LORD! IT'S FOR REAL!
THERE'S A BOY-- A TEEN-AGER-- DRIVING ONTO THE TEST AREA!
I'VE GOT TO GET TO HIM, WARN HIM!
IGOR! DELAY THE COUNTDOWN UNTIL I CAN REACH THAT BOY! HURRY, MAN!
EVERY SECOND COUNTS!
UH... SURE.
THIS MUST BE MY LUCKY DAY!
ALL I HAVE TO DO IS ALLOW THE COUNTDOWN TO PROCEED UNINTERRUPTED...
...AND IT'LL BE THE END OF BRUCE BANNER!

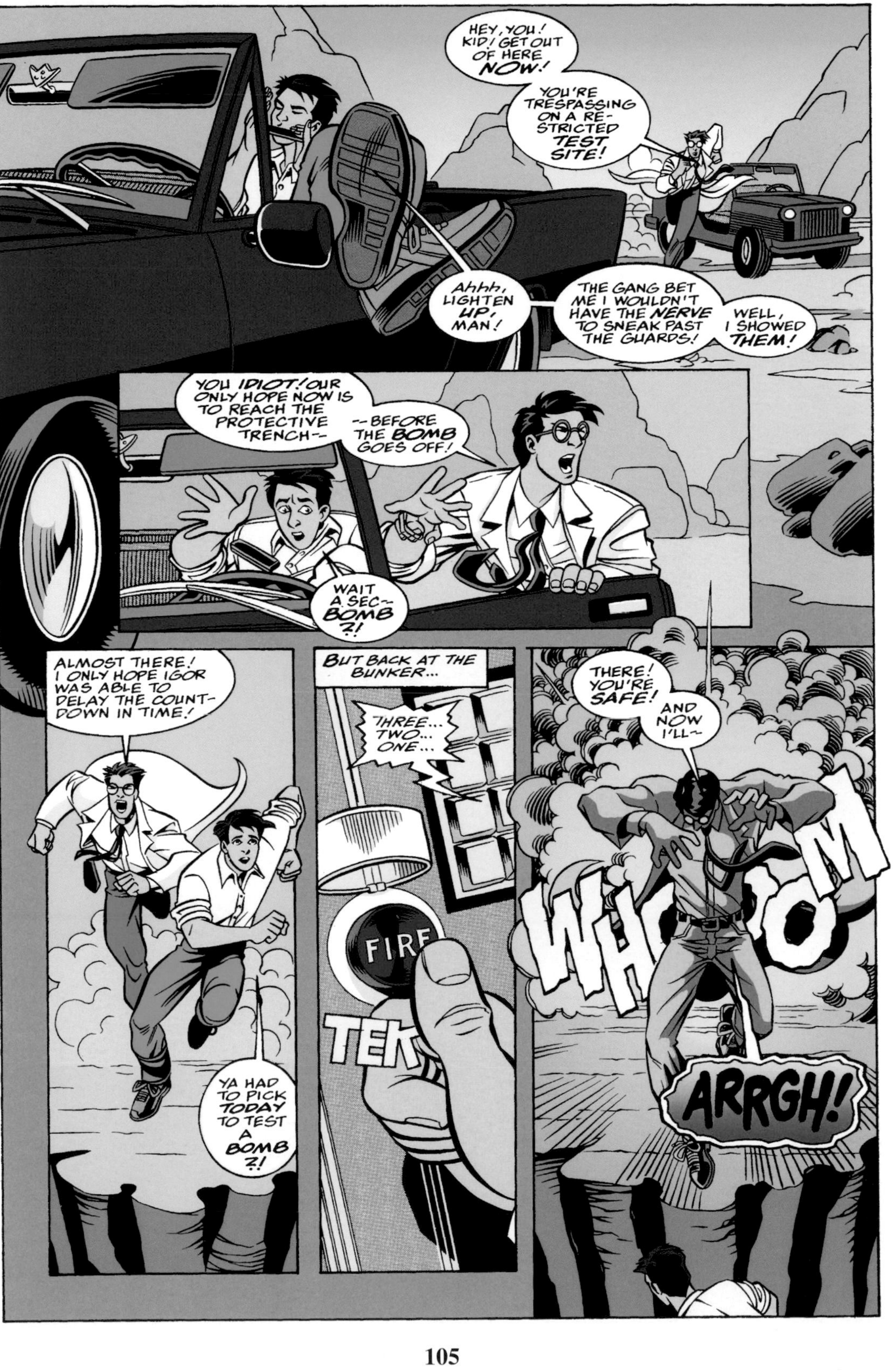
HEY, YOU! KID! GET OUT OF HERE NOW!
YOU'RE TRESPASSING ON A RE-STRICTED TEST SITE!
Ahhh, LIGHTEN UP, MAN!
THE GANG BET ME I WOULDN'T HAVE THE NERVE TO SNEAK PAST THE GUARDS!
WELL, I SHOWED THEM!
YOU IDIOT! OUR ONLY HOPE NOW IS TO REACH THE PROTECTIVE TRENCH--
--BEFORE THE BOMB GOES OFF!
WAIT A SEC-- BOMB?!
ALMOST THERE! I ONLY HOPE IGOR WAS ABLE TO DELAY THE COUNT-DOWN IN TIME!
YA HAD TO PICK TODAY TO TEST A BOMB?!
BUT BACK AT THE BUNKER...
THREE... TWO... ONE...
FIRE
TEK
THERE! YOU'RE SAFE!
AND NOW I'LL--
ARRGH!

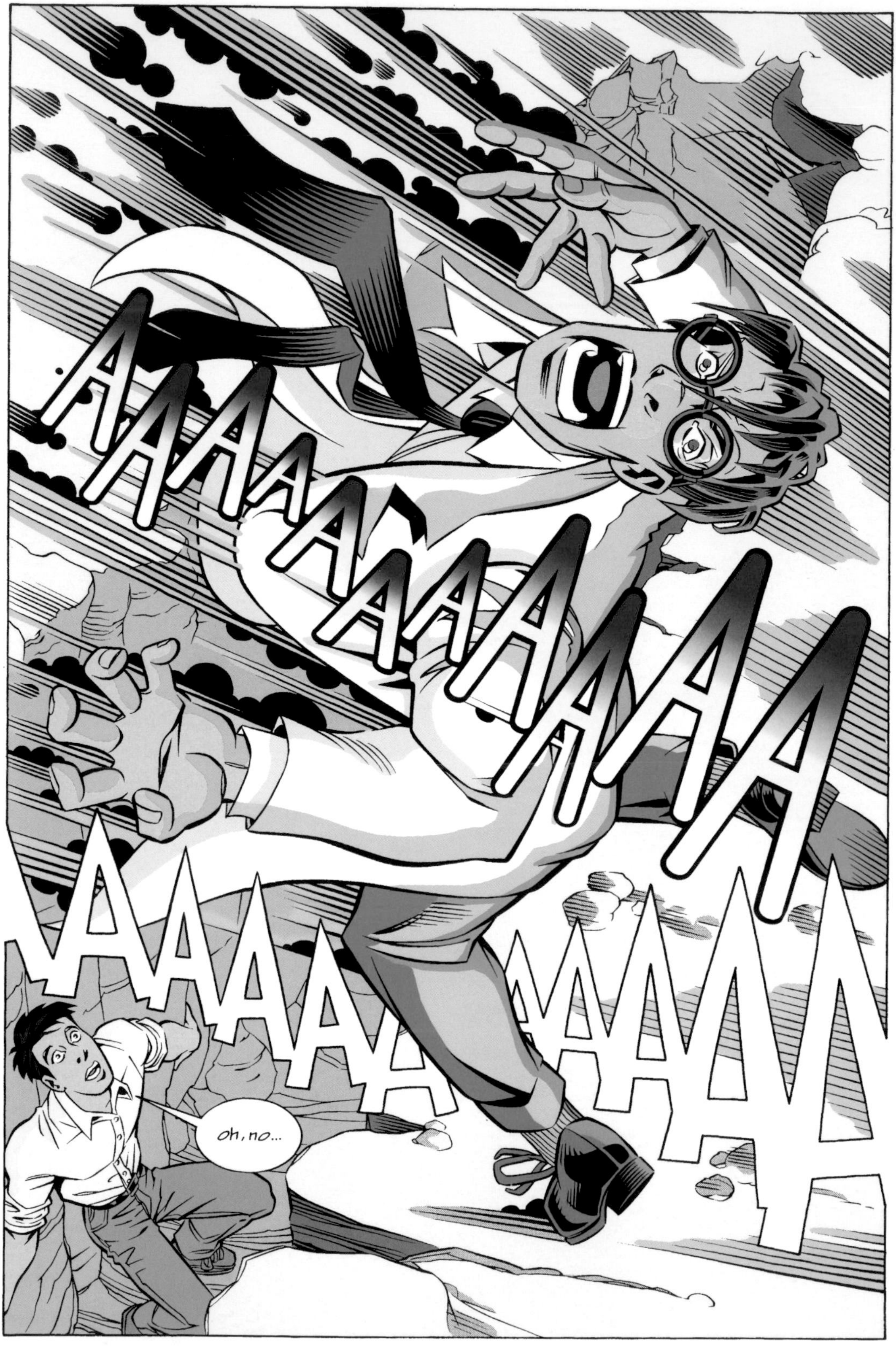
AAAAAAAAAAAAAAA
AAAAAAAAAAAAAAAAA
oh, no...

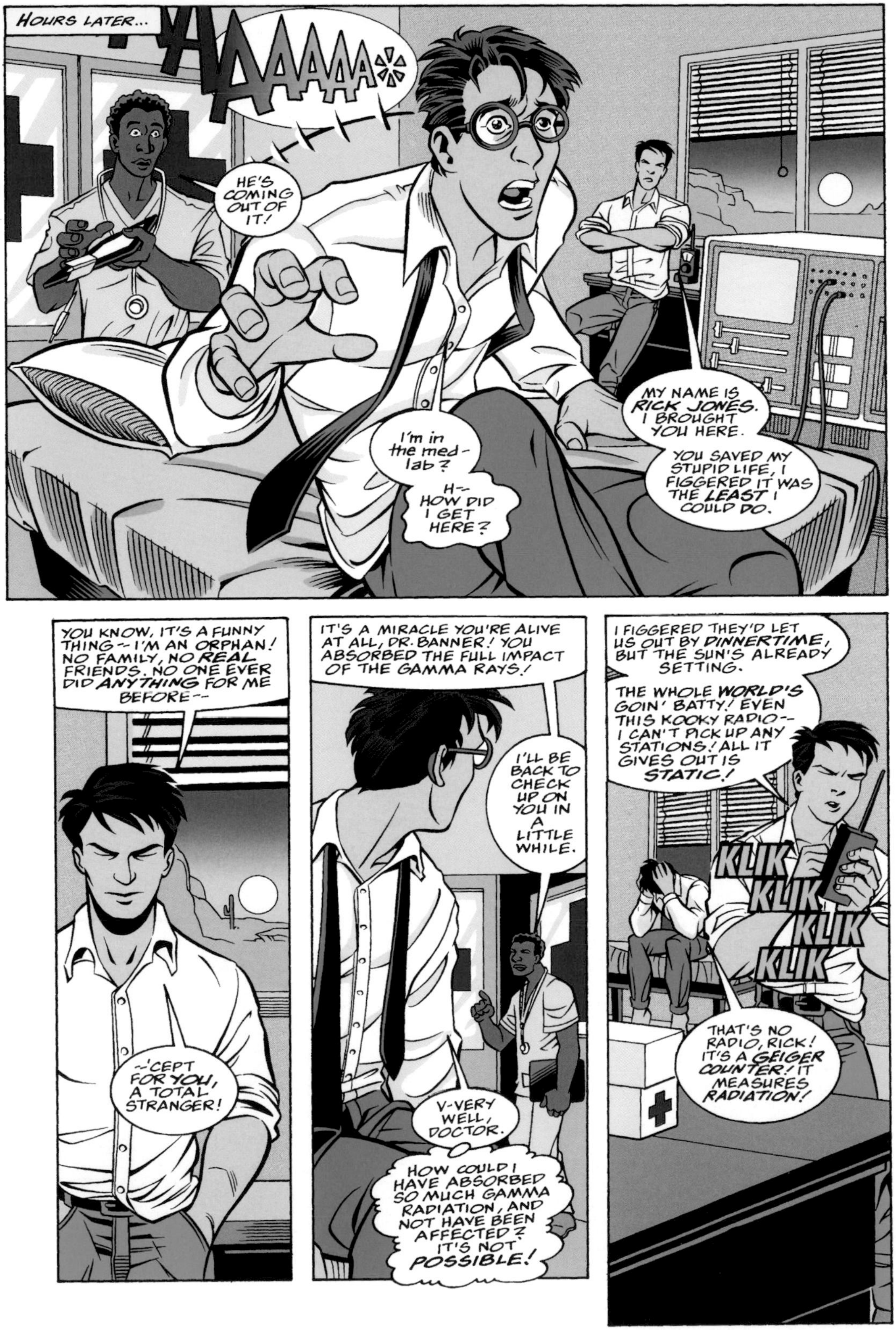

HOURS LATER...
YAAAAAA*!
HE'S COMING OUT OF IT!
I'm in the med-lab?
H-- HOW DID I GET HERE?
MY NAME IS RICK JONES. I BROUGHT YOU HERE.
YOU SAVED MY STUPID LIFE, I FIGGERED IT WAS THE LEAST I COULD DO.
YOU KNOW, IT'S A FUNNY THING-- I'M AN ORPHAN! NO FAMILY, NO REAL FRIENDS. NO ONE EVER DID ANYTHING FOR ME BEFORE--
--'CEPT FOR YOU, A TOTAL STRANGER!
IT'S A MIRACLE YOU'RE ALIVE AT ALL, DR. BANNER! YOU ABSORBED THE FULL IMPACT OF THE GAMMA RAYS!
I'LL BE BACK TO CHECK UP ON YOU IN A LITTLE WHILE.
V-VERY WELL, DOCTOR.
HOW COULD I HAVE ABSORBED SO MUCH GAMMA RADIATION, AND NOT HAVE BEEN AFFECTED? IT'S NOT POSSIBLE!
I FIGGERED THEY'D LET US OUT BY DINNERTIME, BUT THE SUN'S ALREADY SETTING.
THE WHOLE WORLD'S GOIN' BATTY! EVEN THIS KOOKY RADIO-- I CAN'T PICK UP ANY STATIONS! ALL IT GIVES OUT IS STATIC!
KLIK KLIK KLIK KLIK
THAT'S NO RADIO, RICK! IT'S A GEIGER COUNTER! IT MEASURES RADIATION!

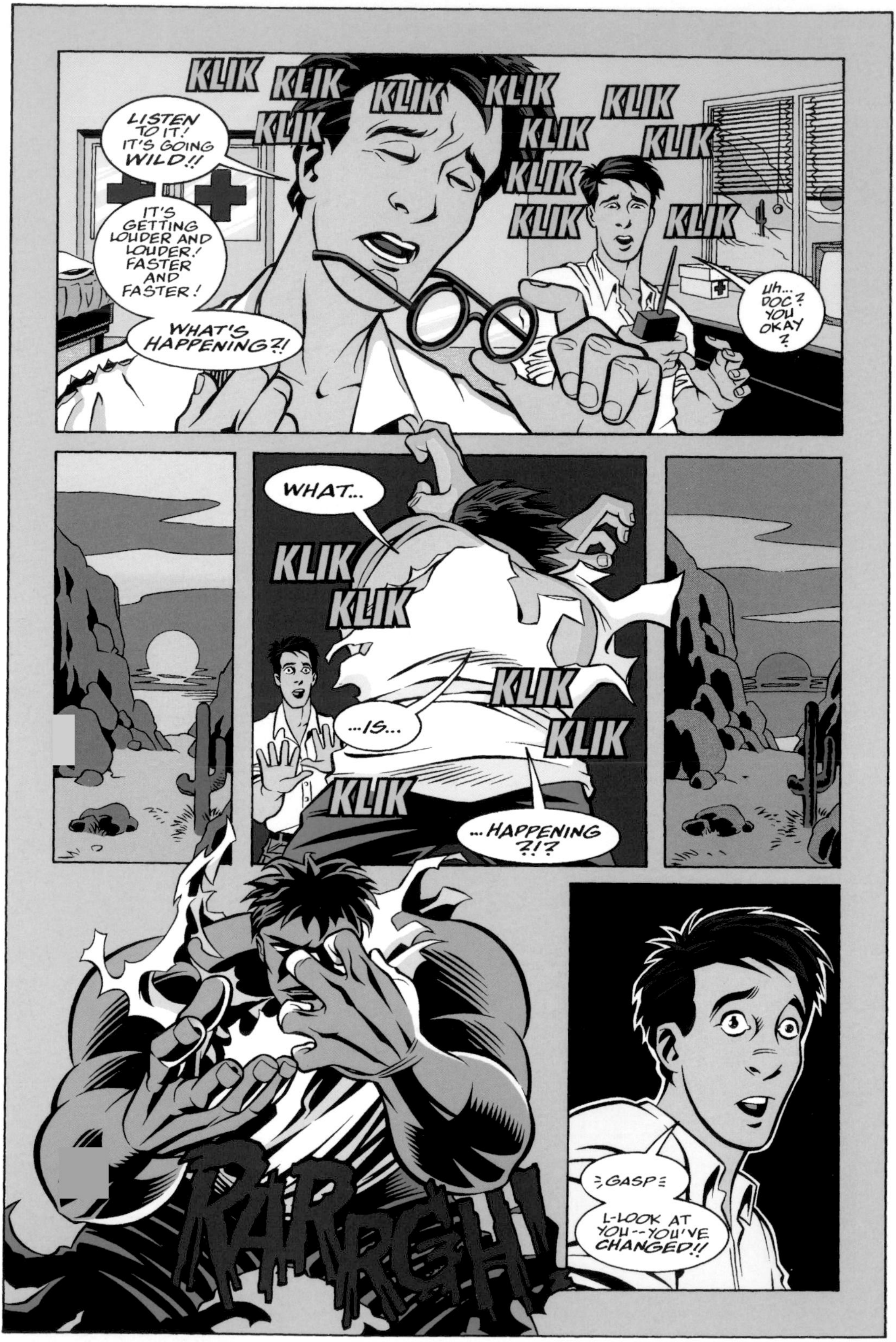
KLIK KLIK KLIK KLIK KLIK
KLIK
LISTEN TO IT! IT'S GOING WILD!!
IT'S GETTING LOUDER AND LOUDER! FASTER AND FASTER!
WHAT'S HAPPENING?!
KLIK KLIK KLIK KLIK KLIK KLIK
UH... DOC? YOU OKAY?
WHAT...
KLIK
KLIK
...IS...
KLIK
KLIK
KLIK
...HAPPENING?!?
RARRGH!
GASP
L-LOOK AT YOU--YOU'VE CHANGED!!

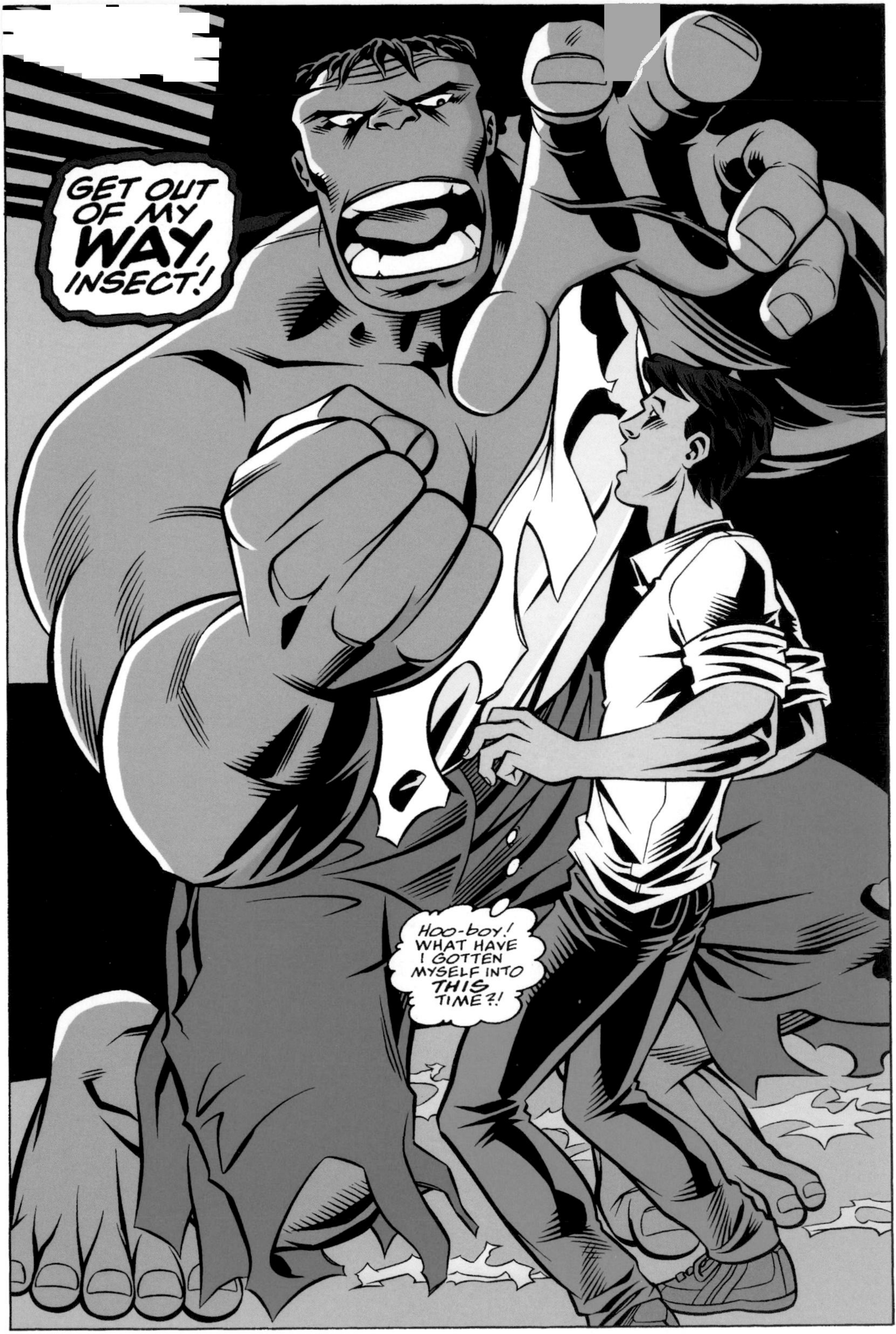
GET OUT OF MY WAY, INSECT!
HOO-BOY! WHAT HAVE I GOTTEN MYSELF INTO THIS TIME?!

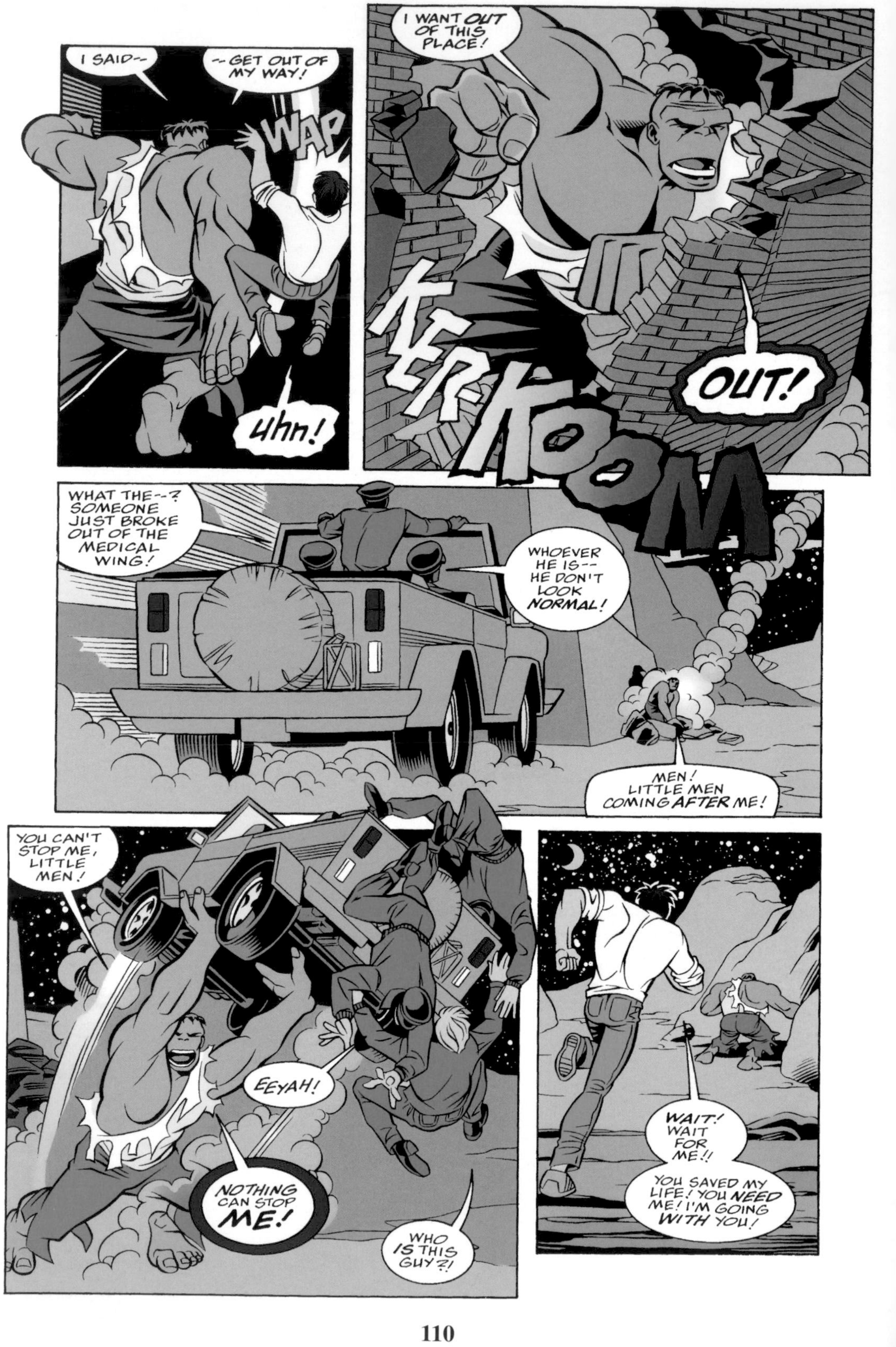
I SAID--
--GET OUT OF MY WAY!
WAP
uhn!
I WANT OUT OF THIS PLACE!
KERKOOOM
OUT!
WHAT THE--? SOMEONE JUST BROKE OUT OF THE MEDICAL WING!
WHOEVER HE IS--HE DON'T LOOK NORMAL!
MEN! LITTLE MEN COMING AFTER ME!
YOU CAN'T STOP ME, LITTLE MEN!
EEYAH!
NOTHING CAN STOP ME!
WHO IS THIS GUY?!
WAIT! WAIT FOR ME!!
YOU SAVED MY LIFE! YOU NEED ME! I'M GOING WITH YOU!

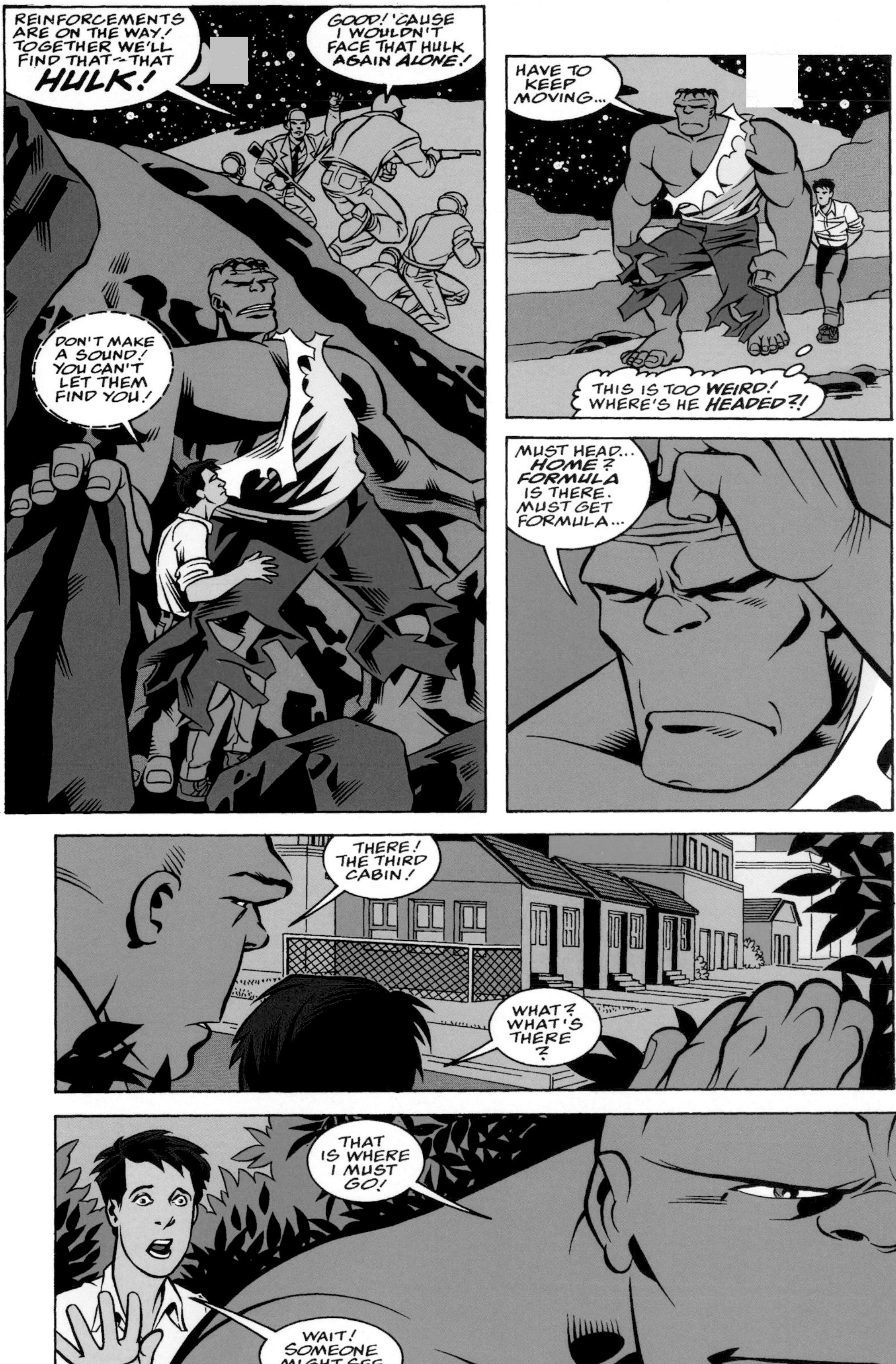
REINFORCEMENTS ARE ON THE WAY! TOGETHER WE'LL FIND THAT--THAT HULK!
GOOD! 'CAUSE I WOULDN'T FACE THAT HULK AGAIN ALONE!
DON'T MAKE A SOUND! YOU CAN'T LET THEM FIND YOU!
HAVE TO KEEP MOVING...
THIS IS TOO WEIRD! WHERE'S HE HEADED?!
MUST HEAD... HOME? FORMULA IS THERE. MUST GET FORMULA...
THERE! THE THIRD CABIN!
WHAT? WHAT'S THERE?
THAT IS WHERE I MUST GO!
WAIT! SOMEONE MIGHT SEE YOU!

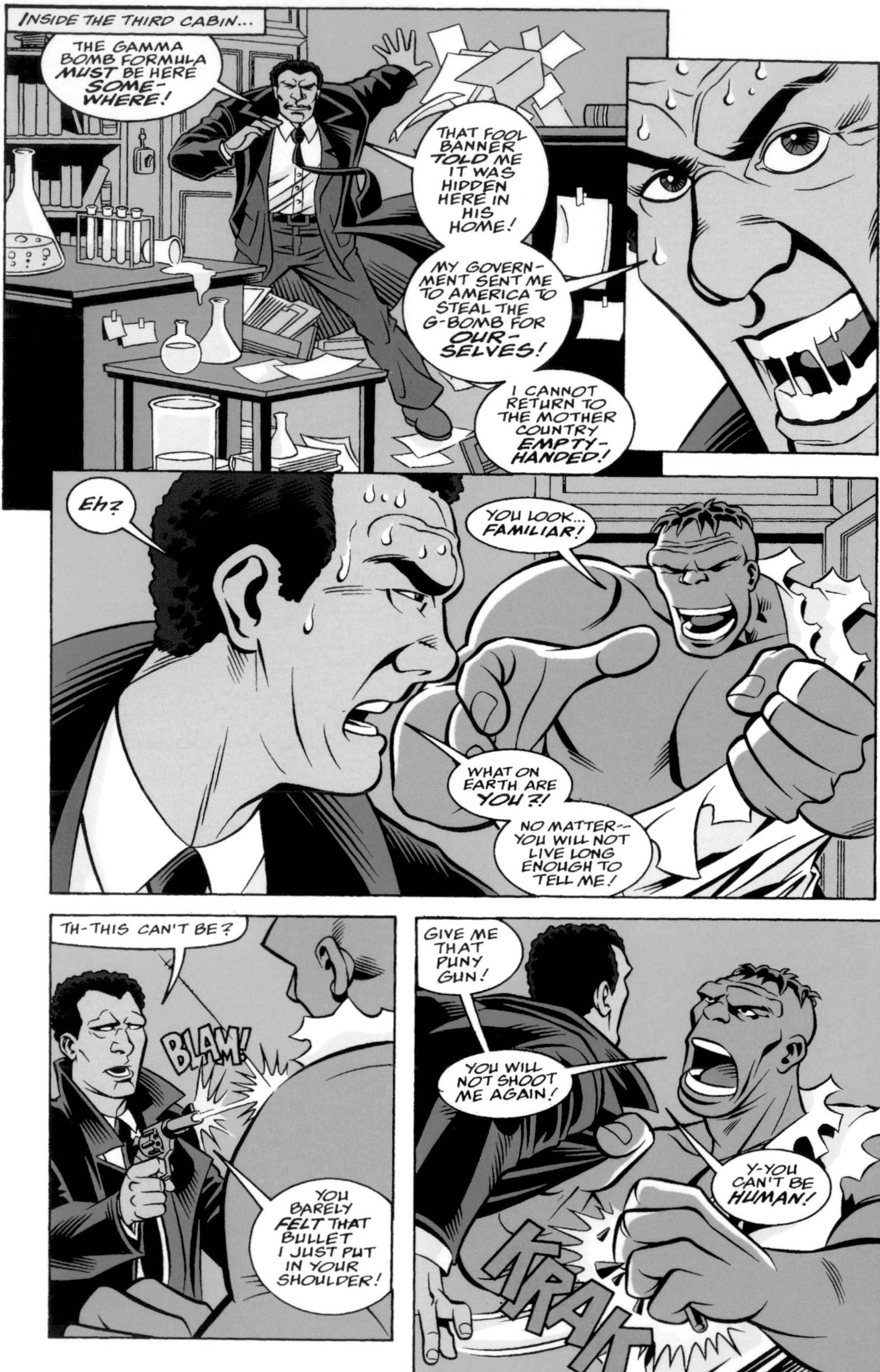
INSIDE THE THIRD CABIN...
THE GAMMA BOMB FORMULA MUST BE HERE SOME-WHERE!
THAT FOOL BANNER TOLD ME IT WAS HIDDEN HERE IN HIS HOME!
MY GOVERNMENT SENT ME TO AMERICA TO STEAL THE G-BOMB FOR OUR-SELVES!
I CANNOT RETURN TO THE MOTHER COUNTRY EMPTY-HANDED!
Eh?
YOU LOOK... FAMILIAR!
WHAT ON EARTH ARE YOU?!
NO MATTER-- YOU WILL NOT LIVE LONG ENOUGH TO TELL ME!
TH-THIS CAN'T BE?
BLAM!
YOU BARELY FELT THAT BULLET I JUST PUT IN YOUR SHOULDER!
GIVE ME THAT PUNY GUN!
YOU WILL NOT SHOOT ME AGAIN!
Y-YOU CAN'T BE HUMAN!
KRAK

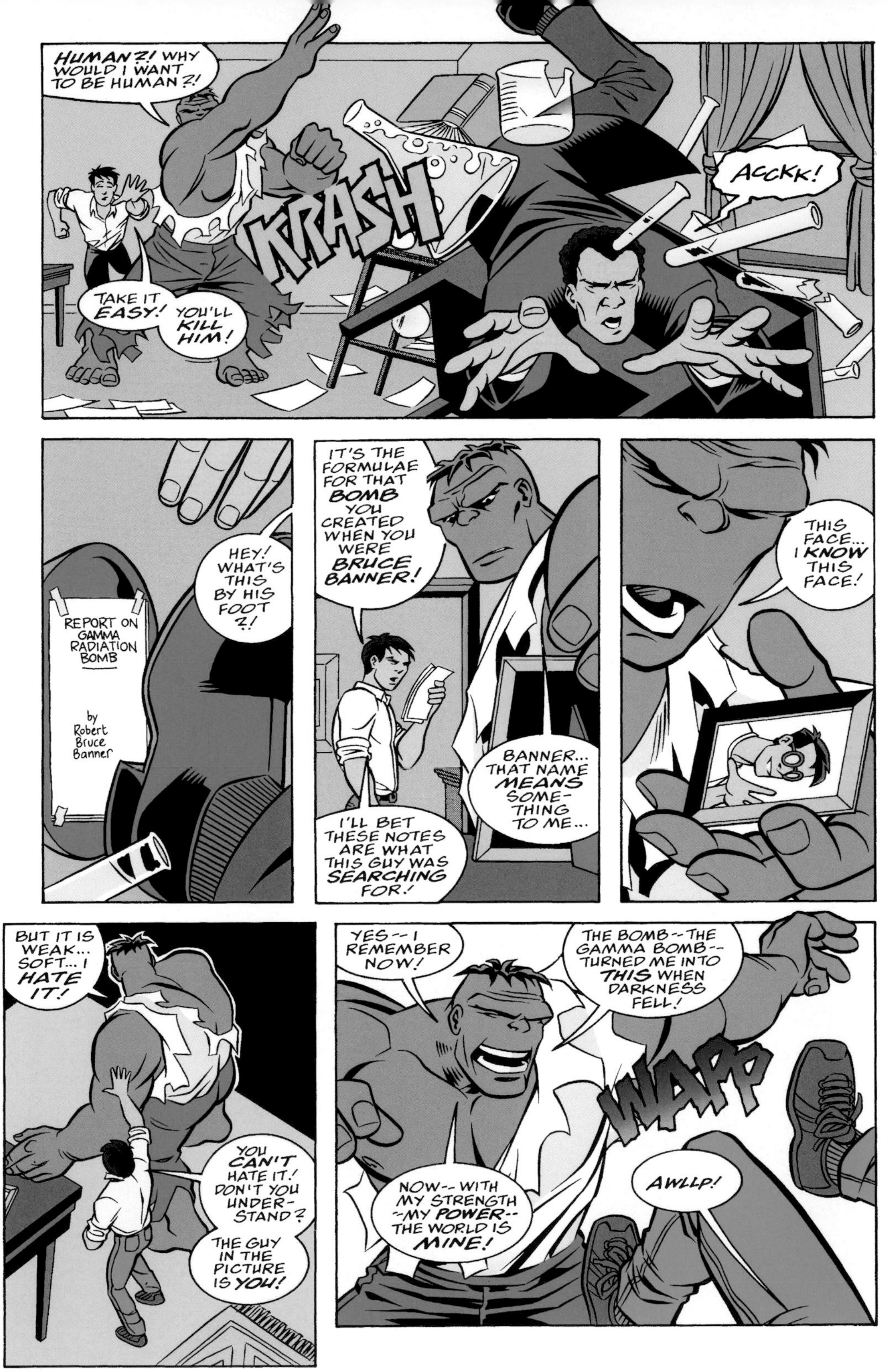
HUMAN?! WHY WOULD I WANT TO BE HUMAN?!
KRASH
ACCKK!
TAKE IT EASY!
YOU'LL KILL HIM!
HEY! WHAT'S THIS BY HIS FOOT?!
REPORT ON GAMMA RADIATION BOMB
by Robert Bruce Banner
IT'S THE FORMULAE FOR THAT BOMB YOU CREATED WHEN YOU WERE BRUCE BANNER!
BANNER... THAT NAME MEANS SOMETHING TO ME...
I'LL BET THESE NOTES ARE WHAT THIS GUY WAS SEARCHING FOR!
THIS FACE... I KNOW THIS FACE!
BUT IT IS WEAK... SOFT... I HATE IT!
YOU CAN'T HATE IT! DON'T YOU UNDERSTAND?
THE GUY IN THE PICTURE IS YOU!
YES--I REMEMBER NOW!
THE BOMB--THE GAMMA BOMB--TURNED ME INTO THIS WHEN DARKNESS FELL!
WAPP
NOW--WITH MY STRENGTH--MY POWER--THE WORLD IS MINE!
AWLLP!

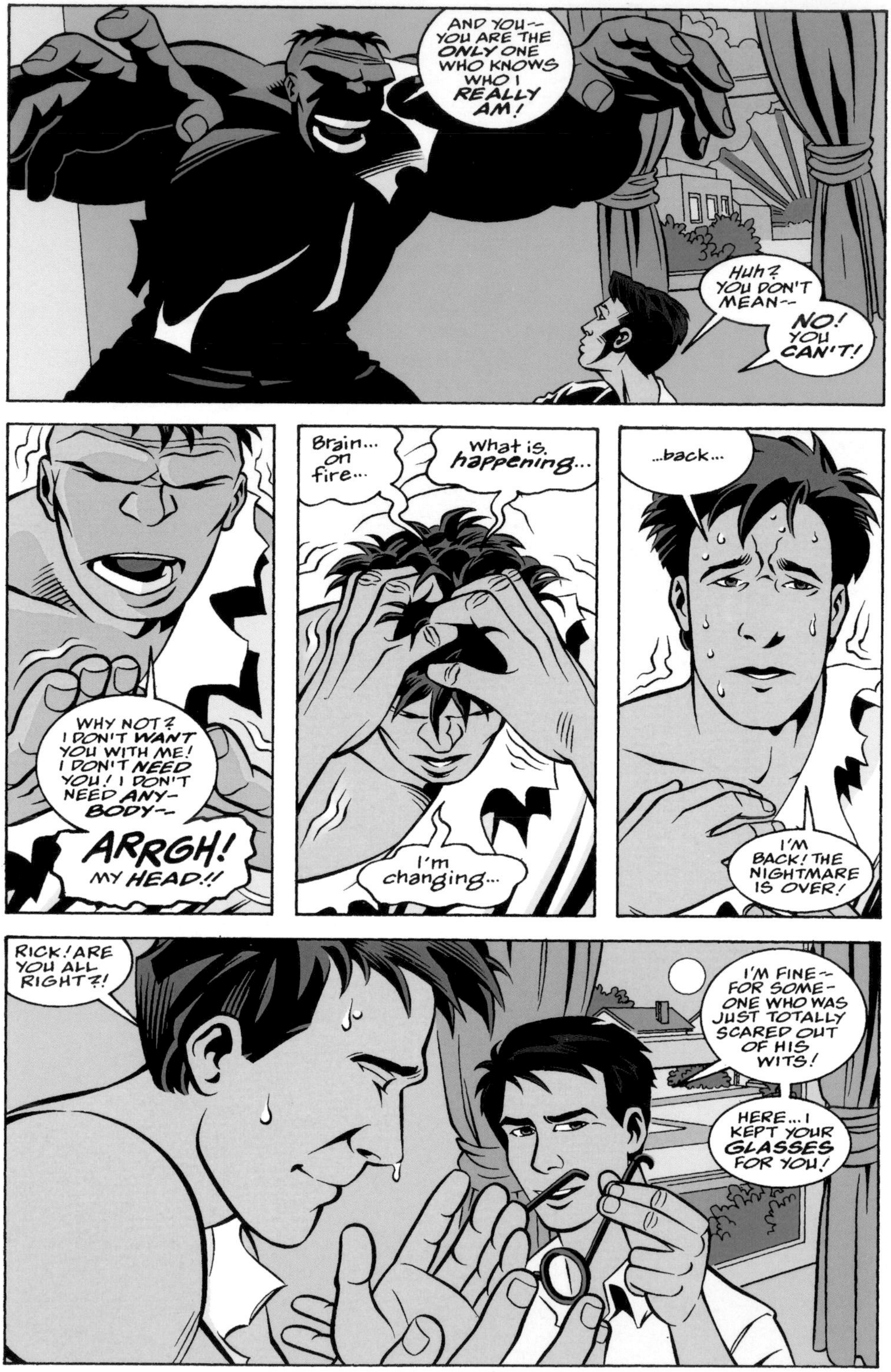
AND YOU--
YOU ARE THE ONLY ONE WHO KNOWS WHO I REALLY AM!
HUH? YOU DON'T MEAN--
NO! YOU CAN'T!
WHY NOT? I DON'T WANT YOU WITH ME! I DON'T NEED YOU! I DON'T NEED ANY-BODY--
ARRGH! MY HEAD!!
Brain... on fire...
What is happening...
I'm changing...
...back...
I'M BACK! THE NIGHTMARE IS OVER!
RICK! ARE YOU ALL RIGHT?!
I'M FINE--FOR SOME-ONE WHO WAS JUST TOTALLY SCARED OUT OF HIS WITS!
HERE... I KEPT YOUR GLASSES FOR YOU!

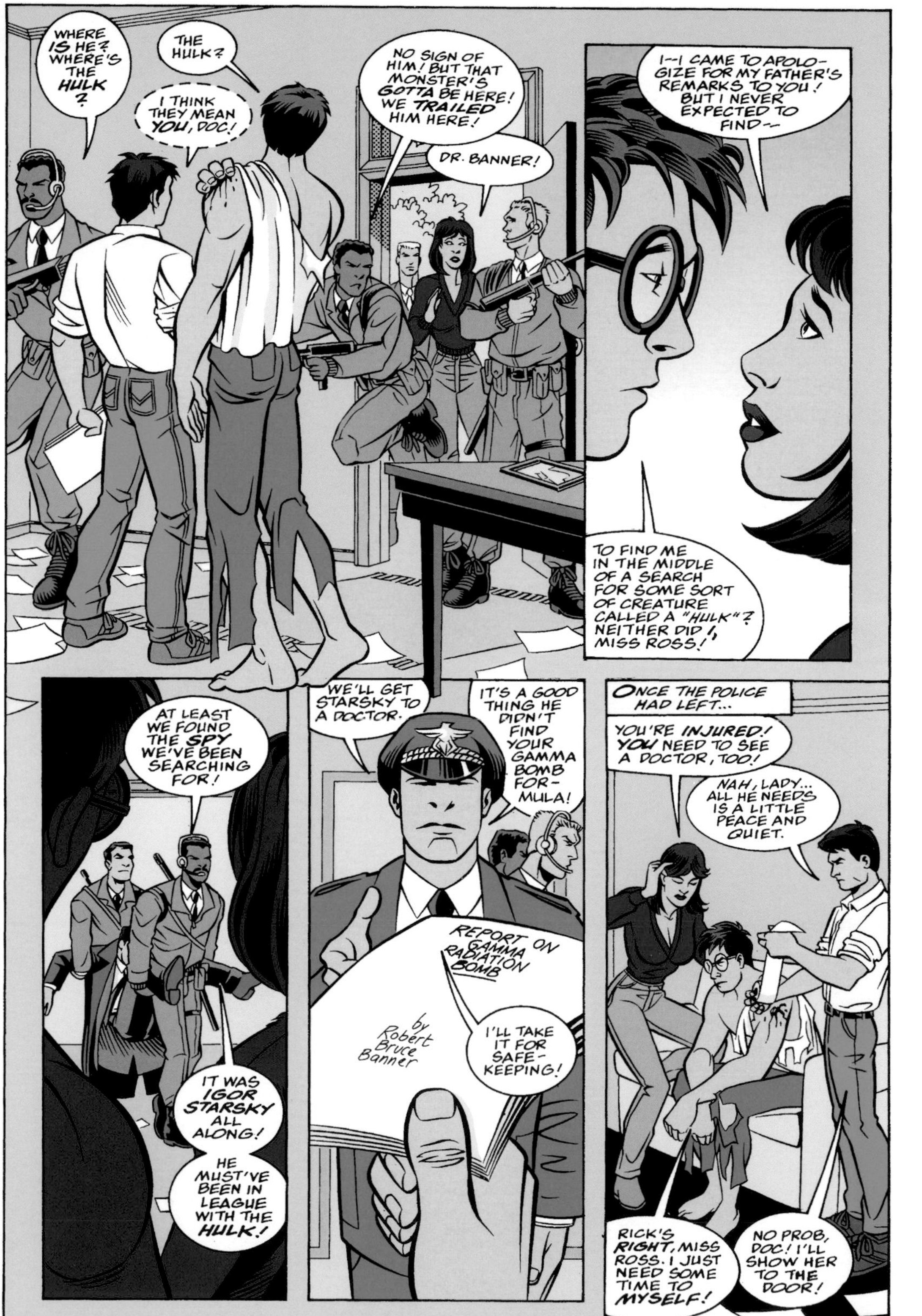
WHERE IS HE? WHERE'S THE HULK?
THE HULK?
I THINK THEY MEAN YOU, DOC!
NO SIGN OF HIM! BUT THAT MONSTER'S GOTTA BE HERE! WE TRAILED HIM HERE!
DR. BANNER!
I--I CAME TO APOLOGIZE FOR MY FATHER'S REMARKS TO YOU! BUT I NEVER EXPECTED TO FIND--
TO FIND ME IN THE MIDDLE OF A SEARCH FOR SOME SORT OF CREATURE CALLED A "HULK"? NEITHER DID I, MISS ROSS!
AT LEAST WE FOUND THE SPY WE'VE BEEN SEARCHING FOR!
IT WAS IGOR STARSKY ALL ALONG!
HE MUST'VE BEEN IN LEAGUE WITH THE HULK!
WE'LL GET STARSKY TO A DOCTOR.
IT'S A GOOD THING HE DIDN'T FIND YOUR GAMMA BOMB FORMULA!
REPORT ON GAMMA RADIATION BOMB
by Robert Bruce Banner
I'LL TAKE IT FOR SAFE-KEEPING!
ONCE THE POLICE HAD LEFT...
YOU'RE INJURED! YOU NEED TO SEE A DOCTOR, TOO!
NAH, LADY... ALL HE NEEDS IS A LITTLE PEACE AND QUIET.
RICK'S RIGHT, MISS ROSS. I JUST NEED SOME TIME TO MYSELF!
NO PROB, DOC! I'LL SHOW HER TO THE DOOR!

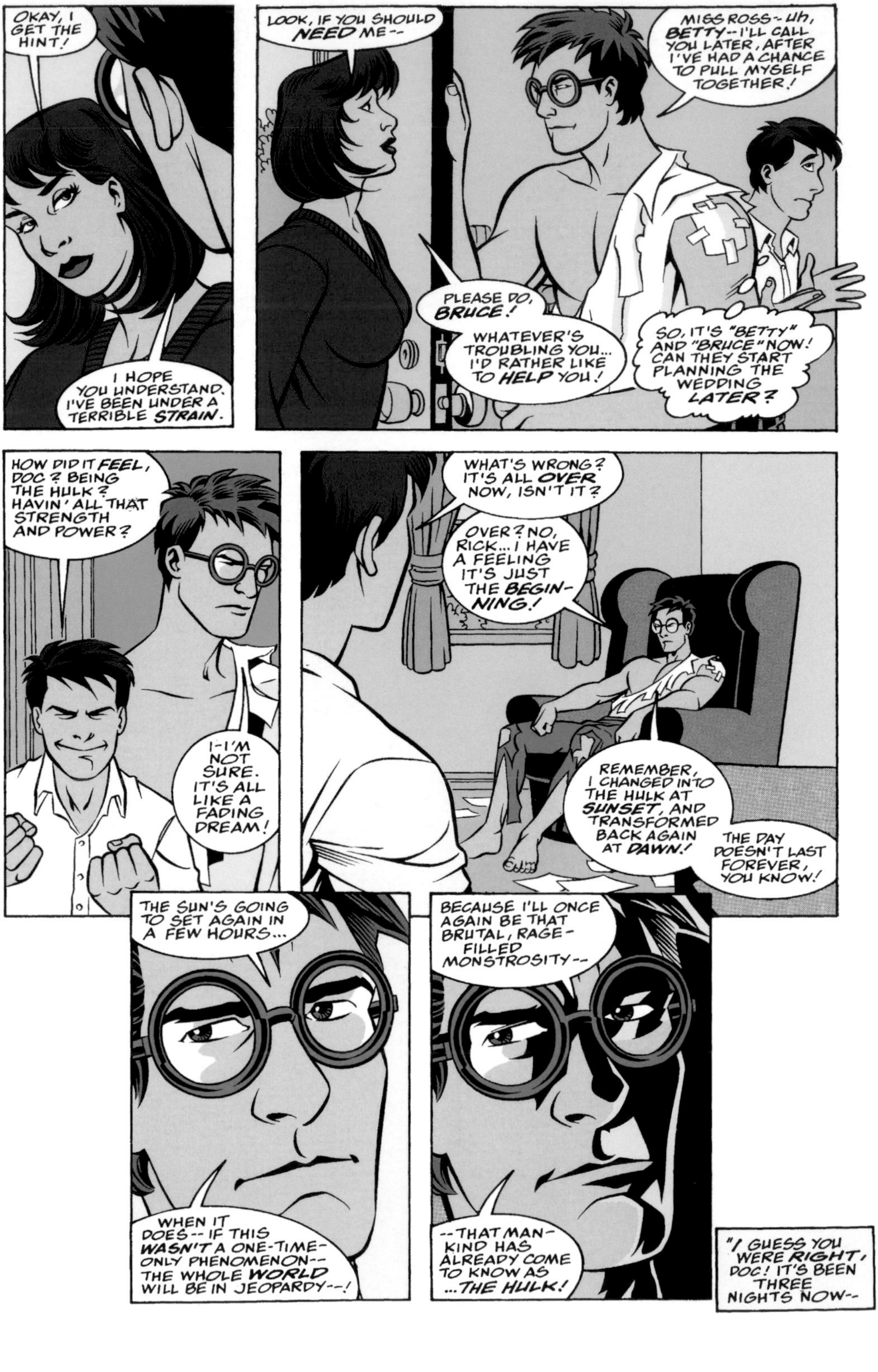
OKAY, I GET THE HINT!
I HOPE YOU UNDERSTAND. I'VE BEEN UNDER A TERRIBLE STRAIN.
LOOK, IF YOU SHOULD NEED ME--
MISS ROSS-- UH, BETTY-- I'LL CALL YOU LATER, AFTER I'VE HAD A CHANCE TO PULL MYSELF TOGETHER!
PLEASE DO, BRUCE!
WHATEVER'S TROUBLING YOU... I'D RATHER LIKE TO HELP YOU!
SO, IT'S "BETTY" AND "BRUCE" NOW! CAN THEY START PLANNING THE WEDDING LATER?
HOW DID IT FEEL, DOC? BEING THE HULK? HAVIN' ALL THAT STRENGTH AND POWER?
I-I'M NOT SURE. IT'S ALL LIKE A FADING DREAM!
WHAT'S WRONG? IT'S ALL OVER NOW, ISN'T IT?
OVER? NO, RICK... I HAVE A FEELING IT'S JUST THE BEGIN-NING!
REMEMBER, I CHANGED INTO THE HULK AT SUNSET, AND TRANSFORMED BACK AGAIN AT DAWN!
THE DAY DOESN'T LAST FOREVER, YOU KNOW!
THE SUN'S GOING TO SET AGAIN IN A FEW HOURS...
WHEN IT DOES-- IF THIS WASN'T A ONE-TIME-ONLY PHENOMENON-- THE WHOLE WORLD WILL BE IN JEOPARDY--!
BECAUSE I'LL ONCE AGAIN BE THAT BRUTAL, RAGE-FILLED MONSTROSITY--
--THAT MAN-KIND HAS ALREADY COME TO KNOW AS ...THE HULK!
"I GUESS YOU WERE RIGHT, DOC! IT'S BEEN THREE NIGHTS NOW--

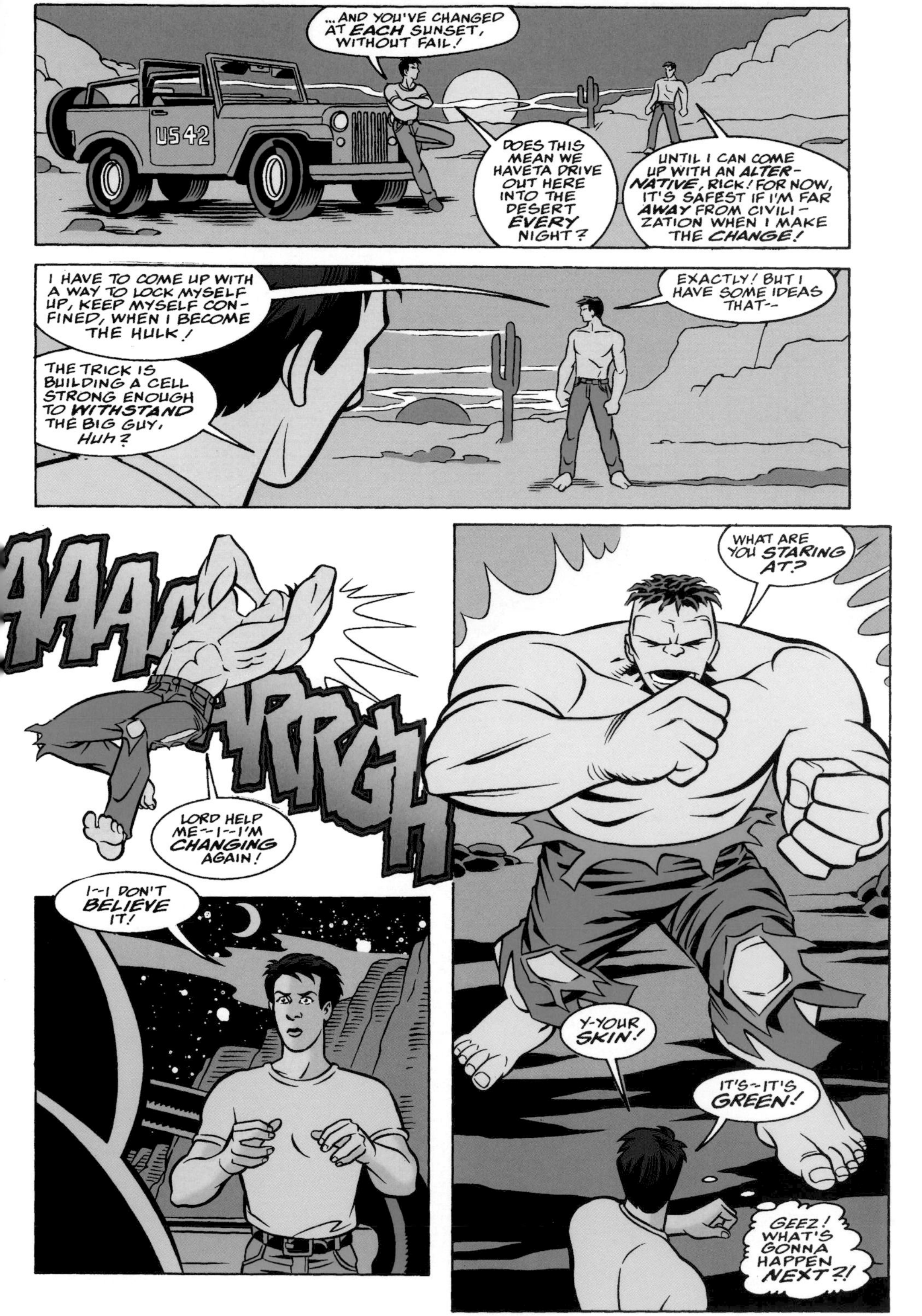
...AND YOU'VE CHANGED AT EACH SUNSET, WITHOUT FAIL!
US 42
DOES THIS MEAN WE HAVETA DRIVE OUT HERE INTO THE DESERT EVERY NIGHT?
UNTIL I CAN COME UP WITH AN ALTER-NATIVE, RICK! FOR NOW, IT'S SAFEST IF I'M FAR AWAY FROM CIVILI-ZATION WHEN I MAKE THE CHANGE!
I HAVE TO COME UP WITH A WAY TO LOCK MYSELF UP, KEEP MYSELF CON-FINED, WHEN I BECOME THE HULK!
THE TRICK IS BUILDING A CELL STRONG ENOUGH TO WITHSTAND THE BIG GUY, Huh?
EXACTLY! BUT I HAVE SOME IDEAS THAT--
AAAARRGH
LORD HELP ME--I--I'M CHANGING AGAIN!
WHAT ARE YOU STARING AT?
I--I DON'T BELIEVE IT!
Y-YOUR SKIN!
IT'S--IT'S GREEN!
GEEZ! WHAT'S GONNA HAPPEN NEXT?!

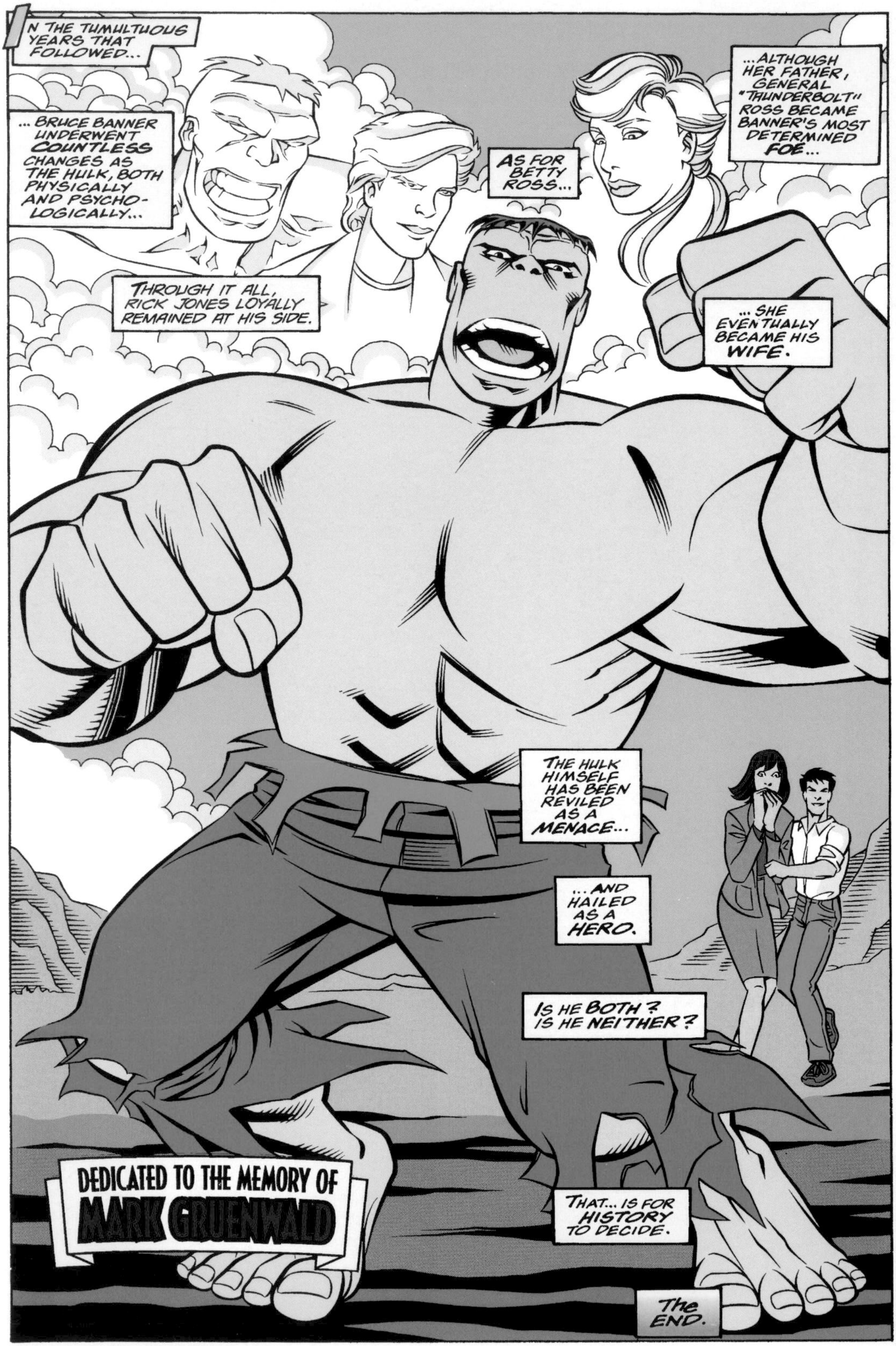
IN THE TUMULTUOUS YEARS THAT FOLLOWED...
...BRUCE BANNER UNDERWENT COUNTLESS CHANGES AS THE HULK, BOTH PHYSICALLY AND PSYCHO-LOGICALLY...
THROUGH IT ALL, RICK JONES LOYALLY REMAINED AT HIS SIDE.
AS FOR BETTY ROSS...
...ALTHOUGH HER FATHER, GENERAL "THUNDERBOLT" ROSS BECAME BANNER'S MOST DETERMINED FOE...
...SHE EVENTUALLY BECAME HIS WIFE.
THE HULK HIMSELF HAS BEEN REVILED AS A MENACE...
...AND HAILED AS A HERO.
IS HE BOTH? IS HE NEITHER?
THAT... IS FOR HISTORY TO DECIDE.
DEDICATED TO THE MEMORY OF MARK GRUENWALD
The END.

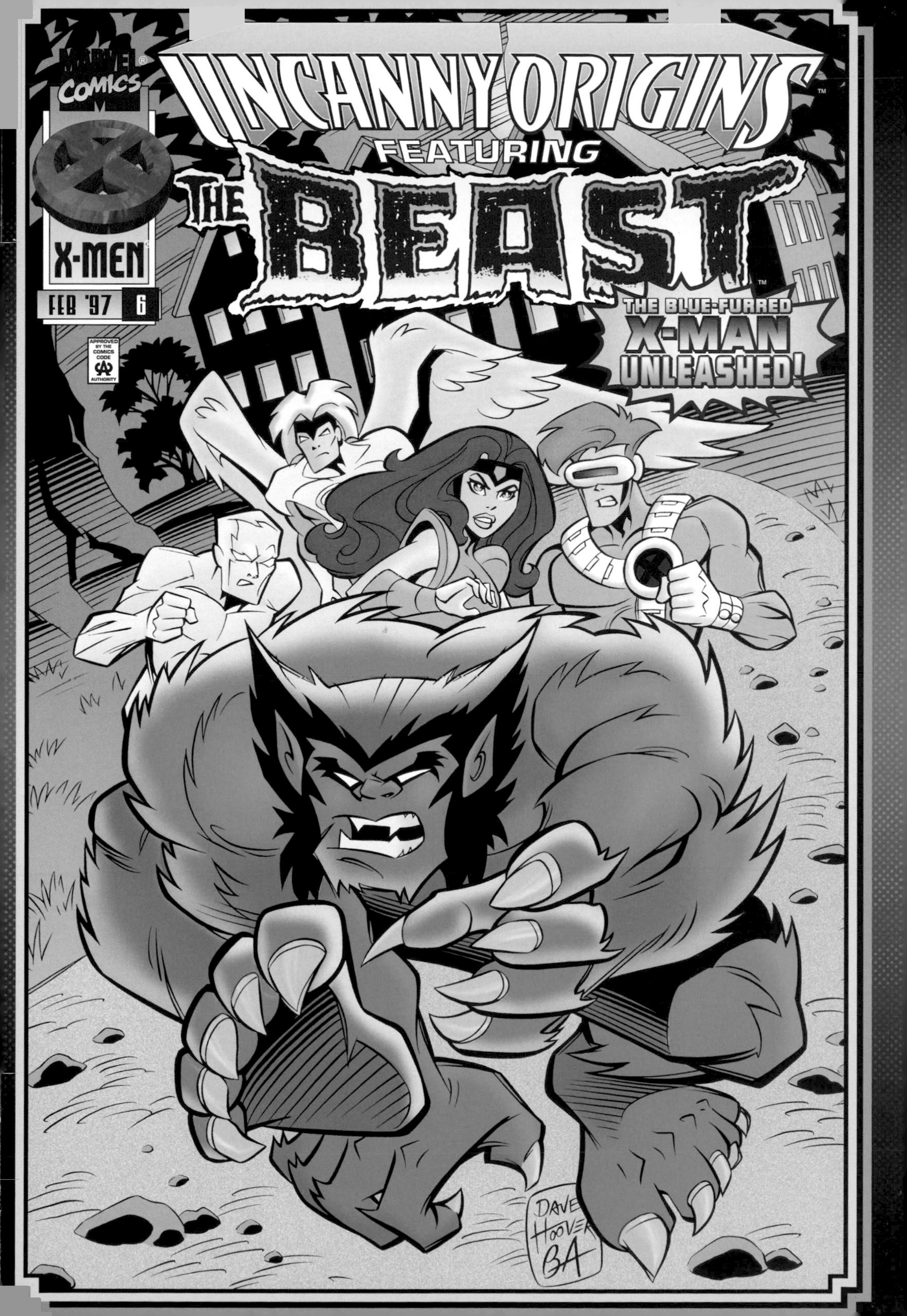
MARVEL COMICS
UNCANNY ORIGINS
FEATURING
THE BEAST
X-MEN
FEB '97 6
APPROVED BY THE COMICS CODE AUTHORITY
THE BLUE-FURRED X-MAN UNLEASHED!
DAVE HOOVER BA

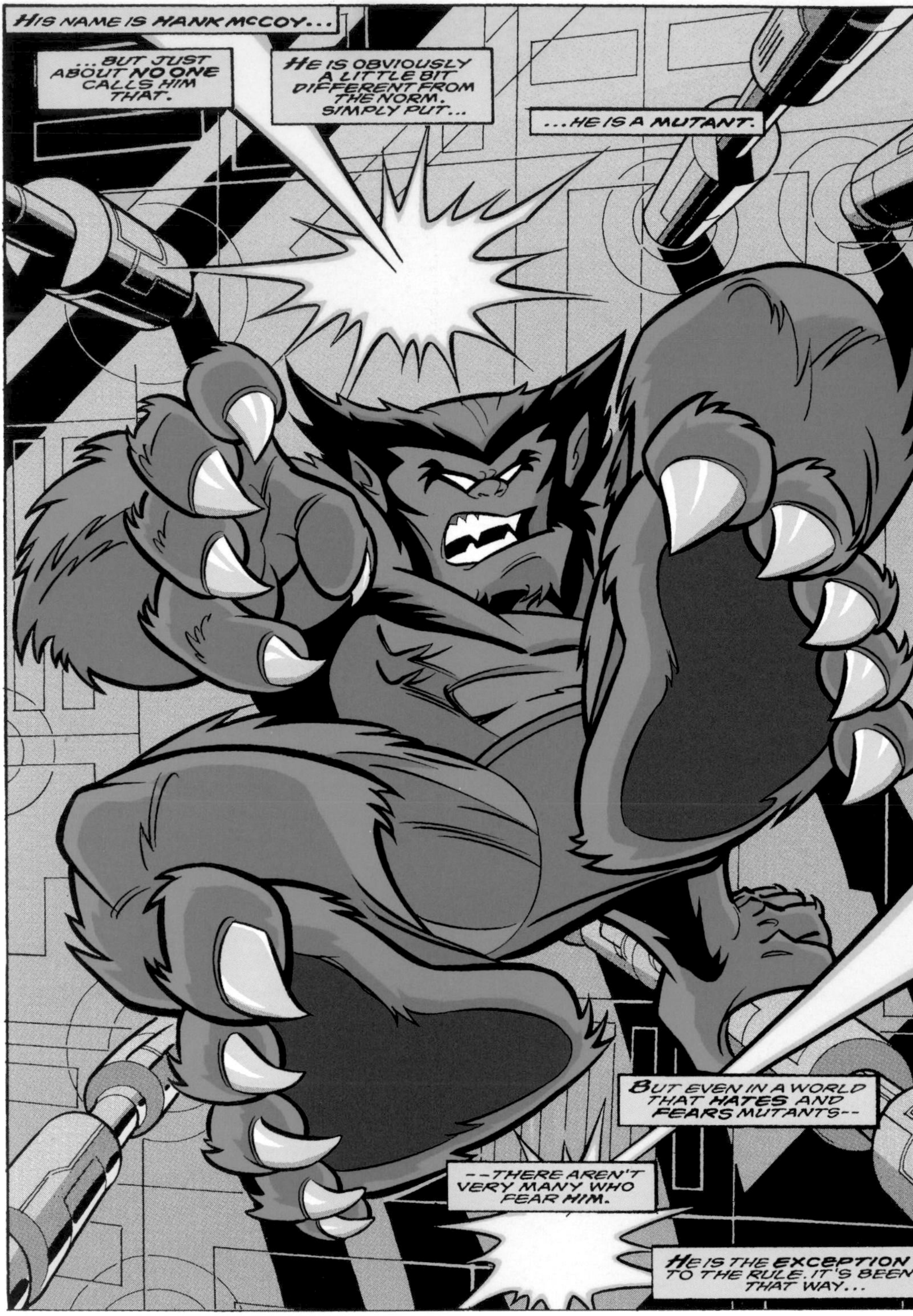
HIS NAME IS HANK McCOY...
...BUT JUST ABOUT NO ONE CALLS HIM THAT.
HE IS OBVIOUSLY A LITTLE BIT DIFFERENT FROM THE NORM. SIMPLY PUT...
...HE IS A MUTANT.
BUT EVEN IN A WORLD THAT HATES AND FEARS MUTANTS--
--THERE AREN'T VERY MANY WHO FEAR HIM.
HE IS THE EXCEPTION TO THE RULE. IT'S BEEN THAT WAY...

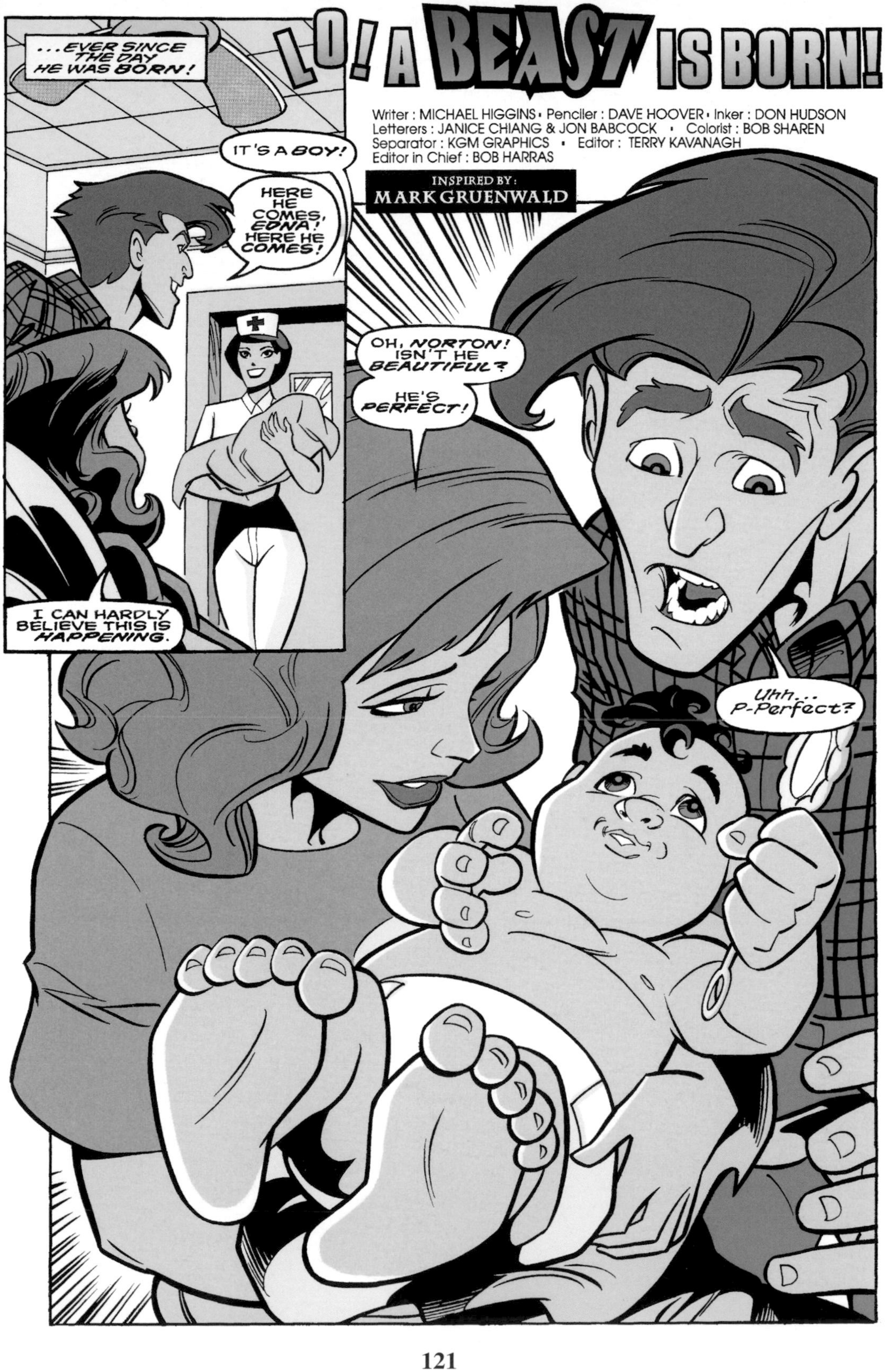
LO! A BEAST IS BORN!
Writer : MICHAEL HIGGINS • Penciler : DAVE HOOVER • Inker : DON HUDSON
Letterers : JANICE CHIANG & JON BABCOCK • Colorist : BOB SHAREN
Separator : KGM GRAPHICS • Editor : TERRY KAVANAGH
Editor in Chief : BOB HARRAS
INSPIRED BY: MARK GRUENWALD
...EVER SINCE THE DAY HE WAS BORN!
IT'S A BOY!
HERE HE COMES, EDNA! HERE HE COMES!
I CAN HARDLY BELIEVE THIS IS HAPPENING.
OH, NORTON! ISN'T HE BEAUTIFUL?
HE'S PERFECT!
Uhh... P-Perfect?

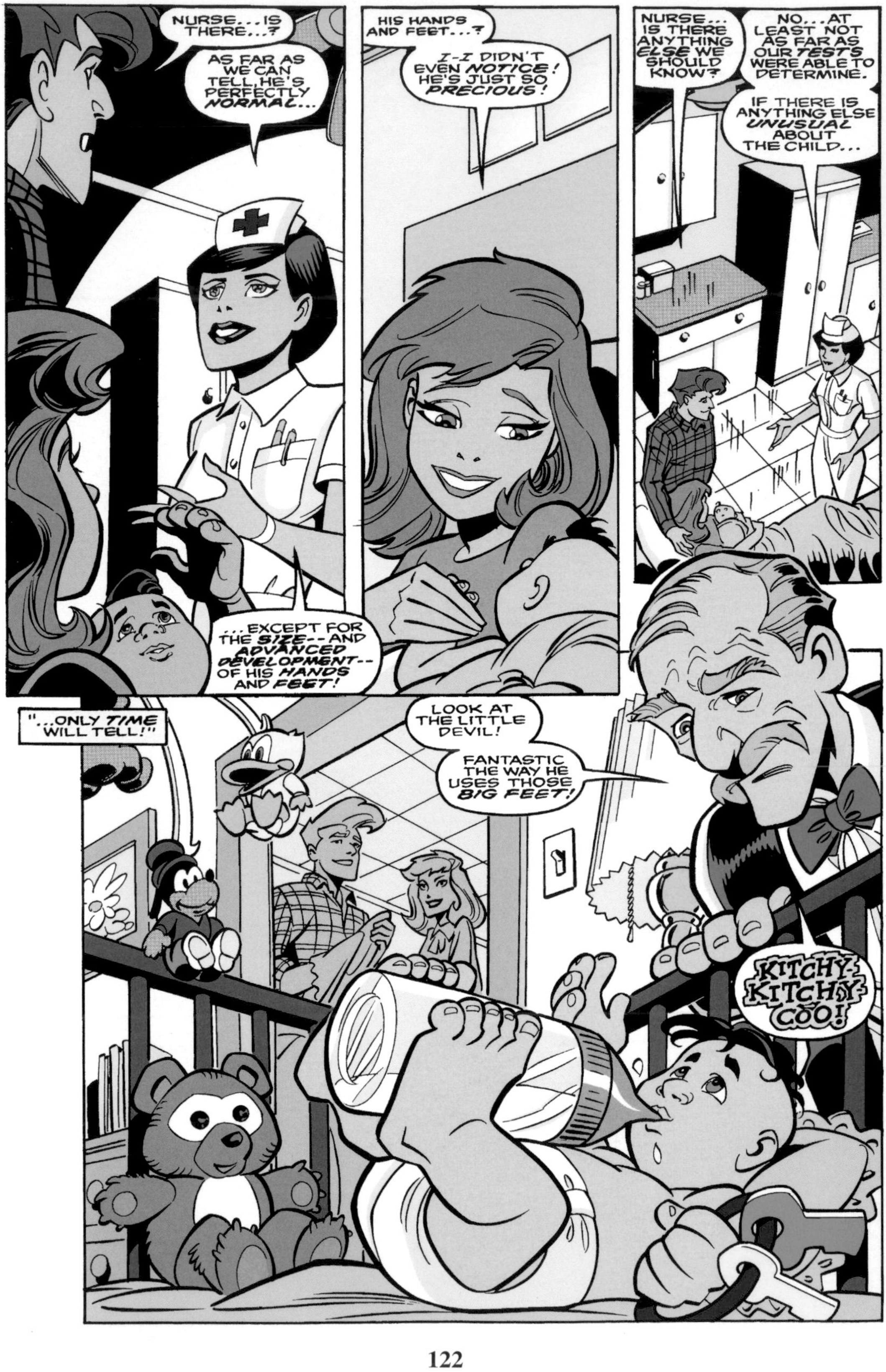
NURSE...IS THERE...?
AS FAR AS WE CAN TELL, HE'S PERFECTLY NORMAL...
...EXCEPT FOR THE SIZE--AND ADVANCED DEVELOPMENT--OF HIS HANDS AND FEET!
HIS HANDS AND FEET...?
I-I DIDN'T EVEN NOTICE! HE'S JUST SO PRECIOUS!
NURSE... IS THERE ANYTHING ELSE WE SHOULD KNOW?
NO...AT LEAST NOT AS FAR AS OUR TESTS WERE ABLE TO DETERMINE.
IF THERE IS ANYTHING ELSE UNUSUAL ABOUT THE CHILD...
"...ONLY TIME WILL TELL!"
LOOK AT THE LITTLE DEVIL!
FANTASTIC THE WAY HE USES THOSE BIG FEET!
KITCHY-KITCHY-COO!

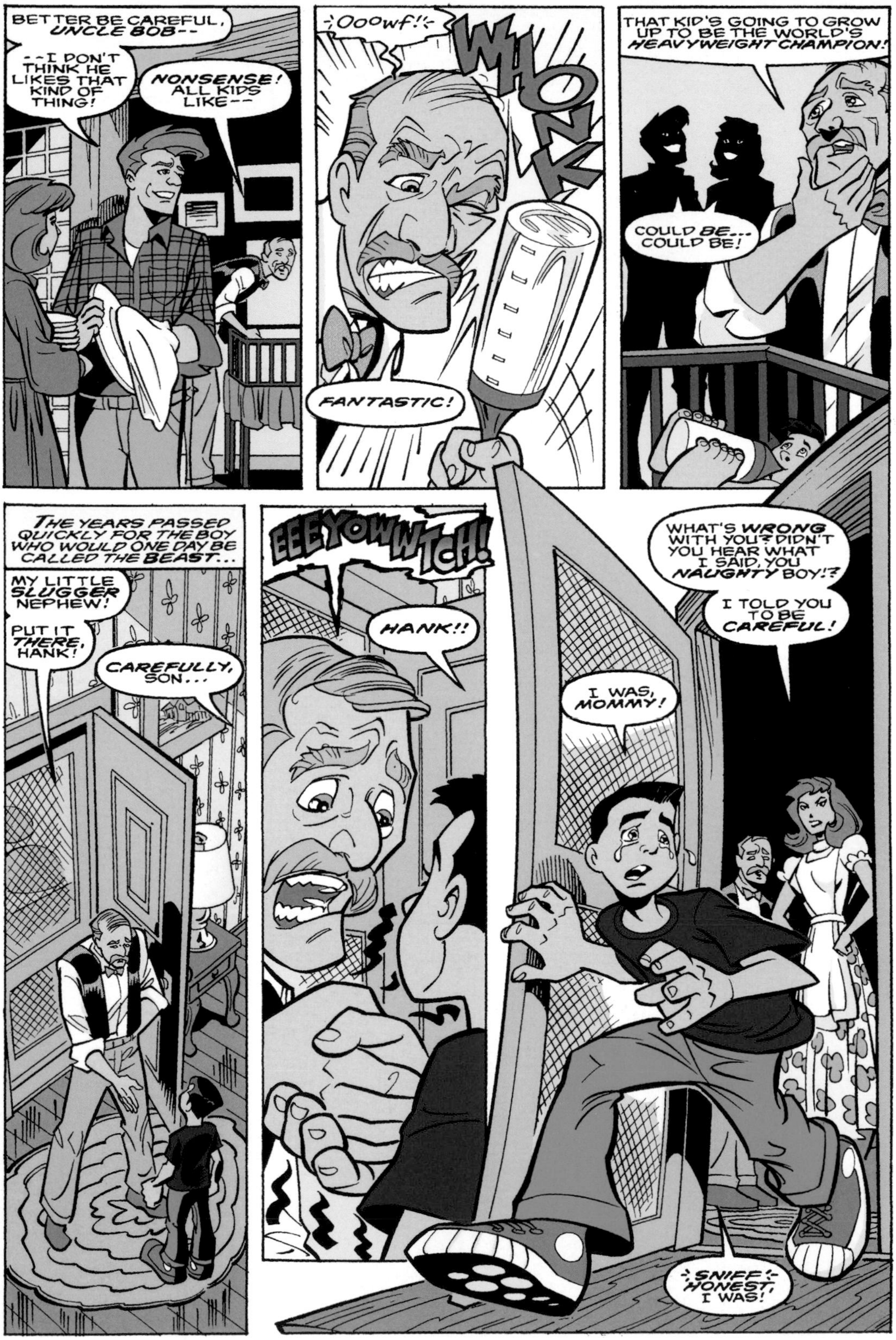
BETTER BE CAREFUL, UNCLE BOB--
--I DON'T THINK HE LIKES THAT KIND OF THING!
NONSENSE! ALL KIDS LIKE--
OOOWF!
WHONK
FANTASTIC!
THAT KID'S GOING TO GROW UP TO BE THE WORLD'S HEAVYWEIGHT CHAMPION!
COULD BE... COULD BE!
THE YEARS PASSED QUICKLY FOR THE BOY WHO WOULD ONE DAY BE CALLED THE BEAST...
MY LITTLE SLUGGER NEPHEW!
PUT IT THERE, HANK!
CAREFULLY, SON...
EEEYOWWTCH!
HANK!!
WHAT'S WRONG WITH YOU? DIDN'T YOU HEAR WHAT I SAID, YOU NAUGHTY BOY!?
I TOLD YOU TO BE CAREFUL!
I WAS, MOMMY!
SNIFF HONEST, I WAS!

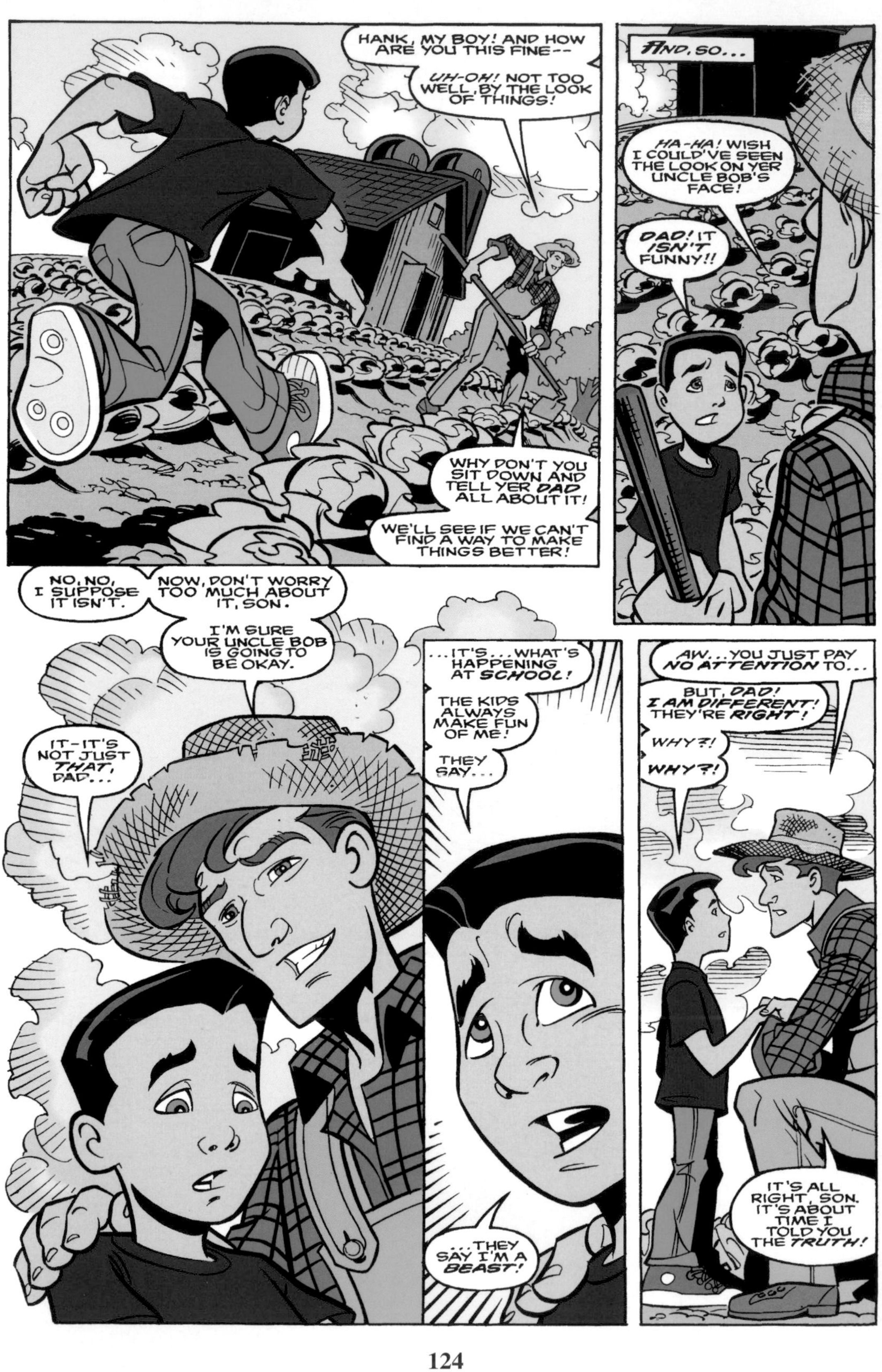
HANK, MY BOY! AND HOW ARE YOU THIS FINE--
UH-OH! NOT TOO WELL, BY THE LOOK OF THINGS!
WHY DON'T YOU SIT DOWN AND TELL YER DAD ALL ABOUT IT!
WE'LL SEE IF WE CAN'T FIND A WAY TO MAKE THINGS BETTER!
AND, SO...
HA-HA! WISH I COULD'VE SEEN THE LOOK ON YER UNCLE BOB'S FACE!
DAD! IT ISN'T FUNNY!!
NO, NO, I SUPPOSE IT ISN'T.
NOW, DON'T WORRY TOO MUCH ABOUT IT, SON.
I'M SURE YOUR UNCLE BOB IS GOING TO BE OKAY.
IT-IT'S NOT JUST THAT, DAD...
...IT'S...WHAT'S HAPPENING AT SCHOOL!
THE KIDS ALWAYS MAKE FUN OF ME!
THEY SAY...
...THEY SAY I'M A BEAST!
AW...YOU JUST PAY NO ATTENTION TO...
BUT, DAD! I AM DIFFERENT! THEY'RE RIGHT!
WHY?!
WHY?!
IT'S ALL RIGHT, SON. IT'S ABOUT TIME I TOLD YOU THE TRUTH!

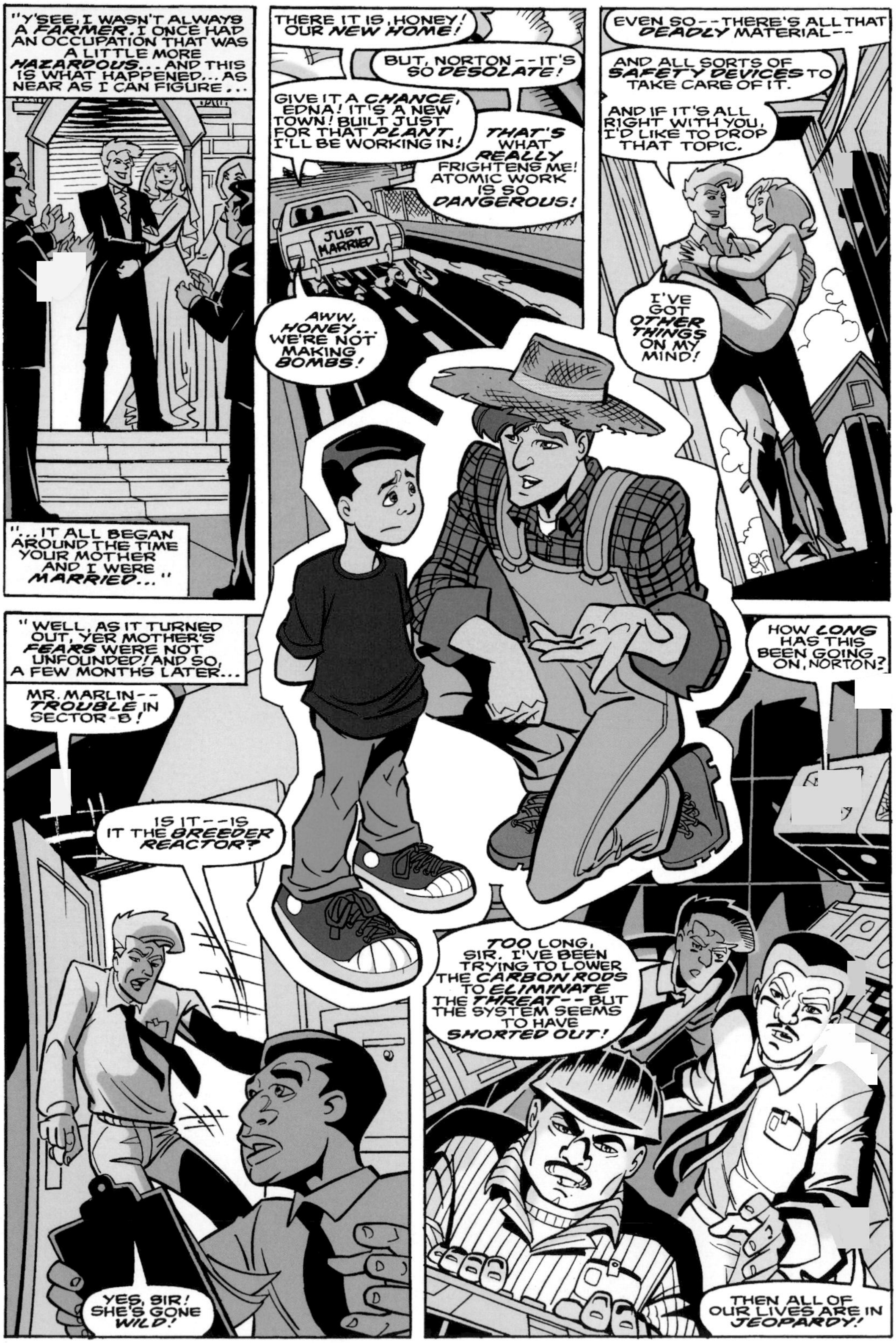
"Y'SEE, I WASN'T ALWAYS A FARMER. I ONCE HAD AN OCCUPATION THAT WAS A LITTLE MORE HAZARDOUS... AND THIS IS WHAT HAPPENED... AS NEAR AS I CAN FIGURE...
"...IT ALL BEGAN AROUND THE TIME YOUR MOTHER AND I WERE MARRIED..."
THERE IT IS, HONEY! OUR NEW HOME!
BUT, NORTON--IT'S SO DESOLATE!
GIVE IT A CHANCE, EDNA! IT'S A NEW TOWN! BUILT JUST FOR THAT PLANT I'LL BE WORKING IN!
THAT'S WHAT REALLY FRIGHTENS ME! ATOMIC WORK IS SO DANGEROUS!
JUST MARRIED
AWW, HONEY... WE'RE NOT MAKING BOMBS!
EVEN SO--THERE'S ALL THAT DEADLY MATERIAL--
AND ALL SORTS OF SAFETY DEVICES TO TAKE CARE OF IT.
AND IF IT'S ALL RIGHT WITH YOU, I'D LIKE TO DROP THAT TOPIC.
I'VE GOT OTHER THINGS ON MY MIND!
" WELL, AS IT TURNED OUT, YER MOTHER'S FEARS WERE NOT UNFOUNDED! AND SO, A FEW MONTHS LATER...
MR. MARLIN--TROUBLE IN SECTOR-B!
IS IT--IS IT THE BREEDER REACTOR?
YES, SIR! SHE'S GONE WILD!
HOW LONG HAS THIS BEEN GOING ON, NORTON?
TOO LONG, SIR. I'VE BEEN TRYING TO LOWER THE CARBON RODS TO ELIMINATE THE THREAT--BUT THE SYSTEM SEEMS TO HAVE SHORTED OUT!
THEN ALL OF OUR LIVES ARE IN JEOPARDY!

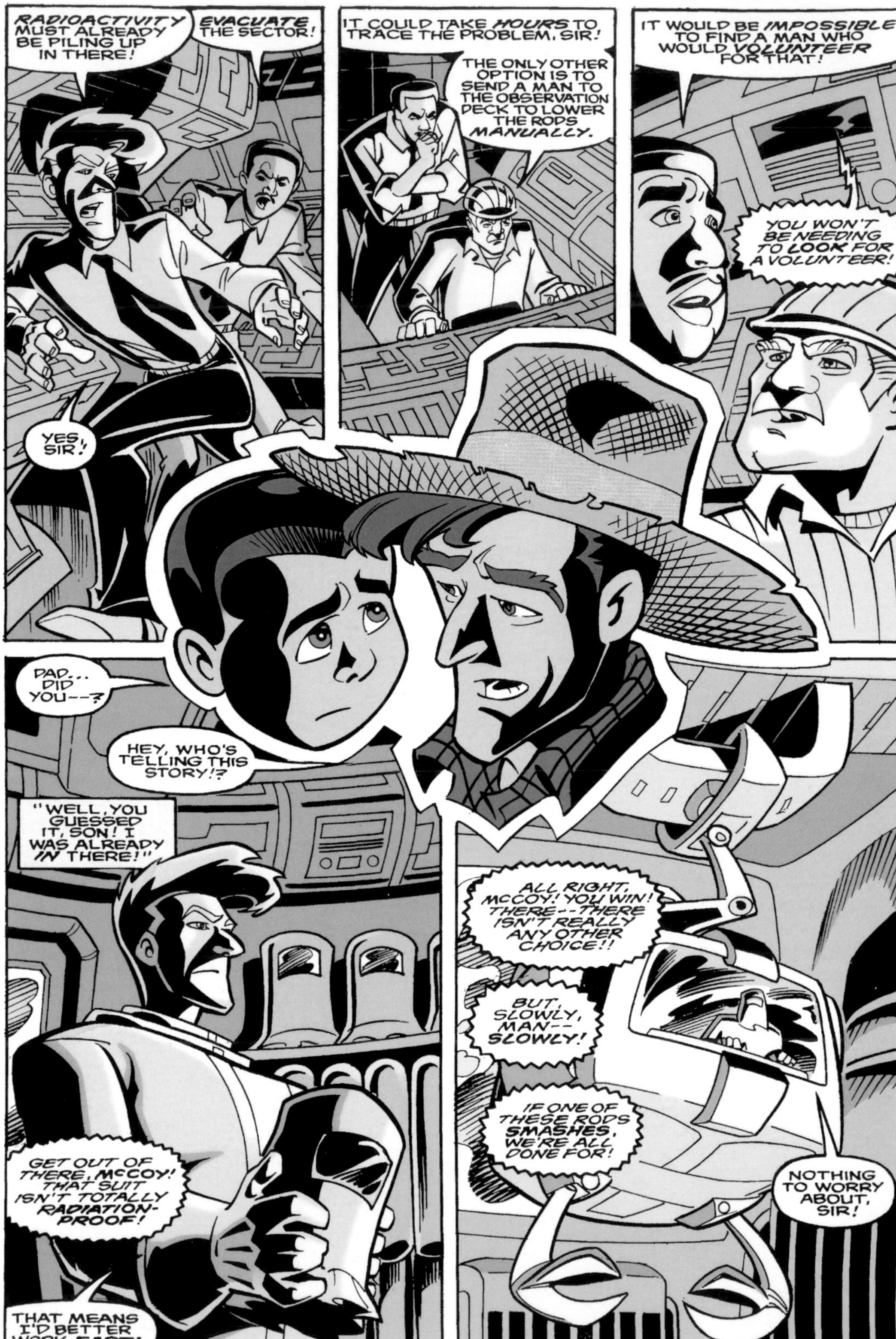
RADIOACTIVITY MUST ALREADY BE PILING UP IN THERE!
EVACUATE THE SECTOR!
YES, SIR!
IT COULD TAKE HOURS TO TRACE THE PROBLEM, SIR!
THE ONLY OTHER OPTION IS TO SEND A MAN TO THE OBSERVATION DECK TO LOWER THE RODS MANUALLY.
IT WOULD BE IMPOSSIBLE TO FIND A MAN WHO WOULD VOLUNTEER FOR THAT!
YOU WON'T BE NEEDING TO LOOK FOR A VOLUNTEER!
DAD... DID YOU--?
HEY, WHO'S TELLING THIS STORY!?
"WELL, YOU GUESSED IT, SON! I WAS ALREADY IN THERE!"
GET OUT OF THERE, McCOY! THAT SUIT ISN'T TOTALLY RADIATION-PROOF!
THAT MEANS I'D BETTER WORK FAST!
ALL RIGHT, McCOY! YOU WIN! THERE--THERE ISN'T REALLY ANY OTHER CHOICE!!
BUT, SLOWLY, MAN-- SLOWLY!
IF ONE OF THESE RODS SMASHES, WE'RE ALL DONE FOR!
NOTHING TO WORRY ABOUT, SIR!

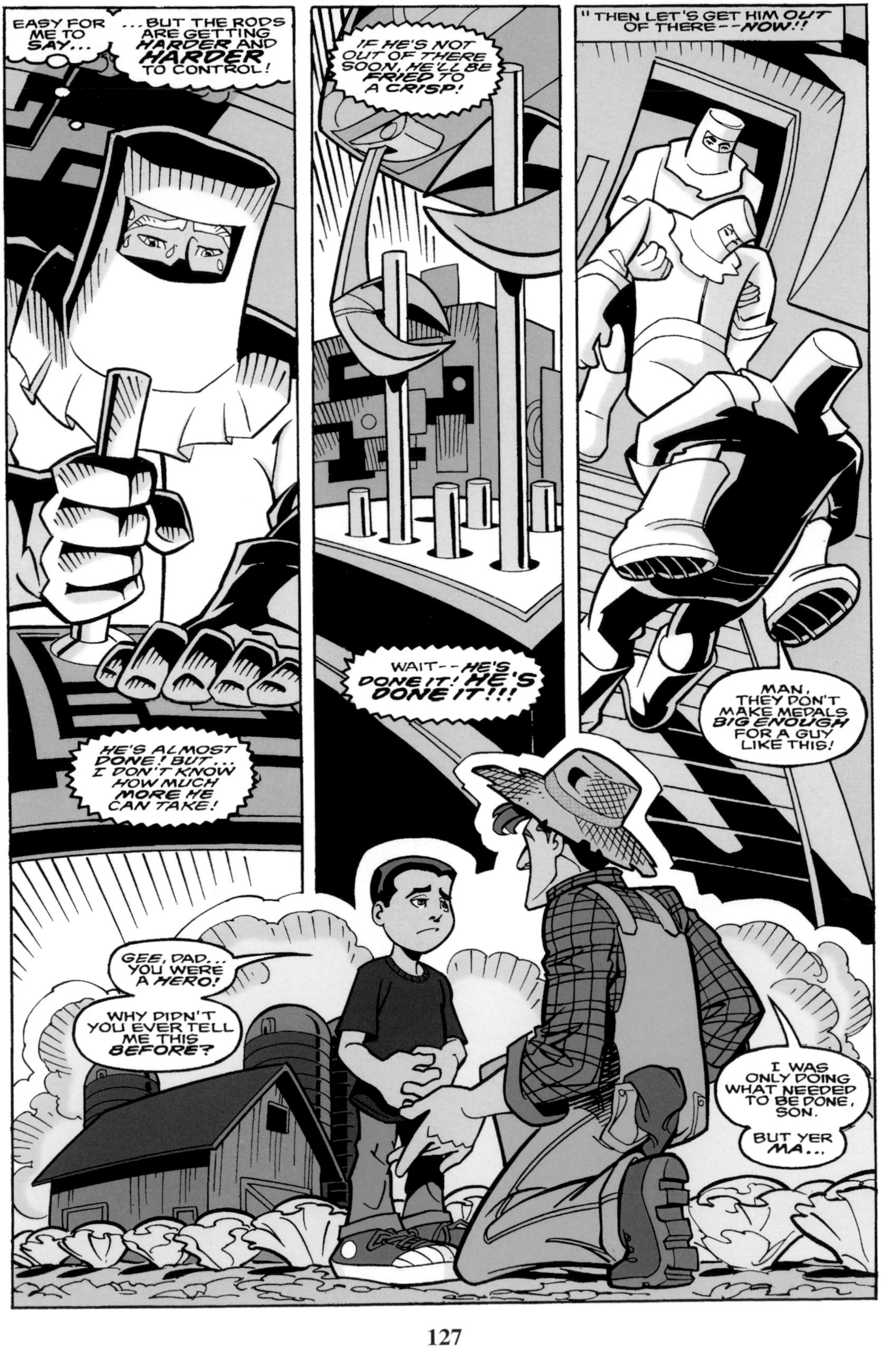
EASY FOR ME TO SAY...
...BUT THE RODS ARE GETTING HARDER AND HARDER TO CONTROL!
IF HE'S NOT OUT OF THERE SOON, HE'LL BE FRIED TO A CRISP!
"THEN LET'S GET HIM OUT OF THERE--NOW!!
HE'S ALMOST DONE! BUT... I DON'T KNOW HOW MUCH MORE HE CAN TAKE!
WAIT--HE'S DONE IT! HE'S DONE IT!!!
MAN, THEY DON'T MAKE MEDALS BIG ENOUGH FOR A GUY LIKE THIS!
GEE, DAD... YOU WERE A HERO!
WHY DIDN'T YOU EVER TELL ME THIS BEFORE?
I WAS ONLY DOING WHAT NEEDED TO BE DONE, SON.
BUT YER MA...

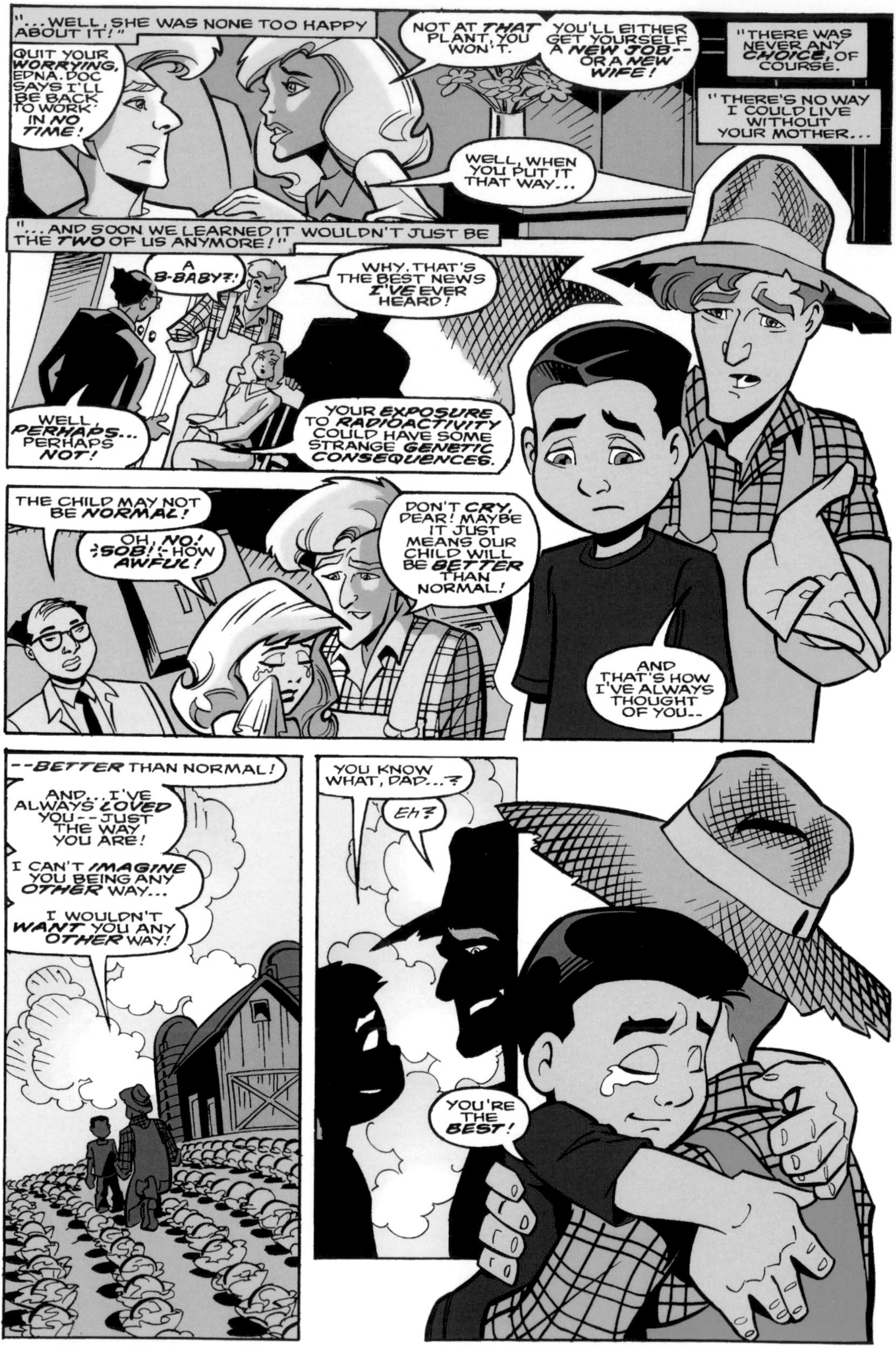
"...WELL, SHE WAS NONE TOO HAPPY ABOUT IT!"
QUIT YOUR WORRYING, EDNA. DOC SAYS I'LL BE BACK TO WORK IN NO TIME!
NOT AT THAT PLANT, YOU WON'T.
YOU'LL EITHER GET YOURSELF A NEW JOB-- OR A NEW WIFE!
WELL, WHEN YOU PUT IT THAT WAY...
"THERE WAS NEVER ANY CHOICE, OF COURSE.
"THERE'S NO WAY I COULD LIVE WITHOUT YOUR MOTHER...
"...AND SOON WE LEARNED IT WOULDN'T JUST BE THE TWO OF US ANYMORE!"
A B-BABY?!
WHY, THAT'S THE BEST NEWS I'VE EVER HEARD!
WELL, PERHAPS... PERHAPS NOT!
YOUR EXPOSURE TO RADIOACTIVITY COULD HAVE SOME STRANGE GENETIC CONSEQUENCES.
THE CHILD MAY NOT BE NORMAL!
OH, NO! -SOB!- HOW AWFUL!
DON'T CRY, DEAR! MAYBE IT JUST MEANS OUR CHILD WILL BE BETTER THAN NORMAL!
AND THAT'S HOW I'VE ALWAYS THOUGHT OF YOU--
--BETTER THAN NORMAL!
AND... I'VE ALWAYS LOVED YOU--JUST THE WAY YOU ARE!
I CAN'T IMAGINE YOU BEING ANY OTHER WAY...
I WOULDN'T WANT YOU ANY OTHER WAY!
YOU KNOW WHAT, DAD...?
Eh?
YOU'RE THE BEST!

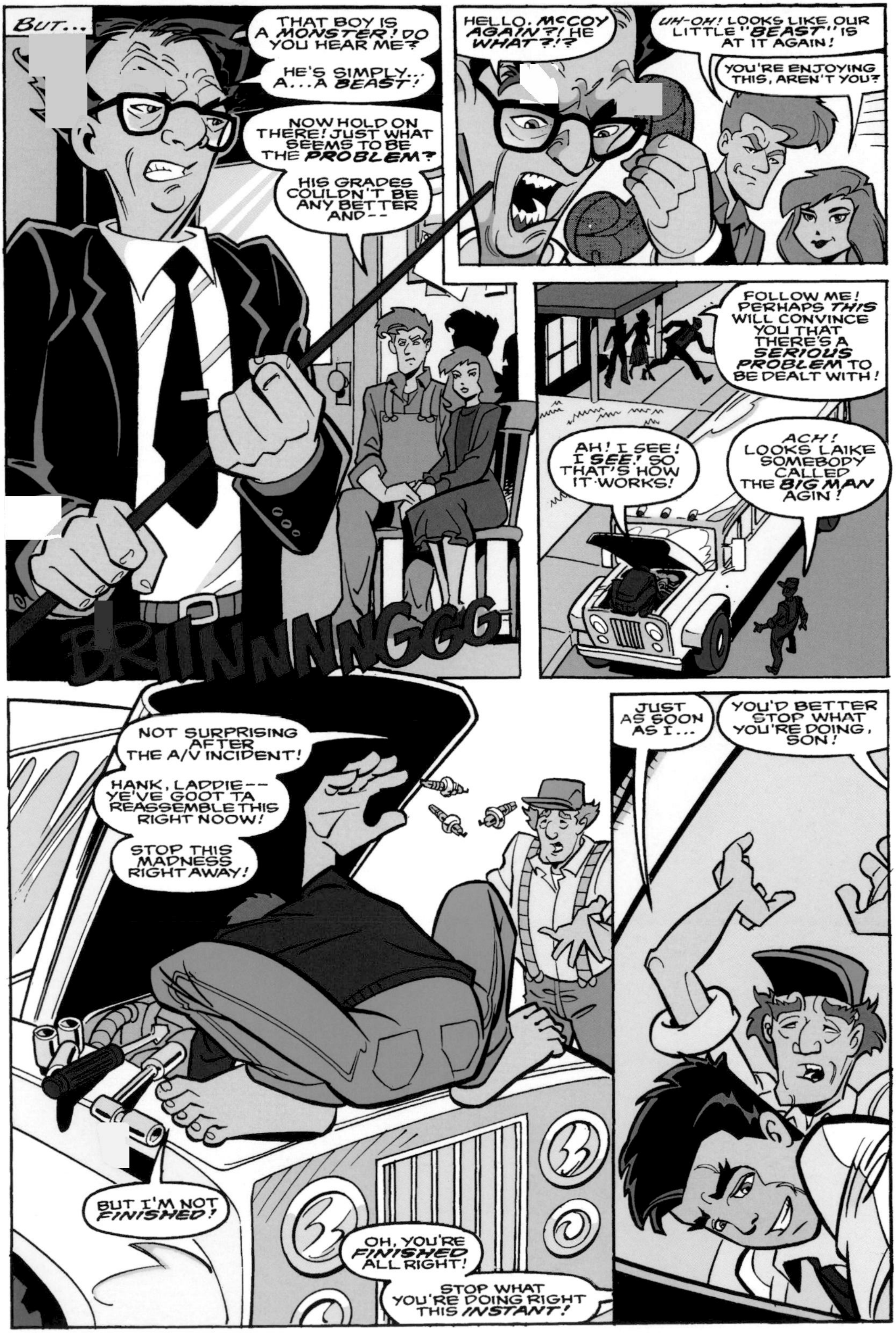
BUT...
THAT BOY IS A MONSTER! DO YOU HEAR ME?
HE'S SIMPLY... A...A BEAST!
NOW HOLD ON THERE! JUST WHAT SEEMS TO BE THE PROBLEM?
HIS GRADES COULDN'T BE ANY BETTER AND--
BRIIINNNNGGG
HELLO, McCOY AGAIN?! HE WHAT?!?
UH-OH! LOOKS LIKE OUR LITTLE "BEAST" IS AT IT AGAIN!
YOU'RE ENJOYING THIS, AREN'T YOU?
FOLLOW ME! PERHAPS THIS WILL CONVINCE YOU THAT THERE'S A SERIOUS PROBLEM TO BE DEALT WITH!
AH! I SEE! I SEE! SO THAT'S HOW IT WORKS!
ACH! LOOKS LAIKE SOMEBODY CALLED THE BIG MAN AGIN!
NOT SURPRISING AFTER THE A/V INCIDENT!
HANK, LADDIE-- YE'VE GOOT TA REASSEMBLE THIS RIGHT NOOW!
STOP THIS MADNESS RIGHT AWAY!
BUT I'M NOT FINISHED!
OH, YOU'RE FINISHED ALL RIGHT!
STOP WHAT YOU'RE DOING RIGHT THIS INSTANT!
JUST AS SOON AS I...
YOU'D BETTER STOP WHAT YOU'RE DOING, SON!

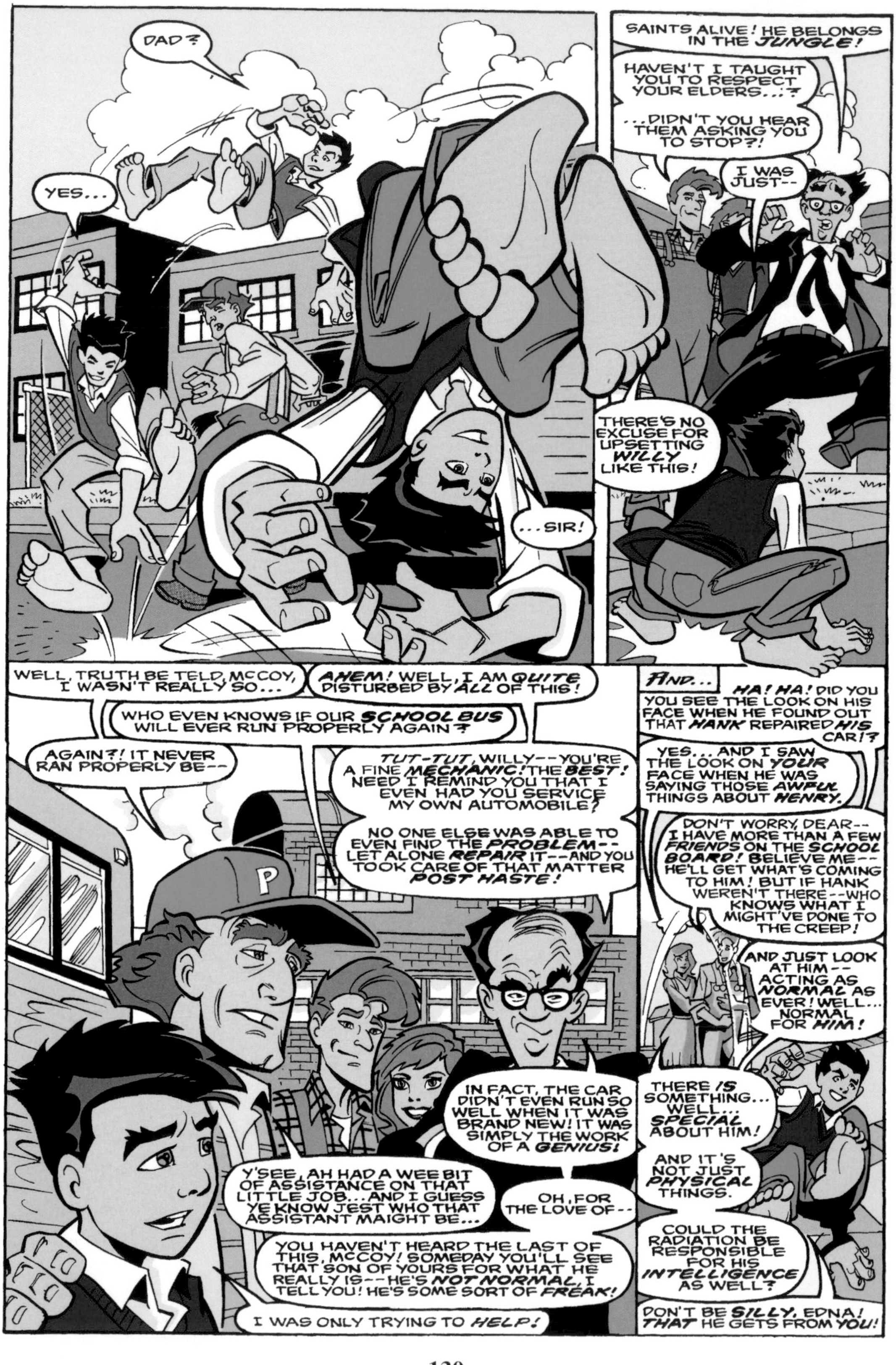
DAD?
YES...
...SIR!
SAINTS ALIVE! HE BELONGS IN THE JUNGLE!
HAVEN'T I TAUGHT YOU TO RESPECT YOUR ELDERS...?
...DIDN'T YOU HEAR THEM ASKING YOU TO STOP?!
I WAS JUST--
THERE'S NO EXCUSE FOR UPSETTING WILLY LIKE THIS!
WELL, TRUTH BE TELD, McCOY, I WASN'T REALLY SO...
AHEM! WELL, I AM QUITE DISTURBED BY ALL OF THIS!
WHO EVEN KNOWS IF OUR SCHOOL BUS WILL EVER RUN PROPERLY AGAIN?
AGAIN?! IT NEVER RAN PROPERLY BE--
TUT-TUT, WILLY--YOU'RE A FINE MECHANIC! THE BEST! NEED I REMIND YOU THAT I EVEN HAD YOU SERVICE MY OWN AUTOMOBILE?
NO ONE ELSE WAS ABLE TO EVEN FIND THE PROBLEM--LET ALONE REPAIR IT--AND YOU TOOK CARE OF THAT MATTER POST HASTE!
IN FACT, THE CAR DIDN'T EVEN RUN SO WELL WHEN IT WAS BRAND NEW! IT WAS SIMPLY THE WORK OF A GENIUS!
Y'SEE, AH HAD A WEE BIT OF ASSISTANCE ON THAT LITTLE JOB...AND I GUESS YE KNOW JEST WHO THAT ASSISTANT MAIGHT BE...
OH, FOR THE LOVE OF--
YOU HAVEN'T HEARD THE LAST OF THIS, McCOY! SOMEDAY YOU'LL SEE THAT SON OF YOURS FOR WHAT HE REALLY IS--HE'S NOT NORMAL, I TELL YOU! HE'S SOME SORT OF FREAK!
I WAS ONLY TRYING TO HELP!
AND...
HA! HA! DID YOU YOU SEE THE LOOK ON HIS FACE WHEN HE FOUND OUT THAT HANK REPAIRED HIS CAR!?
YES... AND I SAW THE LOOK ON YOUR FACE WHEN HE WAS SAYING THOSE AWFUL THINGS ABOUT HENRY.
DON'T WORRY, DEAR--I HAVE MORE THAN A FEW FRIENDS ON THE SCHOOL BOARD! BELIEVE ME--HE'LL GET WHAT'S COMING TO HIM! BUT IF HANK WEREN'T THERE--WHO KNOWS WHAT I MIGHT'VE DONE TO THE CREEP!
AND JUST LOOK AT HIM--ACTING AS NORMAL AS EVER! WELL... NORMAL FOR HIM!
THERE IS SOMETHING... WELL... SPECIAL ABOUT HIM!
AND IT'S NOT JUST PHYSICAL THINGS.
COULD THE RADIATION BE RESPONSIBLE FOR HIS INTELLIGENCE AS WELL?
DON'T BE SILLY, EDNA! THAT HE GETS FROM YOU!

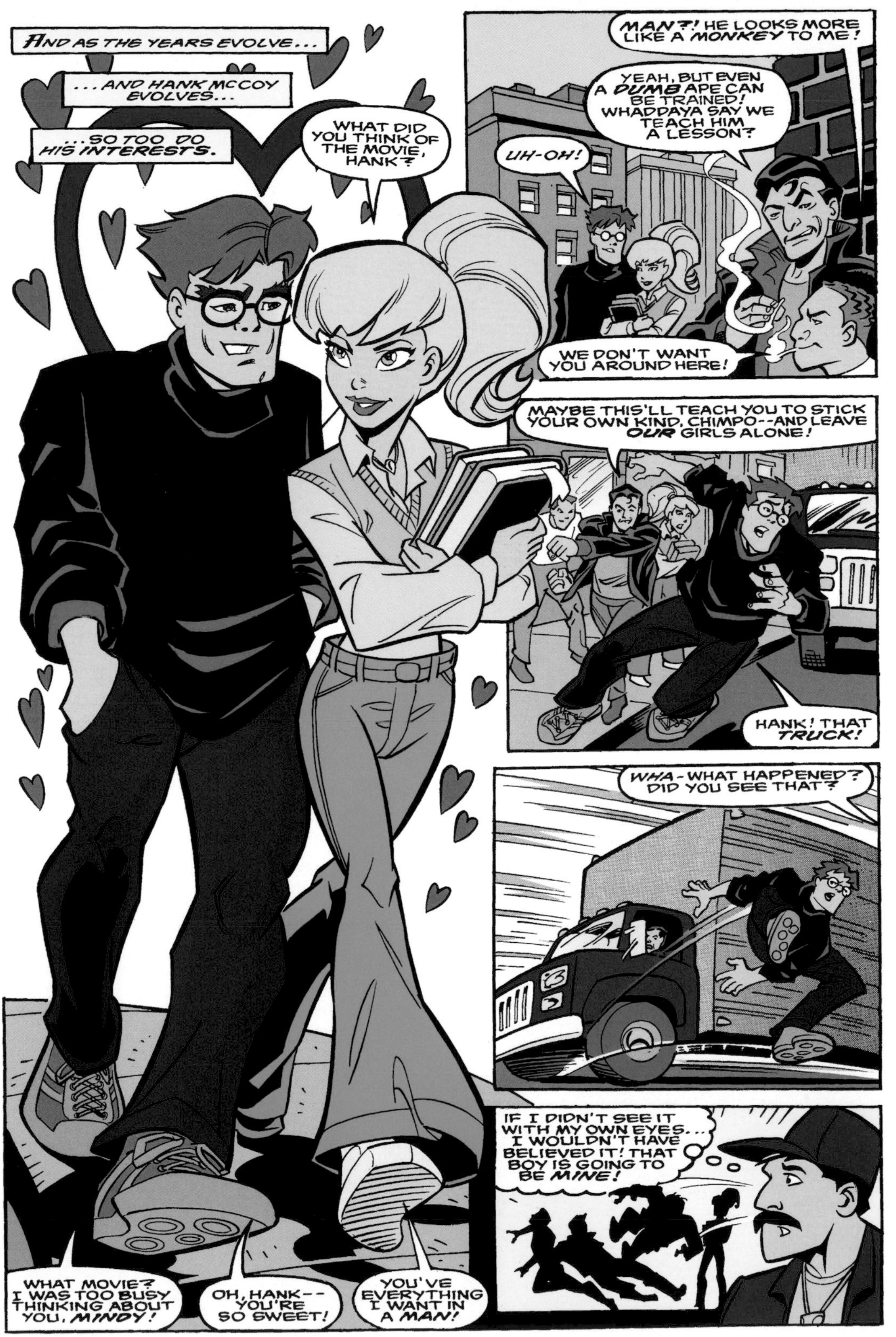
AND AS THE YEARS EVOLVE...
...AND HANK McCOY EVOLVES...
...SO TOO DO HIS INTERESTS.
WHAT DID YOU THINK OF THE MOVIE, HANK?
WHAT MOVIE? I WAS TOO BUSY THINKING ABOUT YOU, MINDY!
OH, HANK-- YOU'RE SO SWEET!
YOU'VE EVERYTHING I WANT IN A MAN!
MAN?! HE LOOKS MORE LIKE A MONKEY TO ME!
YEAH, BUT EVEN A DUMB APE CAN BE TRAINED! WHADDAYA SAY WE TEACH HIM A LESSON?
UH-OH!
WE DON'T WANT YOU AROUND HERE!
MAYBE THIS'LL TEACH YOU TO STICK YOUR OWN KIND, CHIMPO--AND LEAVE OUR GIRLS ALONE!
HANK! THAT TRUCK!
WHA-WHAT HAPPENED? DID YOU SEE THAT?
IF I DIDN'T SEE IT WITH MY OWN EYES... I WOULDN'T HAVE BELIEVED IT! THAT BOY IS GOING TO BE MINE!

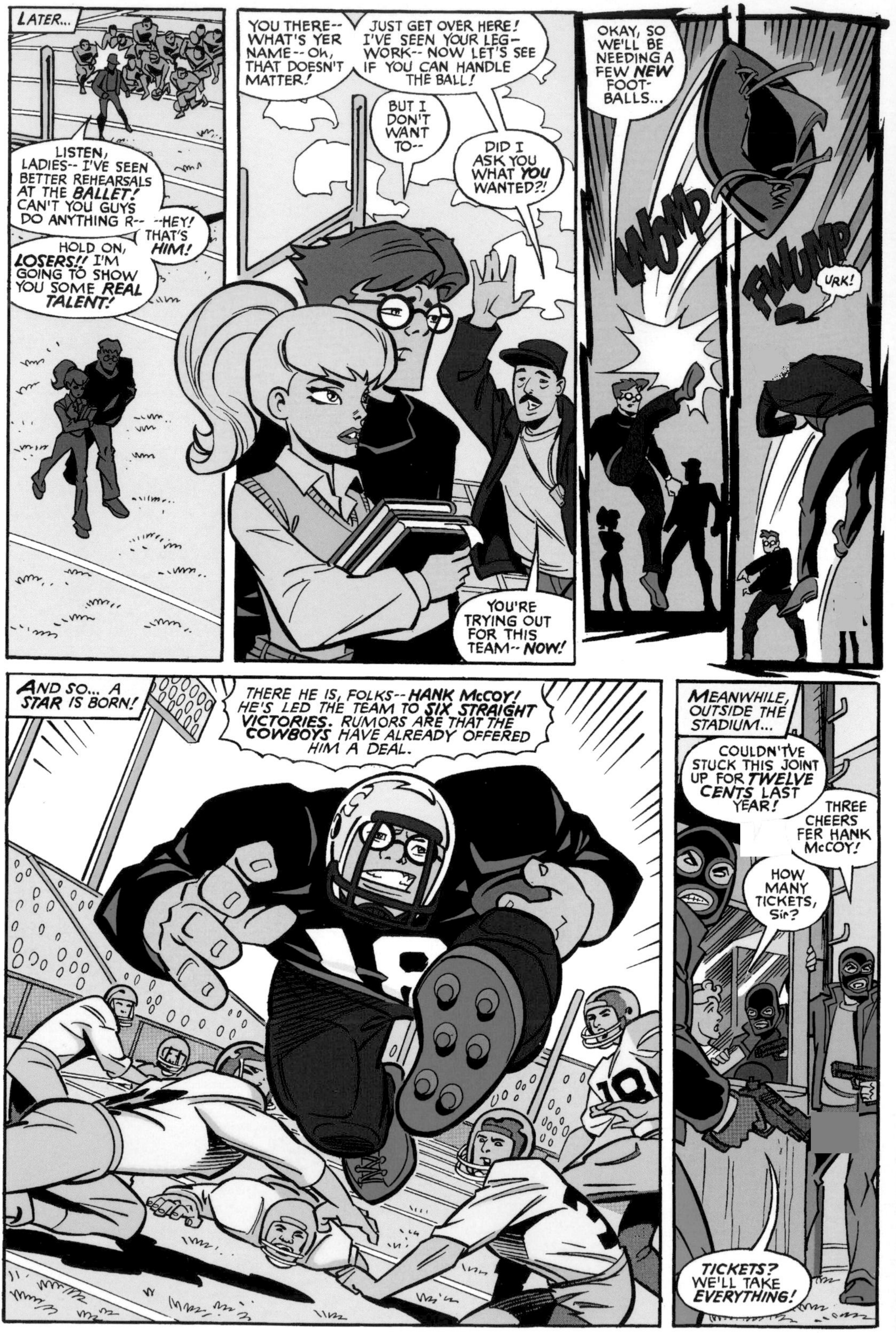
LATER...
LISTEN, LADIES-- I'VE SEEN BETTER REHEARSALS AT THE BALLET! CAN'T YOU GUYS DO ANYTHING R--
--HEY! THAT'S HIM!
HOLD ON, LOSERS!! I'M GOING TO SHOW YOU SOME REAL TALENT!
YOU THERE-- WHAT'S YER NAME-- OH, THAT DOESN'T MATTER!
JUST GET OVER HERE! I'VE SEEN YOUR LEG-WORK-- NOW LET'S SEE IF YOU CAN HANDLE THE BALL!
BUT I DON'T WANT TO--
DID I ASK YOU WHAT YOU WANTED?!
YOU'RE TRYING OUT FOR THIS TEAM-- NOW!
OKAY, SO WE'LL BE NEEDING A FEW NEW FOOT-BALLS...
WOMP
FWUMP
URK!
AND SO... A STAR IS BORN!
THERE HE IS, FOLKS--HANK McCOY! HE'S LED THE TEAM TO SIX STRAIGHT VICTORIES. RUMORS ARE THAT THE COWBOYS HAVE ALREADY OFFERED HIM A DEAL.
MEANWHILE, OUTSIDE THE STADIUM...
COULDN'T'VE STUCK THIS JOINT UP FOR TWELVE CENTS LAST YEAR!
THREE CHEERS FER HANK McCOY!
HOW MANY TICKETS, Sir?
TICKETS? WE'LL TAKE EVERYTHING!

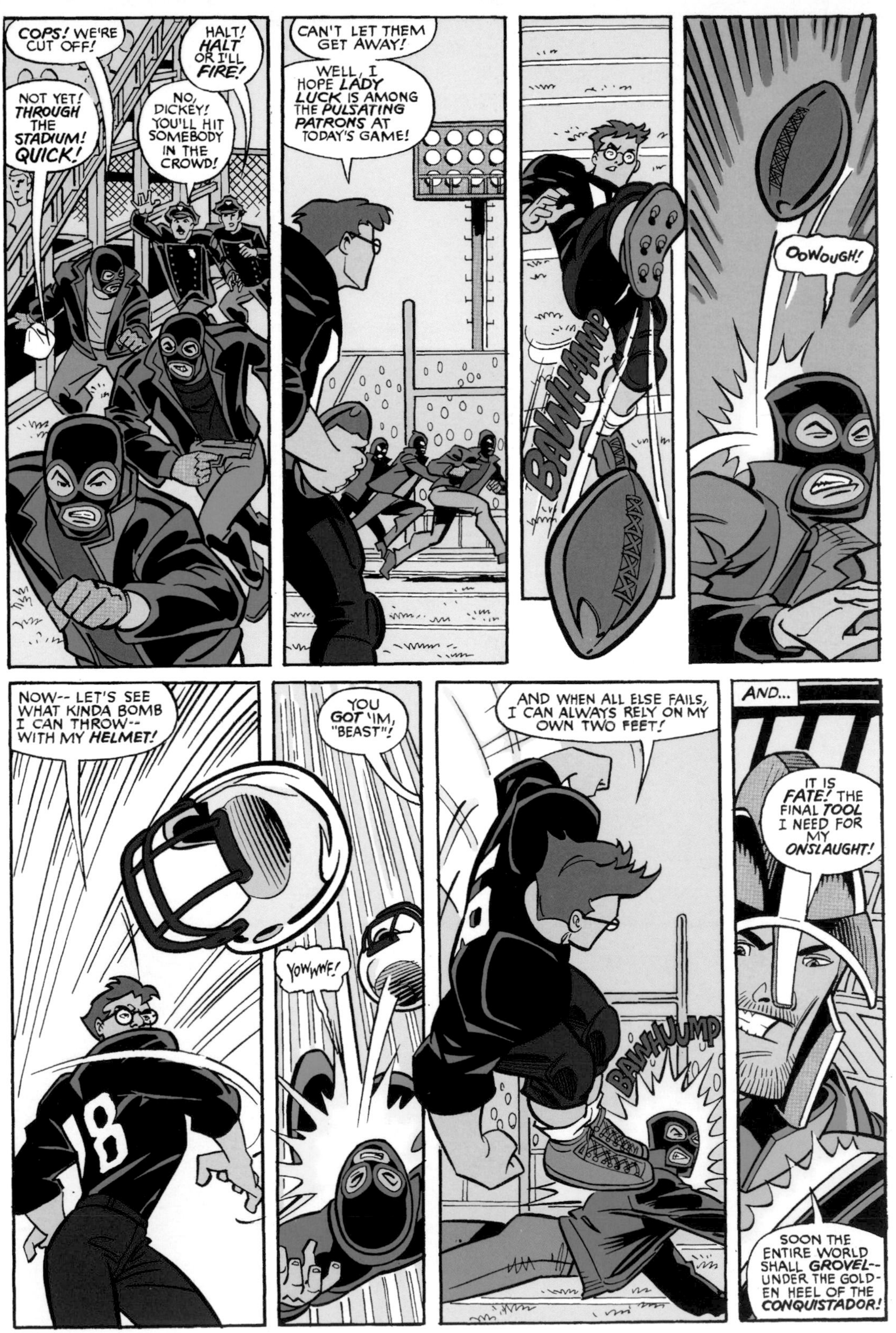
COPS! WE'RE CUT OFF!
HALT! HALT OR I'LL FIRE!
NOT YET! THROUGH THE STADIUM! QUICK!
NO, DICKEY! YOU'LL HIT SOMEBODY IN THE CROWD!
CAN'T LET THEM GET AWAY!
WELL, I HOPE LADY LUCK IS AMONG THE PULSATING PATRONS AT TODAY'S GAME!
BAWHAMP
OOWOUGH!
NOW-- LET'S SEE WHAT KINDA BOMB I CAN THROW-- WITH MY HELMET!
YOU GOT 'IM, "BEAST"!
YOWWF!
AND WHEN ALL ELSE FAILS, I CAN ALWAYS RELY ON MY OWN TWO FEET!
BAWHUUMP
AND...
IT IS FATE! THE FINAL TOOL I NEED FOR MY ONSLAUGHT!
SOON THE ENTIRE WORLD SHALL GROVEL-- UNDER THE GOLDEN HEEL OF THE CONQUISTADOR!

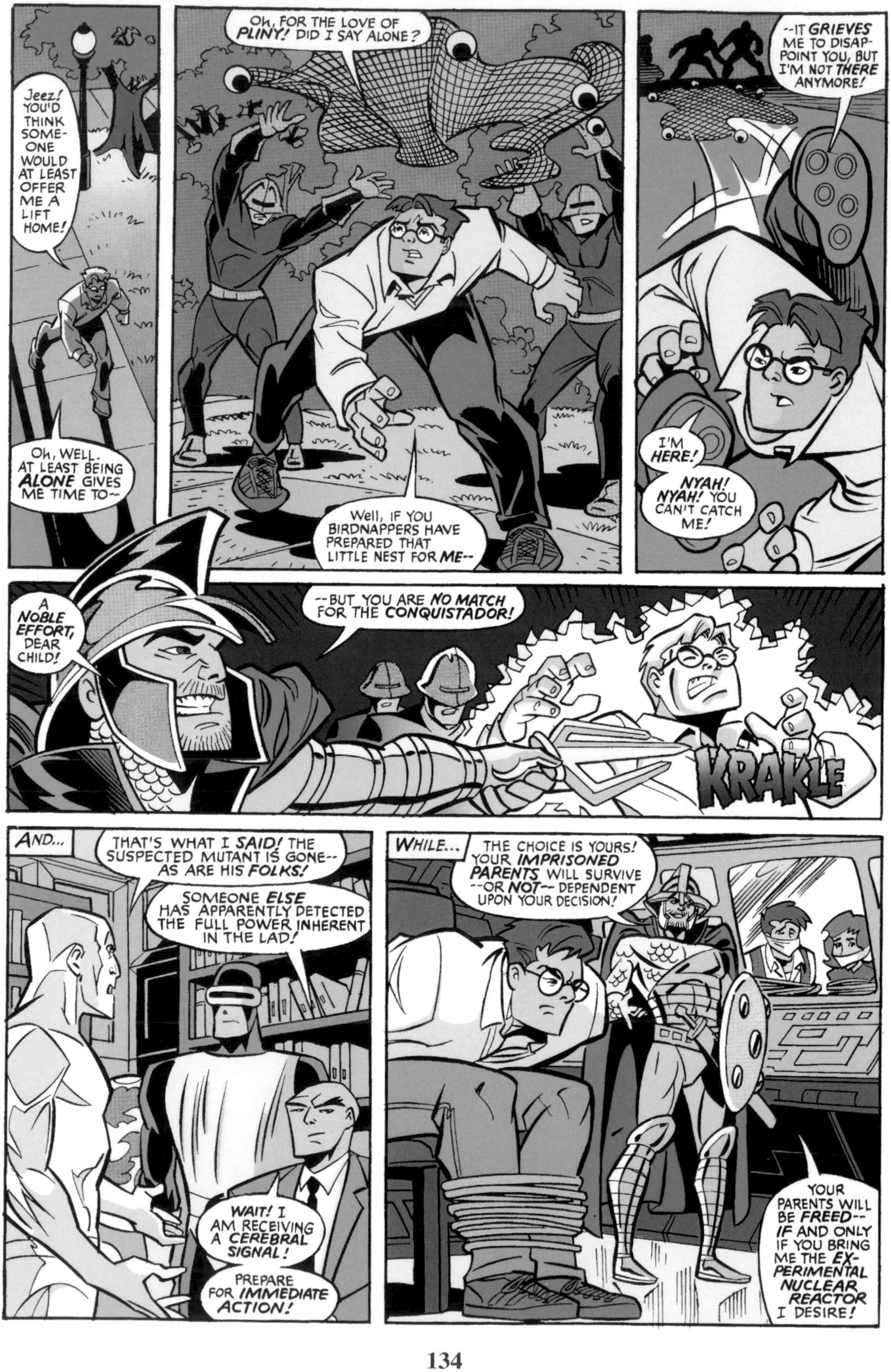
Jeez! YOU'D THINK SOMEONE WOULD AT LEAST OFFER ME A LIFT HOME!
Oh, WELL. AT LEAST BEING ALONE GIVES ME TIME TO--
Oh, FOR THE LOVE OF PLINY! DID I SAY ALONE?
Well, IF YOU BIRDNAPPERS HAVE PREPARED THAT LITTLE NEST FOR ME--
--IT GRIEVES ME TO DISAPPOINT YOU, BUT I'M NOT THERE ANYMORE!
I'M HERE!
NYAH! NYAH! YOU CAN'T CATCH ME!
A NOBLE EFFORT, DEAR CHILD!
--BUT YOU ARE NO MATCH FOR THE CONQUISTADOR!
KRAKLE
AND...
THAT'S WHAT I SAID! THE SUSPECTED MUTANT IS GONE-- AS ARE HIS FOLKS!
SOMEONE ELSE HAS APPARENTLY DETECTED THE FULL POWER INHERENT IN THE LAD!
WAIT! I AM RECEIVING A CEREBRAL SIGNAL!
PREPARE FOR IMMEDIATE ACTION!
WHILE...
THE CHOICE IS YOURS! YOUR IMPRISONED PARENTS WILL SURVIVE --OR NOT-- DEPENDENT UPON YOUR DECISION!
YOUR PARENTS WILL BE FREED-- IF AND ONLY IF YOU BRING ME THE EXPERIMENTAL NUCLEAR REACTOR I DESIRE!

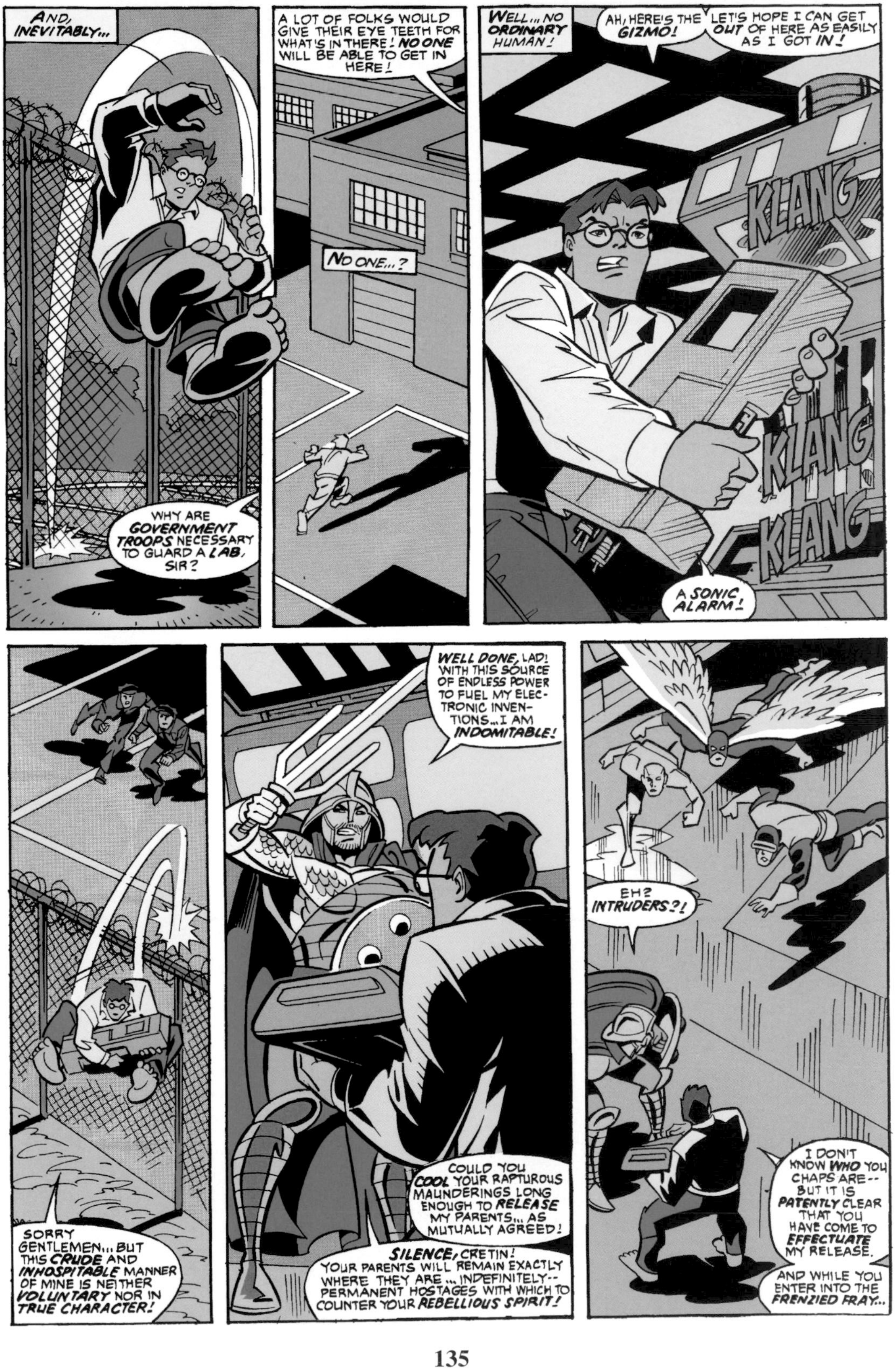
AND, INEVITABLY...
WHY ARE GOVERNMENT TROOPS NECESSARY TO GUARD A LAB, SIR?
A LOT OF FOLKS WOULD GIVE THEIR EYE TEETH FOR WHAT'S IN THERE! NO ONE WILL BE ABLE TO GET IN HERE!
NO ONE...?
WELL... NO ORDINARY HUMAN!
AH, HERE'S THE GIZMO!
LET'S HOPE I CAN GET OUT OF HERE AS EASILY AS I GOT IN!
KLANG
KLANG
KLANG
A SONIC ALARM!
SORRY GENTLEMEN... BUT THIS CRUDE AND INNOSPITABLE MANNER OF MINE IS NEITHER VOLUNTARY NOR IN TRUE CHARACTER!
WELL DONE, LAD! WITH THIS SOURCE OF ENDLESS POWER TO FUEL MY ELECTRONIC INVENTIONS... I AM INDOMITABLE!
COULD YOU COOL YOUR RAPTUROUS MAUNDERINGS LONG ENOUGH TO RELEASE MY PARENTS... AS MUTUALLY AGREED!
SILENCE, CRETIN! YOUR PARENTS WILL REMAIN EXACTLY WHERE THEY ARE... INDEFINITELY-- PERMANENT HOSTAGES WITH WHICH TO COUNTER YOUR REBELLIOUS SPIRIT!
EH? INTRUDERS?!
I DON'T KNOW WHO YOU CHAPS ARE-- BUT IT IS PATENTLY CLEAR THAT YOU HAVE COME TO EFFECTUATE MY RELEASE.
AND WHILE YOU ENTER INTO THE FRENZIED FRAY...

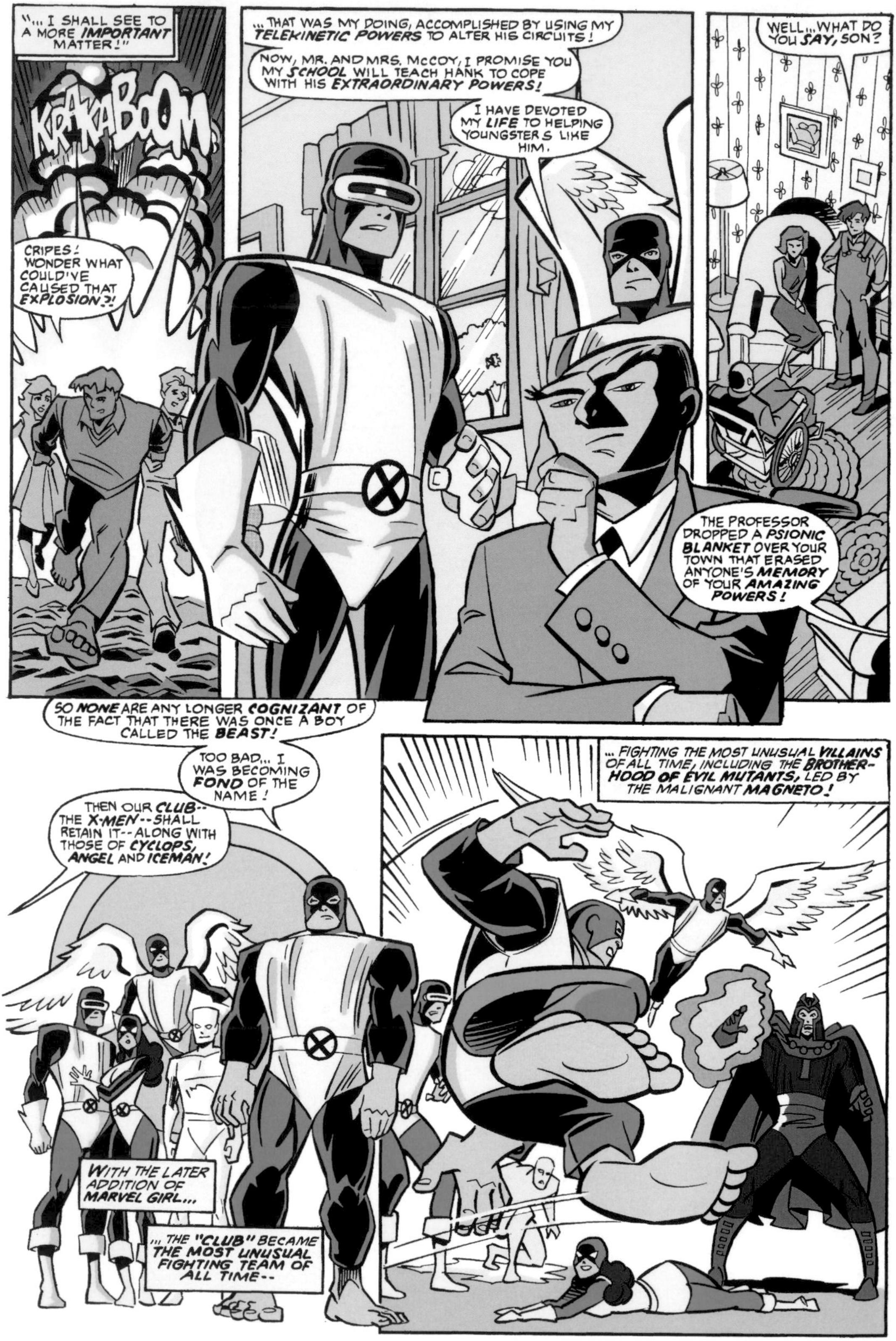
"... I SHALL SEE TO A MORE IMPORTANT MATTER!"
KRAKABOOM
CRIPES! WONDER WHAT COULD'VE CAUSED THAT EXPLOSION?!
... THAT WAS MY DOING, ACCOMPLISHED BY USING MY TELEKINETIC POWERS TO ALTER HIS CIRCUITS!
NOW, MR. AND MRS. McCOY, I PROMISE YOU MY SCHOOL WILL TEACH HANK TO COPE WITH HIS EXTRAORDINARY POWERS!
I HAVE DEVOTED MY LIFE TO HELPING YOUNGSTERS LIKE HIM.
WELL... WHAT DO YOU SAY, SON?
THE PROFESSOR DROPPED A PSIONIC BLANKET OVER YOUR TOWN THAT ERASED ANYONE'S MEMORY OF YOUR AMAZING POWERS!
SO NONE ARE ANY LONGER COGNIZANT OF THE FACT THAT THERE WAS ONCE A BOY CALLED THE BEAST!
TOO BAD... I WAS BECOMING FOND OF THE NAME!
THEN OUR CLUB-- THE X-MEN--SHALL RETAIN IT--ALONG WITH THOSE OF CYCLOPS, ANGEL AND ICEMAN!
WITH THE LATER ADDITION OF MARVEL GIRL...
... THE "CLUB" BECAME THE MOST UNUSUAL FIGHTING TEAM OF ALL TIME--
... FIGHTING THE MOST UNUSUAL VILLAINS OF ALL TIME, INCLUDING THE BROTHERHOOD OF EVIL MUTANTS, LED BY THE MALIGNANT MAGNETO!

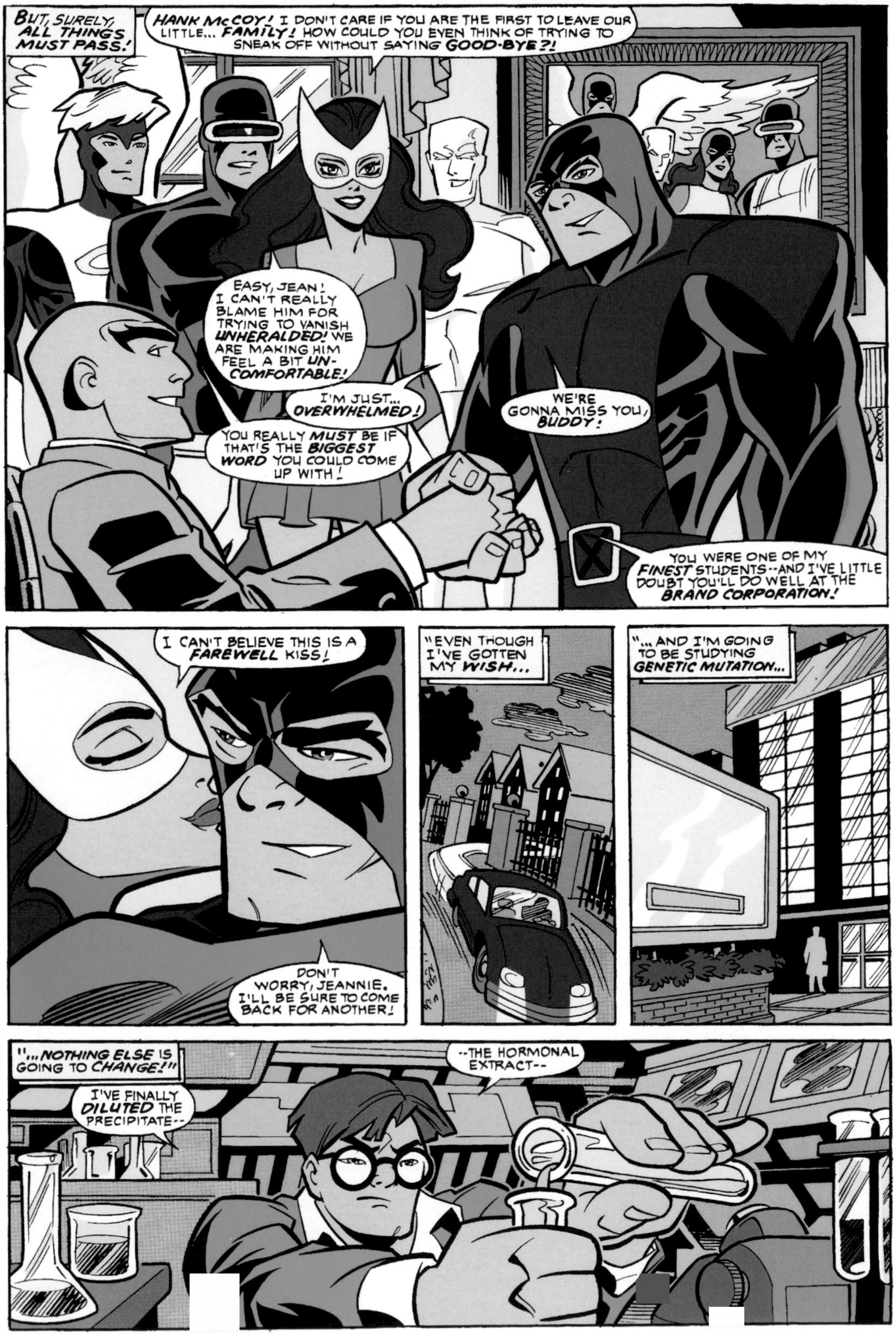
BUT, SURELY, ALL THINGS MUST PASS!
HANK McCOY! I DON'T CARE IF YOU ARE THE FIRST TO LEAVE OUR LITTLE... FAMILY! HOW COULD YOU EVEN THINK OF TRYING TO SNEAK OFF WITHOUT SAYING GOOD-BYE?!
EASY, JEAN! I CAN'T REALLY BLAME HIM FOR TRYING TO VANISH UNHERALDED! WE ARE MAKING HIM FEEL A BIT UN-COMFORTABLE!
I'M JUST... OVERWHELMED!
YOU REALLY MUST BE IF THAT'S THE BIGGEST WORD YOU COULD COME UP WITH!
WE'RE GONNA MISS YOU, BUDDY!
YOU WERE ONE OF MY FINEST STUDENTS--AND I'VE LITTLE DOUBT YOU'LL DO WELL AT THE BRAND CORPORATION!
I CAN'T BELIEVE THIS IS A FAREWELL KISS!
DON'T WORRY, JEANNIE. I'LL BE SURE TO COME BACK FOR ANOTHER!
"EVEN THOUGH I'VE GOTTEN MY WISH...
"...AND I'M GOING TO BE STUDYING GENETIC MUTATION...
"...NOTHING ELSE IS GOING TO CHANGE!"
I'VE FINALLY DILUTED THE PRECIPITATE--
--THE HORMONAL EXTRACT--

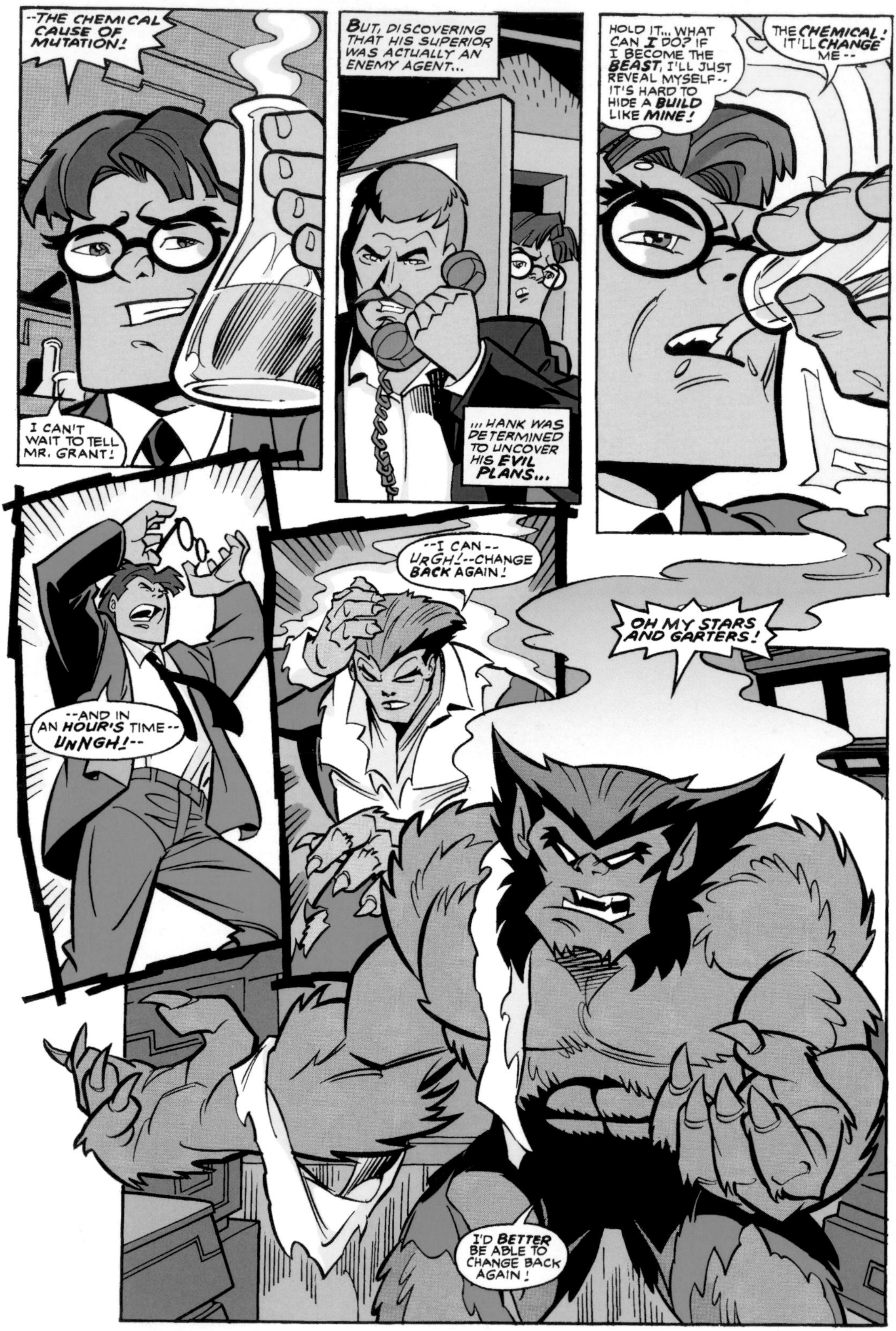
--THE CHEMICAL CAUSE OF MUTATION!
I CAN'T WAIT TO TELL MR. GRANT!
BUT, DISCOVERING THAT HIS SUPERIOR WAS ACTUALLY AN ENEMY AGENT...
...HANK WAS DETERMINED TO UNCOVER HIS EVIL PLANS...
HOLD IT... WHAT CAN I DO? IF I BECOME THE BEAST, I'LL JUST REVEAL MYSELF-- IT'S HARD TO HIDE A BUILD LIKE MINE!
THE CHEMICAL! IT'LL CHANGE ME--
--AND IN AN HOUR'S TIME-- UNNGH!--
--I CAN-- URGH!--CHANGE BACK AGAIN!
OH MY STARS AND GARTERS!
I'D BETTER BE ABLE TO CHANGE BACK AGAIN!

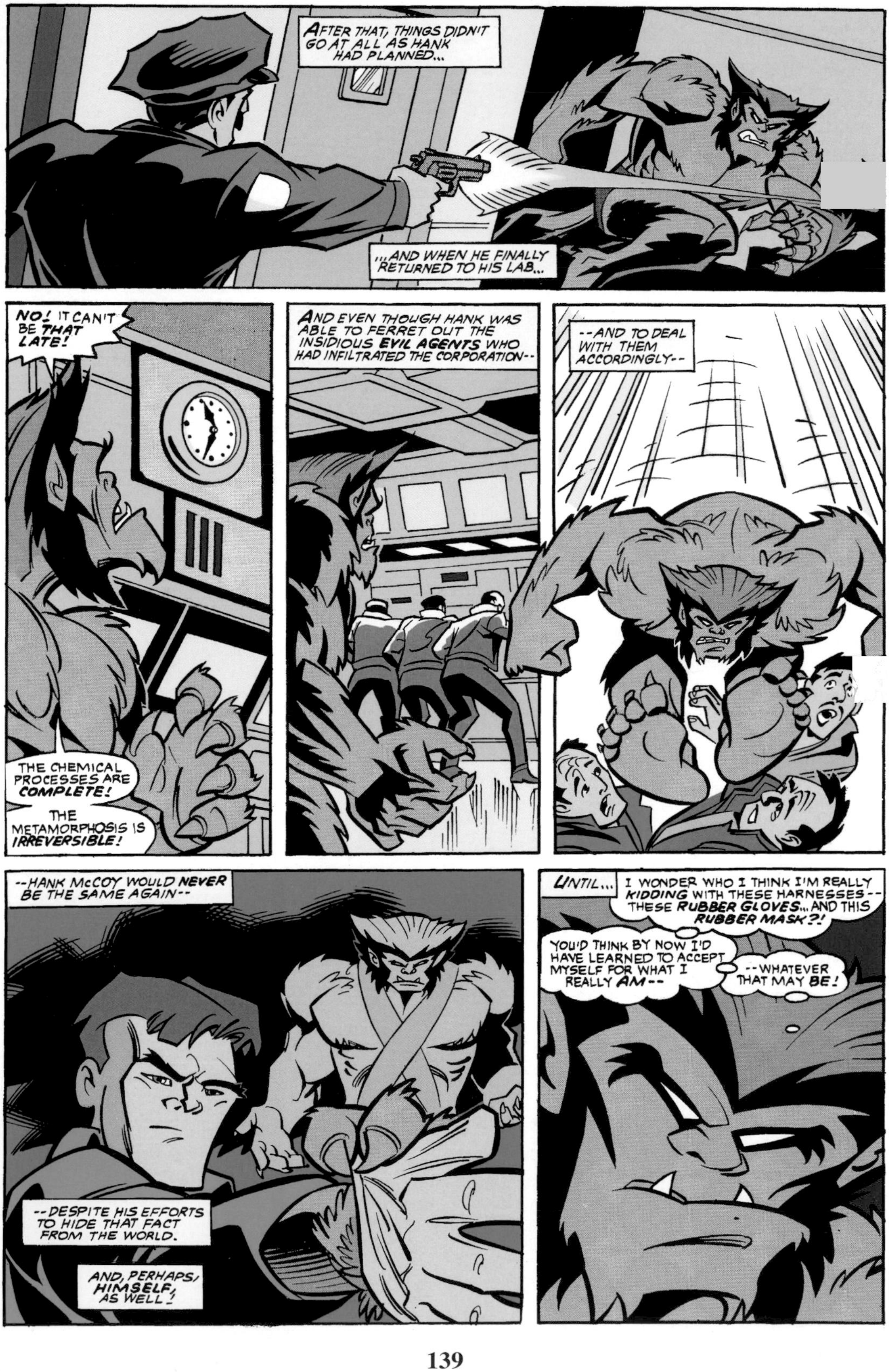

AFTER THAT, THINGS DIDN'T GO AT ALL AS HANK HAD PLANNED...
...AND WHEN HE FINALLY RETURNED TO HIS LAB...
NO! IT CAN'T BE THAT LATE!
THE CHEMICAL PROCESSES ARE COMPLETE!
THE METAMORPHOSIS IS IRREVERSIBLE!
AND EVEN THOUGH HANK WAS ABLE TO FERRET OUT THE INSIDIOUS EVIL AGENTS WHO HAD INFILTRATED THE CORPORATION--
--AND TO DEAL WITH THEM ACCORDINGLY--
--HANK McCOY WOULD NEVER BE THE SAME AGAIN--
--DESPITE HIS EFFORTS TO HIDE THAT FACT FROM THE WORLD.
AND, PERHAPS, HIMSELF, AS WELL!
UNTIL...
I WONDER WHO I THINK I'M REALLY KIDDING WITH THESE HARNESSES--THESE RUBBER GLOVES... AND THIS RUBBER MASK?!
YOU'D THINK BY NOW I'D HAVE LEARNED TO ACCEPT MYSELF FOR WHAT I REALLY AM--
--WHATEVER THAT MAY BE!

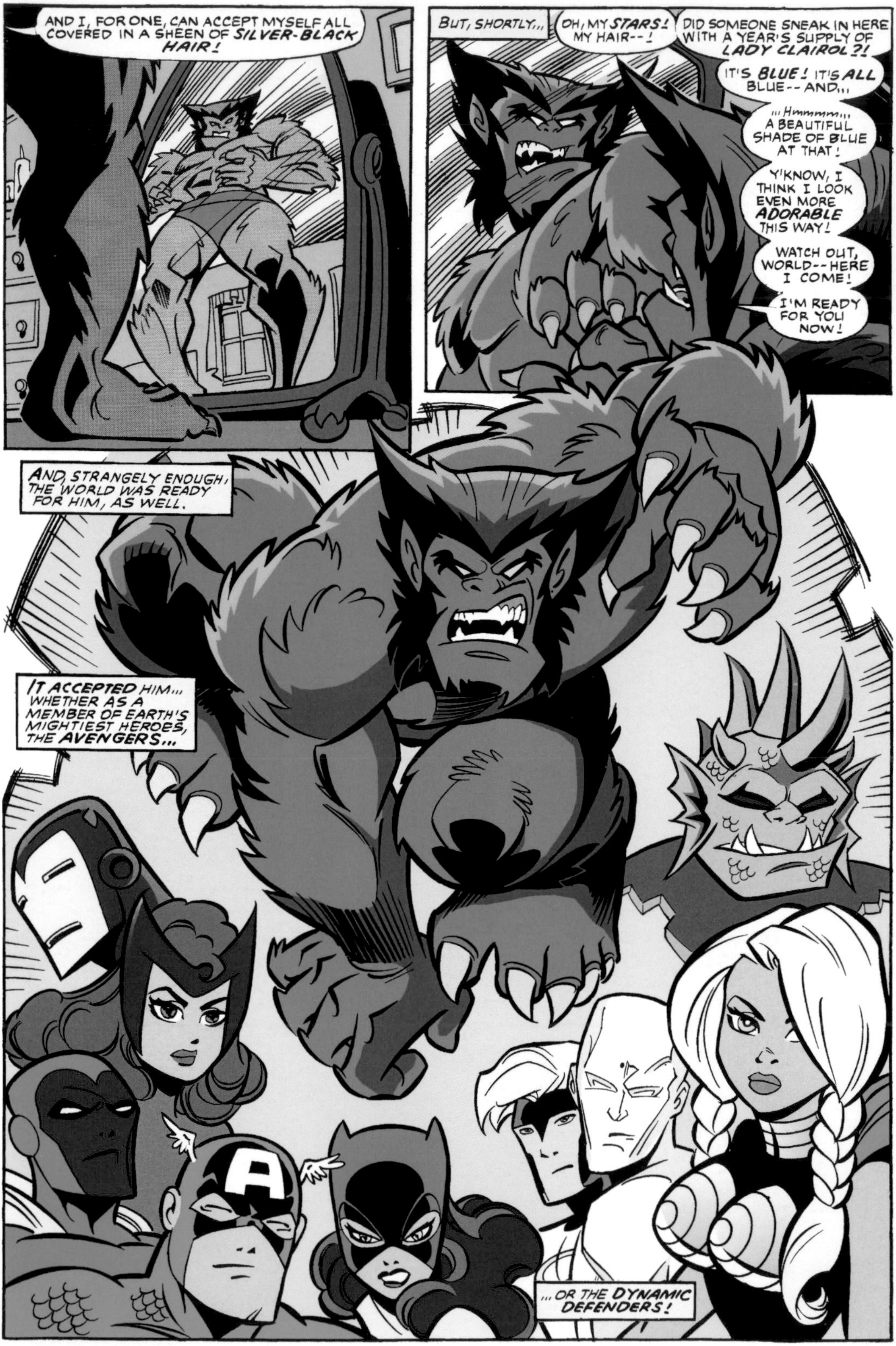
AND I, FOR ONE, CAN ACCEPT MYSELF ALL COVERED IN A SHEEN OF SILVER-BLACK HAIR!
BUT, SHORTLY...
OH, MY STARS! MY HAIR--!
DID SOMEONE SNEAK IN HERE WITH A YEAR'S SUPPLY OF LADY CLAIROL?!
IT'S BLUE! IT'S ALL BLUE-- AND...
...Hmmmm... A BEAUTIFUL SHADE OF BLUE AT THAT!
Y'KNOW, I THINK I LOOK EVEN MORE ADORABLE THIS WAY!
WATCH OUT, WORLD-- HERE I COME!
I'M READY FOR YOU NOW!
AND, STRANGELY ENOUGH, THE WORLD WAS READY FOR HIM, AS WELL.
IT ACCEPTED HIM... WHETHER AS A MEMBER OF EARTH'S MIGHTIEST HEROES, THE AVENGERS...
...OR THE DYNAMIC DEFENDERS!

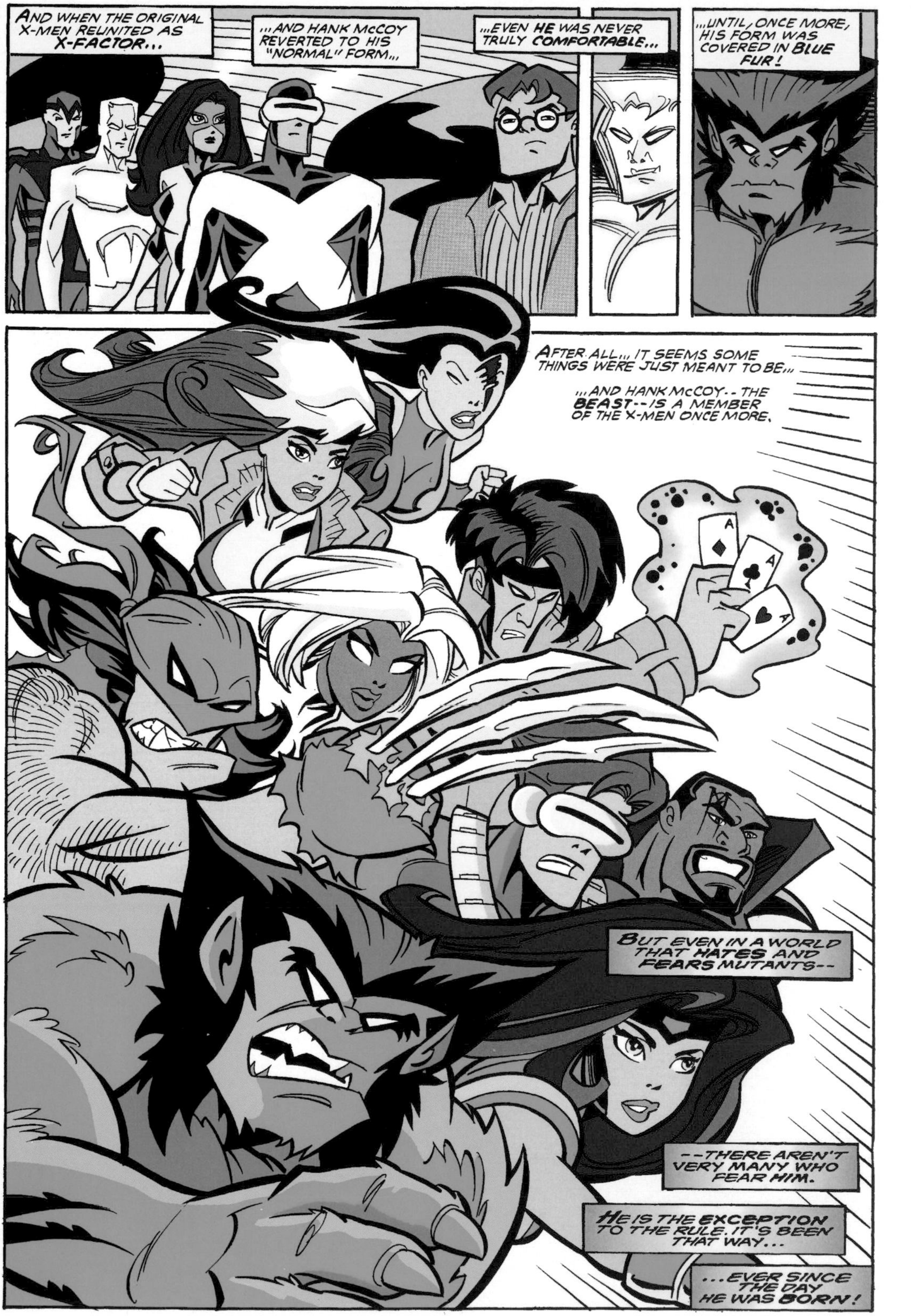
AND WHEN THE ORIGINAL X-MEN REUNITED AS X-FACTOR...
...AND HANK McCOY REVERTED TO HIS "NORMAL" FORM...
...EVEN HE WAS NEVER TRULY COMFORTABLE...
...UNTIL, ONCE MORE, HIS FORM WAS COVERED IN BLUE FUR!
AFTER ALL... IT SEEMS SOME THINGS WERE JUST MEANT TO BE...
...AND HANK McCOY--THE BEAST--IS A MEMBER OF THE X-MEN ONCE MORE.
BUT EVEN IN A WORLD THAT HATES AND FEARS MUTANTS--
--THERE AREN'T VERY MANY WHO FEAR HIM.
HE IS THE EXCEPTION TO THE RULE. IT'S BEEN THAT WAY...
...EVER SINCE THE DAY HE WAS BORN!

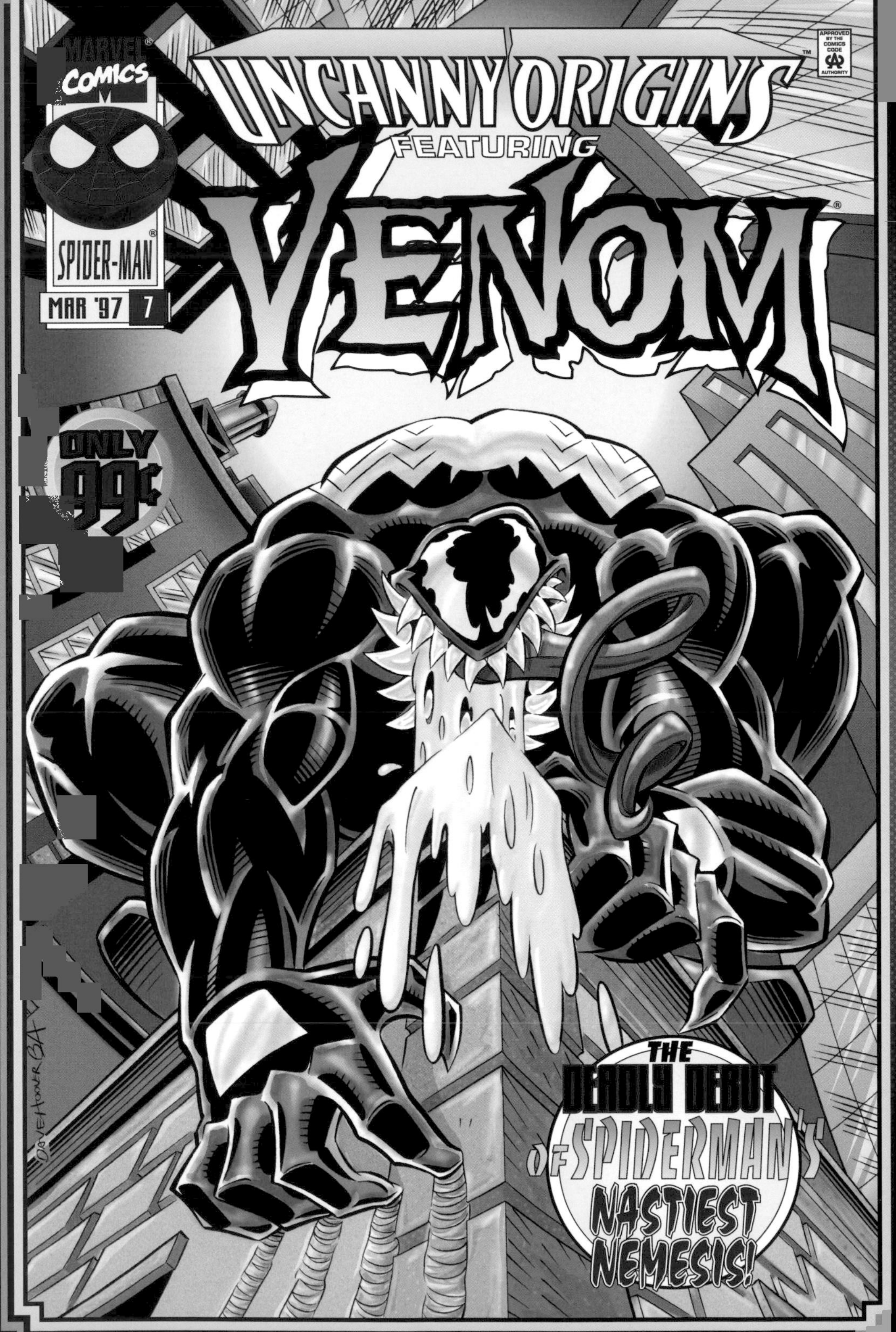
MARVEL COMICS
SPIDER-MAN
MAR '97 7
APPROVED BY THE COMICS CODE AUTHORITY
UNCANNY ORIGINS
FEATURING
VENOM
ONLY 99¢
THE DEADLY DEBUT OF SPIDERMAN'S NASTIEST NEMESIS!

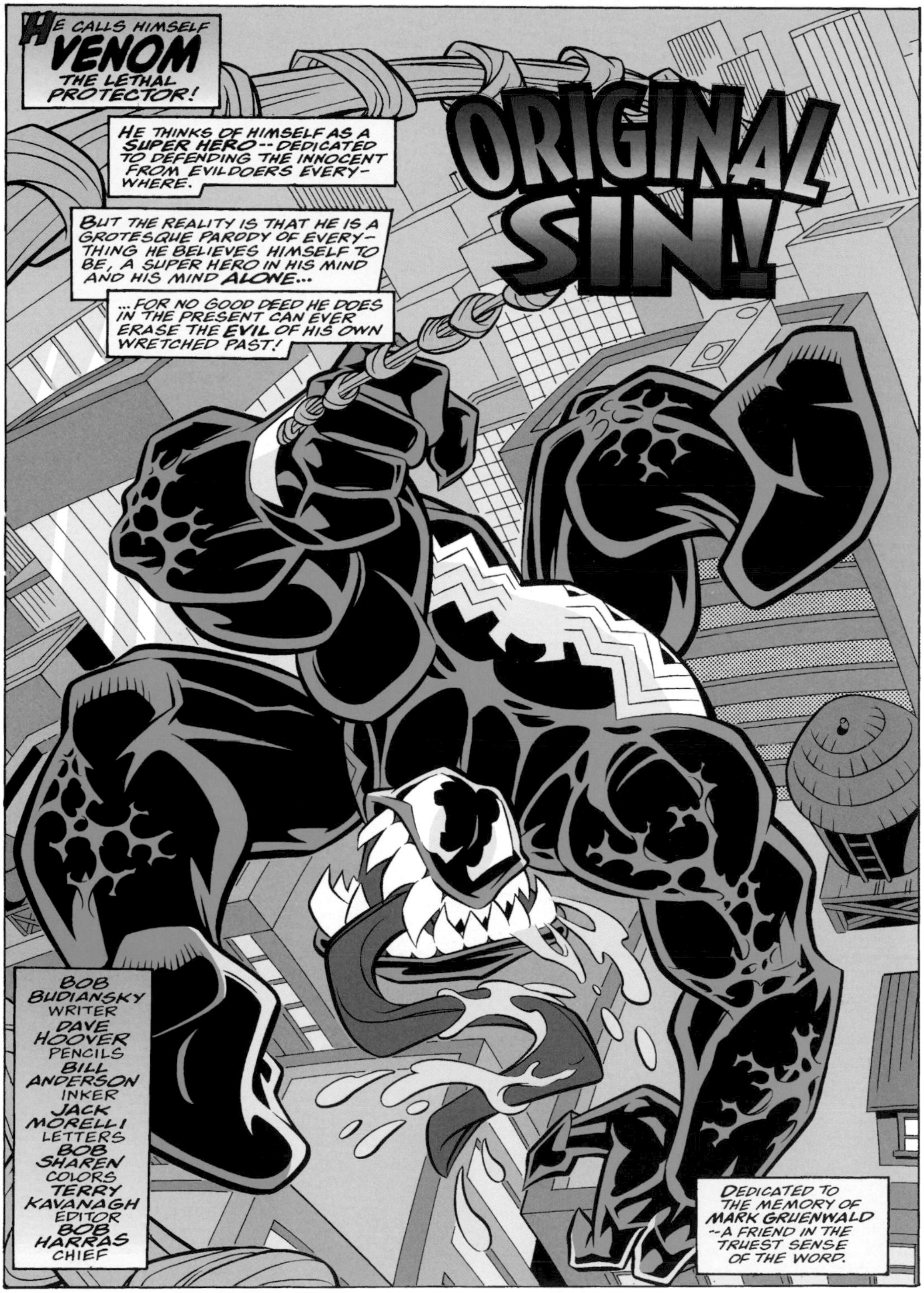
HE CALLS HIMSELF VENOM THE LETHAL PROTECTOR!
HE THINKS OF HIMSELF AS A SUPER HERO-- DEDICATED TO DEFENDING THE INNOCENT FROM EVILDOERS EVERY-WHERE.
ORIGINAL SIN!
BUT THE REALITY IS THAT HE IS A GROTESQUE PARODY OF EVERY-THING HE BELIEVES HIMSELF TO BE, A SUPER HERO IN HIS MIND AND HIS MIND ALONE...
...FOR NO GOOD DEED HE DOES IN THE PRESENT CAN EVER ERASE THE EVIL OF HIS OWN WRETCHED PAST!
BOB BUDIANSKY WRITER DAVE HOOVER PENCILS BILL ANDERSON INKER JACK MORELLI LETTERS BOB SHAREN COLORS TERRY KAVANAGH EDITOR BOB HARRAS CHIEF
DEDICATED TO THE MEMORY OF MARK GRUENWALD --A FRIEND IN THE TRUEST SENSE OF THE WORD.

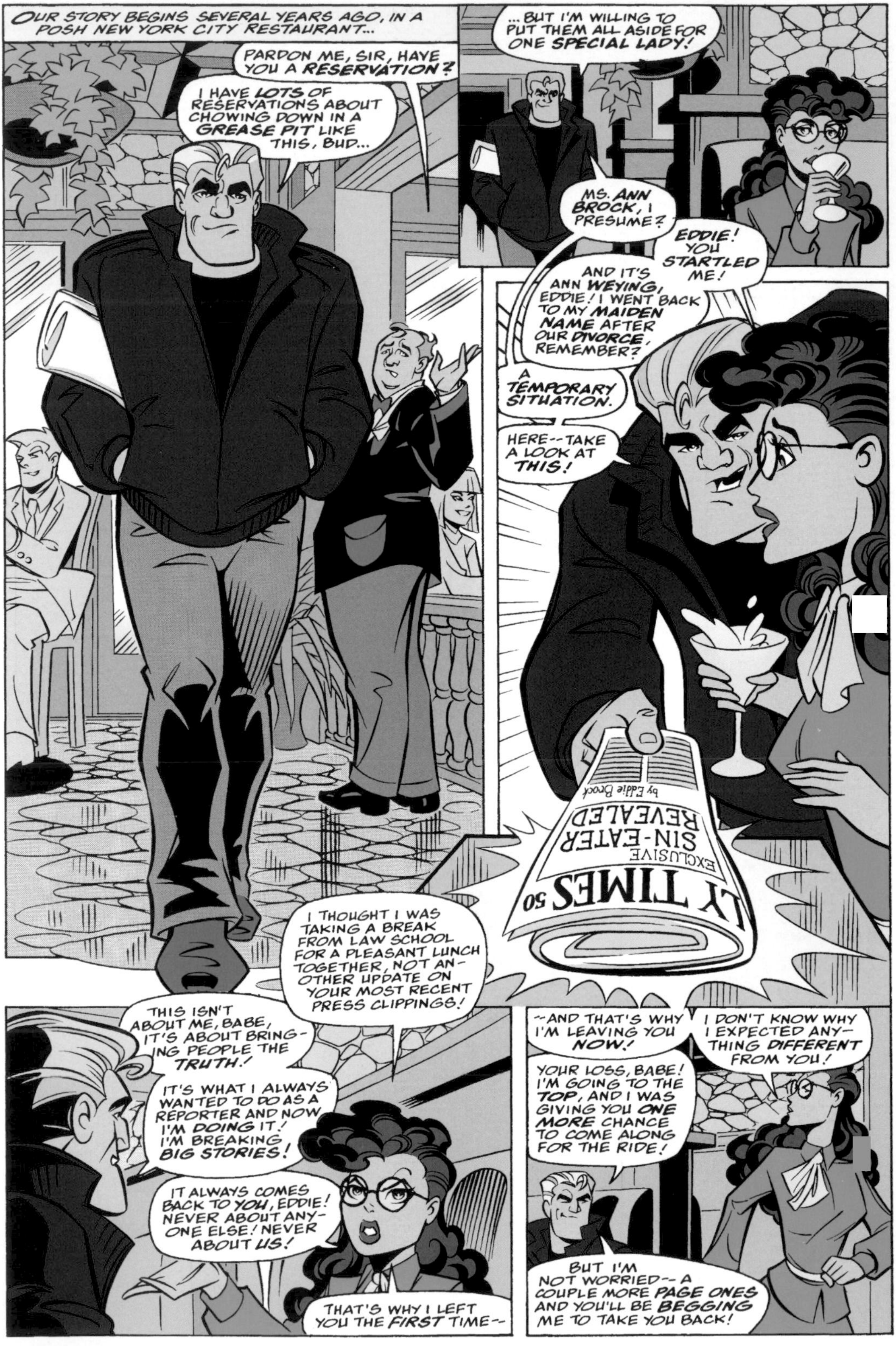

OUR STORY BEGINS SEVERAL YEARS AGO, IN A POSH NEW YORK CITY RESTAURANT...
PARDON ME, SIR, HAVE YOU A RESERVATION?
I HAVE LOTS OF RESERVATIONS ABOUT CHOWING DOWN IN A GREASE PIT LIKE THIS, BUD...
...BUT I'M WILLING TO PUT THEM ALL ASIDE FOR ONE SPECIAL LADY!
MS. ANN BROCK, I PRESUME?
EDDIE! YOU STARTLED ME!
AND IT'S ANN WEYING, EDDIE! I WENT BACK TO MY MAIDEN NAME AFTER OUR DIVORCE, REMEMBER?
A TEMPORARY SITUATION.
HERE--TAKE A LOOK AT THIS!
LY TIMES 50
EXCLUSIVE
SIN-EATER REVEALED
by Eddie Brock
I THOUGHT I WAS TAKING A BREAK FROM LAW SCHOOL FOR A PLEASANT LUNCH TOGETHER, NOT AN-OTHER UPDATE ON YOUR MOST RECENT PRESS CLIPPINGS!
THIS ISN'T ABOUT ME, BABE, IT'S ABOUT BRING-ING PEOPLE THE TRUTH!
IT'S WHAT I ALWAYS WANTED TO DO AS A REPORTER AND NOW I'M DOING IT! I'M BREAKING BIG STORIES!
IT ALWAYS COMES BACK TO YOU, EDDIE! NEVER ABOUT ANY-ONE ELSE! NEVER ABOUT US!
THAT'S WHY I LEFT YOU THE FIRST TIME--
--AND THAT'S WHY I'M LEAVING YOU NOW!
I DON'T KNOW WHY I EXPECTED ANY-THING DIFFERENT FROM YOU!
YOUR LOSS, BABE! I'M GOING TO THE TOP, AND I WAS GIVING YOU ONE MORE CHANCE TO COME ALONG FOR THE RIDE!
BUT I'M NOT WORRIED-- A COUPLE MORE PAGE ONES AND YOU'LL BE BEGGING ME TO TAKE YOU BACK!

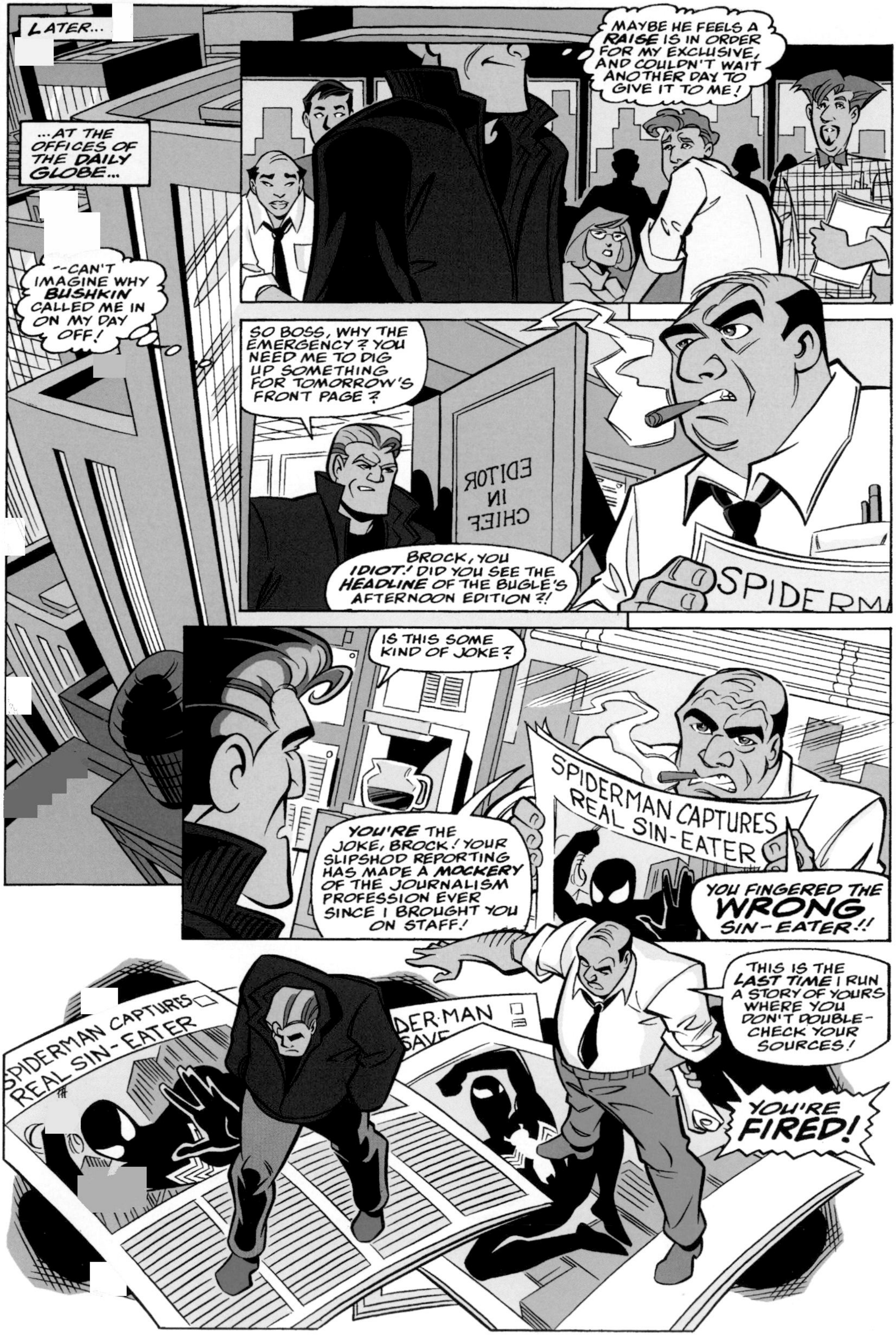
LATER...
...AT THE OFFICES OF THE DAILY GLOBE...
--CAN'T IMAGINE WHY BUSHKIN CALLED ME IN ON MY DAY OFF!
MAYBE HE FEELS A RAISE IS IN ORDER FOR MY EXCLUSIVE, AND COULDN'T WAIT ANOTHER DAY TO GIVE IT TO ME!
SO BOSS, WHY THE EMERGENCY? YOU NEED ME TO DIG UP SOMETHING FOR TOMORROW'S FRONT PAGE?
EDITOR IN CHIEF
BROCK, YOU IDIOT! DID YOU SEE THE HEADLINE OF THE BUGLE'S AFTERNOON EDITION?!
SPIDERM
IS THIS SOME KIND OF JOKE?
SPIDERMAN CAPTURES REAL SIN-EATER
YOU'RE THE JOKE, BROCK! YOUR SLIPSHOD REPORTING HAS MADE A MOCKERY OF THE JOURNALISM PROFESSION EVER SINCE I BROUGHT YOU ON STAFF!
YOU FINGERED THE WRONG SIN-EATER!!
SPIDERMAN CAPTURES REAL SIN-EATER
DER-MAN SAVE
THIS IS THE LAST TIME I RUN A STORY OF YOURS WHERE YOU DON'T DOUBLE-CHECK YOUR SOURCES!
YOU'RE FIRED!

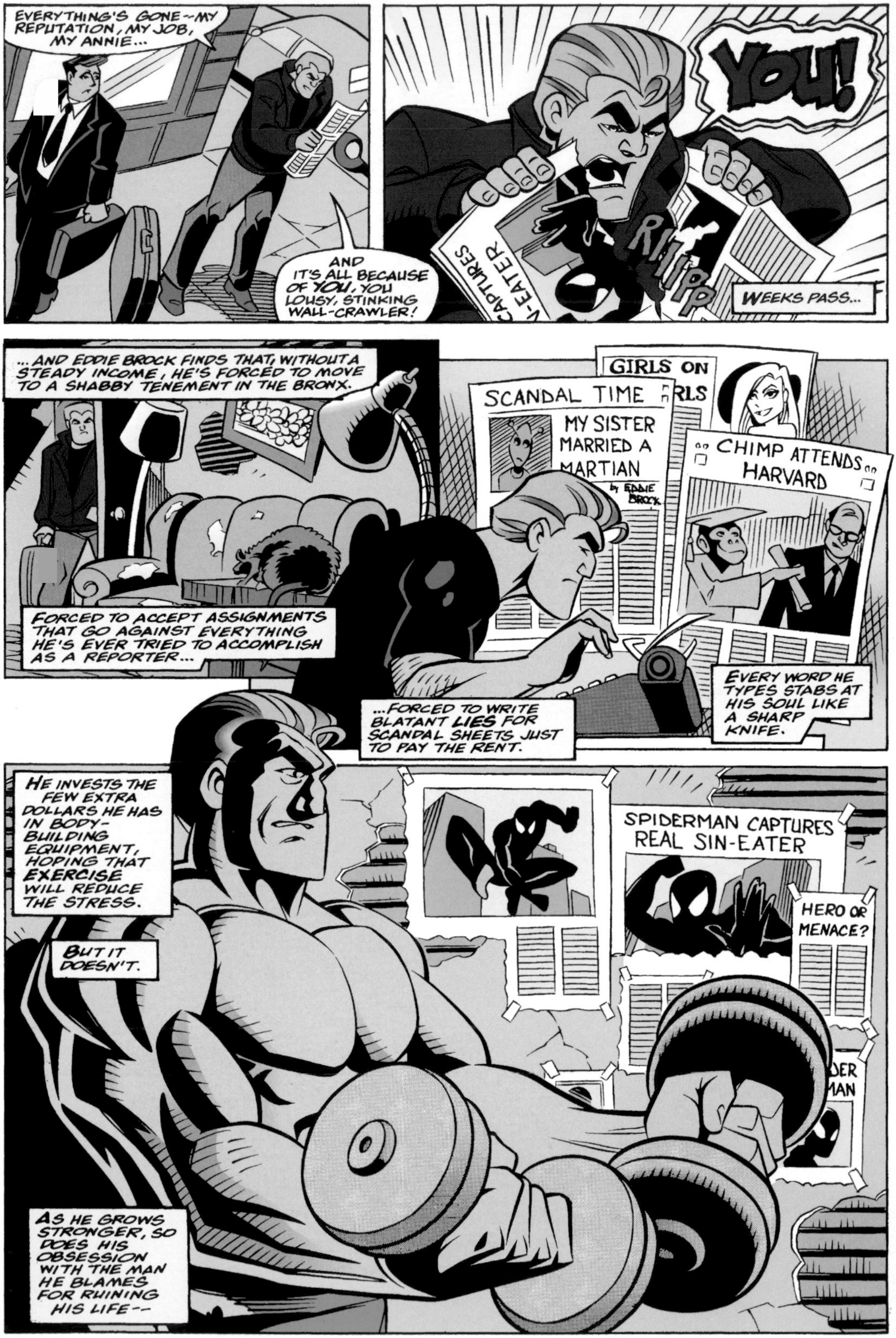
EVERYTHING'S GONE--MY REPUTATION, MY JOB, MY ANNIE...
AND IT'S ALL BECAUSE OF YOU, YOU LOUSY, STINKING WALL-CRAWLER!
YOU!
RIIIPP
WEEKS PASS...
...AND EDDIE BROCK FINDS THAT, WITHOUT A STEADY INCOME, HE'S FORCED TO MOVE TO A SHABBY TENEMENT IN THE BRONX.
GIRLS ON
SCANDAL TIME
MY SISTER MARRIED A MARTIAN
by EDDIE BROCK
CHIMP ATTENDS HARVARD
FORCED TO ACCEPT ASSIGNMENTS THAT GO AGAINST EVERYTHING HE'S EVER TRIED TO ACCOMPLISH AS A REPORTER...
...FORCED TO WRITE BLATANT LIES FOR SCANDAL SHEETS JUST TO PAY THE RENT.
EVERY WORD HE TYPES STABS AT HIS SOUL LIKE A SHARP KNIFE.
HE INVESTS THE FEW EXTRA DOLLARS HE HAS IN BODY-BUILDING EQUIPMENT, HOPING THAT EXERCISE WILL REDUCE THE STRESS.
BUT IT DOESN'T.
SPIDERMAN CAPTURES REAL SIN-EATER
HERO OR MENACE?
AS HE GROWS STRONGER, SO DOES HIS OBSESSION WITH THE MAN HE BLAMES FOR RUINING HIS LIFE--

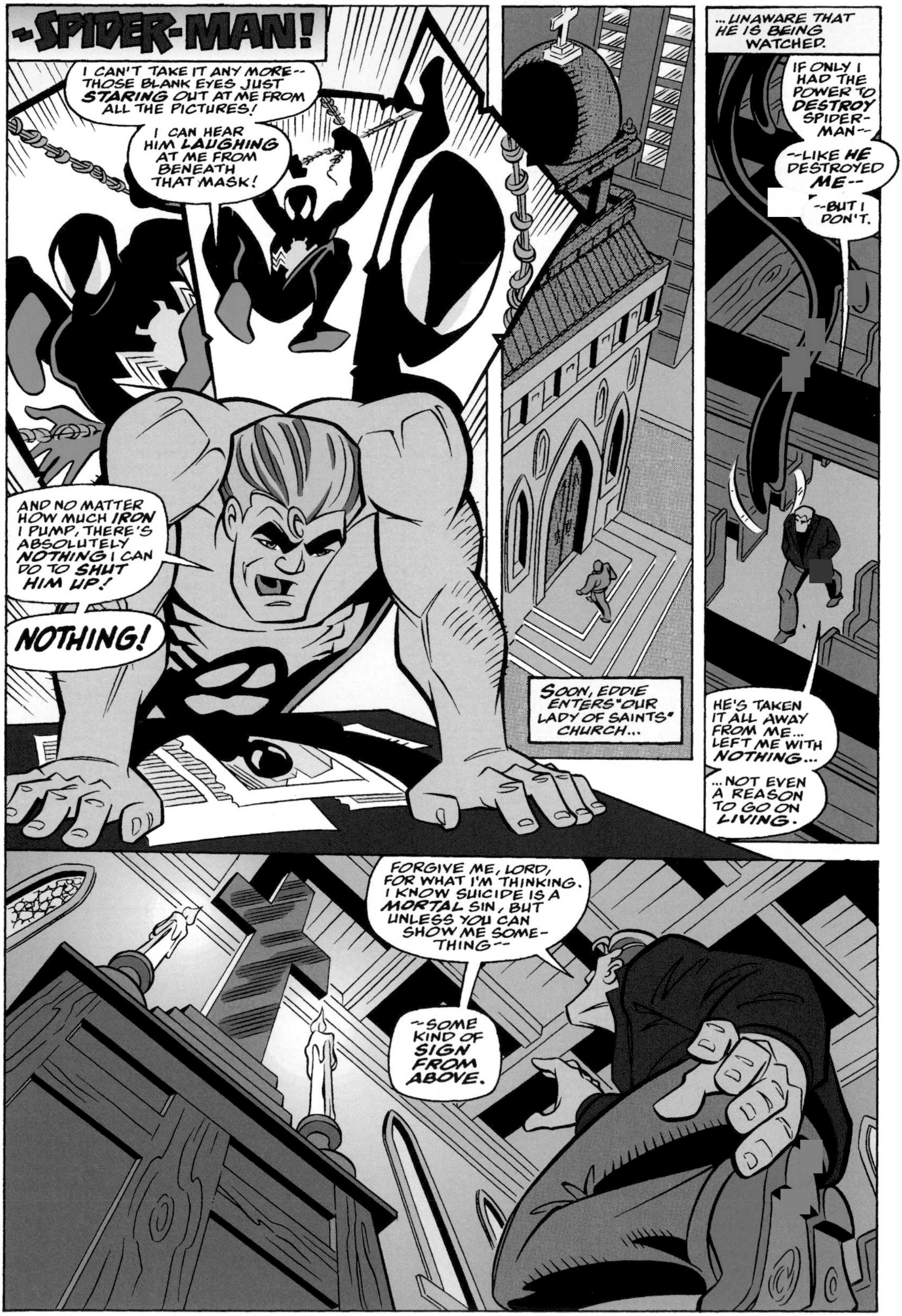
-SPIDER-MAN!
I CAN'T TAKE IT ANY MORE-- THOSE BLANK EYES JUST STARING OUT AT ME FROM ALL THE PICTURES!
I CAN HEAR HIM LAUGHING AT ME FROM BENEATH THAT MASK!
AND NO MATTER HOW MUCH IRON I PUMP, THERE'S ABSOLUTELY NOTHING I CAN DO TO SHUT HIM UP!
NOTHING!
SOON, EDDIE ENTERS "OUR LADY OF SAINTS" CHURCH...
...UNAWARE THAT HE IS BEING WATCHED.
IF ONLY I HAD THE POWER TO DESTROY SPIDER-MAN--
--LIKE HE DESTROYED ME--
--BUT I DON'T.
HE'S TAKEN IT ALL AWAY FROM ME... LEFT ME WITH NOTHING...
...NOT EVEN A REASON TO GO ON LIVING.
FORGIVE ME, LORD, FOR WHAT I'M THINKING. I KNOW SUICIDE IS A MORTAL SIN, BUT UNLESS YOU CAN SHOW ME SOME-THING--
--SOME KIND OF SIGN FROM ABOVE.

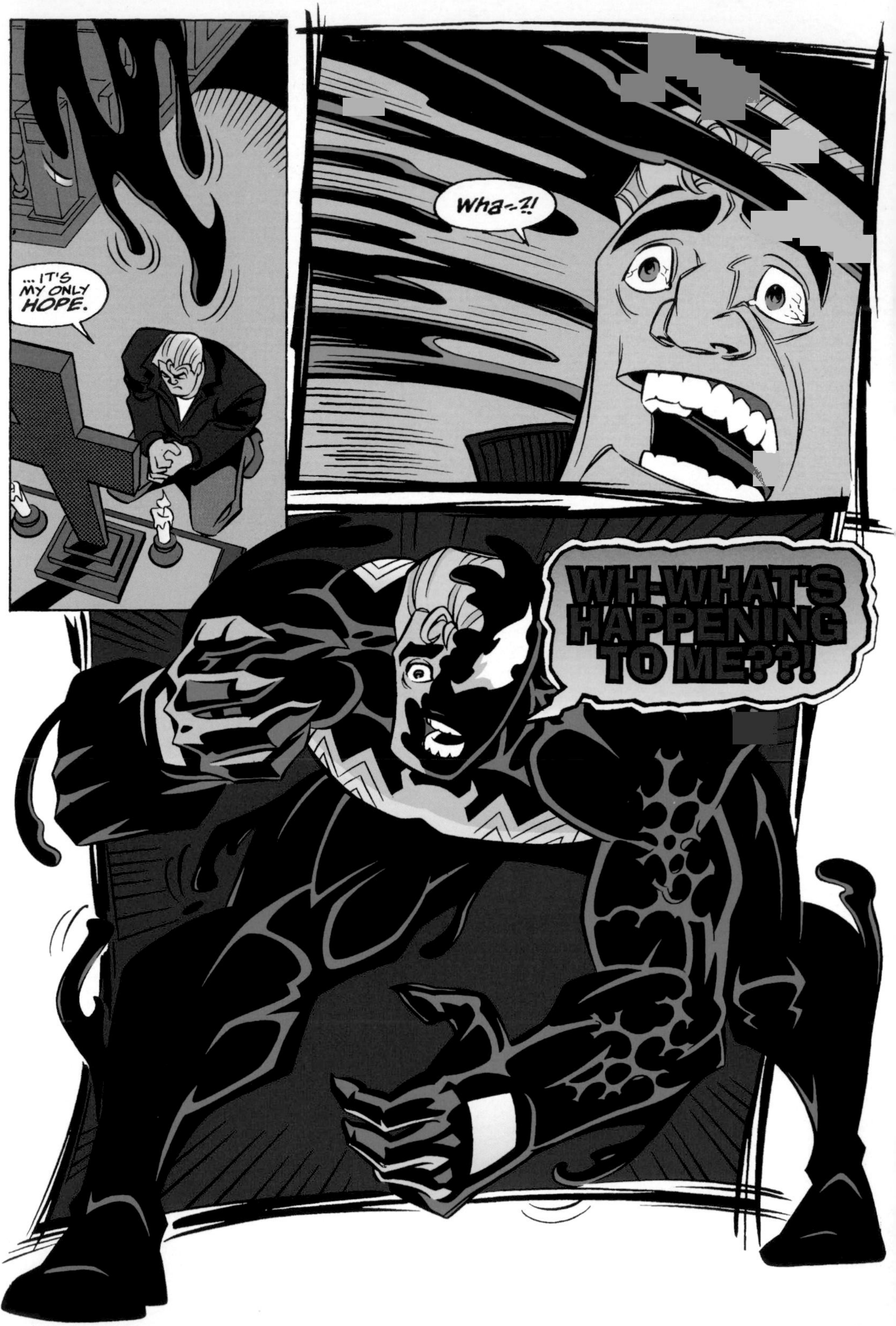
...IT'S MY ONLY HOPE.
Wha--?!
WH-WHAT'S HAPPENING TO ME??!

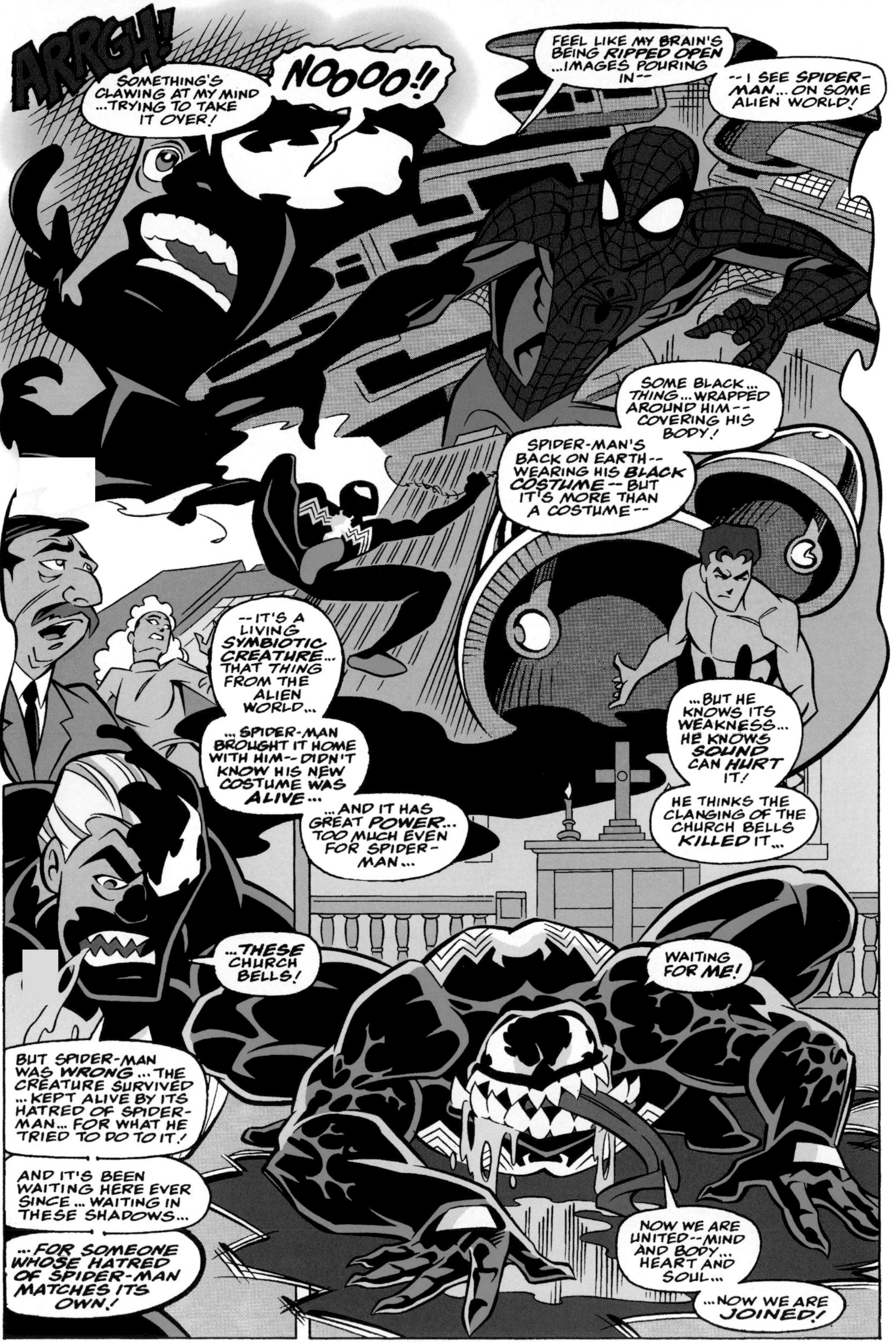
ARRGH!!
SOMETHING'S CLAWING AT MY MIND ...TRYING TO TAKE IT OVER!
NOOOO!!
FEEL LIKE MY BRAIN'S BEING RIPPED OPEN ...IMAGES POURING IN--
--I SEE SPIDER-MAN... ON SOME ALIEN WORLD!
SOME BLACK... THING... WRAPPED AROUND HIM-- COVERING HIS BODY!
SPIDER-MAN'S BACK ON EARTH-- WEARING HIS BLACK COSTUME--BUT IT'S MORE THAN A COSTUME--
--IT'S A LIVING SYMBIOTIC CREATURE... THAT THING FROM THE ALIEN WORLD...
...SPIDER-MAN BROUGHT IT HOME WITH HIM--DIDN'T KNOW HIS NEW COSTUME WAS ALIVE...
...AND IT HAS GREAT POWER... TOO MUCH EVEN FOR SPIDER-MAN...
...BUT HE KNOWS ITS WEAKNESS... HE KNOWS SOUND CAN HURT IT!
HE THINKS THE CLANGING OF THE CHURCH BELLS KILLED IT...
...THESE CHURCH BELLS!
WAITING FOR ME!
BUT SPIDER-MAN WAS WRONG... THE CREATURE SURVIVED ...KEPT ALIVE BY ITS HATRED OF SPIDER-MAN... FOR WHAT HE TRIED TO DO TO IT!
AND IT'S BEEN WAITING HERE EVER SINCE... WAITING IN THESE SHADOWS...
...FOR SOMEONE WHOSE HATRED OF SPIDER-MAN MATCHES ITS OWN!
NOW WE ARE UNITED--MIND AND BODY... HEART AND SOUL...
...NOW WE ARE JOINED!

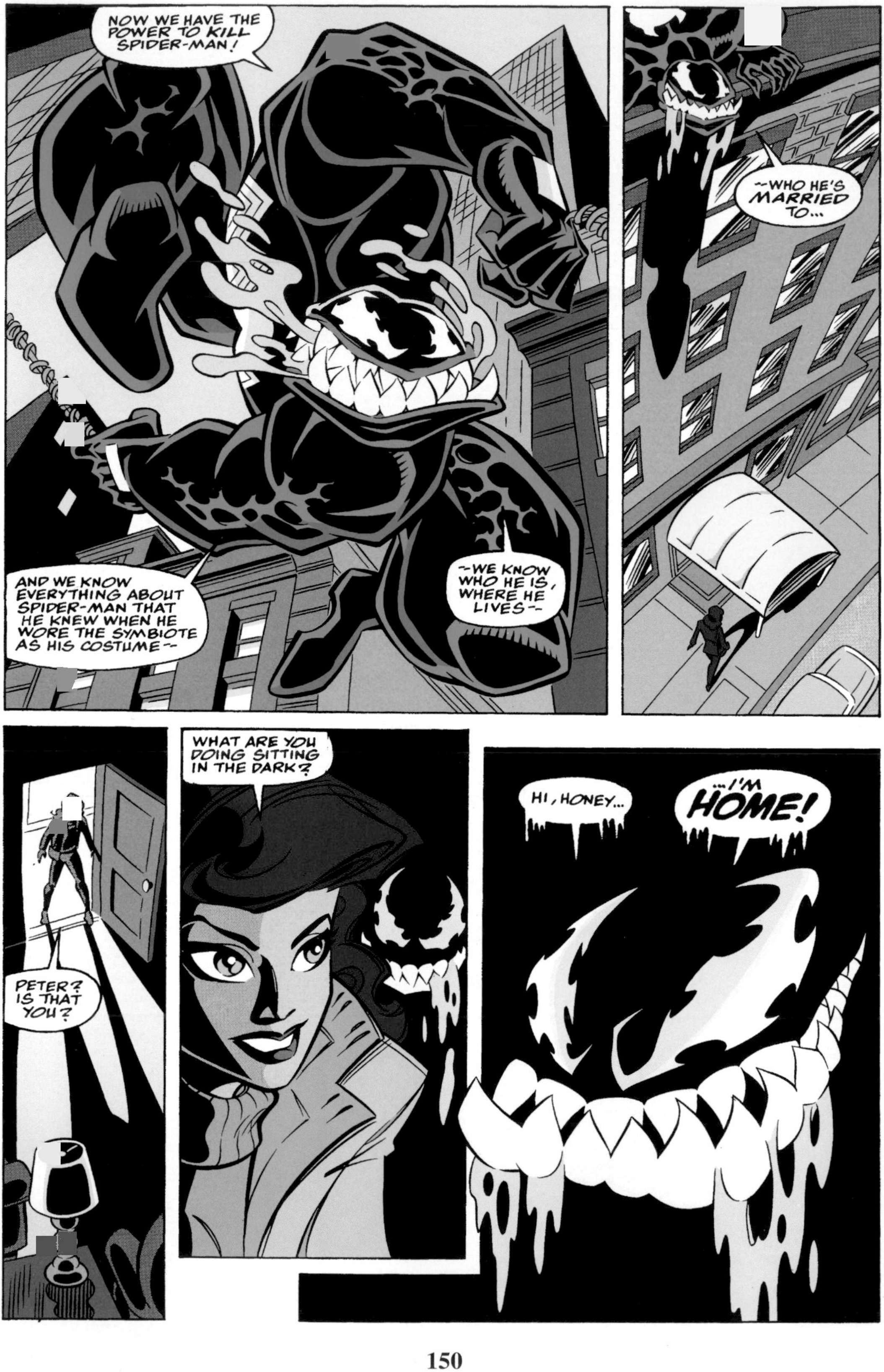
NOW WE HAVE THE POWER TO KILL SPIDER-MAN!
AND WE KNOW EVERYTHING ABOUT SPIDER-MAN THAT HE KNEW WHEN HE WORE THE SYMBIOTE AS HIS COSTUME--
--WE KNOW WHO HE IS, WHERE HE LIVES--
--WHO HE'S MARRIED TO...
PETER? IS THAT YOU?
WHAT ARE YOU DOING SITTING IN THE DARK?
HI, HONEY...
...I'M HOME!

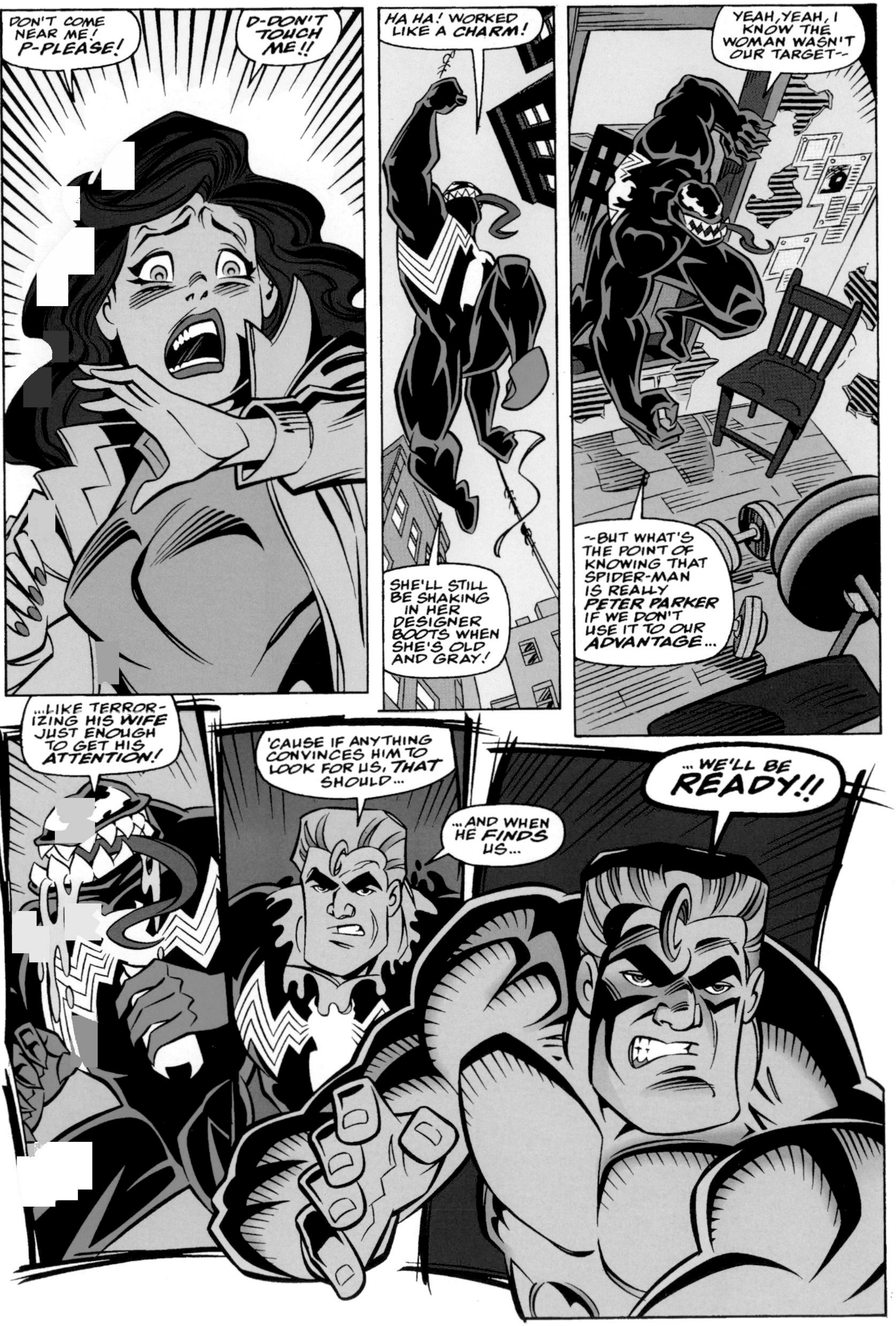
DON'T COME NEAR ME! P-PLEASE!
D-DON'T TOUCH ME!!
HA HA! WORKED LIKE A CHARM!
SHE'LL STILL BE SHAKING IN HER DESIGNER BOOTS WHEN SHE'S OLD AND GRAY!
YEAH, YEAH, I KNOW THE WOMAN WASN'T OUR TARGET--
--BUT WHAT'S THE POINT OF KNOWING THAT SPIDER-MAN IS REALLY PETER PARKER IF WE DON'T USE IT TO OUR ADVANTAGE...
...LIKE TERRORIZING HIS WIFE JUST ENOUGH TO GET HIS ATTENTION!
'CAUSE IF ANYTHING CONVINCES HIM TO LOOK FOR US, THAT SHOULD...
...AND WHEN HE FINDS US...
...WE'LL BE READY!!

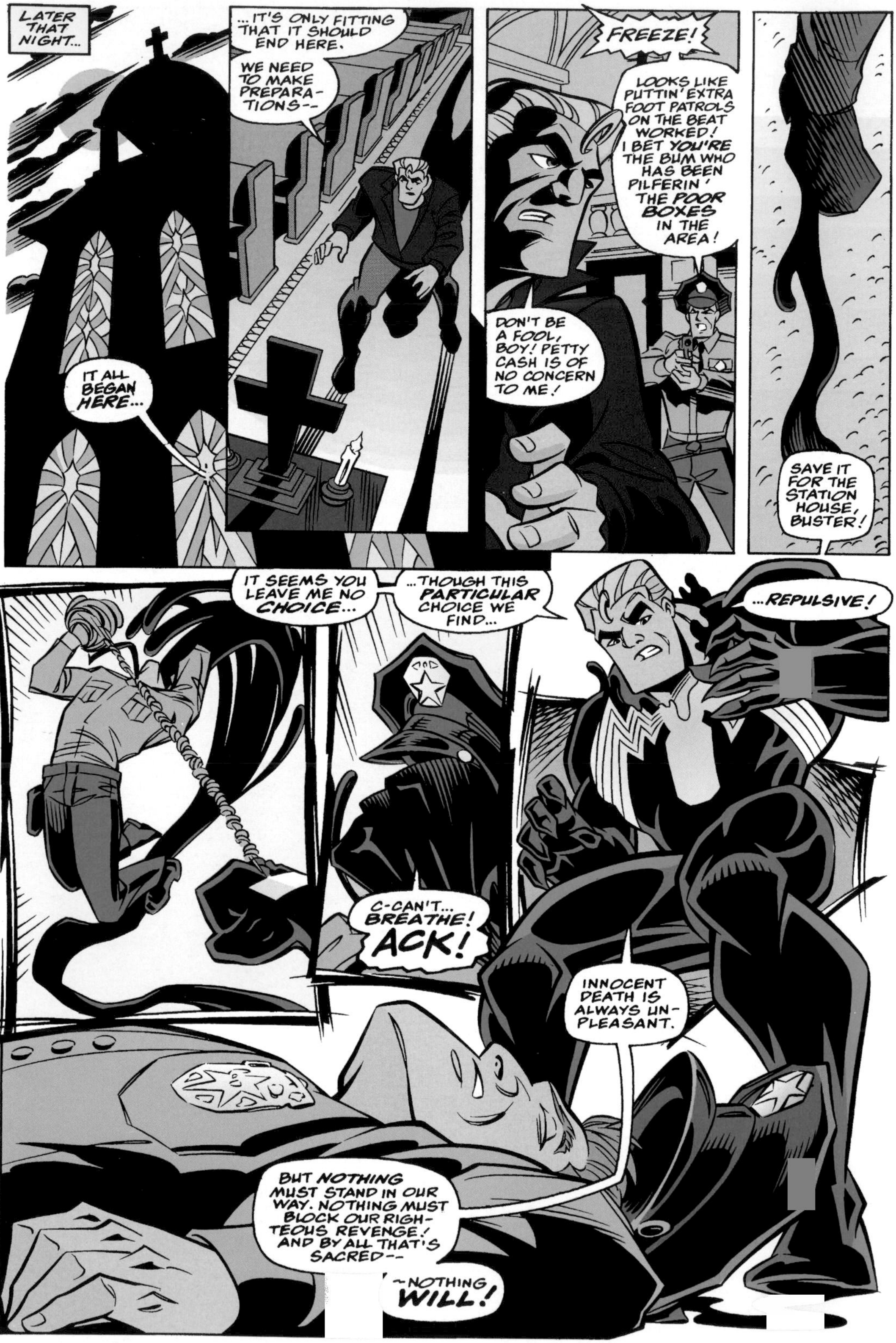
LATER THAT NIGHT...
IT ALL BEGAN HERE...
...IT'S ONLY FITTING THAT IT SHOULD END HERE.
WE NEED TO MAKE PREPARATIONS--
FREEZE!
LOOKS LIKE PUTTIN' EXTRA FOOT PATROLS ON THE BEAT WORKED! I BET YOU'RE THE BUM WHO HAS BEEN PILFERIN' THE POOR BOXES IN THE AREA!
DON'T BE A FOOL, BOY! PETTY CASH IS OF NO CONCERN TO ME!
SAVE IT FOR THE STATION HOUSE, BUSTER!
IT SEEMS YOU LEAVE ME NO CHOICE...
...THOUGH THIS PARTICULAR CHOICE WE FIND...
...REPULSIVE!
C-CAN'T... BREATHE! ACK!
INNOCENT DEATH IS ALWAYS UN-PLEASANT.
BUT NOTHING MUST STAND IN OUR WAY. NOTHING MUST BLOCK OUR RIGHTEOUS REVENGE! AND BY ALL THAT'S SACRED--
--NOTHING WILL!

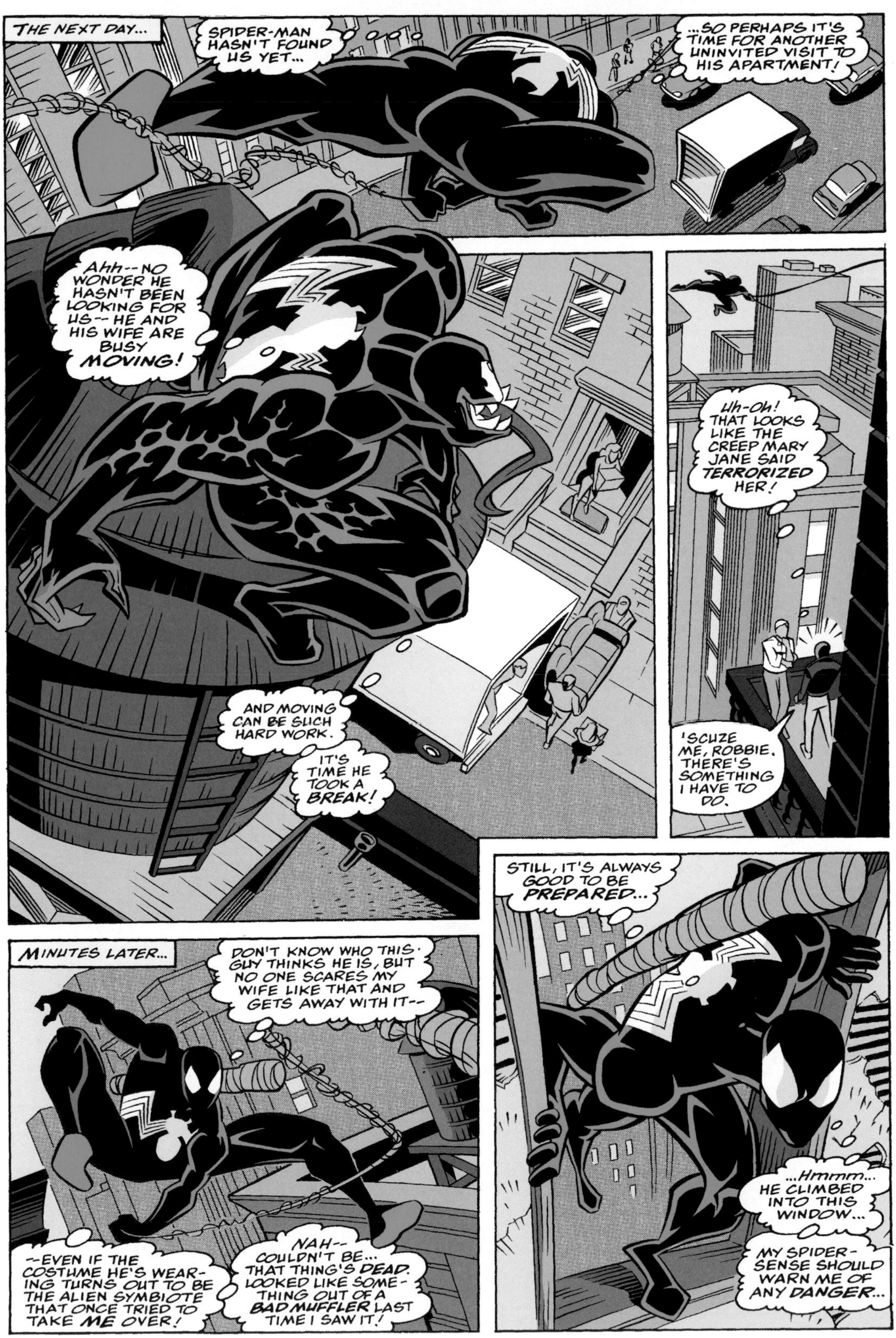
THE NEXT DAY...
SPIDER-MAN HASN'T FOUND US YET...
...SO PERHAPS IT'S TIME FOR ANOTHER UNINVITED VISIT TO HIS APARTMENT!
Ahh--NO WONDER HE HASN'T BEEN LOOKING FOR US--HE AND HIS WIFE ARE BUSY MOVING!
AND MOVING CAN BE SUCH HARD WORK.
IT'S TIME HE TOOK A BREAK!
Uh-Oh! THAT LOOKS LIKE THE CREEP MARY JANE SAID TERRORIZED HER!
'SCUZE ME, ROBBIE. THERE'S SOMETHING I HAVE TO DO.
MINUTES LATER...
DON'T KNOW WHO THIS GUY THINKS HE IS, BUT NO ONE SCARES MY WIFE LIKE THAT AND GETS AWAY WITH IT--
--EVEN IF THE COSTUME HE'S WEARING TURNS OUT TO BE THE ALIEN SYMBIOTE THAT ONCE TRIED TO TAKE ME OVER!
NAH--COULDN'T BE... THAT THING'S DEAD. LOOKED LIKE SOMETHING OUT OF A BAD MUFFLER LAST TIME I SAW IT!
STILL, IT'S ALWAYS GOOD TO BE PREPARED...
...Hmmm... HE CLIMBED INTO THIS WINDOW...
MY SPIDER-SENSE SHOULD WARN ME OF ANY DANGER...

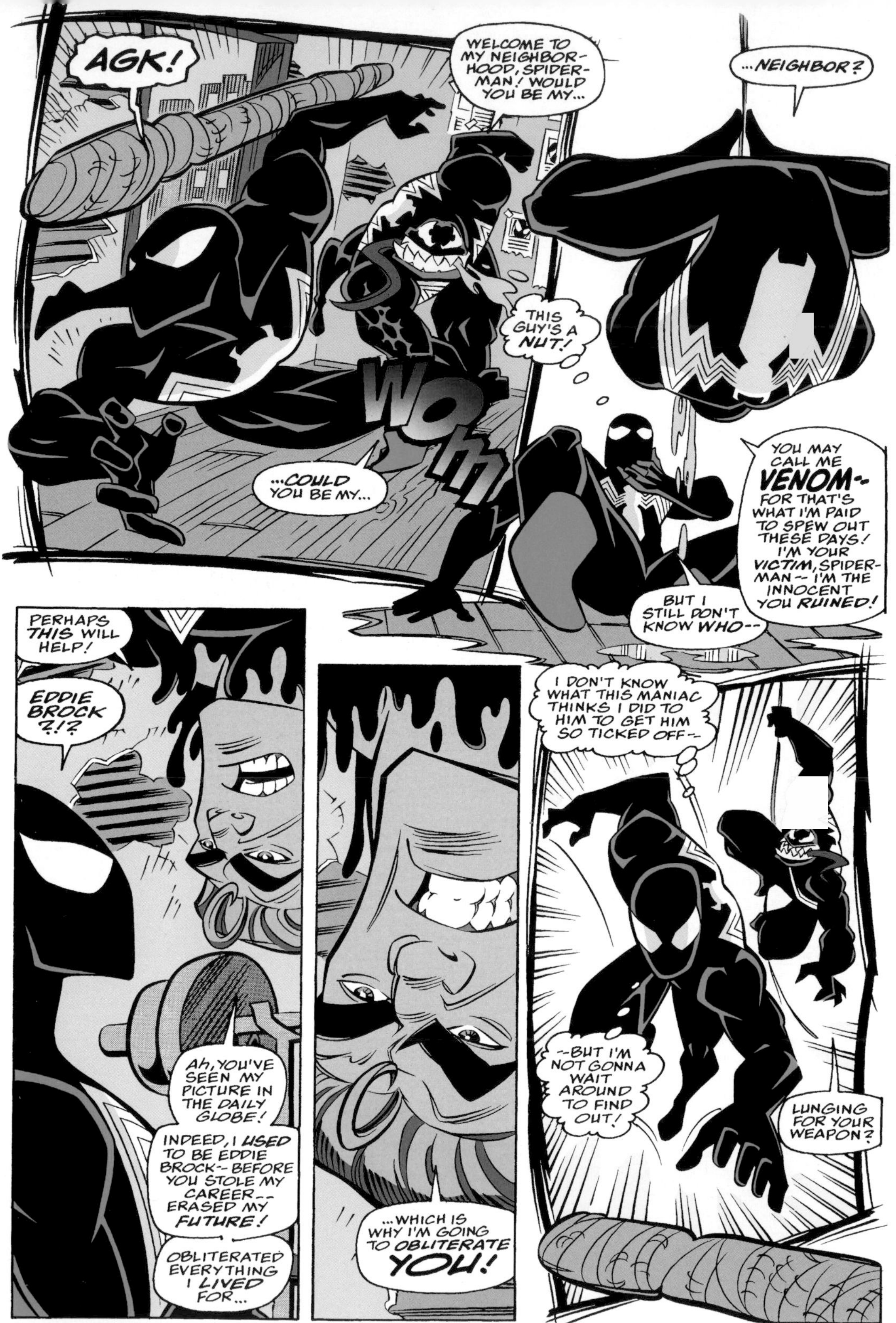
AGK!
WELCOME TO MY NEIGHBOR-HOOD, SPIDER-MAN! WOULD YOU BE MY...
...NEIGHBOR?
THIS GUY'S A NUT!
WOM
...COULD YOU BE MY...
YOU MAY CALL ME VENOM-- FOR THAT'S WHAT I'M PAID TO SPEW OUT THESE DAYS! I'M YOUR VICTIM, SPIDER-MAN-- I'M THE INNOCENT YOU RUINED!
BUT I STILL DON'T KNOW WHO--
PERHAPS THIS WILL HELP!
EDDIE BROCK ?!?
Ah, YOU'VE SEEN MY PICTURE IN THE DAILY GLOBE!
INDEED, I USED TO BE EDDIE BROCK-- BEFORE YOU STOLE MY CAREER-- ERASED MY FUTURE!
OBLITERATED EVERYTHING I LIVED FOR...
...WHICH IS WHY I'M GOING TO OBLITERATE YOU!
I DON'T KNOW WHAT THIS MANIAC THINKS I DID TO HIM TO GET HIM SO TICKED OFF--
--BUT I'M NOT GONNA WAIT AROUND TO FIND OUT!
LUNGING FOR YOUR WEAPON?

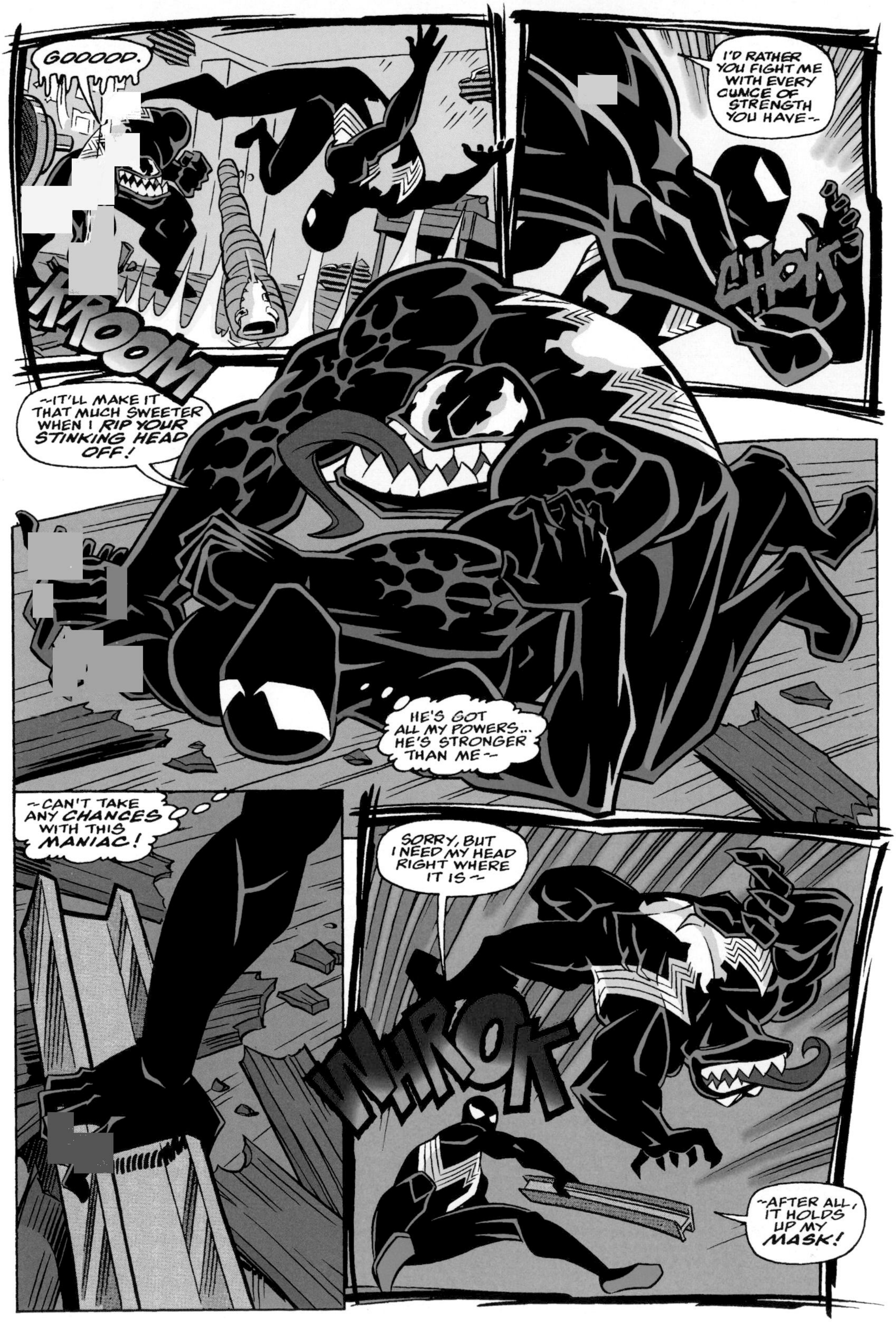
GOOOOOD.
KROOM
I'D RATHER YOU FIGHT ME WITH EVERY OUNCE OF STRENGTH YOU HAVE--
CHOK
--IT'LL MAKE IT THAT MUCH SWEETER WHEN I RIP YOUR STINKING HEAD OFF!
HE'S GOT ALL MY POWERS... HE'S STRONGER THAN ME--
--CAN'T TAKE ANY CHANCES WITH THIS MANIAC!
SORRY, BUT I NEED MY HEAD RIGHT WHERE IT IS--
WHROK
--AFTER ALL, IT HOLDS UP MY MASK!

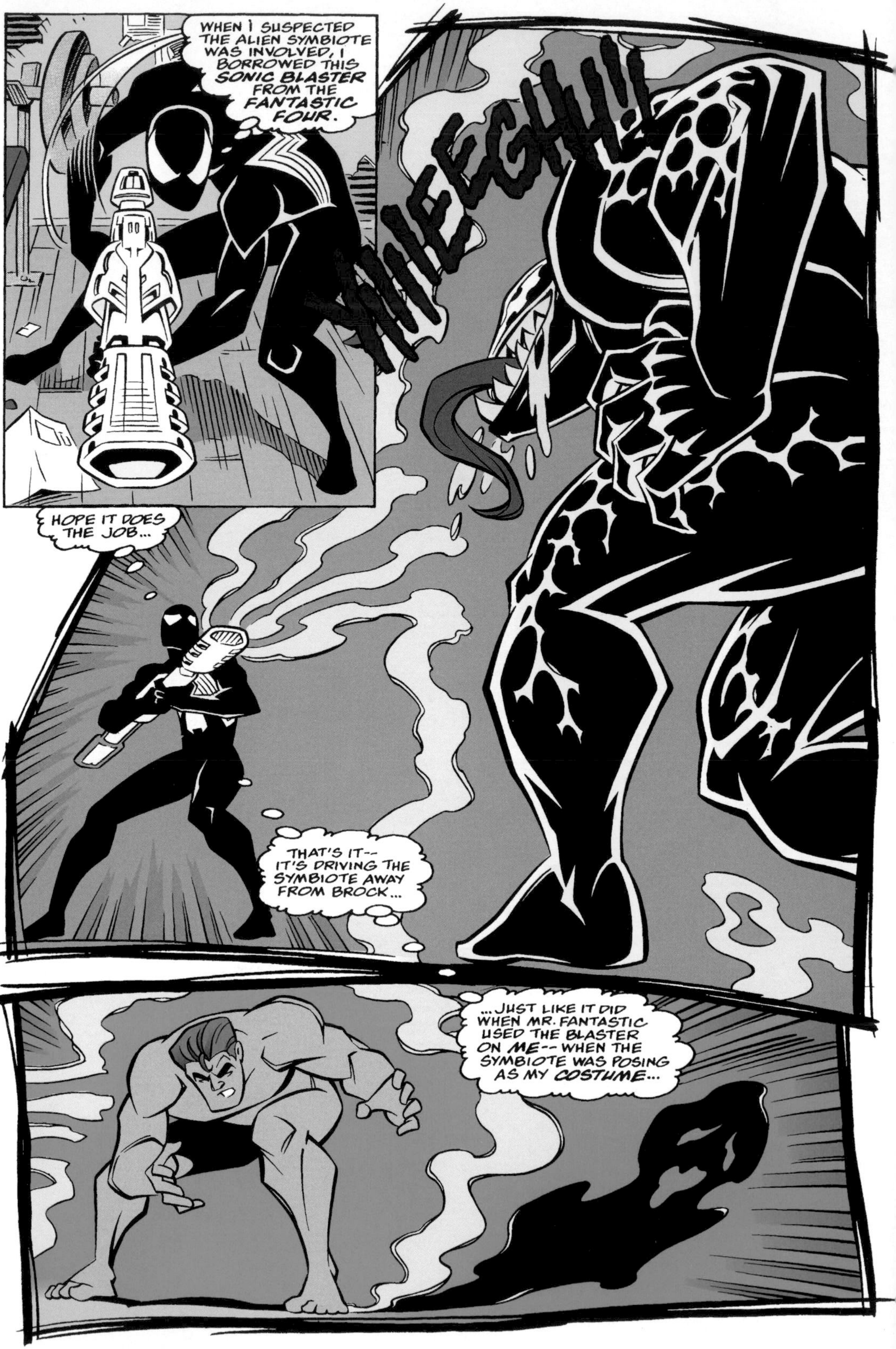

WHEN I SUSPECTED THE ALIEN SYMBIOTE WAS INVOLVED, I BORROWED THIS SONIC BLASTER FROM THE FANTASTIC FOUR.
WHEEGH!!!
HOPE IT DOES THE JOB...
THAT'S IT-- IT'S DRIVING THE SYMBIOTE AWAY FROM BROCK...
...JUST LIKE IT DID WHEN MR. FANTASTIC USED THE BLASTER ON ME-- WHEN THE SYMBIOTE WAS POSING AS MY COSTUME...

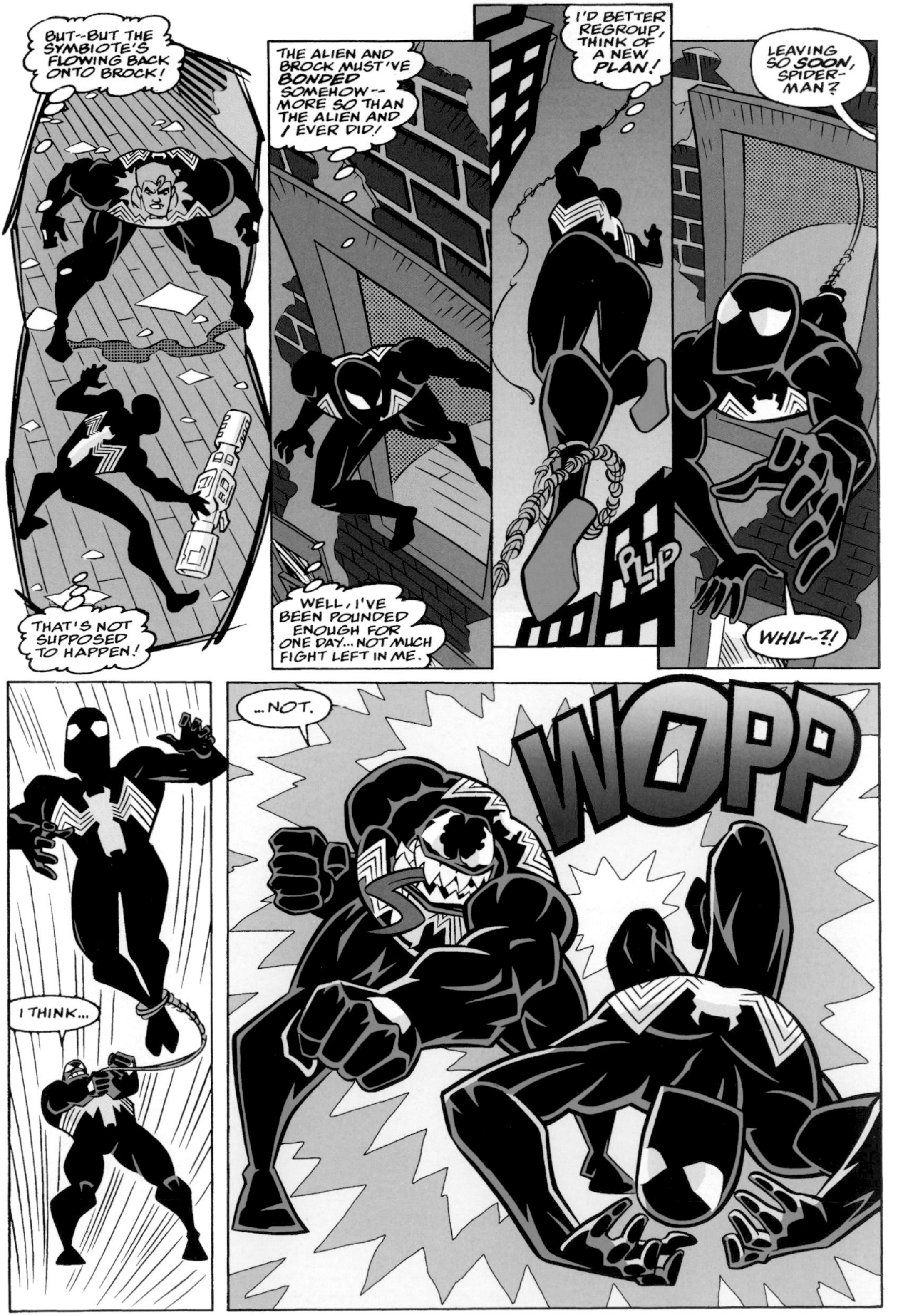
BUT--BUT THE SYMBIOTE'S FLOWING BACK ONTO BROCK!
THAT'S NOT SUPPOSED TO HAPPEN!
THE ALIEN AND BROCK MUST'VE BONDED SOMEHOW-- MORE SO THAN THE ALIEN AND I EVER DID!
WELL, I'VE BEEN POUNDED ENOUGH FOR ONE DAY... NOT MUCH FIGHT LEFT IN ME.
I'D BETTER REGROUP, THINK OF A NEW PLAN!
PLIP
LEAVING SO SOON, SPIDER-MAN?
WHU--?!
I THINK...
...NOT.
WOPP

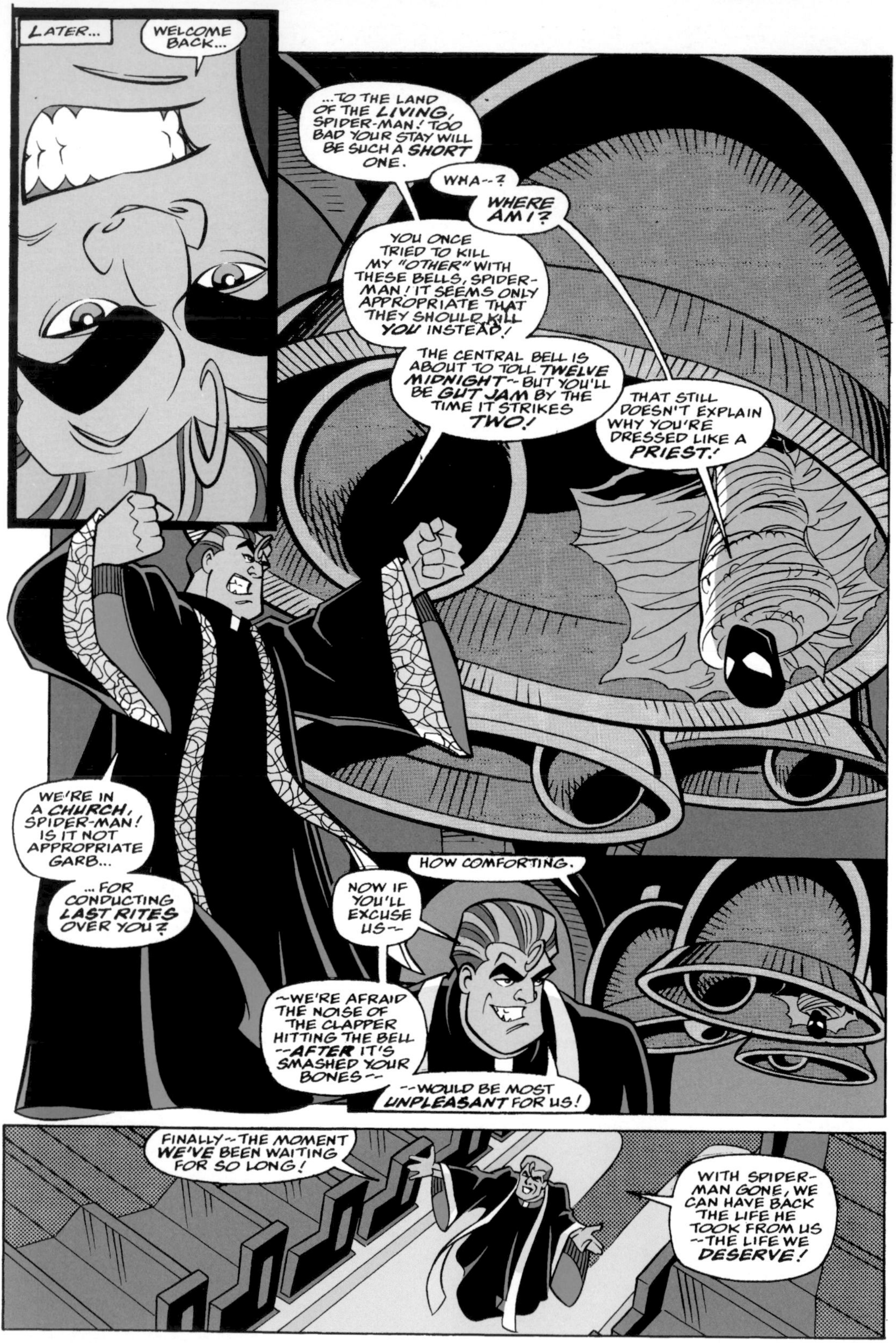
LATER...
WELCOME BACK...
...TO THE LAND OF THE LIVING, SPIDER-MAN! TOO BAD YOUR STAY WILL BE SUCH A SHORT ONE.
WHA--?
WHERE AM I?
YOU ONCE TRIED TO KILL MY "OTHER" WITH THESE BELLS, SPIDER-MAN! IT SEEMS ONLY APPROPRIATE THAT THEY SHOULD KILL YOU INSTEAD!
THE CENTRAL BELL IS ABOUT TO TOLL TWELVE MIDNIGHT-- BUT YOU'LL BE GUT JAM BY THE TIME IT STRIKES TWO!
THAT STILL DOESN'T EXPLAIN WHY YOU'RE DRESSED LIKE A PRIEST!
WE'RE IN A CHURCH, SPIDER-MAN! IS IT NOT APPROPRIATE GARB...
...FOR CONDUCTING LAST RITES OVER YOU?
HOW COMFORTING.
NOW IF YOU'LL EXCUSE US--
--WE'RE AFRAID THE NOISE OF THE CLAPPER HITTING THE BELL --AFTER IT'S SMASHED YOUR BONES--
--WOULD BE MOST UNPLEASANT FOR US!
FINALLY--THE MOMENT WE'VE BEEN WAITING FOR SO LONG!
WITH SPIDER-MAN GONE, WE CAN HAVE BACK THE LIFE HE TOOK FROM US --THE LIFE WE DESERVE!

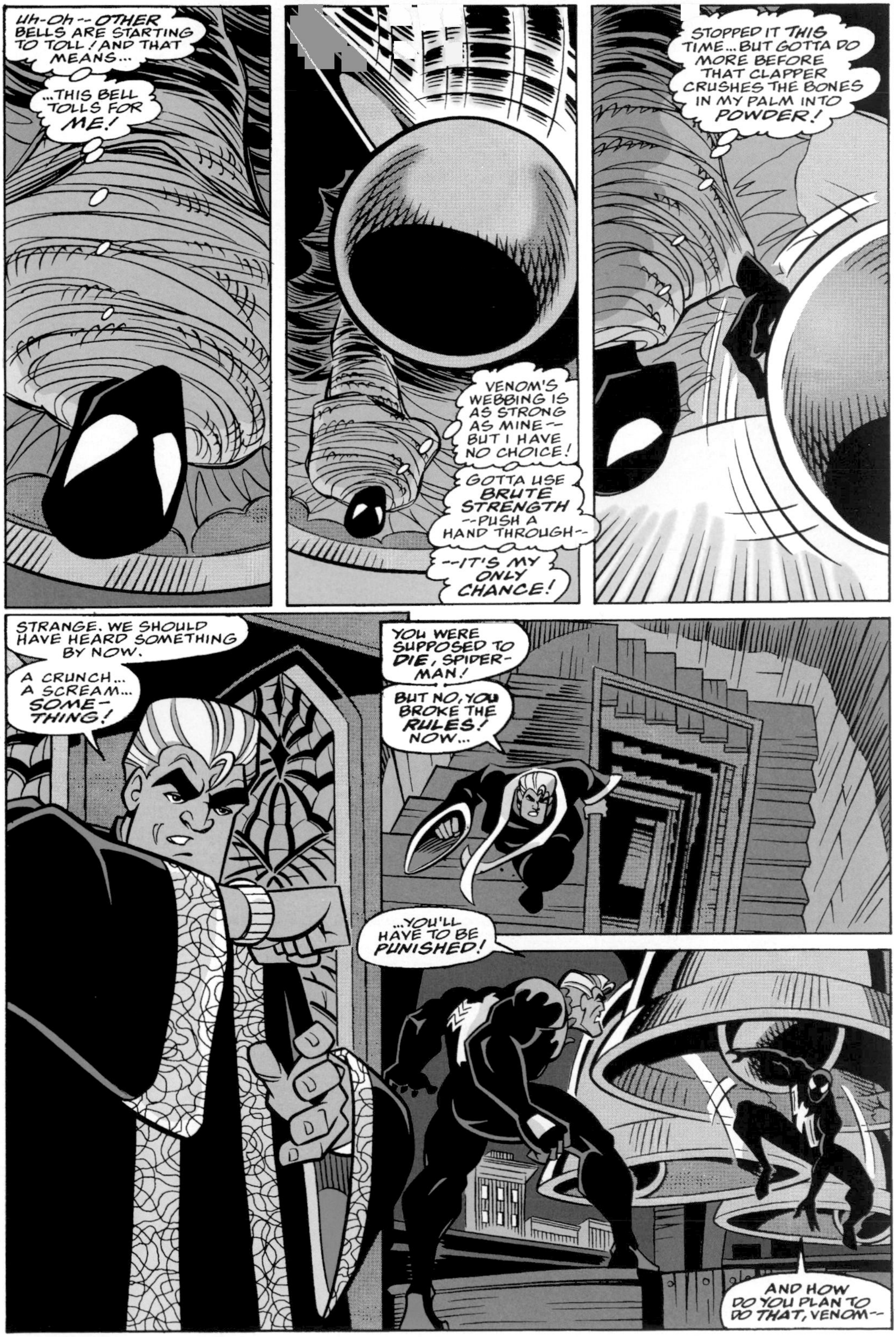
UH-OH -- OTHER BELLS ARE STARTING TO TOLL! AND THAT MEANS...
...THIS BELL TOLLS FOR ME!
VENOM'S WEBBING IS AS STRONG AS MINE -- BUT I HAVE NO CHOICE!
GOTTA USE BRUTE STRENGTH -- PUSH A HAND THROUGH --
-- IT'S MY ONLY CHANCE!
STOPPED IT THIS TIME... BUT GOTTA DO MORE BEFORE THAT CLAPPER CRUSHES THE BONES IN MY PALM INTO POWDER!
STRANGE. WE SHOULD HAVE HEARD SOMETHING BY NOW.
A CRUNCH... A SCREAM... SOMETHING!
YOU WERE SUPPOSED TO DIE, SPIDER-MAN!
BUT NO, YOU BROKE THE RULES! NOW...
...YOU'LL HAVE TO BE PUNISHED!
AND HOW DO YOU PLAN TO DO THAT, VENOM --

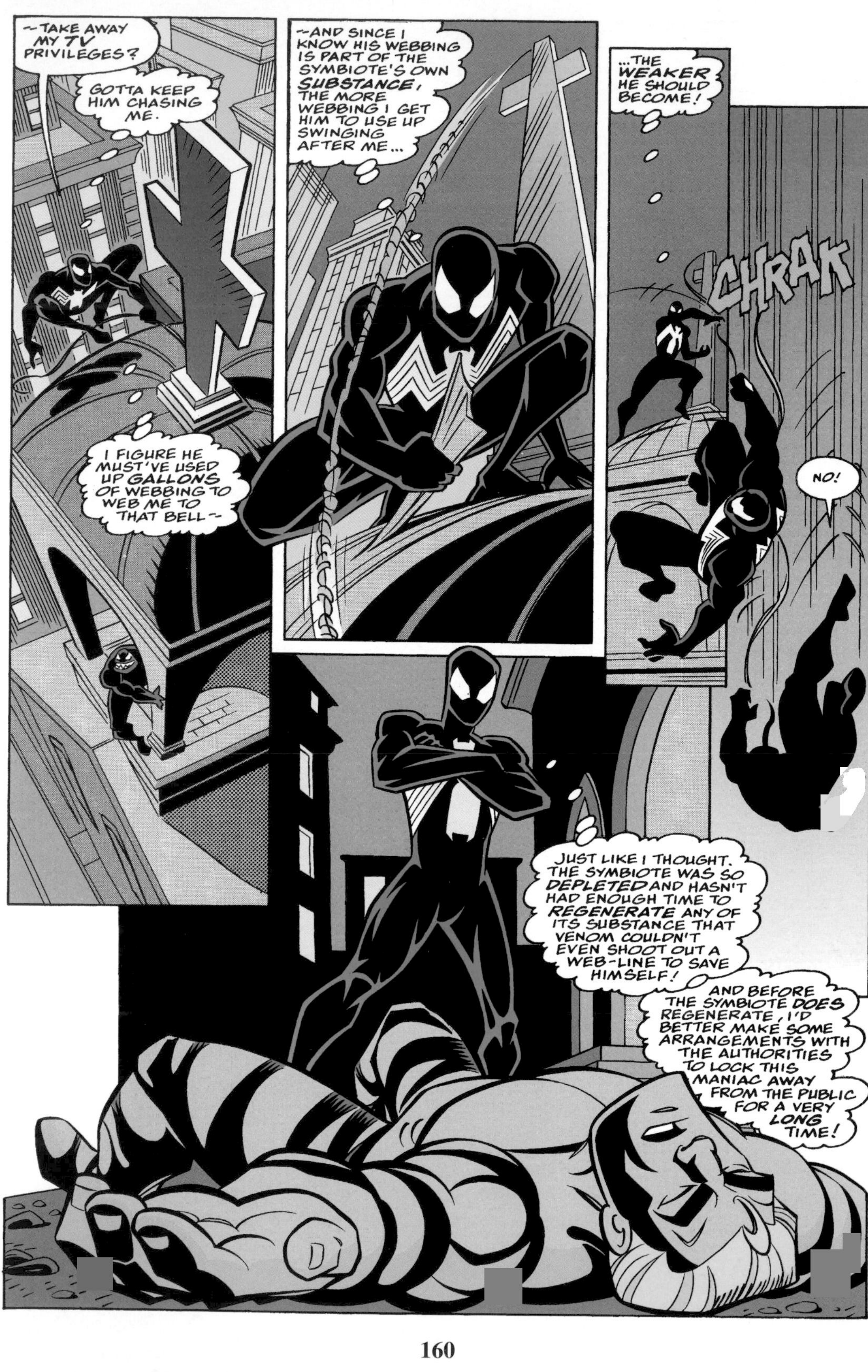
--TAKE AWAY MY TV PRIVILEGES?
GOTTA KEEP HIM CHASING ME.
I FIGURE HE MUST'VE USED UP GALLONS OF WEBBING TO WEB ME TO THAT BELL--
--AND SINCE I KNOW HIS WEBBING IS PART OF THE SYMBIOTE'S OWN SUBSTANCE, THE MORE WEBBING I GET HIM TO USE UP SWINGING AFTER ME...
...THE WEAKER HE SHOULD BECOME!
CHRAK
NO!
JUST LIKE I THOUGHT. THE SYMBIOTE WAS SO DEPLETED AND HASN'T HAD ENOUGH TIME TO REGENERATE ANY OF ITS SUBSTANCE THAT VENOM COULDN'T EVEN SHOOT OUT A WEB-LINE TO SAVE HIMSELF!
AND BEFORE THE SYMBIOTE DOES REGENERATE, I'D BETTER MAKE SOME ARRANGEMENTS WITH THE AUTHORITIES TO LOCK THIS MANIAC AWAY FROM THE PUBLIC FOR A VERY LONG TIME!

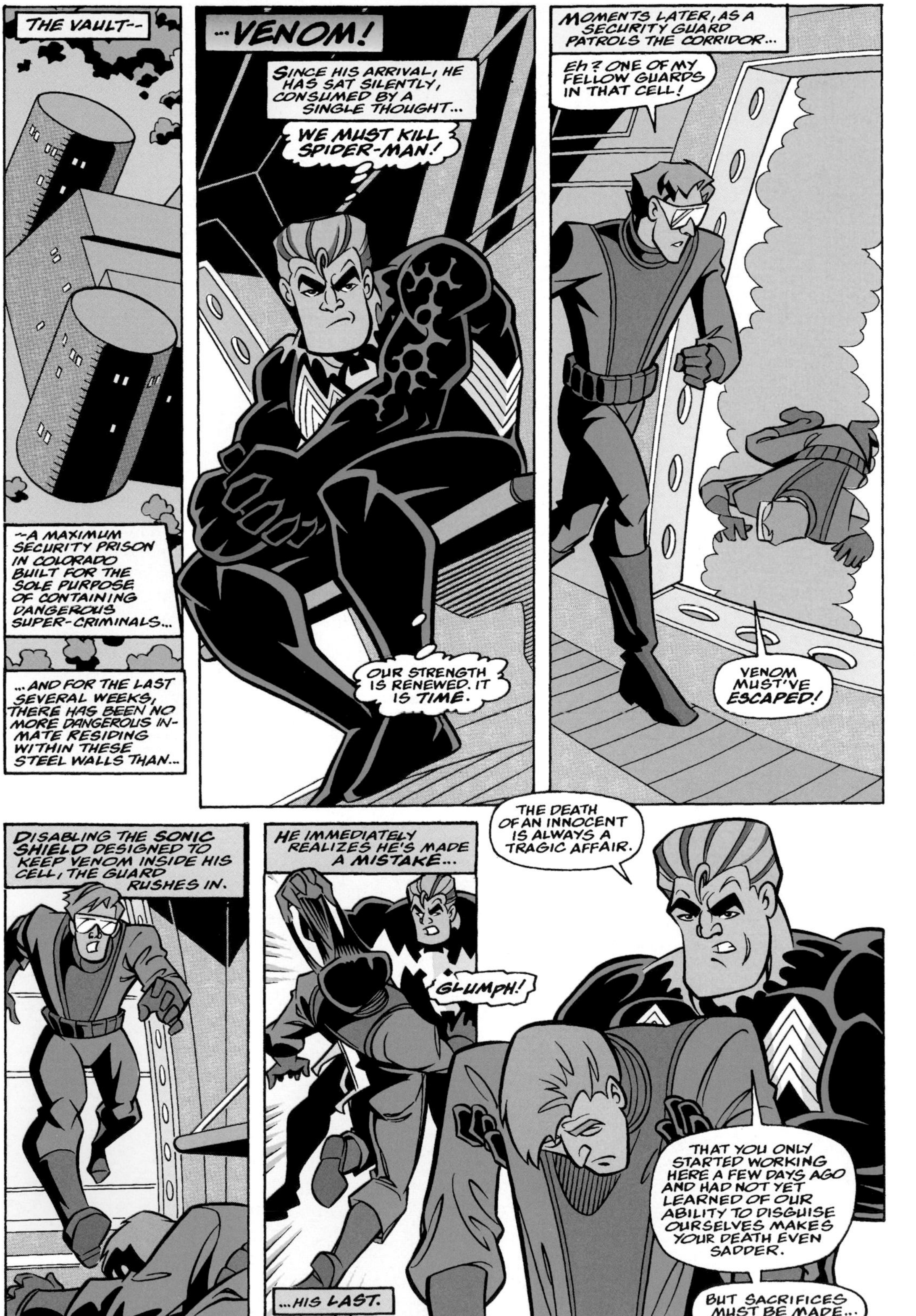
THE VAULT--
--A MAXIMUM SECURITY PRISON IN COLORADO BUILT FOR THE SOLE PURPOSE OF CONTAINING DANGEROUS SUPER-CRIMINALS...
...AND FOR THE LAST SEVERAL WEEKS, THERE HAS BEEN NO MORE DANGEROUS IN-MATE RESIDING WITHIN THESE STEEL WALLS THAN...
...VENOM!
SINCE HIS ARRIVAL, HE HAS SAT SILENTLY, CONSUMED BY A SINGLE THOUGHT...
WE MUST KILL SPIDER-MAN!
OUR STRENGTH IS RENEWED. IT IS TIME.
MOMENTS LATER, AS A SECURITY GUARD PATROLS THE CORRIDOR...
Eh? ONE OF MY FELLOW GUARDS IN THAT CELL!
VENOM MUST'VE ESCAPED!
DISABLING THE SONIC SHIELD DESIGNED TO KEEP VENOM INSIDE HIS CELL, THE GUARD RUSHES IN.
HE IMMEDIATELY REALIZES HE'S MADE A MISTAKE...
GLUMPH!
...HIS LAST.
THE DEATH OF AN INNOCENT IS ALWAYS A TRAGIC AFFAIR.
THAT YOU ONLY STARTED WORKING HERE A FEW DAYS AGO AND HAD NOT YET LEARNED OF OUR ABILITY TO DISGUISE OURSELVES MAKES YOUR DEATH EVEN SADDER.
BUT SACRIFICES MUST BE MADE...

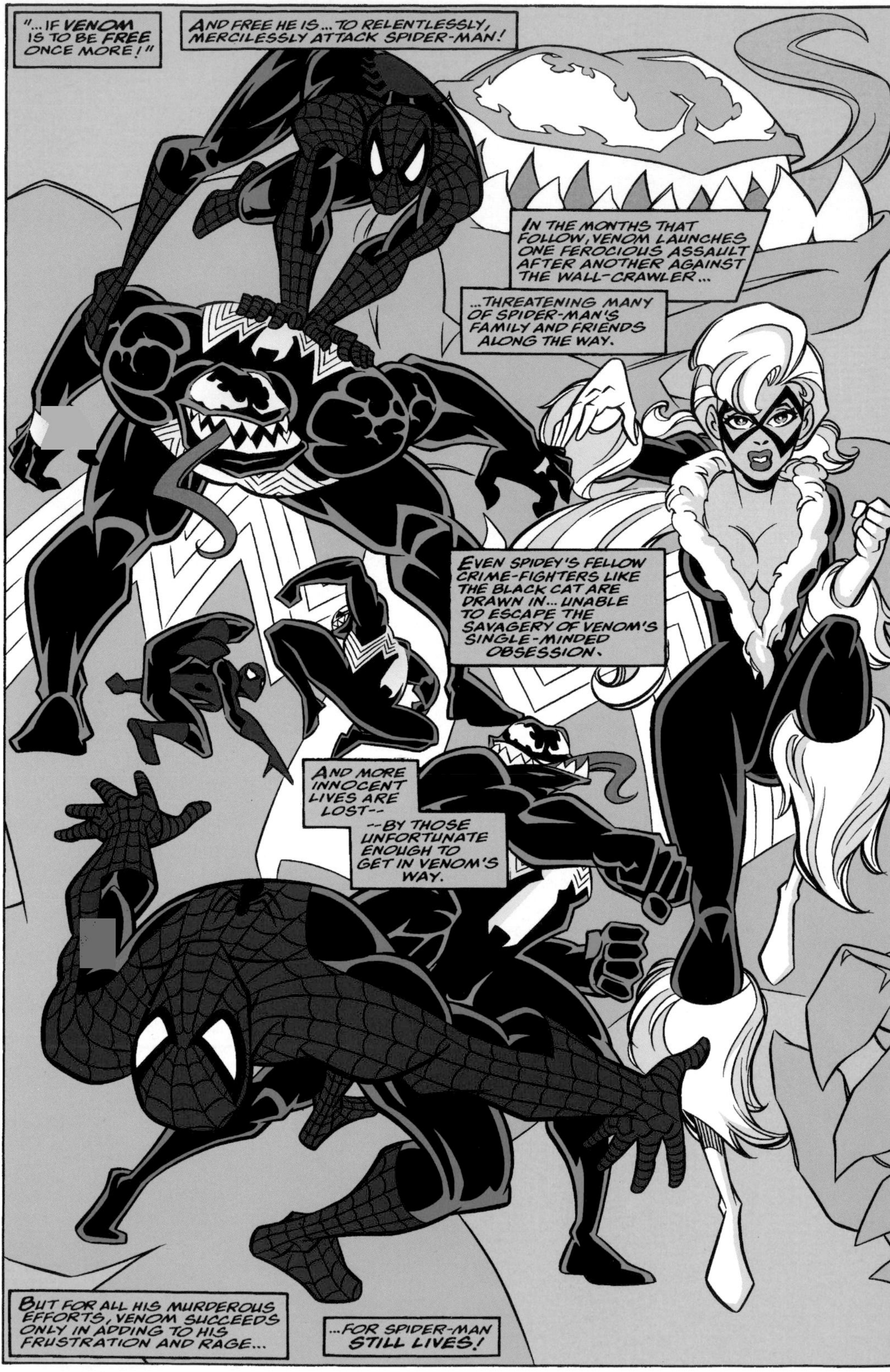
"...IF VENOM IS TO BE FREE ONCE MORE!"
AND FREE HE IS... TO RELENTLESSLY, MERCILESSLY ATTACK SPIDER-MAN!
IN THE MONTHS THAT FOLLOW, VENOM LAUNCHES ONE FEROCIOUS ASSAULT AFTER ANOTHER AGAINST THE WALL-CRAWLER...
...THREATENING MANY OF SPIDER-MAN'S FAMILY AND FRIENDS ALONG THE WAY.
EVEN SPIDEY'S FELLOW CRIME-FIGHTERS LIKE THE BLACK CAT ARE DRAWN IN... UNABLE TO ESCAPE THE SAVAGERY OF VENOM'S SINGLE-MINDED OBSESSION.
AND MORE INNOCENT LIVES ARE LOST--
--BY THOSE UNFORTUNATE ENOUGH TO GET IN VENOM'S WAY.
BUT FOR ALL HIS MURDEROUS EFFORTS, VENOM SUCCEEDS ONLY IN ADDING TO HIS FRUSTRATION AND RAGE...
...FOR SPIDER-MAN STILL LIVES!

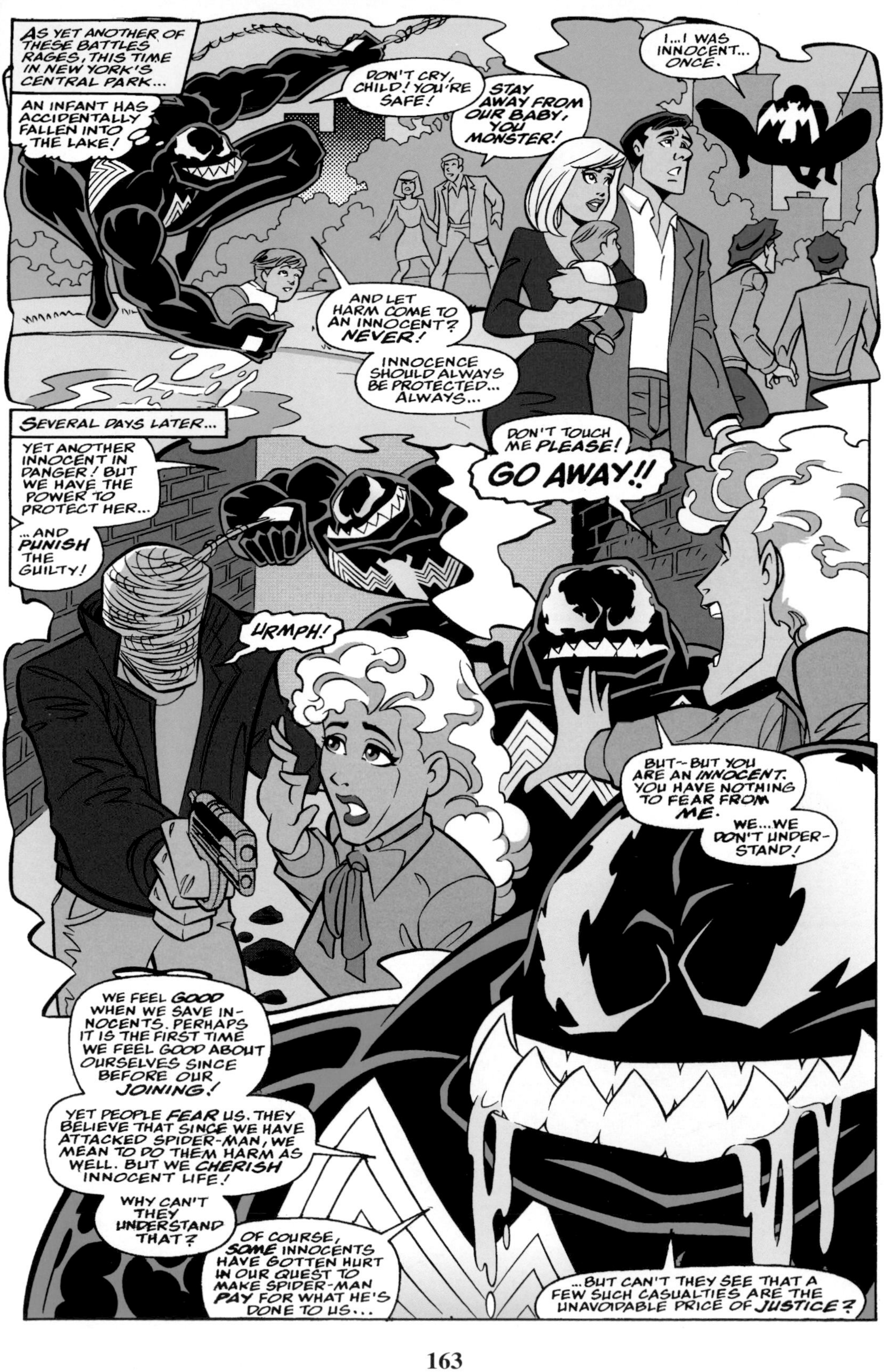
AS YET ANOTHER OF THESE BATTLES RAGES, THIS TIME IN NEW YORK'S CENTRAL PARK...
AN INFANT HAS ACCIDENTALLY FALLEN INTO THE LAKE!
DON'T CRY, CHILD! YOU'RE SAFE!
STAY AWAY FROM OUR BABY, YOU MONSTER!
AND LET HARM COME TO AN INNOCENT? NEVER!
INNOCENCE SHOULD ALWAYS BE PROTECTED... ALWAYS...
I...I WAS INNOCENT... ONCE.
SEVERAL DAYS LATER...
YET ANOTHER INNOCENT IN DANGER! BUT WE HAVE THE POWER TO PROTECT HER...
...AND PUNISH THE GUILTY!
URMPH!
DON'T TOUCH ME PLEASE! GO AWAY!!
BUT--BUT YOU ARE AN INNOCENT. YOU HAVE NOTHING TO FEAR FROM ME.
WE...WE DON'T UNDERSTAND!
WE FEEL GOOD WHEN WE SAVE INNOCENTS. PERHAPS IT IS THE FIRST TIME WE FEEL GOOD ABOUT OURSELVES SINCE BEFORE OUR JOINING!
YET PEOPLE FEAR US. THEY BELIEVE THAT SINCE WE HAVE ATTACKED SPIDER-MAN, WE MEAN TO DO THEM HARM AS WELL. BUT WE CHERISH INNOCENT LIFE!
WHY CAN'T THEY UNDERSTAND THAT?
OF COURSE, SOME INNOCENTS HAVE GOTTEN HURT IN OUR QUEST TO MAKE SPIDER-MAN PAY FOR WHAT HE'S DONE TO US...
...BUT CAN'T THEY SEE THAT A FEW SUCH CASUALTIES ARE THE UNAVOIDABLE PRICE OF JUSTICE?

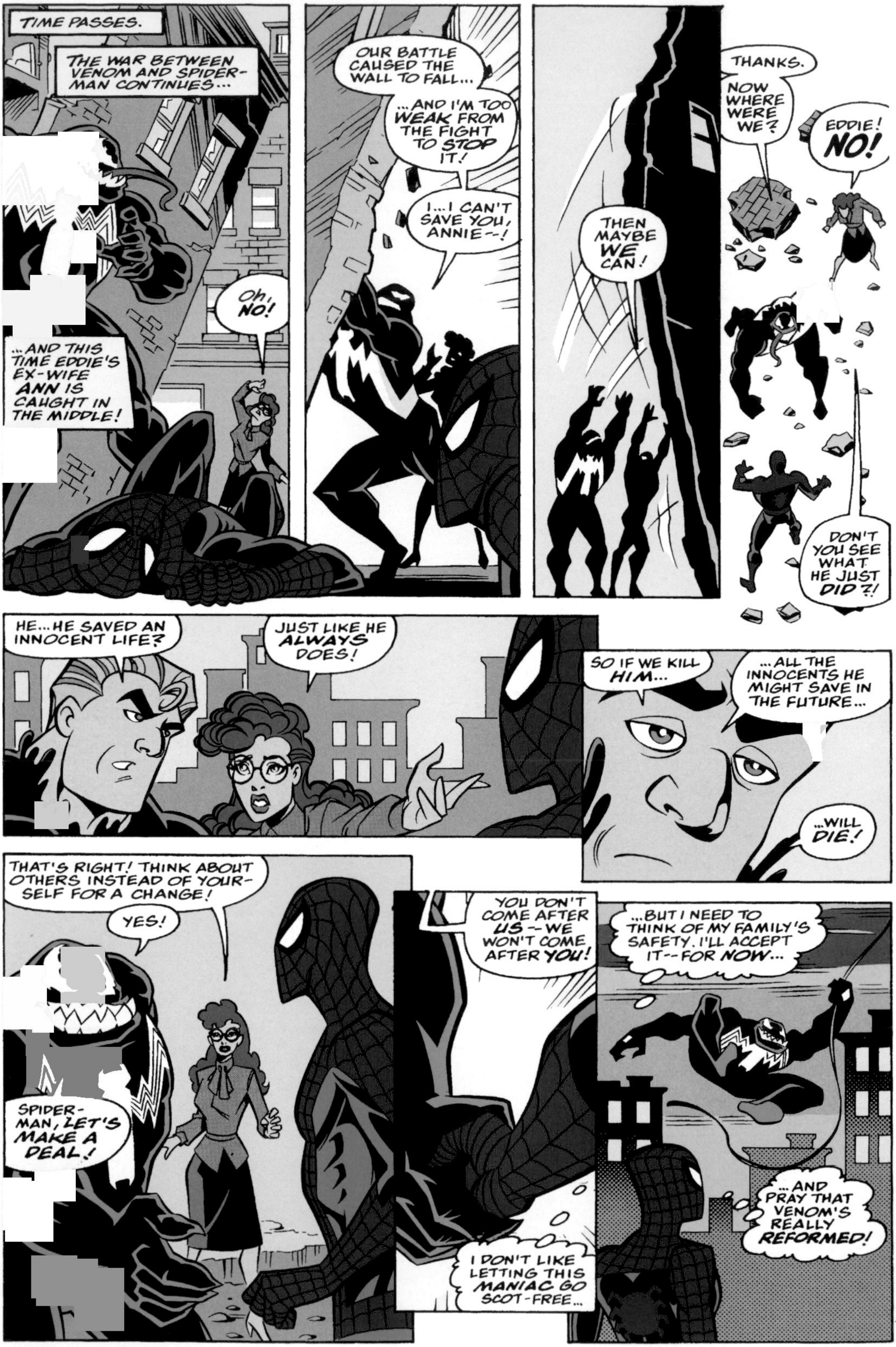
TIME PASSES.
THE WAR BETWEEN VENOM AND SPIDER-MAN CONTINUES...
...AND THIS TIME EDDIE'S EX-WIFE ANN IS CAUGHT IN THE MIDDLE!
Oh, NO!
OUR BATTLE CAUSED THE WALL TO FALL...
...AND I'M TOO WEAK FROM THE FIGHT TO STOP IT!
I...I CAN'T SAVE YOU, ANNIE--!
THEN MAYBE WE CAN!
THANKS.
NOW WHERE WERE WE?
EDDIE! NO!
DON'T YOU SEE WHAT HE JUST DID?!
HE...HE SAVED AN INNOCENT LIFE?
JUST LIKE HE ALWAYS DOES!
SO IF WE KILL HIM...
...ALL THE INNOCENTS HE MIGHT SAVE IN THE FUTURE...
...WILL DIE!
THAT'S RIGHT! THINK ABOUT OTHERS INSTEAD OF YOURSELF FOR A CHANGE!
YES!
SPIDER-MAN, LET'S MAKE A DEAL!
YOU DON'T COME AFTER US -- WE WON'T COME AFTER YOU!
I DON'T LIKE LETTING THIS MANIAC GO SCOT-FREE...
...BUT I NEED TO THINK OF MY FAMILY'S SAFETY. I'LL ACCEPT IT-- FOR NOW...
...AND PRAY THAT VENOM'S REALLY REFORMED!

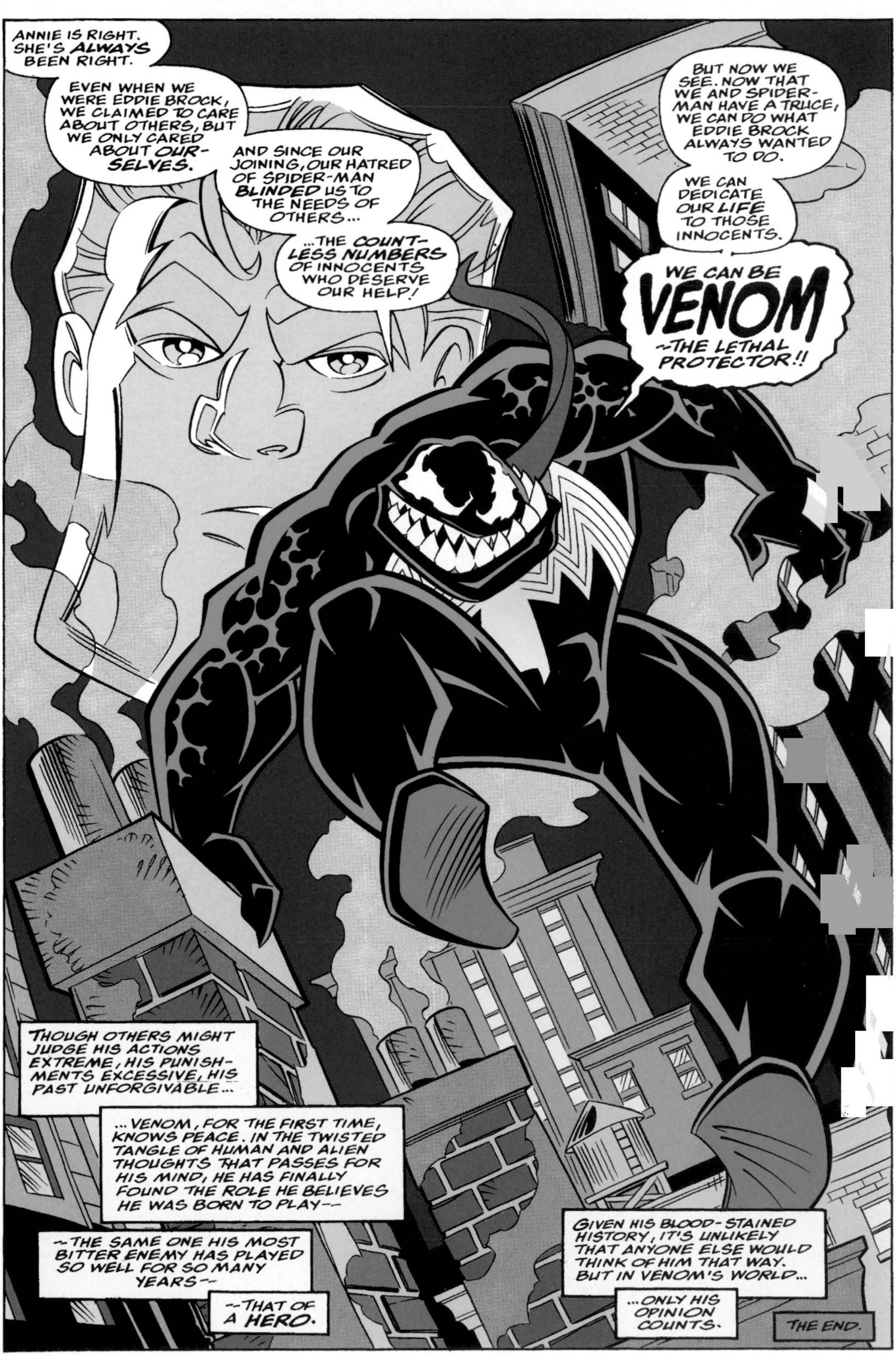
ANNIE IS RIGHT. SHE'S ALWAYS BEEN RIGHT.
EVEN WHEN WE WERE EDDIE BROCK, WE CLAIMED TO CARE ABOUT OTHERS, BUT WE ONLY CARED ABOUT OURSELVES.
AND SINCE OUR JOINING, OUR HATRED OF SPIDER-MAN BLINDED US TO THE NEEDS OF OTHERS...
...THE COUNTLESS NUMBERS OF INNOCENTS WHO DESERVE OUR HELP!
BUT NOW WE SEE. NOW THAT WE AND SPIDER-MAN HAVE A TRUCE, WE CAN DO WHAT EDDIE BROCK ALWAYS WANTED TO DO.
WE CAN DEDICATE OUR LIFE TO THOSE INNOCENTS.
WE CAN BE VENOM --THE LETHAL PROTECTOR!!
THOUGH OTHERS MIGHT JUDGE HIS ACTIONS EXTREME, HIS PUNISHMENTS EXCESSIVE, HIS PAST UNFORGIVABLE...
...VENOM, FOR THE FIRST TIME, KNOWS PEACE. IN THE TWISTED TANGLE OF HUMAN AND ALIEN THOUGHTS THAT PASSES FOR HIS MIND, HE HAS FINALLY FOUND THE ROLE HE BELIEVES HE WAS BORN TO PLAY--
--THE SAME ONE HIS MOST BITTER ENEMY HAS PLAYED SO WELL FOR SO MANY YEARS--
--THAT OF A HERO.
GIVEN HIS BLOOD-STAINED HISTORY, IT'S UNLIKELY THAT ANYONE ELSE WOULD THINK OF HIM THAT WAY. BUT IN VENOM'S WORLD...
...ONLY HIS OPINION COUNTS.
THE END.

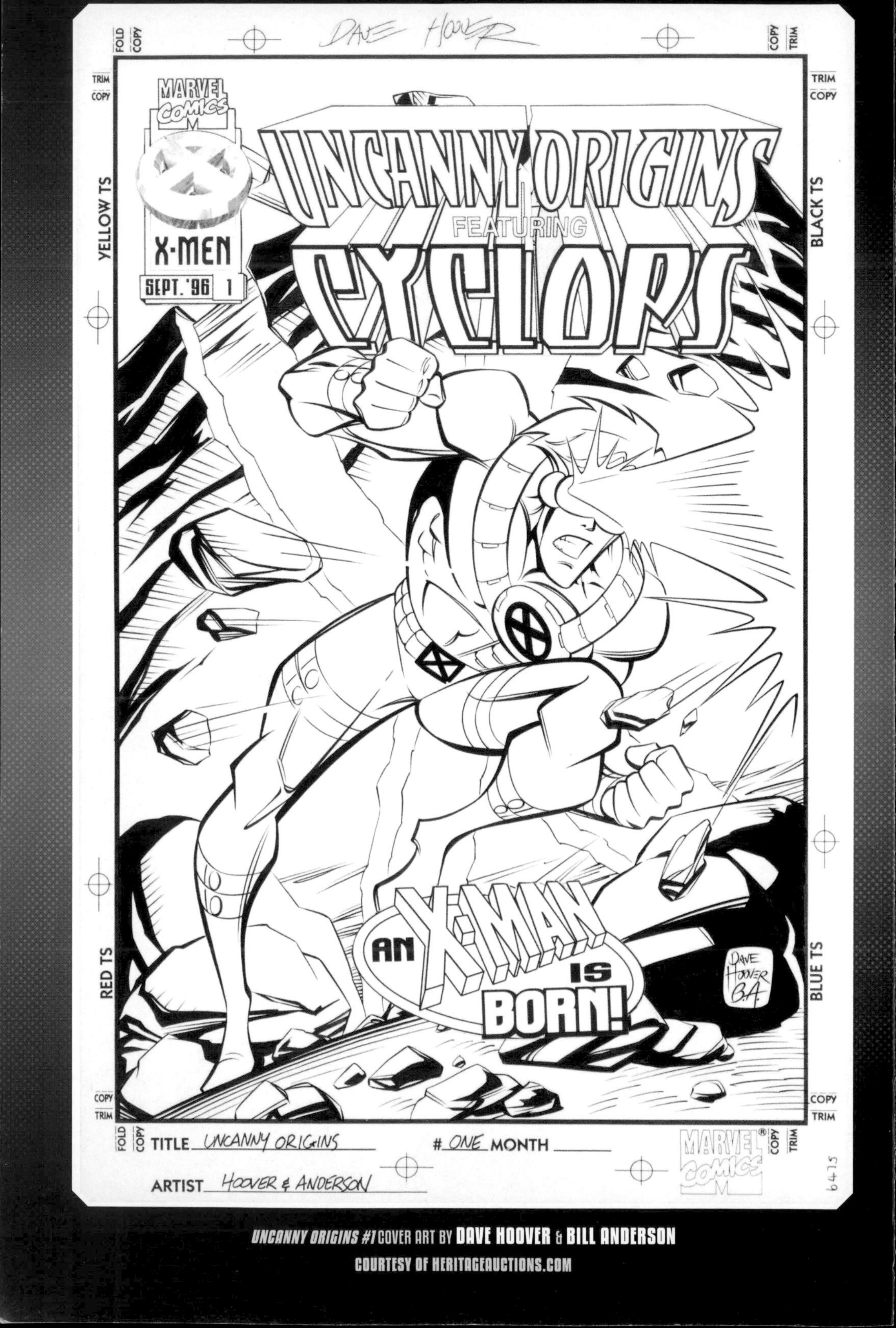
DAVE HOOVER
MARVEL COMICS
X-MEN
SEPT. '96 1
UNCANNY ORIGINS
FEATURING
CYCLOPS
AN X-MAN IS BORN!
DAVE HOOVER B.A.
TITLE UNCANNY ORIGINS
ONE MONTH
ARTIST HOOVER & ANDERSON
MARVEL COMICS

***UNCANNY ORIGINS* #1 COVER ART BY DAVE HOOVER & BILL ANDERSON**

COURTESY OF HERITAGEAUCTIONS.COM

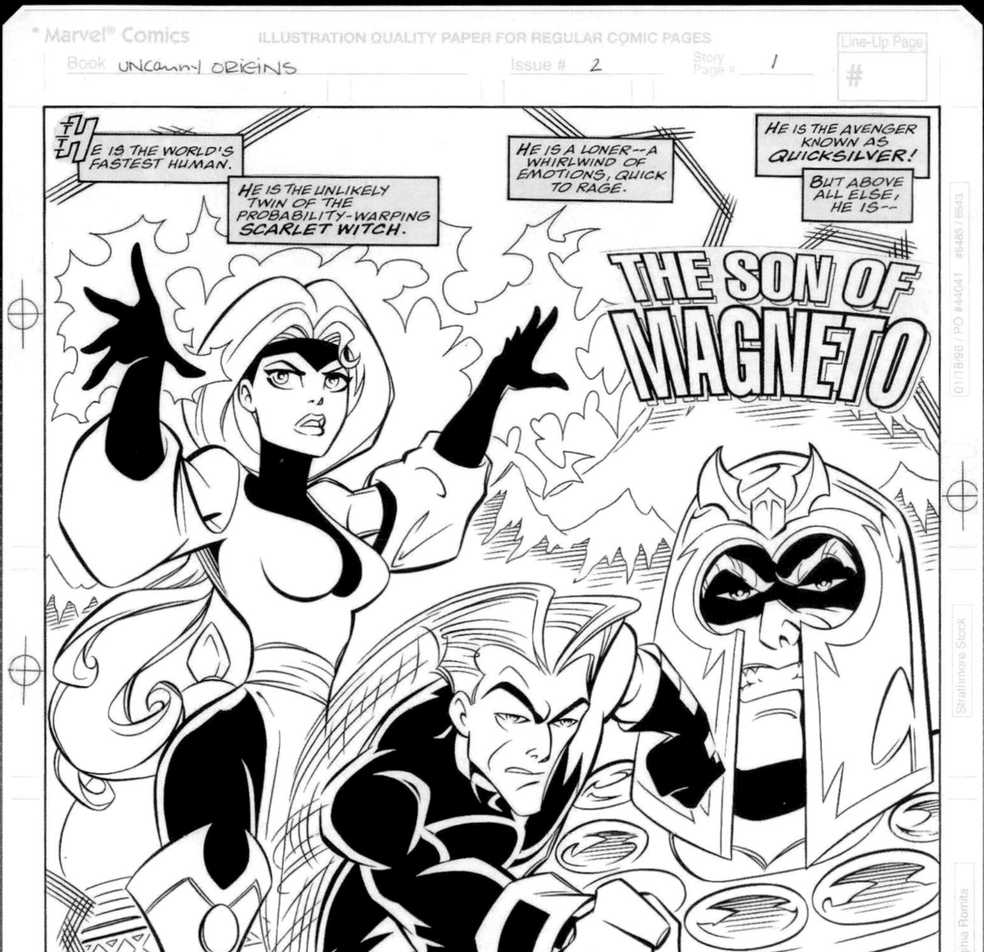
Marvel® Comics
ILLUSTRATION QUALITY PAPER FOR REGULAR COMIC PAGES
Line-Up Page
#
Book UNCANNY ORIGINS
Issue # 2
Story Page # 1
HE IS THE WORLD'S FASTEST HUMAN.
HE IS THE UNLIKELY TWIN OF THE PROBABILITY-WARPING SCARLET WITCH.
HE IS A LONER--A WHIRLWIND OF EMOTIONS, QUICK TO RAGE.
HE IS THE AVENGER KNOWN AS QUICKSILVER!
BUT ABOVE ALL ELSE, HE IS--
THE SON OF MAGNETO
GLENN HERDLING WRITER
DAVE HOOVER PENCILS
BILL ANDERSON INKS
JACK MORELLI LETTERS
BOB SHAREN COLORS
MARK GRUENWALD EDITOR
BOB HARRAS CHIEF
UNCANNY ORIGINS™ Vol. 1, No. 2, October, 1996. Published by MARVEL COMICS, Gerard Calabrese, President. Stan Lee, Publisher. OFFICE OF PUBLICATION: 387 PARK AVENUE SOUTH, NEW YORK, N.Y. 10016. Application to mail at second class postage is pending at New York, N.Y. and at additional mailing offices. Published bi-monthly. Copyright © 1996 Marvel Characters, Inc. All rights reserved. Price $.99 per copy in the U.S. and $1.38 in Canada. Subscription rate for 12 issues: U.S. $12.00. Foreign: $24.00. Canadian subscribers must add $10.00 for postage and GST. GST #R127032852. No similarity between any of the names, characters, persons, and/or institutions in this magazine with those of any living or dead person or institution is intended, and any such similarity which may exist is purely coincidental. This periodical may not be sold except by authorized dealers and is sold subject to the condition that it shall not be sold or distributed with any part of its cover or markings removed, nor in a mutilated condition. UNCANNY ORIGINS (and all prominent characters featured in this issue and the distinctive likenesses thereof) is a trademark of MARVEL CHARACTERS, INC. POSTMASTER: SEND ADDRESS CHANGES TO UNCANNY ORIGINS, c/o MARVEL DIRECT MARKETING INC./SUBSCRIPTION DEPT. P.O. BOX 1979, DANBURY, CT. 06813-1979. TELEPHONE # (203) 743-5331. Printed in the U.S.A.

UNCANNY ORIGINS #2, PAGE 1 ART BY **DAVE HOOVER** & **BILL ANDERSON**

COURTESY OF HERITAGEAUCTIONS.COM

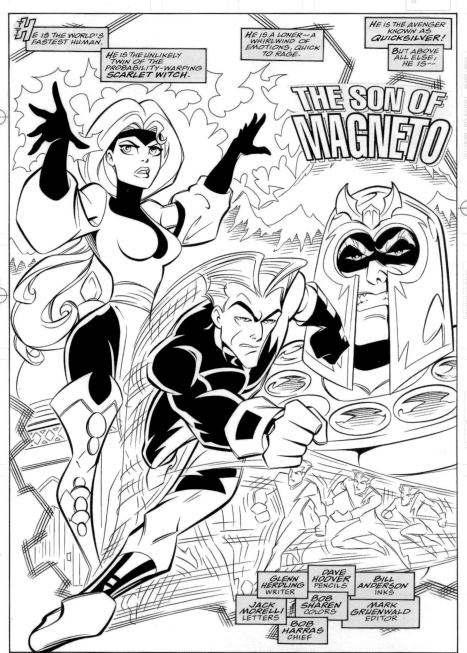

Marvel Comics
ILLUSTRATION QUALITY PAPER FOR REGULAR COMIC PAGES
Uncanny Origins
6
13
18
LATER...
LISTEN, LADIES-- I'VE SEEN BETTER REHEARSALS AT THE BALLET! CAN'T YOU GUYS DO ANYTHING R--
--HEY! THAT'S HIM!
HOLD ON, LOSERS!! I'M GOING TO SHOW YOU SOME REAL TALENT!
YOU THERE-- WHAT'S YER NAME-- OH, THAT DOESN'T MATTER!
JUST GET OVER HERE! I'VE SEEN YOUR LEG-WORK-- NOW LET'S SEE IF YOU CAN HANDLE THE BALL!
BUT I DON'T WANT TO--
DID I ASK YOU WHAT YOU WANTED?!
YOU'RE TRYING OUT FOR THIS TEAM-- NOW!
OKAY, SO WE'LL BE NEEDING A FEW NEW FOOT-BALLS...
WOMP
FWUMP
URK!
AND SO... A STAR IS BORN!
THERE HE IS, FOLKS-- HANK McCOY! HE'S LED THE TEAM TO SIX STRAIGHT VICTORIES. RUMORS ARE THAT THE COWBOYS HAVE ALREADY OFFERED HIM A DEAL.
MEANWHILE, OUTSIDE THE STADIUM...
COULDN'T'VE STUCK THIS JOINT UP FOR TWELVE CENTS LAST YEAR!
THREE CHEERS FER HANK McCOY!
HOW MANY TICKETS, Sir?
TICKETS? WE'LL TAKE EVERYTHING!

UNCANNY ORIGINS #6, PAGE 13 ART BY **DAVE HOOVER** & **DON HUDSON**

COURTESY OF HERITAGEAUCTIONS.COM

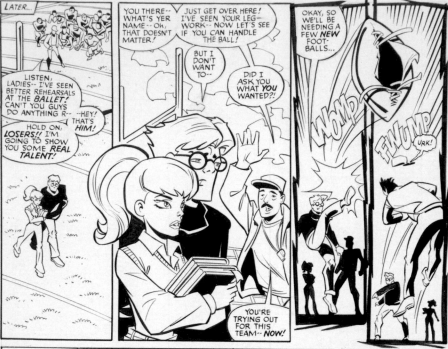

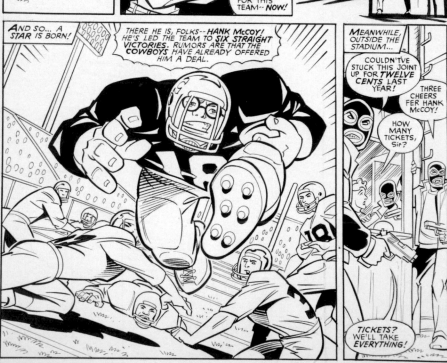